Helen Hollick lives in London with her husband
researching the background information for her
series about Jesamiah Acorne, she spends most c
who is a semi-professional show jumper, as chie
She has a university diploma in early medieval hist\

C000242878

For up-to-date information visit Helen's Website: <u>www.helenhollick.net</u>

Praise for Helen Hollick's novels:

"A spellbinding novel...a fabulous read and one to be recommended unreservedly. If
only all historical fiction could be this good!"
Historical Novels Review

"Hollick juggles a large cast of characters and a bloody, tangled plot with great
skill."
Publishers Weekly

"Helen Hollick has a powerful talent for bringing the past vividly to life"
Bestselling author - Elizabeth Chadwick

"Compelling, convincing and unforgettable"
Bestselling author – Sharon Penman

"An epic re-telling of events leading to the Norman Conquest – most impressive."
The Lady

"Don't miss Helen Hollick's colourful recreation of events leading up to the Norman
Conquest"
Daily Mail

"Uniquely Compelling... bound to have a resounding and lasting impact on Arthurian
fiction"
Books Magazine

"Helen Hollick joins the ranks of Rosemary Sutcliff, Mary Stewart and Marion
Bradley with this splendid novel"
Pendragon Magazine

Also by Helen Hollick, Published by Discovered Authors

Historical Fiction:

The Pendragon's Banner Series: a trilogy about Arthurian Britain
    The Kingmaking
    Pendragon's Banner
    Shadow of the King

~~~

Harold the King: the story of the Battle of Hastings

~~~

A Hollow Crown: the story of Emma, Queen of Saxon England
Published by Arrow Books (Random House UK)

For Children:

Come and Tell Me – a keep yourself safe book
Published by Happy Cat Books

Sea Witch

Helen Hollick

Being the First Voyage of
Cpt. Jesamiah Acorne & his ship, Sea Witch

First edition published in Great Britain in 2006
By Discovered Authors

A Discovered Authors Diamond
from
Imagination Books

ISBN 1-90510-814-1

Printed by BookForce UK

BookForce UK's policy is to use papers that are natural, renewable
and recyclable products and made from wood grown in sustainable
forests where ever possible

Discovered Authors
50 Albemarle Street
London W1S 4BD
www.bookforce.co.uk
www.discoveredauthors.co.uk

For Mal

Who has sailed the seven seas
and who is my best friend.

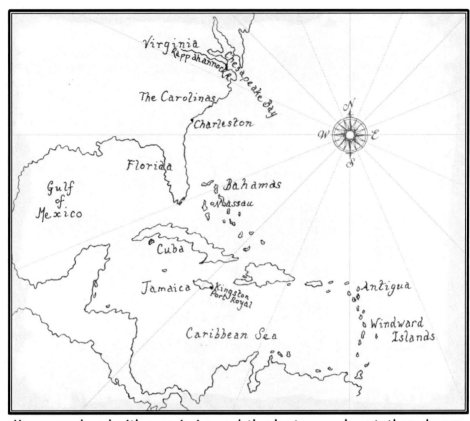

Map reproduced with permission and thanks to www.keeptothecode.com

Plan of the sails and masts of a square-rigged ship

Sails

1 Flying Jib
2 Jib
3 Fore Staysail
4 Fore Topgallant sail (pronounced *t'gan's'l*)
5 Fore Topsail (pronounced *tops'l*)
6 Foresail or Fore Course

7 Main Topgallant
8 Main Topsail
9 Mainsail or Main Course
10 Mizzen Topgallant
11 Mizzen Topsail
12 Mizzen Sail

Masts

A Bowsprit/Jib-boom
B Foremast
C Fore Topmast
D Fore Topgallant Mast
E Main Mast

F Main Topmast
G Main Topgallant Mast
H Mizzenmast
I Mizzen Topmast
J Ensign and Ensign Staff

Acknowledgements

Priority for appreciation must go to Mal and Aly for their unswerving support, and for his professional help to James L. Nelson, author of the *Brethren of the Coast* series and *Revolution At Sea* Saga - among other excellent maritime novels. Unlike myself, Jim (also known as Black Jim Spudcake, the fourth most fearsome pirate in the Caribbean) is an experienced sailor, he was so patient with answering my naive questions about sailing and ships. However, I must take full credit for any errors - they are all my own work!

My gratitude to Jo for her copy-editing skills and our "interesting" telephone discussions; I appreciate your time and enthusiasm.

Thank you also to everyone who has helped me with the early drafts of *Sea Witch*, her launching has been long and arduous but worth it. To Jansy, Sue and Katie; Adrienne, Caz, Connie and the "crew" members of the P.O.C. Interactive. Also to Nathan for his humour and sensible advice, and Yolanda, Fran and Merle for their aid with Dutch, French and German. - and of course, my thanks to Jennie and the team at BookForce UK.

I am especially grateful to historical fiction authors Elizabeth Chadwick and Sharon Kay Penman for their support and friendship, and to Karen who explored the Sebastian Inlet State Park on my behalf. I would have liked to have undertaken my own research here - but unfortunately the Florida Coast is a little too far for a day-trip excursion from London!

My appreciation also to the staff of the Whydah Exhibition Centre, the National Maritime Museum, Greenwich, and those aboard the Cutty Sark and H.M.S. Victory - and to *Google*. Where would writers be without the Internet for those urgent and obscure research questions that must be immediately answered?

Finally, thank you to Johnny Depp for his wonderful role as Captain Jack Sparrow - without him the exciting world of pirates would not have been rekindled and my Jesamiah would never have been created.

*

*In the depths, in the abyss of darkness at the very
bottom of the oceans Tethys stirred.
She was the soul of the sea, the spirit of the waves
and was capable, as the mood took her, of benign
complaisance or malicious rage.*

*She was without form or solidity yet she saw, heard, and
became aware of everything within her jurisdiction.
And she ruled her water realm with unchallenged power
and a terrible omnipotence.*

~ *Jesamiah* ~

"Beware of Pirates,
for danger can lurk behind their smiles."

January 1716

- One -

Mermaid was moving fast, the ship bowling along with her sails filled, the canvas billowing, cordage creaking and straining. She climbed over the next wave, her bow lifting to linger a moment before swooping down into another deluge of spray. Completing the seesaw movement her stern soared high as the roller trundled beneath her keel. The wind smelt of hot, dry and dusty land, of jungle and grass savannah. Of Africa.

The look out, clad in an old shirt and sailor's breeches was perched high in the crosstrees, one hundred and thirty feet above the deck. Excited, he pointed to the horizon. "Over there Jesamiah, that's where I saw 'er. I swear I saw a sail!"

With the ease of years of practice, Jesamiah Acorne stepped from the rigging on to the narrow platform that swayed with the lift and plunge of the ship. He hooked his arm through a t'gallant shroud and brought his telescope to his eye, scanned the ocean. Nothing. Nothing except a flat expanse of blue emptiness going on, unbroken, for twenty miles. And beyond that? Another twenty, and another.

These were the waters of the Gulf of Guinea, the huge stretch of sea beneath the bulb of land where the trade wealth of West Africa was turned into fat profit: gold, ivory and slaves. The African coast, where merchants found their plentiful supply of human misery and where an entire ships' crew could be wiped out by fever within a week.

Where pirates hunted in search of easy prey.

The crew of the *Mermaid* were not interested in slavers or the foetid coast. Their rough-voiced, ragged-faced captain, Malachias Taylor, had more lucrative things in mind - the sighting of another ship, preferably a full-laden, poorly manned merchantman with a rich cargo worth plundering.

"What can y'see?" he shouted from the deck, squinting upwards at his quartermaster, the relentless sun dazzling his eyes. His second-in-command, Jesamiah, like his father before him, was one of the best seamen Taylor knew.

"Nothing! If young Daniel here did see a sail he has better sight than I 'ave," Jesamiah called down, the frustration clear in his voice. All the same, he studied the sea again with the telescope.

Jesamiah Acorne. Quick to smile, yet formidable when angered. Tall, tanned, with strong arms and a seaman's tar-stained and callused hands. His black hair fell as an untidy chaos of natural curls to his shoulders, laced into it, lengths of blue ribbon which streamed about his face in the wind, the whipping ends stinging his cheeks. The ladies ashore thought them a wonderful prize when he occasionally offered one as a keepsake.

If there was a ship, Daniel would only have glimpsed her highest sails, the topgallants; the rest of her would still be hull down, unseen below the curve of the horizon. "I think you had too much rum last night, my lad," Jesamiah grinned. "Your eyes are playing tricks on you."

Young Daniel was adamant. "I saw her I say. I'll wager m'next wedge of baccy I did!"

"You know I cannot abide the stuff," Jesamiah chuckled good-natured as he stretched out his arm to ruffle the lad's mop of hair. He had turned his back on anything to do with tobacco – except stealing it – seven years ago when his elder brother had thrown him off their dead father's plantation, with the threat he would hang if ever he returned. But then, Phillipe Mereno was only a half brother and he had always been a cheat and a bully. One day, for the misery of his childhood, Jesamiah would find the opportunity to go back and finish beating the bastard to a pulp.

Out of habit he touched the gold charm dangling from his right earlobe: an acorn, to match the signet ring he had worn since early youth. Given to him by his Spanish mother, God rest her soul. She had always thought the acorn, the fruit of the solid and dependable oak tree to be lucky. It had been the first word to come to mind when he had needed a new name in a hurry.

Acorne, with an "e" to make the name unique, and his own.

About to shut the telescope a flash caught his eye and Jesamiah whisked the bring-it-close upwards again. The sun reflecting on something?

"Wait... Damn it, Daniel - I've got her!" The sudden enthusiasm carried in an eager flurry as he shouted down to the deck, his words greeted by a hollered cheer from the rag-tag of men who made the *Mermaid's* crew.

Even the usually dour-faced Malachias Taylor managed a smile. "Probably a slaver," he muttered, "but we'll set all sail an' pay her a visit." His gap-toothed smile broadened into a grin. "She might be wantin' company, eh lads?"

Aye she might, but not the sort of company the *Mermaid* would be offering. Respectable traders and East India Company merchantmen did not care for pirates.

Half an hour. Three-quarters. The sand trickled through the half-hour glass as if it were sticky with tar, and although the *Mermaid* was under full sail the distance between the two ships seemed to take an interminable time to lessen. Each man was trying to pretend he did not care whether they were on to a possible Prize or not, but for all that, finding a variety of excuses to be up on deck or clambering about the rigging. In the end Jesamiah put a stop to it, cursing them for the dregs they were.

"Looking ain't going to bring us closer to a Chase any the quicker!" he barked, resisting the temptation to have yet another squint through the telescope for himself. "Cease this 'opping about as if you've an army of ants crawling up yer backsides! We stay on this course and make out we're minding our own business. We ain't interested in her, savvy?" All the same, he touched his gold earring for luck.

From his high vantage point Daniel finally put them out of their misery. "On deck there! She's a trader!" he shouted. "A dirty great, huge, East Indiaman – God's breath, would you believe it? There's something smaller following in her wake." He cursed again and spat chewed tobacco into the sea. "We wait all this damned time, then get two Chases at once!"

The Captain climbed aloft himself, a satisfied smile spread over his weatherworn face as he lifted the telescope to his eye. The Indiaman must have been keeping lookout too, for as he watched she showed her identity, the tri-coloured Dutch ensign clearly hoisted to her main mast. Britain was not at war with the Dutch. A minor fact which did not perturb Taylor in the slightest.

Privateering during periods of declared war was legal, providing the captain carried a Letter of Marque giving him government permission to harass enemy ships. Naturally, Captain Taylor possessed his formal letter, and naturally, he preyed on any Spanish or French enemy ship daring to show a sail over the horizon. He saw no reason to ignore everything else also coming within range of his cannon though, British or Dutch ships included. Now that was not privateering, but piracy - a crime punished by the death penalty of hanging.

"Show British colours, let her think we're friendly," he called down. He winked at Daniel. "We take the trader, put a scratch crew aboard then think about chasing after the other one as well, eh? What say you, young Wickersley?"

Daniel grinned a half-moon smile at Taylor, a fairer, more profitable captain than his previous one aboard an English Royal Navy frigate. "Aye sir, sounds good t'me!"

Jesamiah was waiting for orders, fingers curled loosely around the hilt of a cutlass slung from a leather baldric worn aslant across his faded waistcoat, the strap concealing a rough-patched, blood-stained hole where some while ago a pistol's lead shot had penetrated. He wore canvas breeches as soft and comfortable as moleskin, knee-high boots and a cotton shirt that had once been white but was now a dirty grey. One cuff was beginning to fray into a ragged edge. He stood, his other hand fiddling with his blue ribbons, legs straddled, balancing against the rise and fall of the ship.

Taylor slid, hand over hand down the backstay; watching him Jesamiah ran his finger and thumb across the moustache trailing each side of his mouth into a beard trimmed close along his jaw. He lifted his chin slightly as Taylor's feet touched the deck. The Captain looked towards his second-in-command. "If you please, Mr. Acorne."

Acknowledging, Jesamiah paused, knowing the crew of eighty rogues were set to jump at his command. He held them a moment... "All hands! Clear for action!"

A whoop of delight, a scuffing patter of bare feet on the sun-hot deck, the tarred caulking sticky between the boards, the men scattering in various directions to ready the ship for fighting. A task they could do day or night, drunk or sober.

As captain of a pirate ship Taylor only held unquestionable command when it came to the engagement of an enemy ship. At other times decisions were made by discussion and a vote. And if a captain got it wrong too often? The crew simply elected another one.

Taylor was safe. He was skilled at piracy, his achievements obvious by his long standing as master of the *Mermaid* over a contented crew.

"Make ready the guns," he called to Jesamiah, "but don't run out yet. Keep some of the crew out o' sight, too. I want this Dutchman thinkin' we're a poorly manned merchant, no threat, for as long as possible."

Jesamiah grinned, the light of easy laughter darting into his face. He wanted that too. The easier the chase, and the fight at the end of it, the better.

He had no fear of dying for everyone had to go some day. Hoped when his turn came it would be quick and painless, for it was the long, drawn-out agony he and any pirate, any man, dreaded.

But today? This fine, clear blue day was not a day for dying. This was a day for taking treasure!

- Two -

Aboard the *Christina Giselle,* a girl, Tiola, stood peering over the rail, mesmerised by the foaming water churning away along the side of the hull. Yesterday a school of dolphins had kept them company for several miles, their silver bodies leaping and glistening as they flashed and darted. Today, it seemed they had a different companion, one unwanted and uninvited.

Tiola. Fifteen. Named for her grandmother, an old, old name, *Tio-la,* short and quick, not Ti-*oh*-la as some, wrongly, said. She was slim and not very tall; a tumble of midnight-black hair, with eyes as dark. Her features were fine, almost delicate, her mother used to jest she was a fairy child. She was, in a way.

England, Cornwall, was many miles, many weeks and many tears behind. She would not see her home or brothers again. Nor her mother. Mother was already in the next world, gone to God, except while she hanged the jeering mob had shouted that a woman who plunged a knife into the heart of her own husband was of the Devil's breeding and would burn in Hell. From there it had been an easy step for someone to shout "witch" and for the blood-fever of superstition to spread. Had it not been for one of her elder brothers hurrying her to safety, Tiola would also have been lynched. Her father's blood had been spattered on her clothes too.

The irony? It was not Mother who was the witch.

Tiola's guardian, Jenna Pendeen, shielded her eyes against the glare of the sun and peered at the approaching vessel. "Is it not a British flag she flies? Surely, she is of no threat to us?"

Behind her the Dutchman, Captain van Noord, shrugged. "I grant she may be British," he proclaimed in perfect English, "but if that is all she is, then I am the King of Spain!" His manner was easy and confident; neatly dressed and polite he roamed the decks of his ship, hands clasped behind his back, his darting eyes missing nothing. Rightly, he took pride in the sleek vessel he commanded.

Realising what he meant Jenna squeaked alarm. "You suspect her to be a pirate?" Her hand jerked to her throat. "Are we in danger?"

The captain offered a polite bow. "Ah no, ma'am, I do not *suspect* them to be pirates, I am *certain* of it. From experience, I know her crew for what they are; rogues and thieves. Degenerates who deserve to kick from the gallows. As no doubt they shall one day."

Tiola said nothing. No one deserved to hang, it was a wicked death. Only if the victim had friends or relatives to act as hangers on, to add their weight to the jerking torso, was the slow strangulation hastened to its gruesome end.

"Ought we not show more speed?" Jenna asked nervously, glancing up at the billow of the sails. She fluttered her hand at Tiola. "You understand, my concern is for my ward Miss Oldstagh, not for myself. I promised her mother I would take care of her. In the hands of pirates I dread to think what indecencies she may suffer."

Jenna, unable to do anything to save her beloved mistress had transferred her devotion and duty to the only daughter instead. Someone had to accompany the child she had insisted, she could not leave England, flee for her life, alone.

"It would be interesting to meet a pirate," Tiola announced, turning to smile at van Noord. "Do they all have eye patches and gold teeth?"

The Captain smiled at her naive innocence. "Alas child, the pirates I have had the misfortune to cross a course with have all been dirt-grimed drunkards with black, foul teeth and even fouler language and manners."

Jenna drew in her breath, horrified.

"You have my word, dear lady, they will not be setting foot upon *this* ship." Van Noord half saluted his two passengers and strolled astern, issuing calm, unhurried orders as he went.

Tiola linked her arm through Jenna's. "He knows what he is doing, we must trust him."

The older woman snorted. For all he was a gentleman, through most of her forty years of life she had never found a reason to trust a man.

Almost leisurely, the Dutch crew were reducing the spread of canvas to fighting sail. A ship had to be balanced, the height of her masts to the length and weight of her hull. Full sail would give them speed but not manoeuvrability. And in a fight, it was being able to turn that counted. That, and the power of her guns and the efficiency of her gunners.

Excitement was shivering down Tiola's spine. *Real* pirates! All the stories she had read of daring adventurers: Sir Francis Drake and his expeditions against the Spanish; Captain Morgan's famous sacking of Panama and Portobello. William Dampier, whose exploits had led him to sail twice around the seas of the world, and who was even now on a third journey. And Captain William Kidd, whose pirate bones had bleached from where they dangled on the gallows at London's Wapping docks. They had pushed him off from the wagon twice. The first time the rope had snapped and he had tumbled, shaken but unharmed, to the mud of the low tide. The misfortune had not served him well for they tied another noose and pushed him off again. To the end he had shrilled his innocence, claiming he was a privateer with a royal commission, not the scoundrel of a pirate.

Tiola shivered again. She was not afraid, the child she was had too much liking for the romance of adventure, and the ageless woman, the part of her that carried the inherited gift of Craft passed down through alternate generations, grandmother to granddaughter, was not afraid of anything. Aside, Captain van Noord knew exactly what he was doing. Equally however, these men rapidly closing on the *Christina Giselle,* appeared to be as competent in their trade.

At first sight of the cannons being run out, Jenna fled to the sanctuary of their cramped cabin situated forward on the lower deck. Tiola remained above, although prudently she moved to the taffrail along the stern, out of the way of the scurrying men busy rigging protective netting. Several of the crew shouted at her to go below, including Captain van Noord, but with determined stubbornness she pretended not to hear, and they did not have opportunity to bother with her again.

Her throat dry, breath coming short and quick, Tiola's emotions were tumbling together, alarm mixing with exhilaration. She was determined to stay and watch, for there was something here – someone – stirring her excitement. She stood, her hands tightly gripping the rail as the pirate ship ran closer, studying the men aboard her as the smaller vessel began to overhaul the *Christina Giselle.* Her sight enhanced by her ability of Craft she needed no telescope to put to her eye.

Pirates. A ragged bunch, most of them barefoot and unwashed with greasy, unkempt hair and dressed in loose woollen shirts and seaman's striped trousers. Astern on the quarterdeck, stood their captain, smarter dressed than his crew, a buckram coat, white breeches; a red, feathered plume in his cocked hat. His hands were clasped behind his back, his face grim as he glowered, steadfast, ahead.

Her gaze slid over him, dismissive. No, it was not his spirit calling to hers - there must be someone else. Someone who...

And then she saw the man with the black hair and the blue ribbons.

Three

Jesamiah counted twelve gun ports along the starboard side of the ship. *Mermaid* carried twelve cannon in all; minions, three to four pounders. Twelve against twenty four.

"Shit," he muttered, beneath his breath, his mind rapidly considering several questions. What poundage were they? A vessel her size, nine? Surely not powerful twelve pounder guns? And the big question, was she nothing more than brazen show? This air of could-not-care-less, was it all sham? The *Christina Giselle* - her name was painted across her stern - was not running from them nor, beyond reducing to the more manageable fighting sail, had she made any attempt at defence; just keeping steady on her course, almost stubbornly ignoring them. Her captain must be damned sure of himself, few ships could muster the bravado to outface a pirate.

The distance rapidly decreasing, Jesamiah, standing beside Taylor on the quarterdeck, was beginning to feel the first niggling of doubt. He considered whether to voice his unease aloud or keep the thoughts to himself. "Why are they not responding to our presence with more alarm?" he murmured under his breath. Then, louder, "I wonder what crew she has? These Dutch merchantmen are usually undermanned. All owners think of is profit, employing a decent crew eats too far into it."

His thumbs tucked through his pistol belt, Taylor was vigilantly studying the ship looming larger ahead of them. Now they were closing, her size was more apparent; at least twice the length of *Mermaid* he reckoned. As long as she did not have twice the gun power.

"Or she might be adequately crewed." Jesamiah continued his commentary, nervously running the fingers and thumb down his moustache, the hairs at the nape of his neck prickling. "Not all owners are imbeciles. She don't appear to be poorly manned, she shortened sail efficiently."

Taylor answered gruffly. He had been thinking the same thoughts but was not as confident at airing them aloud. "Well, Jes lad, when we engage, we shall find out, eh?"

A quarter of a mile away as if the *Christina Giselle* had heard, her gun ports casually opened, her cannons run out. Walking forward to the rail Taylor called his order to the crew down in the waist. Time for the *Mermaid* to also reduce sail. "Clew up there!"

"Malachias," Jesamiah said quietly at his side, his hand lightly touching the captain's arm to gain his attention. "I have a bad feeling about this. Something ain't right here. Why not pass her up? Go for that Spaniard trying to scuttle away?"

Did Taylor hear? If he did, he ignored the suggestion, shouted instead, "Gunners, we'll rake her on my command. Sail trimmers stand by. Mr Acorne, I would be obliged if you were to run up our colours."

Jesamiah shrugged; he had said his piece, so be it. He twirled the flag halyard off the belaying pin and brought in the decoy British ensign, in its place, hauled up the pirate flag of the *Jolie Rouge* – most pirates had their own design, Taylor's being a red flag adorned with a grinning skeleton and an almost empty hour-glass. Death and time running out.

The distance between the two ships was closing rapidly; Taylor nodded to the helmsman, his plan, to run in rake her with a few well-aimed shots from the starboard battery, force her to heave to and surrender, then make ready to board.

But the Dutchman fired first, a single shot that plumed towards the *Mermaid* and missed her bowsprit by a matter of inches.

"Damn his hide!" Taylor roared, indignant, and in the next breath bellowed, "Fire all!"

Six guns boomed in a rippling howl of noise that rent apart the quiet of the ocean, sending it into a fair representation of Hell. The *Mermaid's* deck shook from the recoil and smoke belched in a thick, choking fog that swirled and lingered a moment before drifting off downwind. The men, used to the incredible noise and the acrid stink, took no notice, began running in and re-loading with barely a pause.

At the same moment the Dutch captain ordered the release of his own rage of destruction. Protruding from her white-painted hull the cavernous muzzles of the *Christina Giselle's* guns were stark and ominous - and then fire and smoke roared in a broadside from all twelve as if they were a single, terrible weapon, the sound splitting the air with its mighty force, like the crash of an overhead thunderclap. Only, this unleashed storm brought with it the heavy iron of deadly round shot whistling across the gap between the two vessels, to punch holes in sails, rip away great sections of railing and tear apart mens' bodies. To leave behind the gush of blood and the scream of death.

Mermaid rocked, then shrugged herself free of the damage and the swirl of smoke enveloping her, sailed on, plunging gallantly forward. Jesamiah swore colourfully, his hope of this being an easy fight totally gone. Two of those guns were mighty eighteen pounders!

Pray God, he thought, *she's not as well manned as she's making out....* He let the thought drift off with the smoke. The merchant had either to turn or swab, reload and run out again. If she was bluffing, had a ragged crew, poorly commanded, *Mermaid* might stand a chance. If not...

Jesamiah's deafened ears were ringing from the sound of the guns and the screams of wounded and dying men, but there was no time for concern - the merchant was tacking away from them, apparently unharmed save for minor damage to her rails and one hole in her fore topsail. Was she leaving? Making a run for it now she had made her defiant gesture?

Again Jesamiah swore. Was she heck - her sails were coming aback as her crew hauled the topsails around. If *Mermaid* did not meet her, any compassion he held for his dying crewmates would be worthless, for within a few minutes they might all be dead.

He glanced across the quarterdeck at Malachias, expecting him to shout orders to tack, saw him slumped across the binnacle box, his head in his hands, blood streaming between his fingers.

"Taylor!" Jesamiah ran to him, was relieved to be waved aside. The Captain lifted his head, showing a great, bloody gouge along his cheek. "I'm alright, give me a moment, I'll be alright."

But there was no time for delay; without pause Jesamiah took command. "Hands to stations for stays!" he yelled. "Tack, for God's sake! We need to bloody bring her round!" Men were running to their places, looking towards him for orders, while the gunners continued to reload and run out, making ready to fire the next blast once the Prize came into their sights again.

His concentration set on the leeches, the vertical edges of the fore topsail, Jesamiah waited, impatient, for the tell-tale flutter of the wind to touch them. "Come on, fok you, come on," he muttered, casting a swift glance at the *Christina Giselle* as she completed her turn.

Calmly the Dutch ship continued to turn, coming around in an elongated circle, presenting her opposite, larboard, side and any moment now, a second deadly barrage of cannon fire.

"Tops'l haul!" Jesamiah bellowed, and as the sail came aback the yards were hauled around. "Turn, you fickle bitch!" he muttered "do not miss stays, for pity's sake, don't bloody miss!" And as the second blast of fire and smoke tore from the merchant, *Mermaid* responded with her fore topsail pressed against the mast; was swinging through the wind. "Keep falling off!" Jesamiah shouted to the helmsman, to the men, "Meet her, damn you! Come on, move yourselves, you're too bloody slow! Square up!"

He ducked as another round of shot whistled through rails, rigging and canvas. The fore topgallant mast fell away, crashing to the deck, hands racing aloft to cut away the tangled mess. The merchant's cannons were firing one after the other, a non stop barrage, the gunners professional, experienced men, with an excellent aim.

"Get those guns reloaded!" Jesamiah bellowed, "run out, run out!"

And the Merchant got a taste of her own medicine. Holes appeared in her sails and the torn woodwork sent up sprays of flying splinters, but her captain had rigged his netting well and there was little harm done to her crew. He knew what he was about and showed it, as with cold efficiency he began to make ready to swoop around and cut behind the *Mermaid's* stern.

Jesamiah's blood froze as he watched, thought, *If he knows what he's doing, then God help us!* He issued a stream of orders. Sod Taylor – they were ending this. Now!

Appalled at the carnage she was witnessing, Tiola cried out in dismay; blood was running every where on the decks, draining out the scuppers, leaving a trail of red to mar the white foam of her wake. Each shot of the *Christina Giselle's* fire found a mark, men were being flung into the air and the sea. Limbs were severed, heads decapitated; bodies dreadfully mutilated. Those men, pirates they may be, but they were being butchered like cattle at the autumn slaughter!

Tiola's gifts, her inherited knowledge, was for healing and bringing life into the world, not to see it so wantonly and bloodily snuffed out. This was naught but Hell set loose! What drove these men to do this? Surely not the lure of silver and gold alone? Sickened by the sight and the noise and the smell, Tiola put her hand over her nose and mouth to avoid breathing in the choking, acrid smoke, tightly shut her eyes, felt the heave of the deck from the thrust of the great guns' recoil; heard the noise, smelt the smoke and gunpowder. Not being able to see exaggerated the other senses, making the horror worse - the noises louder, the cries of dying and wounded men more inhuman. She had to look! She had to watch that man with the black hair and the blue ribbons, something was drawing her to him, something over which she had no control. *Like a bee is attracted to honey*, she thought, then snorted mild self contempt. *Or a moth is seduced to the lure of a flame, only to find its wings get burnt.*

The dead and dying were sprawled in distorted heaps, some no longer recognisable as men, others remained at their guns, running them out, firing, hauling in, swabbing, ramming, reloading; running out, firing. Gun after gun as the *Christina Giselle* began to sweep in a wide curve behind the *Mermaid's* stern and immediately took her wind, leaving her crippled with no means of forward movement or escape. At least now Tiola could read the smaller ship's name, painted in gold across her stern.

Briefly, she diverted her attention to Captain Van Noord standing behind his helmsman, his hand raised, holding the gunners ready, not permitting them to fire in the tawdry, haphazard order that the Pirate had been doing. With rising horror, she realised he intended to use the full effective force of his gunnery to put an end to what he considered an inconvenient nuisance. He waited, then released his larboard guns to rake the pirate from stern to stem, a consecutive barrage of destruction, each gun firing one after the other as they came to bear. Firing straight along the *Mermaid's* deck with a mixture of round shot, chain shot, grape and langrage that took away the rudder and ripped through the great cabin below the quarterdeck, shattering the glass of the stern windows and everything in its path. Round shot tore through the bulkheads and men alike.

Blast after blast the cannon spat death and destruction in a roll of fire, one, two, three, four, five – all twelve guns, the men aboard the *Mermaid* steeling themselves as the *Christina Giselle* swept on past, some falling to their knees to pray, others curling into a protective ball. This was not a good way to die. Chain shot tangled in the *Mermaid's* already damaged rigging and wrapped around the main mast, while the small, jagged pieces of scrap iron that was langrage ploughed through flesh and bone, sail and wood alike. The resulting splinters, some several inches long, causing as much destruction as the shot itself.

Unhurried, unconcerned, her twelve guns emptied, the Dutch East Indiaman forged onward beginning to leave the pirates astern. Tiola's fingernails dug into the taffrail, tears streaming down her face as she swivelled her head to keep her gaze on the dark haired man as he jumped from the quarterdeck down into the waist.

He stumbled over the torn mess of tackle, was urgently pointing upward as he ran, shouting. Blood was staining his left bicep, seeping further into the sleeve as he gestured frantically, unaware he had been wounded by a length of splintered wood. Tiola could see it thrusting through his torn shirt and the bloodied flesh beneath. She flinched, feeling the pain he was ignoring.

Following his pointing fingers upwards, she heard, above all the noise, a distinct creak from the main topmast. Then something snapped, a loud, sharp, bang and standing and running rigging was pinging apart, wood was splitting - the whole uppermost part of the mast was groaning, sounding as if a tree was about to fall. And then the pole began to topple, slowly, so very slowly at first, leaning ponderously for a moment to one side. A cable parted and the topmast and t'gallant mast, spars, sails and rigging all tipped through the centre of balance and fell, everything coming down, crashing across the deck to drape into the sea, trailing like a bird's broken wing.

The pirates were firing muskets and pistols as if nothing else mattered, and were frantically working the two lightweight swivel guns mounted on the quarterdeck's rails but their efforts were futile. The black haired man was desperately shouting at men to clear the wreckage, to free the tangled rigging, using his cutlass to hack at the damage. With the *Christina Giselle's* stern now past the *Mermaid's* they had a wind again; but what use the wind with a shattered mast? If the Dutch Captain should turn and hit them again they would all be dead men.

Jesamiah slashed at the tangle that had once been a topmast. One more broadside and they would be finished. His arm was screeching pain, blood slithering, wet and sticky, down his arm. He ignored it, would tend it later - if he survived that long. If he had not bled to death or stopped another shot of iron.

"Keep firing!" he bellowed at the men in the waist – although only two guns were now intact. "Gunners, forget this mess just keep bloody firing! You other men, get aloft and help cut those shrouds free!" Anger stormed in his eyes, despair shrieking in his deep, husky, voice. He paused from his hacking, wiped sweat and grime from his forehead with the back of his sleeve, spreading blood grotesquely across his face. *Mermaid* lay wounded and sluggish, as if along with the broken mast her heart had been torn from her. Their only hope was to keep fighting, for she could not run. Jesamiah closed his eyes, not wanting to witness her agony. She was a good ship, she did not deserve to die so ignobly.

With a cheer of relief and success, the men managed to hack through the last cable and the mast fell away with a plume of spray into the sea. They had a chance now, a slight chance to hold their own when the Dutch Indiaman next fired, when she tacked to run alongside, board and finish the job.

Except she did not. The *Christina Giselle* was sailing away as if the *Mermaid* did not exist; her guns were being run in and as Jesamiah continued to watch, stunned, open-mouthed in furious disbelief, her maincourse fell in a billowing cloud of canvas from the yard and topmen were racing aloft to loosen off the topgallants. Sailing away as if nothing out of the ordinary had happened. Not bothering to waste her time or effort in finishing off an unworthy opponent.

Jesamiah swore, the sweat trickled down his face, beneath his armpits and the small of his back. He sheathed his cutlass, wincing, clamped his hand over the wound in his arm, watched, incredulous, as sedately returning to her original course the *Christina Giselle* put water between them.

The entire engagement had taken no more then fifteen short minutes.

"Bastard!" he yelled as he stood amid the chaos of broken wreckage, the shattered mast, the dead and the dying. No time just yet to feel for them; that must came later – they all knew the risks of a fight, survive and hope to become rich, or die poor. That was the deal. Death stared them all in the face, whether it was from the raking of a cannon's shot or the tightening of the hangman's noose. The close proximity of death was not an easy companion, but while pirates lived, the life was good and the rewards when they came along, worthwhile.

The wounded needed tending, a necessary task that Jesamiah hated but was another of his responsibilities as quartermaster. They needed a surgeon aboard. When they reached Cape Town he would have to remind Malachias about finding one.

Glancing along the shambles of the deck he ran his hand through his hair, unsure where to make a start. Looked again at the departing ship. *Damn you!* he thought. *Damn you to Hell and back!* Then he paused, stared, not believing what he was seeing. Was that a child? A sodding child was standing at the merchant's taffrail! Had that Dutch captain been so confident he had allowed a passenger to observe the whole debacle? Cocky bastard! Jesamiah narrowed his eyes to see more clearly, but from this distance detail was distorted. All he could see was the shape of a girl with dark hair - a girl for God's sake!

Annoyed, he glowered, but as he turned away to get on with what he ought to be doing he had the uneasy feeling she was watching him, and him alone. The hairs at the nape of his neck prickled and his spine shivered. Sound faded from his ears; the moans and pleas for help from the wounded, Malachias calling orders - everything blurring in his mind as if nothing else mattered, as if there was nothing else outside the existence of himself and this girl. She was staring at him and he felt naked and vulnerable beneath her gaze, as if she had stripped him of his rough, hard exterior, the necessary façade of a pirate. As if she could see the private hidden person. He found his hands were shaking, had the strangest feeling this girl, whoever she was, knew everything about him. Everything.

Stranger still, he did not mind her knowing his secrets, felt almost relieved that at last he could share them with someone. Her presence was not intrusive but comforting - and suddenly a suppressed memory of the past flooded into his mind, a memory of experiencing something similar to this before!

He had been on his knees spewing his guts into wet earth puddled with his own urine; was distraught, crying and gasping for breath. He was not yet fifteen years old and his brother was behind him carolling vicious and vindictive laughter. And through the shame and fear he had distinctly felt a hand resting between his shoulder blades: a sensation filled with love and protection. And a voice had entered his head, breaking through the utter, bereft and lonely despair.

~ Fight him! ~

Words he was sure, later, he had imagined, for everything that dark night had been tainted with bewildering distress. Yet, squinting across the widening gap of the sea at this girl he questioned his assumption. Had he imagined it?

He felt – how did he feel? Odd, as if someone was standing beside him, smiling. As if a smile was in his head – not words, not thoughts, just a friendly, protective smile.

- 24 -

He looked down at the splinter of wood stabbing into his arm, at the blood soaking his shirt. Was this nonsense because of blood loss? Making him light headed? Yet, beyond this stupid idea that someone was standing here with him, there was no disorientation, no confusion.

He had a sudden urge to look at that child properly; spun on his heel and hurried up the companionway steps to the shattered chaos of the quarterdeck, claimed the telescope from beside the ship's compass, mercifully, both still intact. Extending the tube to its full length, was about to raise it to his eye when Malachias, his face covered in blood, called his name and distracted his attention. The spell was broken. Jesamiah turned to answer, and when he looked again she was gone; no one stood at the stern of the *Christina Giselle*. There was no girl. He shrugged, perhaps he had imagined her after all? Perhaps it was the smoke, the noise, the anguished cries of the wounded begging for help – his anger – playing tricks on his mind? He shook his head to clear his senses, set his attention to concentrating on more important things; getting this sliver of wood out of his arm, tending the wounded – there would be amputations to do. The dead to see to, a few words of respect to be spoken over them before the corpses were sent overboard. The *Mermaid* to be salvaged, somehow.

Busy, his mind occupied, he forgot the girl.

As Tiola, with her gift of Craft, had intended him to.

*

Tethys rippled, annoyed at the fluctuations of sound thumping and echoing, intrusive, through her vast domain of the oceans. She stared upward at the faint glimmer that was the sparkle of the sun on the surface of the sea. Two ships. Men. Stupid, irreverent, irrelevant men. She had no time or patience with the world of humans. The thud of cannon oscillated the water. Was that all they thought about? Killing and maiming each other? She shifted position, her great amorphous mass disturbing the sand, stirring the bones of the dead, her collected trophies, and flushing the fishes into swarms of iridescent panic. Noticed as she went, turning away from the pathetic self-destruction going on high above her, a gleam of gold and a flutter of blue. She halted, intrigued. She liked pretty, shiny things, for there was only limited colour and light down here in the deep.

Tethys looked again, closer, projecting her senses into the confined world of the pirate ship. She heard the moans of the wounded, the shouting, the confusion; smelt the pungent odour of cannon smoke and seared flesh; the sickly-sweet stench of spilt blood. Found the presence of the man with the blue ribbons and scanned deeper, infiltrating and exploring his body and his mind, touching his deliberately concealed loneliness. Her probing, beyond a strong, sudden smell of the sea and the stink of rotting fish, quite undetected.

Assigning him and everything about him to her infinite memory she sank down satisfied, into the gloom of her own timeless existence. A man, a handsome, seductive man of passion and charm. A man of the sea who wore blue ribbons in his hair and a golden acorn, a trinket of the land, that other place, dangling from his ear.

She knew little of the land, it was beyond her interest or care, but her understanding did encompass the life-seed of the oak, a tree of longevity and imposing stature, of dignity, endurance and strength. She knew of oak because ships were made from its wood, and she knew of acorns because the sailors aboard those ships believed they brought luck, protection and fertility.

She quite fancied an acorn for herself. Either one would do. The earring was pretty - but the man would be the better prize.

- Four -

Mermaid had been heeling slightly, as they rounded the point protecting the natural harbour of Cape Town she steadied on an even keel and then rolled to starboard. With cordage and timber complaining, the wheel was put over.

"Tops'l sheets," Jesamiah shouted as the ship glided into her destined anchorage to the western edge of the Bay. "Tops'l clew lines... Helm-a-lee!" And *Mermaid* turned into the wind, her sails coming aback, her forward motion ceasing as she eased sedately to a halt.

The lime-whitened walls of buildings with their green shutters and tiled or thatched roofs, sprawled between the sea and the rugged, upward sweep of the flat-topped, aptly named Table Mountain. Flanking the dominant plateau was the smaller cone of Devil's Peak and the elongated Signal Hill, the lower extension of the Lion's Head, a mass of rock rearing two thousand feet high that did indeed resemble a crouching lion. Jesamiah found himself staring, awe-struck. The panorama was spectacular.

Driven by the relentless wind howling up from the ice-ridden lands of Antarctica, the Atlantic swept in to spume against tumbled rocks and run against the wide, sweeping curve of sand. Jesamiah had expected Cape Town to be as he imagined all of Africa; impenetrable jungle or empty desert shimmering in a haze of blistering heat. Yes, it was hot, for this was January the southern hemisphere summer, but apart from the bareness of the mountain tops, everything was flushed with a vibrant green.

The famous gardens of the Dutch East India Company, covering all of forty-five acres, were vivid against the backdrop of Table Mountain. The Dutch had planted them specifically; trees and bushes for fruit, and every kind of vegetable that would grow in this climate. The object, to create a trade post for the

Vereenigde Oost-Indische Compagnie, the V.O.C., to provide a convenient place for Dutch ships to make repairs, for sailors to rest and stores to be replenished. The trade post had become a settlement, and the settlement had rapidly expanded into a town of more than one thousand permanent residents. Of the fluid population, there was no count. Probably three times as many again.

The crew, leaning over the rails or hanging from the shrouds were gossiping, excited. Jesamiah ignored the buzz of conversation; there was always this lift of expectation at coming into harbour. He felt the euphoria himself, going ashore was suddenly very appealing. They had been at sea a long time. *Mermaid* desperately needed careening, to be safely beached somewhere for the barnacles, weed and the worm boring into her wooden hull to be scraped clean. A ship that was not careened was a slow ship, and pirate craft by necessity of their trade needed to be fast. It would have to wait a while though, until they sailed on to Madagascar where pirates were welcome and an anchorage was safe. As for the entertainment? Jesamiah grinned, anticipating the delights on offer to a healthy young man who had been at sea for more weeks than he cared to tally.

"Let go!" he yelled, and the fluked anchor, twice the height of a man, splashed down into the water, its cable chuntering busily out through the hawse-hole. They were securely anchored and Jesamiah did not mind admitting he was relieved to be here in more or less one piece. Repairing the *Mermaid* after that tangle with the *Christina Giselle* had been a frustrating, time-consuming delay, but as it turned out, not too much of a nuisance. There had been no need to pretend distress to lure another vessel in, the damage to both ship and men had been real enough.

Fortunately, they had struck lucky with a second Spanish trader homeward bound from the East Indies, full laden and worth waiting for. Hoisting Spanish colours - with Jesamiah being half the breed and able to speak the language fluently, his black hair making him look every inch a Spaniard from Cadiz, they had shouted for aid, claiming they had been attacked by pirates. Had taken the unsuspecting victim without a single shot fired from cannon or pistol. That was the art of piracy, to successfully dupe or threaten; to give the impression of horrors that could be unleashed if there was no immediate surrender. As with the *Christina Giselle* threats did not always work, usually they did - very effectively.

With the two ships made fast to one another they had taken all they required at their leisure: a new rudder, replacement sails; topmast, spars, yards, cordage, blocks – and the ship's surgeon. He had protested at being forced to work aboard a pirate craft, but once they had made sail again had knuckled down to his job. It was that or starve. He would not be permitted ashore, of course. Surgeons were hard to come by, for the duration of their stay in Cape Town harbour he was shackled and incarcerated in the forward sail locker. Well out of sight and sound of any prying eyes and ears.

For their purpose in Cape Town they had painted out the *Mermaid's* name, and added subtle disguises; rigging different sails and fixing two more ornate lanterns, procured from the Spaniard, to either side of the single lamp on the stern taffrail. She was now the highly respectable *Mary Anne,* a British trader bound for India, anchoring in harbour to take on essential supplies.

Half an hour later, the ship tidied and made ready for when she was to next sail, and wearing his best, not too faded coat and favoured three-cornered hat, Jesamiah was sauntering along the jetty towards the pentagonal fortress protecting both town and harbour. A prerequisite of all trading harbours, especially those dominated by the Dutch, to verify a ship's papers. Failure to do so could result in being blasted out of the water by the several cannon aimed directly at the hull.

He followed the tree-lined canal that ran down from the gardens to flow into the sea beside the fort. A pleasant stroll, except for what leered behind him at the end of the jetty down on the muddy sand of the shore. The gallows. Empty and forlorn, malevolently waiting for a man, a pirate, to decorate the cross-beam.

Tipping his hat backwards slightly and puffing his cheeks, he halted at the fort's archway, a dark-shadowed mouth gaping black against the white of lime-washed walls. Above, an impressive bell tower; he peered at a brass plaque announcing the bell had been cast in Amsterdam in 1697. Beneath it, the coat of arms of the V.O.C. All of it intent on making a statement of invincible strength. In the bright sun on the far side of the tunnel stretching beneath the arch, Dutch soldiers were drilling, muskets aslant across their shoulders. There were dungeons inside this fort. Jesamiah took a fortifying breath, straightened his hat, smoothed his moustache and touched his earring. Best get the job done, present the papers to the harbourmaster. That they were false was immaterial, they looked authentic. The task had fallen to Jesamiah because Taylor had been here before, several times. On the last occasion, only by a stroke of good fortune had he avoided an intimate friendship with those gallows.

Garrison quarters, blacksmith, sailmaker, cooper's bothies. Kitchens, bakery, armoury - the usual cramped bustle of a full-strength fortress. Jesamiah found the harbourmaster's office tucked two doors along, with Erik Vorst seated behind a desk awash with a glut of papers and documents. A sullen, fat-bellied man with bad breath, and from the way he continuously belched, a martyr to chronic indigestion.

"Where is your captain then?" Vorst asked testily as he squinted at the illegible writing of the two documents Jesamiah handed him. "It is usual for the captain to present these, not his subordinate."

"As it is usual for the *Mary Anne's* captain to be drunk in his cot. He will not emerge for another four and twenty hours yet," Jesamiah answered smoothly, his deep, husky voice losing the clipped pirate accent he used when aboard with the men. Jesamiah was educated, able to read, write, tally numbers and knew the intricacies of navigation. It came in useful to be able to change his speech patterns as necessity demanded.

Vorst belched again and scratched beneath his armpit, releasing a pungent smell of body odour. Drunk? *Ja,* he had heard the same before. "Where are you bound?"

"Bombay, Calcutta. Might cruise on down to Sumatra or Java." Jesamiah lied as he perched one buttock on the corner of the desk, ignoring the ensuing frown of disapproval. "What I would prefer to do is go on to New Holland – Australia some are calling it now, are they not? Have a go at circumnavigation. Round the world, eh? What an adventure!" He narrowed his eyes and peered into an imaginary distance, enjoying the false embellishment of conversation.

He could think of nothing more dreadful than sailing all the way around the globe. Pitting ship and soul against those monstrous seas off Cape Horn? No thank you! Bravado might suit some, but he had all the excitement he needed in the existence he already had. He sighed, slapped his hands against his thighs, rubbed them along the worn canvas of his breeches. "The *Mary Anne* is not suitably equipped for such a journey, and our captain is not," he paused rubbed his moustache, his embarrassment apparently genuine. "I was going to say competent, but that sounds disloyal. Intrepid, perhaps?"

Failing to see the lie, shrugging, the harbourmaster rolled the ship's papers and handed them back to Jesamiah along with the document giving permission to be anchored. "*Dank u.* Hand this in at the gate as you leave, it'll ensure the guns are stood down. In my opinion for such a venture you either have to be barking mad or an utter bore. We have both lack-lustre qualities residing here in Cape Town at the moment. Captain Woodes Rogers put in two months ago." He vaguely gestured over his shoulder. "His ships are in harbour, you must have noticed them? *Duke* and *Duchess.* I wish to God he'd stay his mouth, return aboard and clear off back to England. If I hear one more account of how he captured the *Acapulco Galleon* or *Nuestra Señora*, I'll cut my throat," muttered quietly under his breath, "Or his."

Jesamiah frowned. He had noticed the ships, had taken a careful look at what was anchored as they sailed into harbour to ensure the *Christina Giselle* was not among them. It would not do to be recognised. "Rogers? Never heard of him."

"Nor do you want to. He seems to have made a profitable job of his privateering commission against Spain and is determined to ensure everyone knows about it. His holds are stuff-packed with Spanish bullion, so he claims. Don't believe a word of it myself."

Carefully, Jesamiah schooled his face to remain neutral, although it was difficult to keep the gleam of lust from his eyes. Two rich pickings right here in front of them? Best leave them alone, they would never get past the fort's battery, not while the *Mermaid* was worm-riddled and encrusted with barnacles. Now, if they had already careened? Ah well.

"Privateer eh?" He said with a shrug. "A British commission to legally plunder anything flying a Spanish ensign? I don't suppose the Spanish see it that way. They'd say he was nothing but a scamp of a pirate."

"We don't hold with pirates in these waters," Vorst answered huffily, affronted at the offensive word, *pirate*.

"Rightly so, but the distinction between privateering and pirating depends on which side the wind is blowing from, does it not?" Jesamiah smiled, friendly, at ease. "If I were Spanish for example, I could blast the shit out of *Duke* and *Duchess* and claim I had every right to do so."

"Except the heavy artillery of this fort would be blowing you to kingdom come before you could get more than one shot fired."

Conceding the point, Jesamiah grinned, adding, "Unless the Dutch government decide to change alliance and side with Spain."

At the disapproving glare he thought it prudent to alter tack. "You said one is mad?"

"As one of your English March hares. Dampier. William Dampier. Had too much of the sun boiling his brains if you ask me. Obsessed with detailing every living thing he comes across, always scribbling in his note-book. I saw him flat on his belly down on the beach the other day, wig askew, studying a crab would you believe? I mean, for God's sake, the things are only fit for eating. What point in drawing the little sods?"

Jesamiah's eyes had lit up, glowing with excitement. "Dampier? Now him I *have* heard of." William Dampier here in Cape Town? The most famous, most successful buccaneer to torment the Spanish – a man who had drawn a very fine line between legitimate privateering and the hanging offence of piracy! He had first rounded Cape Horn and crossed the Pacific to the East Indies in 1680, had circumnavigated the World yet again since then – three occasions if this Woodes Rogers had indeed commanded another successful expedition. Jesamiah's copy of Dampier's book, so well read it was dog-eared and falling apart. To meet him? Ah, the questions he would ask! He had no intention of attempting such a venture, but that did not deter Jesamiah's enthralment of reading about it.

Vorst was weary of the subject. He pushed himself from his chair, his hand holding the bulge of his belly. "Talking of crabs, I would not recommend too many of the blighters. Give you belly ache." He gestured Jesamiah towards the door. "If you would excuse me, I need to sit on the comfort stool a while. If you are a follower of adventure try presenting yourself at the *Golden Hind,* one of our more respectable taverns. Rogers is billeted there, no doubt he will delight in boring the wax out of a fresh ear."

Sketching a half-hearted salute to the harbourmaster's disappearing back Jesamiah casually rummaged through the scatter of papers on the desk, found a few documents that might prove useful in the future and stuffed them into his coat's cavernous inner pocket, along with a bag of coin and an attractive pocket watch left lying there on the desk for anyone to pick up.

Outside, standing on the civilian side of the arch he considered what to do next. The brothel first or a tavern? He turned up the street, away from the range of buildings that served as slave quarters for inbound wretches. The wealth of South Africa as with the Caribbean islands of the West Indies and the tobacco and cotton colonies of the Americas, were being built by the captive labour of Irish and British convicts and African blacks. Only on a pirate ship were men treated as equal. The Sweet Trade, where a man could be free of the law and bigotry.

A neat, pretty town with streets set in an orderly grid pattern, the overall effect spoilt by the rough roads, wandering animals and the stink of an open sewage system. Warehouses, ship yards, chandlers and carpenters were arrayed along the sea-front. Behind them the more wealthy townhouses were double-storied, typical Dutch in design, all standing alongside taverns, lodgings and workshops. A scatter of churches, a few mosques. And brothels. There were always brothels.

The uphill ground swayed and dipped as he walked, a common problem for those who had been a while at sea, the movement of the ship staying with the body even on solid land. From experience Jesamiah knew to keep his eyes looking straight ahead and ignore the uncomfortable feeling that he was about to fall, but all the same, his gait rolled and he almost tripped up twice when misjudging the height of steps. He turned left and the street suddenly widened into a market square cluttered with stalls and bothies, a multitude of people, buyers, sellers, browsers, beggars and thieves.

Buying a coconut-shell bowl of minced lamb and rice he strolled along while eating, scooping the food with his fingers, enjoying the delicious mess it made. Wiping his hands every so often down the front of his coat he casually glanced at the trade stalls, wondered how Malachias was faring with selling some of the cargo wharf-side. That was his problem, Jesamiah had played his part. He stopped to inspect a few bedraggled parrots and wandered on. He was tempted to make his way to the *Golden Hind,* it would be wonderful to meet Dampier. Would such a move be sailing too close to the wind? If anyone could spot a pirate masquerading as a trader it would be Dampier. Jesamiah sighed, he would have enjoyed personally meeting the man. Best not.

Enthusiasm for these few precious hours ashore was draining away, his mood turning sour, the prospect of sport in bed with one of Cape Town's doxies losing its appeal. Perhaps a tot or two of rum would rekindle his interest?

Dismally, he inspected the several taverns on the uphill side of the square. Nothing seemed inspiring. He wove his way through the crowd, seemingly, every race, colour and creed from every continent; a babble of languages, a variety of costume and clothing. Was it any wonder Cape Town had earned for itself the title *Tavern of the Seas?*

He paused at a stall where a German was enquiring after the tobacco pipes for sale, picking each one up to closely inspect it with a squinting short-sightedness. Jesamiah slid in beside him, feigning interest in purchasing a pipe for himself, his eyes lingering on the fat money pouch the fool had carelessly put down on the table top. His fingers twitching towards it, Jesamiah grimaced. So tempting to quietly take it up, slip it into his pocket... he was not here to draw attention to himself. He withdrew his hand then abruptly changed his mind, swung back to lift the pouch, clasping his fingers neatly around it – just as the German remembered the thing.

Jesamiah's reaction was the quicker.

"Your money, *mein herr?* It is not sensible to leave it where any common cut-purse could so easily steal it." With a smile, he took up the astonished man's hand and put the pouch securely into his palm. Touching his hat in genial salute, Jesamiah strolled on, puffing his cheeks. That had been close! The penalty for stealing was no different than piracy. Hanging.

Turning into a side street he headed back downhill in the direction of the harbour, then frowned at a sudden disturbance outside a blacksmith's bothy at the far end of an intersecting alley. A girl's shrill and furious shout.

"Leave him be! Can you not see he cannot carry you? He is lame!"

A man was beating a sweat-sodden saddle horse about the head with his riding crop, and a dishevelled girl was as vigorously pummelling the man with her fists and feet.

"Damn creature threw me. This be none of your business girl, clear off!" One side of the man's apparel was dusty, the horse's knees were scuffed. He raised the crop again, about to set the lash into the animal's sweating hide - the girl grabbed his arm and bit his hand, her teeth clamping into the pad of soft flesh beneath his thumb. The man turned with a yelp of outrage and started hitting her instead, his curses a stream of blasphemy, the blows coming down on her shoulders and back.

"I will do what I want with my own horse, you little she-devil!"

Tempted to ignore it as none of his business Jesamiah scowled then stepped forward. He disliked bullies. His hand encircled the man's wrist staying the next fall of the crop. "That sir, is not a gentlemanly attitude. She is but a girl and I can see, even if you cannot, despite the fact I am a seaman not a horseman, that this animal is lame. He probably stumbled because he is favouring the off-fore."

The man wrenched his arm free and made to strike Jesamiah's face. With a hiss of steel the pirate's cutlass slid from its scabbard, the tip of the blade pricking through the white cravat beneath the man's double chin.

"Perhaps you did not hear me?" Jesamiah repeated, wearing a charming smile but with menace rasping in the tone of his voice.

"The horse requires attention." He called into the smithy. "Ahoy there!"

The sound of hammering ceasing the smith, a grizzle-haired Dane, sauntered from the shadows of his forge, sweat beading his forehead. He smelt of horse and smoke.

"This animal's unsound," Jesamiah said, not lowering his blade. "My friend here would be obliged if you would kindly investigate the problem."

Grunting indifferently, the smith lifted the gelding's fore-foot and inspected the inside of the hoof. From the pocket of his leather apron, produced a hoof-pick and prised loose a stone wedged beneath the iron shoe. "Been there some while, I reckon," he said as he set the foot down, his hand automatically going to the horse's neck to calm it. "Not surprising he's lame."

"Thank you, I am indebted t'you." Jesamiah felt in his coat pocket for a coin, flipped it at the smith. "I appreciate your service, even if this tub of melted lard don't." He lowered the cutlass, did not sheathe it. "I suggest, sir, the next time you find your fat backside cannot stay in a saddle, you question whether the fault be your own poor ability, not the creature's." He slid the cutlass into its scabbard and touched his hat, with his other hand took hold of the girl's arm and forcefully marched her away before either she or the man realised it. He rounded a corner and set her loose with an aggressive shake.

"And I would suggest to you, young lady, that you stay out of grown men's business or you will come to a sorry and sticky end."

She stared innocently up at him, her head cocked to one side, her dark eyes meeting square with his. "I am not frightened of imbeciles like him. I can look after myself."

"Oh aye?" Jesamiah countered, taking her chin in his hand and twisting her face to the side. The mark was livid across her cheek, spots of blood oozing in several places. "A tad higher and he could have had your eye out, lass."

He moved her face the other way, inspecting it closer. She was no urchin. Her nails were not bitten or dirty, her hair had no sign of lice and her gown, if plain, was of a passable quality. She smelt and looked clean.

Nor was she as young as he had first assumed. Fourteen? He guessed wrongly, a year out. She was as thin as a stick, although not malnourished, more along the line of a late developer - her bosom had not yet rounded, but even in maturity she would probably boast nothing bigger than small apples. Unlike the ripe melons on some of the strumpets he knew. His own height of two inches below six feet exaggerated her petite stature. Frowning, he looked at her more intently. There was something familiar about her though. "Do I know you?" he asked.

"We have not met, surr," she answered truthfully, giving a bobbed curtsey of good manners. "My guardian has employment at the *Golden Hind* but we came here from England." Her hint of a Cornish accent was a slight, burred lilt; pleasant.

The coincidence of the *Golden Hind* was too much to resist. Jesamiah grinned. He firmly believed in grabbing opportunities as they presented themselves. Only, sometimes, you had to forcefully go after them with a club.

"Then, if you will be so kind as to show me the way, I shall escort you to your guardian and strongly suggest he gives your backside a thorough paddling."

Tiola said nothing, trotted meekly at his side, her eyes occasionally lifting to study his handsome face, taking in every subtle detail of the man with the blue ribbons. The pirate.

He did not recall her. She did not expect him to. In his eyes she was nothing more than a lanky, undeveloped child - hardly the sort of female he would normally notice! And here, this moment, was not the right place to be revealing herself to him, to be undoing the manipulated fact that he had completely forgotten her.

- Five -

Jesamiah found Captain Woodes Rogers to be a stout man, full of his own self-importance and liking the sound of his own voice. Unsightly scarring marked what was left of the upper part of his left jaw.

"Pistol ball shot it away," Rogers explained, offering his hand and seeing Jesamiah's eyes stray to the damage. "Can't go capturing the Dons' ships without expecting some form of retaliation, eh lad?" He slapped Jesamiah heartily on the shoulder, ushering him down an unlit corridor towards the private saloon of the tavern.

On behalf of the girl's guardian, Rogers thanked Jesamiah repeatedly. "The dear lady has been frantic with worry about the lass these past two hours – ye'll join m'party for a glass of wine?"

He preferred the taste of rum or brandy, but flattered at being invited, Jesamiah did not refuse.

"I thank you again sir, for your kindness with the young miss," Rogers enthused as he waved Jesamiah ahead of him. He lowered his voice, although even then he had a tone that could carry a quarter of a mile. "Child's been here five weeks, but has already caused no end of disruption. Needs a good thrashing if you ask me. Comes from Cornwall. Rough lot, those Cornish. Like the Welsh, untameable." He shrugged. "Her guardian is a wonderful woman, for all she is of the servile class." Impatient, he gestured for his guest to open the door, go through. In the sudden light of a south facing room, full of sunshine, Jesamiah realised Rogers' foot was swathed in bandaging.

"Another misfortune," the captain explained as he hobbled into the room. "Shot through the heel. Blasted thing has played me up the entire voyage, these two years or so. The girl's guardian, Mistress Pendeen bless her, knows a thing or two about poulticing, almost has it to rights now. Damned good woman." He gestured a large bosom with his hands. "Shame I have a wife, eh?" He laughed. "Come, let me introduce ye. William, we have a saviour of errant young ladies among us! Sir, meet my friend and navigator, William Dampier."

"Er, Acorne," Jesamiah said, politely bowing, unexpectedly flustered. "Jesamiah Acorne, with an 'e', at your service, sir." He could not believe his fortune, here he was making the acquaintance of the great William Dampier himself!

A third man, tall and thin with a grey beard and a head of thick white hair, was rising from a chair. Rogers introduced him also. "Alexander Selkirk. Found him marooned some several hundred miles west of Chile. Been there over four years had ye not, Selkirk?"

Jesamiah did not know whether to gape in admiration or guffaw out loud. Were these men serious? If it were not for the credentials he could merit to Dampier, the conversation would have seemed nothing more than a mother's telling of a fabulous bed-time tale. Marooned for *four* years? How had the man survived?

Seating himself, Rogers, oblivious to Jesamiah's amusement, forged on. "My good friend Defoe, back in England, so his prattling letters mention, cannot wait to meet Selkirk here. He intends to write his experiences down as an adventure story. Says he'll call it *Robinson Crusoe* to protect the innocent involved in the tale. Absurd eh? Ha, ha!" He had a habit of laughing at his own poor jests.

Selkirk had the manners to blush. "Nothing to tell. I had a falling out with the captain and demanded to be put ashore for m'own safety and sanity. Hadn't bargained on another ship not coming by the sooner."

"Now my book," Rogers interrupted, "I shall call '*A Cruising Voyage Round the World: first to the south seas thence to the East Indies and Homeward by the Cape of Good Hope*'. What think you of that? A title to stir the vitals, eh?"

Politely, Jesamiah agreed. What was it the harbourmaster had said? *"I wish to God he'd stay his mouth, and clear off back to England."* With that, too, Jesamiah found himself agreeing. He so wanted to talk to the quiet and polite Dampier, but Rogers was not the sort to heave to in a following wind. Nothing was going to stop him from bending a new ear to his account of heroic privateering.

"It is interesting to hear you talk so freely of your commission," Jesamiah said at one point, while Rogers was issuing a refill of wine. "There are more than a few who insist privateering has much in common with piracy."

Rogers spluttered indignation. "Good God man, pirates are the dregs of this Earth! Rogues the lot of 'em. I took only ships at war with my Country, and every last gold and silver piece shall go back to m'sponsors." He cleared his throat and brushed at the stains he had splashed over his embroidered waistcoat. "Of course, I shall receive my share of the profits. I carry about two million on board, ye know."

"I would not let any self-respecting pirate hear you boast that fact too often," Jesamiah said quietly, with a deceptively charming smile.

"They do not scare me, son. Let 'em come! Let 'em try at me! I'd wipe my arse with them, as easy as pissing."

"Even so..."

"The difference between a pirate and a privateer, my boy, is that of a matter of honour. The former has no idea of the meaning of the word."

Jesamiah was beginning to weary of Rogers' arrogance. "What is the Government to do with all these privateers who carry the excuse of a Letter of Marque, such as yourself, when this current skirmish with Spain is over? As it soon shall be. It is only a matter of time for a treaty of peace to be signed. What do the politicians expect the privateers to do then? Shuffle off home to sit with their feet in the hearth, smoking pipes of heavily taxed tobacco? Or go on the Account?"

"Pirates?" Rogers repeated. "Swabs, the lot of them. Washed up, drunken, swabs. I have no concern for pirates, they hold no threat for me."

Jesamiah was tempted to prove this blustering idiot wrong by suggesting to Malachias they board one of those ships sitting idle in the harbour and strip it of everything of worth. Ah, Rogers was right, no pirate would think of attacking him. Pirates tended to pick on the weak, the stragglers, the undefended merchantmen. Those ships in the harbour? Too many guns and experienced gunners.

"Nevertheless," William Dampier suggested after a silent pause, "Pirates do roam these African waters, and they are a threat. The *Christina Giselle* was attacked, was she not?"

Rogers barked a derisive guffaw. "Attacked, aye, but the cowards came off worse, no match for her superiority. That's it with pirates, y'see, no balls, no guts."

To hide his expression, Jesamiah sipped at the wine, a nasty feeling sinking heavily into the pit of his stomach. He wished he had asked for rum now. He felt his throat run dry, the colour fade from his face. "The *Christina Giselle?*" he asked, hoping they did not hear the unnatural croak that came out.

Rogers answered in his gruff, no-nonsense manner. "Dutch East Indiaman put in here at Cape Town a few weeks past. Had a brush with a bunch of scoundrels. Soon sent them packing. That's where my good lady with her poultices and bandages came from. The Captain, good fellow, well mannered, can't remember his name, recommended her. Passenger on board, making her way here with her ward, bit of a rough child. Always up to something, little madam. You know her of course, you trudged her back to quarters did ye not? Has eyes that follow ye - gives me the shivers frankly. Let me at a pirate over a precocious young wench, any day eh? Ha, ha!"

Jesamiah's skin crawled. He *knew* he had seen her before! He swallowed down the wine, suddenly finding it unpalatably sweet and sickly. Thought perhaps it might be prudent to get back to the *Mermaid.* Wondered how practical it would be to round up the crew.

Hell's tits! If the little brat opened her mouth to sing...

Six

Aboard the *Mermaid*, men were slogging at the capstan, slowly winching the dripping anchor cable in and laboriously stowing it to dry on the slats raised above the bilge in the lower deck. Many pirates, Tiola had heard, did not bother; what did it matter if an anchor cable rotted? They could easily obtain another one. The crew of the *Mermaid*, however, appeared to take pride in their vessel. Was that *his* doing Tiola wondered as she shaded her eyes against the dazzle of the rising sun. Or did they have an exceptionally good captain?

Gulls were riding the swell of the sea, and waders were strung out along the length of the bay busy delving into the sand for shellfish, shrimps and small creatures left exposed by the ebbing tide. To the far side of the harbour men were preparing to take the fishing boats out, the red sails contrasting with the vivid blue of a new day's clean-washed sky.

Clutching the rusting rail, she descended the weed-slimed stairway from the jetty and stepped on to the firm expanse of wet sand; walked, her head dipped against the bullying of the wind to where the surf was receding from the beach. Told herself she was a fool to be blinking away tears. Her cloak, gown and petticoats were flapping in the wind, the sea snagging at the hems, leaving them stained and sodden, making them a heavy weight about her ankles.

Hands were climbing the *Mermaid's* rigging, running out along the yards and dropping to the footropes below, mindless of the possible danger of falling. Tiola heard his voice carried by the wind across the bay.

"Let fall fore tops'l." A pause as the sail mid way up the foremast spilt with a rumbling crackle. Then, "Fores'l!" and the lower sail fell.

They were leaving! She had not expected him to sail away!

As the great expanse of the lower sail on the forward mast unfolded majestically, it sagged a moment then filled, and the *Mermaid*, free of the restraint of her anchor was gliding forwards the canvas catching the wind as she began to lie over and gather way. Thrusting effortlessly into it, she met the first roller and a burst of spray sent a shimmer of rainbow colour across the spar of the bowsprit pointing ahead of her like a finger. She looked beautiful with the first rays of the sun striking on her white hull, sparkling on the churning foam of her rapidly lengthening wake.

Tiola was not a seer, the as yet immature ability of Craft that she possessed did not bestow her with such talent, yet she knew Jesamiah was meant to be with her. Although if he was leaving, perhaps she was wrong? He was handsome – a charming rogue. Was her attraction towards him nothing more than a young girl's idle fancy? At least, now, she knew his name. Jesamiah Acorne.

The *Mermaid* was leaving. *He* was leaving! Irrational disappointment swamped her.

Confusing images had tumbled through her mind during the night. Some as dreams, some as half-awakened thoughts, so that she did not know on fitfully waking, which was real which was nonsense. Was this all nonsense, standing here shivering in the wind as a new day trundled in from the east?

When had he remembered her? Realised her face was the one he had seen staring at him over the stern of the *Christina Giselle?* She had carefully and deliberately blurred his memory, for her instinct had warned her it was too early for them to be together: she was too young, he needed his freedom. But oh! She did not want him to go! What – who - had reminded him? Something had triggered the connection while he had been talking to Captain Rogers. He had taken his leave in haste, the seaman's natural roll obvious in his stride as he had hurried through the door and out into the street. Tiola had been waiting for him, sitting on the narrow flight of stairs where she could see the door to the private saloon, where no one could see her. Had darted after him, wanting to call out, to say he need not fear her, she would not betray him. But he had gone, disappearing into the labyrinth of alleyways. Why, why had she not said something to reassure him as he had walked with her?

Could she do something to stop him? She had always known how to weave simple tricks of slight of hand, had discovered she possessed the other, older and deeper Craft when its use had been desperately needed - when her father had tried to rape her and her mother had killed him for it. Since that night there had been no necessity to test the full strength of her new-awakened power. Was this an opportunity to do so?

Chewing her lip Tiola considered. Could she force Jesamiah to stay? If the ship was damaged ... Raising her hand she fashioned a subtle figure-of-eight motion with her splayed fingers, concentrated on the sails, the expanse of canvas. Think only of those sails. Clear the mind of all else, see only the sails.

Potent energy surged within her, along her spine through her shoulders. Down her arm to her fingers. A great force of controlling, dark, power swelling and expanding within her - and then another thought, one of alarm thundering into her head in an explosion of realisation. This was wrong! Wrong to cause something to happen for want of her own satisfaction. Wrong! She dropped her arm, thrust it behind her back, her fingers crossed to ward off the stink of evil giggling its malevolence all around her.

Mermaid was ploughing forward, dipping and lifting through the sea as if she were the creature she was named for, half woman half fish – and a sharp, sudden, *bang,* like the discharge of a musket being fired in a confined space lurched across the bay, the sound darting off towards the indifferent gaze of Table Mountain. The lower corner of the *Mermaid's* fore topsail was flying loose, sending the entire sail writhing and flapping, tangling itself around the topmast forestay, yawing the boat off-balance and sending her askew.

A wild gasp sped from Tiola's mouth. What had she done!

"Clew up! Move, you buggers!" Jesamiah's voice, shouting, angry and urgent. "Ease the sheets! Ease them away there!"

A man's shadow crossed Tiola's own, stretching over the wet ripples where the sea had washed. "Cordage must have severed. Tops'l sheet worn through, I expect."

Not seeing him arrive Tiola jumped as she realised he was standing beside her. "Master Dampier!" she gasped. "You startled me!" She looked up at the tall, middle-aged man, thankful that if she were to have a companion it was not the patronising Captain Rogers or the dour Mr Selkirk.

"My apologies Miss, that I did not intend to do." He bowed, polite, smiled.

She liked Mr Dampier. He had sailed the world and seen things, people and places, no other had seen, yet he was a modest man with a natural curiosity who never boasted of his cleverness. What he did was for science, not for himself.

Dampier gave a slight inclination to his head. "And I also beg pardon, Miss Oldstagh for using sailor's jargon. A *sheet* is the nautical term for the ropes used to trim – manoeuvre - the sails. We never say 'rope' aboard ship. Its rigging or cordage."

She knew that, did not say so for it was kind of him to explain. Most men either did not bother or assumed because she was female and a child, she would not be interested. She closed her eyes, let her held breath subside, a tear of relief meandering down her cheek. She was not responsible for the rope – sheet - snapping but had come so close to being so utterly stupid!

"There, look now, the crisis is almost over." Mr Dampier indicated the *Mermaid* with his telescope. "They have the sail tamed; the topmen will soon fully sort the problem." He smiled down at her and realised she was silently weeping. Immediately concerned he wiped at the wet trail of a tear with the pad of his thumb.

"Do not fret yourself, puss, they were never in danger."

"I caused it!" Tiola cried, her confused emotions bursting from her.

"You? How could you have caused it, puss? No my dear, a faulty line that was all. Sheets, all cordage wears ragged where it chafes. It is a common problem, we are forever wrapping bandaging of one type or another, or splicing in new hemp if nothing more can be done."

He did not understand her meaning, nor could she tell him there were laws by which she carried and used her Craft. Laws made outside time, at the dawn of time, that forbade her to do intentional harm. She had to say something however, or her silence would lengthen into rudeness. His boots, she noticed, were grimed with sand and sea-water had soaked his stockings. In his hand, as ever, he carried his note book and brass telescope.

She forced brightness into her tone. "You are up early Mr Dampier. Have you been watching the birds?"

He chuckled. "I could say the same for you lass? Nay, I was observing Venus. That orb low on the horizon resembling a very bright star."

Tiola turned her head to look where he pointed.

"Is it not a glorious sight? My hope," he sighed wistfully, "is that one day man shall construct a telescope fine enough to see the six planets in all their full and wondrous detail. Alas, this poor apology of a specimen is all I possess."

"Yet surr, is it not better than your naked eye?" Tiola held her silence on saying more, for she could not be telling him there were not a mere six planets; that there were others beyond the giant of Jupiter.

"Aye lass, it is!" he answered with a laugh, brushing his hand fondly along the brass of his beloved instrument. "Would you care to observe Venus through it? Or perhaps that boat sailing away? See for yourself she is quite unharmed?"

Solemnly he held the telescope out to her. Tiola hesitated, then with a shy smile took it, extended the interlacing tubes to its full length and held the end to her eye.

Jesamiah was at the helm, steering the *Mermaid* into the waves, steadying her into her course as the rest of her canvas was spread to catch the wind. Not just the rescued topsail and the foresail now, the mainsail was filled and the triangular jib sails at the bow, all set and trimmed with efficient speed.

"She is a fine vessel," Dampier remarked at Tiola's shoulder. "You have some special interest in her?"

"Not particularly," Tiola murmured with a false shrug. How could she explain to a stranger the love she felt for someone she did not know? She was certain, now, her soul had brushed against this pirate at some time in his past. Its reason, its happening, the why and the where not yet ready to reveal itself to her. But a little bit of her had stayed with him, although not enough for him to return these same feelings. Not yet.

Her initial instinct while aboard the *Christina Giselle*, and then yesterday evening in the streets here in Cape Town, had been right. She was a witch of the White Craft, she ought to trust her own knowing and accept the serpentine path of their lives had once again crossed, but this was not the occasion for them to become permanently entwined. Would she discover the circumstances of their first meeting? Maybe, maybe not. It could have occurred during any one of their souls' many disguises. For now she would need content herself that there would be another coming together, for once a soul touched with another the two were always attracted. Like a compass swings always towards north, their inner spirits would seek each other and meet again. In a few weeks or many years, or in another lifetime. But not here, not this moment.

Even knowing all this, the disappointment washed through her, she was vulnerable and lonely, had lost everyone she loved and now she was losing him too. The child she was wanted to cry, the adult - ah, to be honest, the adult part of her wanted to weep as well. Loneliness was such a solitary, desperate emotion.

"They had to sail." Dampier said looking down at her with a sideways glance. "A pirate craft can never linger in harbour, she may be too easily recognised."

Tiola turned to gaze at him. How had he known?

Taking the glass from her, he raised it to his own eye to watch the *Mermaid*, nodding approvingly as she began to heel out into the open Atlantic. "I will grant he knows his business, that young man." Dampier lowered the telescope. "A fine mariner. A pity he is on the wrong side of what is legal and what is not."

"How do you know he is a pirate?" Tiola asked with an indrawn breath, realising she was not betraying a confidence to one who already, somehow, knew the truth.

"Oh, I guessed the set of his sail the moment I met him." Dampier smiled, winked at her. "There is too much of the pirate adventurer set dormant in me to not recognise it. He has the smell of freedom clinging to him, the freedom to do what and go where he wants." He sighed heavily. "I envy him."

"Yet you said nothing to Captain Rogers?"

Mr Dampier stood on the rapidly drying sand next to her, observing a crab burrowing its way downwards. "Neither did you, I notice. There would be many a young lass, like yourself, who would be eager to shout wolf in the fold and gain reward of praise for it."

As she gazed across the sparkle of the sea, Tiola was thoughtful. "I have only seen pictures, is the wolf not a handsome beast with his sleek coat and intelligent eyes? A hunter, hunted to extinction in England by those who do not care for things that matter?"

In turn, Mr Dampier was also thoughtful as he regarded the thin-faced girl teetering on the verge of womanhood. "For a young lass you have a wise head on your shoulders, puss. But you should not be shedding tears for a man, not yet; not at your innocent age." He eased the crick of aching muscles from his lower back and said with a teasing chuckle, "And most certainly not for a man who is a scoundrel and a pirate!"

He tucked away a strand of her hair, said, "You must beware of pirates my lady for danger lurks behind their smiles."

Tiola stared across the sea, at the *Mermaid* growing rapidly smaller as she gathered way. "I wanted to tell him he has no need to fear me. I would not have him thinking ill of me. I wish I knew if I will meet him again soon."

Dampier doubted the rascal sailing away so hurriedly would remember this girl for long beyond the forenoon, but to preserve her feelings said nothing. She was young to be experiencing the first stabbing pangs of a passing infatuation, but she was also a sharp, clever girl with a mind and intelligence older than her years and he had to admit, had chosen a most handsome-looking fellow to be smitten with. Ah, innocence. If only he were young again!

"If we could predict the future my dear, what a sorry life we would lead. There would be no expectation, no hope. No looking at the horizon for what may be sailing over it in the next hour, week or month. No excitement for the eager anticipation of a new dawn. If we were to know what is planned for us on our path, what pleasure would there be in making the journey?"

He was right, of course.

"You will not be telling Captain Rogers, will you Mr Dampier? I do not think he has much tolerance of pirates."

"Nay, he has not." Dampier agreed as he held his arm out to Tiola. Companions, they strolled back to the *Golden Hind,* and the prospect of breakfast, through streets coming alive with the business of the new day. Some fortunate fellow was going to find himself with a lucky catch for a wife one day in the not so distant future, Dampier mused. A fellow, he sincerely hoped, with more to offer than the rugged charm of a sea-scoundrel.

"Captain Rogers," he continued saying as they walked, "is the sort of man who, if he were to see a wolf, would shoot it. He would never notice its beauty."

"Where do you suspect they are sailing to?" Tiola asked, taking one last glance over her shoulder down the hill towards the harbour.

"Oh, they could be bound anywhere. Pirates are free to make their own decision. Apart from their agreed Ship's Articles, their rules, which many of them make up as they go along, and the avoidance of any Ship of the Line, they go where they wish; India, the China Seas perhaps? Or back to the wolf pack and their familiar hunting grounds among the islands of the Caribbean."

Dampier too, looked over his shoulder. First though, he guessed, they would sell their plunder at the pirate trade post in Madagascar, careen the hull and only then go home.

He envied them; envied the rogue his youth and his freedom. Envied the attraction he had for a young lass's fancy.

- Seven -

Weed quivered and fishes, disturbed, flashed and darted in exotic, woven patterns their colours illuminated by the distorted shafts of filtered sunlight. A crab scuttled sideways and buried itself rapidly in the soft, yielding sand. But the sand itself was moving, tipping and sliding, funnelling downward faster and faster – and then the depths below, the very crust of the earth, gave a heave and the underwater world that was the bottom of the turquoise, sparkling sea collapsed in upon itself, yawning into a great chasm ripping across the ocean floor. Pulling it apart as easily as a ship ploughs through a wave.

And where the jagged tear of the earthquake gaped, sand and weed, shell and fish plunged into its open jaws and the very sea itself gushed downward into the abyss. Chaos for a few, brief-passing seconds that were as nothing to the millennia of eternal time. Then everything settled and the moment of violence and confusion was past. Forgotten. There was no one to see or feel, or remember it's brief excitement.

Except for Tethys, who was aware of all that happened within her realm.

*

Their business completed in Madagascar, the decision of where to sail next had been put to the vote in democratic pirate tradition. The crew had opted for going "home" to the Caribbean. Jesamiah had not been so certain. As he had predicted to Woodes Rogers, England had negotiated a treaty of peace with France and Spain. It would have been too costly for Parliament not to, like dropping gold coin down a bottomless well.

As he had also predicted privately to Malachias, that same government had no more honesty than the worst liar in London's

Newgate Gaol. With the end of war, pardons had been promised to the sea-roving privateers who had aided the English struggle against the Spanish Dons and the Frenchies. Except, the men who sought these pardons soon discovered they were as rare as two-headed donkeys to procure. Free given, aye, if you had the gold to buy one, and if you could prove you had not committed any debased act of piracy against any vessel not French or Spanish. If you had the gold? You must be a pirate.

Jamaica: aligned east to west, the largest island in the Caribbean; one hundred and forty six miles long by fifty or so wide. Jesamiah knew the facts and could not give a damn about them. Bringing the *Mermaid* here to the Royal Naval harbour of Port Royal in search of one of these pardons was a bad idea. He had said so for the whole of the return voyage across the Atlantic. Now, locked in a dank, rat and cockroach infested prison cell these past four weeks, he wished he had said it louder.

The boredom was the worst of it. There was nothing to do except sleep or walk up and down the few yards to the far end of the cell and back again. Entertaining if you took into account the crunch of the insects beneath your boots and the necessity to step over or around the other fourteen people also incarcerated in the same cell, while avoiding the accumulation of spewed vomit, piddled urine and excreted shit.

There was one small, grilled window at eye level about two feet long by one high. Its view was mostly of the protruding rear wall of Fort Charles' extensive armoury, but Jesamiah had discovered if he stood to the side and screwed his head around he could glimpse a portion of the harbour. Or if he looked upward, the sky.

Watching a single cloud amble across a small patch of blue, he concluded, was as exhilarating as watching a new coat of paint dry on a ship's hull. The harbour view had not been agreeable either. Not since the day he had seen some thief sail the *Mermaid* away. She had been claimed and sold as a Prize by the Royal Navy -

and they did not consider that an act of piracy? Commandeering someone else's ship and selling her for profit without a by your leave?

The fact Malachias had stolen her from someone else originally was beside the point.

Jesamiah scratched at the growth of his beard, he hated having so much clinging to his chin; found a louse, crushed it between his thumb and finger. Wearily he sank down from the window to sit on the musty straw scantily covering the damp, disgusting floor. Today was the eighteenth. He knew that because yesterday, the seventeenth, they had hanged Malachias Taylor and Daniel Wickersley down on the shore below the high-tide line. Their bodies would dangle there until three tides had washed over them and then they would be cut down. Daniel's corpse would be sent for medical dissection at the naval hospital. Malachias, coated in tar, put in tight-fitting iron bars and displayed for all to see until the flesh and bones rotted to nothing. The twentieth would be Jesamiah's own hanging. Not the most enthralling prospect to look forward to.

He sighed, tried to get comfortable and spent ten minutes fidgeting before giving up and getting to his feet again. God's tears the place stank! He frowned down at a drainage hole; s'trewth, even the rats were leaving! He watched as two in succession whisked out, frowned as a third followed. Puzzled, he scanned the cell, the place was normally riddled with vermin. He counted only four - then he felt it, slight, indistinct, unmistakable. The ground was trembling. Tentatively, he put his hands up to the iron bars of the grill. Faint, almost undetectable, but it was there. Movement.

Another man, a Frenchman with a tumble of brown hair and a bush of overgrown beard was on his feet, his expression curious. "What is it do you think?" He put out his hand to touch the wall.

Jesamiah shook his head, tried to remember - 1692 was it? Yes of course, the year before he was born. An earthquake had carelessly shrugged half of Port Royal into the sea. The governor had rebuilt Fort Charles as a military and naval base, the rich moving their mansions across the bay to establish the present town of Kingston, leaving the poor to salvage what they could from the rubble. Stepping back from the wall he stared, fascinated, as a crack appeared above the rat hole and spread upward, zigzagging through the lines of mortar,

"If it's what I think it is," he answered slowly, "we might not have to worry too much about being hanged."

Other men were getting to their feet, some bewildered, others starting to shout their panic. Then Jesamiah was pulling the Frenchman violently aside, yelling a warning as the entire wall began to topple inward, the floor shaking and quivering, heaving itself upward as if the earth was shrugging her shoulders to rid herself of these annoying fleas that dared walk upon her. The sound was of several broadsides being fired at once, a huge cloud of dust adding to the spread of panic and confusion.

It lasted no more than half a minute, although with the walls and roof falling in, the cries of trapped men and Hell apparently opening up beneath their feet, it seemed a lifetime.

Jesamiah stood and stared. There was no longer a wall, only a pile of dust-smoking rubble. Nor was there a north side outer wall to Fort Charles, part of it was nothing more than a gaping hole. Coughing and spluttering he peered out through the swirling fug, dust choking in his throat and nose, coating his face and hands. A great crack had torn across the paving of the courtyard, red-coated militiamen were sprawled dead or injured, others were standing dazed and disorientated.

"*Allez monsieur! Vite! Vite!* Do not stand there – run!" The Frenchman urged as he ducked out into the open air of freedom. "Or do you wish to stay 'ere and 'ang at the governor's pleasure, after all?"

Hesitating, Jesamiah glanced behind into what had been their prison cell. He could see three dead men; good men, good crew, good pirates - were those other two alive? He winced, wrestling with his conscience. If he stayed to help them what could he do? He was no surgeon; one looked as though he had lost a leg, the other was half buried.

"I'm sorry," he muttered as he chose survival and freedom, and hoped the poor beggars, if alive, would die quickly.

In Port Royal's main street people were running in aimless directions like frightened rabbits, others stood or sat, silent and dazed some cradling broken bones and bleeding wounds. More than a few lay dead, crushed beneath collapsed buildings. A small child, shrieking hysterically for her mother, wandered on to the cracked cobbles of the road straight into the path of a bolting horse, its iron shoes sending up a shower of sparks as it galloped, terrified. Without thinking of his own safety Jesamiah plunged forward, grabbed up the child and rolled with her as he hit the ground. Slammed his eyes shut as a hoof came down a hair's breadth from where his head had been a short second ago.

He sat up, the child screeching her indignation in his arms, he stroked her hair, jigged her up and down, did what he could to comfort her while he tried to think what to do. Think man! Think! The officers inside the fort were beginning to get themselves and their men organised. Any moment now they would realise the jail was empty of living men and erupt in search of their prisoners.

"I cannot take you with me, sweetness, I'm sorry lass. Your ma will soon find you." He set the girl down, dragging her clinging fingers from his grimed shirt and ran towards the harbour, forcing himself not to look back at her or he would be sure to regret it.

A two-masted sloop anchored in the harbour had wrenched free of her cable; she would be holed on a reef before long if no one went aboard to set a sail and steer her. Several other small boats had broken their warping lines and were also drifting. Jesamiah knew next to nothing of earthquakes; this one had seemed enormous, but as most of the fort and the ramshackle town was still standing he assumed it had not been anywhere near as massive as the 'quake of '92. Did he not remember his father

- 57 -

saying something about aftershocks and tidal waves? He looked out to sea. Aye, the waves were crashing over the reefs, running at twice the height he would have expected - as if a storm were rumbling beneath the surface.

He recognised two others from his cell, the Frenchman and a black African. He shouted to them, waving his arm. "If there's enough of us, we can get to sea - it'll be rough sailing but that sloop's begging for a crew!"

He jumped for the deck of one of the row boats bumping loose against the jetty, which was leaning drunkenly aslant, one of its supporting pillars given way. Barrels, wicker baskets, crates, were bobbing in the water; a hissing cat clinging wildly to one, squawking chickens cackling in another. He grabbed a line, secured it around a bollard, holding the craft firm.

"Hurry," he called, "the fort will soon be on to us!"

The two men needed no further urging. Five more followed. It took only a matter of moments to row across, scramble up the side and board.

"Hoist sail!" Jesamiah yelled, darting towards the wildly swinging tiller, realised as he shouted five of the men had no idea what to do.

Only the Frenchman and the African were of use. *"Je suis Claude de la Rue,"* the first said, introducing himself without formality as he and his companion grabbed at halyards. *"Mes amis m'appellent Rue* - my friends call me Rue. This is Isiah Roberts. We 'ave roamed the sea together several years. *Merci bien* for saving my life twice over, *monsieur.* When the wall collapsed and now again."

"We're not out of this yet, my friend," Jesamiah grunted. "Can none of you others sail?" Solemnly, they shook their heads. He cursed. Useless land-lubbers!

"Hold this tiller," Jesamiah instructed a man with a red beard, Nathaniel, he thought his name was. They had all been strangers thrown together in a small cell these weeks, exchanging names had never seemed a priority. No point finding out, not when the hangman was all too keen to put an end to new-formed friendships. "Do you feel the wind on your left cheek?" he asked.

Nathaniel frowned, raised his head slightly. "Aye."

"Then keep it there. Do not let it come around to the other cheek, or to the full of your ugly face."

"If I do?"

"I'll kick your fokken arse and toss you overboard!"

The craft was broad of beam and had a slow leak somewhere, peering quickly down into the hold he could hear water sloshing about below. No matter, deal with that later. First thing was to set these fore-and-aft sails and steer a safe course through the reefs. Thank God at least for Rue and Roberts.

At the far tip of the spit of land known as Gallows Point, the cross bar and top half of a gallows showed through the surging high tide. From it, dangled two men their dead and bloated bodies swaying in a grotesque dance, caught in the forward and backward movement of the sea. Jesamiah paused with hauling the sail, stood, his throat choking, brought suddenly to tears..

The Frenchman was a large, well-built man but the touch of his hand upon Jesamiah's shoulder was light. "I did not know 'im, but I 'ave 'eard of Malachias Taylor," he said, his accent unmistakable. "'E was a good man *n'est pas?*"

Jesamiah opened his mouth to answer and found the words would not come. Instead, he nodded. Rue, fully understanding, patted his shoulder.

Respectfully, Jesamiah brought his right hand to his forehead, saluted his friends. *You are free now,* he thought. *None can touch either of you where you have gone. God guard your souls.*

Wiping a hand across his face he took a deep breath, squared his shoulders, carried on hauling, concentrating on what he was doing. Time enough to grieve later. There again, if God was not on the side of pirates he may well be meeting Malachias Taylor and Daniel Wickersley sooner than expected. It was a long way to the nearest safe harbour where he could acquire something more suitable to his needs, and as he soon discovered, the wooden tub leaked more than he had realised, had several holes in her sails and was mostly crewed by men who could not tell the bow from the stern.

Malachias had always said Jesamiah had the luck of the Devil. Out of habit he touched the acorn earring between his finger and thumb. Aye, well, if he did not have it before, he sorely needed it now

- Eight -

For Tiola and Jenna, a living had to be made. The revenue from selling mother's jewellery would not last for ever, nor when Captain Rogers had finally decided to make sail for England, had his generous patronage been of further use. He had been content to pay for their board and lodging in lieu of Jenna's medicinal skills - Tiola's in reality, but she had thought a man such as Rogers would not contemplate receiving treatment from a girl. Easier for all parties if Tiola assisted Jenna and made pretence it was the older woman who possessed the skill.

With only a few days left before the money ran out, and a roof over their heads consequently about to be denied them, the solution was solved by chance coincidence - or ordained providence?

Jenna, not as adventurous as the younger Tiola, tended to use the wider and safer main streets or the East India Company market for food and provisions. Tiola found the maze of alleyways more fascinating to explore, although knowing Jenna disapproved, rarely told of where she had been. Here, the scum of Cape Town scrabbled a living by plying their trades; here, the beggars and whores, the thieves and charlatans eked a meagre existence of day to day drudged survival. Elsewhere, near the grandeur of the fort and the V.O.C. gardens were the well-to-do houses, the estates of the rich merchants and traders, ship owners, slavers. The wealthy. Tiola preferred the honesty of the poor.

Most of them were thieves and scoundrels out for all they could get for free, ready to rob as soon as look at you, but they had honour among their own and judged people for what they were, not for what they alluded to be. Those fat profiteers in their mansions, with their acres of estates, their bulging purses and their conceit? Tiola wanted nothing to do with them, although she realised Jenna would be doing all she could to encourage such acquaintances. Tiola was a gentleman's daughter and would, in Jenna's dutiful opinion, soon be needing a gentleman as a husband. Father? A gentleman? A respected clergyman, a man with an outer veneer of honest decency? Huh! More like a man diseased by mouldering rot!

Early morning found Tiola scrambling over a pile of mildewed cabbage leaves attempting to catch an injured cat. She had been stalking the mangy creature for several days, anxious that the bloodied, maggoty ear needed attention. Jenna had scoffed, saying it would be best to leave the animal to die, one less of the caterwauling little pests would be a blessing. Tiola, as usual, ignored her.

She lunged, caught the cat's tail. He turned yowling his fury and scratched her hand, but she held tight, bundling him quickly into the scrap of sacking she had brought for the purpose. Wrapping it around his body she inspected the ear. Most of it was missing.

"Been fighting have you Tom? You need to move quicker on your paws lad, if you are going to survive that game." Tucking him into a secure grip she turned for home, the single room they would soon be having to vacate on the top floor at the rear of the *Golden Hind*.

In places, the alleys were no more than corridors between buildings, most of them piled with accumulated debris blown there by the persistent wind. Rats scurried, the smell of rot and sewage nauseating. She turned left, then right, aware this was the favoured area for the prostitutes, set near the taverns and the harbour. Sailors were not interested in walking far before they found their eager-awaited entertainment.

She had been accosted on several occasions in these back streets, grappled by men assuming she was a working girl looking for custom. One, this morning, had been blind drunk, easy to push to the ground and leave lying in the garbage, legs and arms waving helplessly as if he were a beetle on its back.

For another she had used her skill of Voice. *"I am not for you. Be on your way."* And he had shambled off looking puzzled, half remembering something that for some reason now eluded him.

The cat was wriggling; Tiola was concentrating on keeping the wild thing confined within the sacking, on not getting scratched again or bitten, then stopped, cocked her head, listening intently.

"Help me!" A desperate plea, faint but urgent. Tiola let the cat go, the moth-eaten tabby streaking off the way they had come. She back-tracked a few yards and peered up a dead-end passage providing a rear entrance to a tavern and a storehouse. It was littered with the usual heaps of strewn rubbish - but at the far end a woman huddled against a brick wall. Not a woman, a girl, not much younger than herself. Thirteen perhaps? A girl with blood and urine staining her petticoats and ragged gown. The girl groaned, sank to her knees, her suffering blowing through her lips and rising into a scream as her arms clutched around her abdomen.

Tiola glanced up and down for aid; this was a rarely used alley. No one was in sight or within hailing distance. What to do?

~ *You know what to do.* ~ The guiding voice of her grandmother, and of all her grandmothers, sharing their knowledge of Craft.

She ran to the girl, put her arms around her shoulders, smoothed aside her sweat-soaked hair. "I am here to help. Be easy, dear-heart." Unobtrusively, Tiola lifted the drape of the girl's clothes, peeped beneath. "For how long have you been like this?"

"Don't know. I've 'ad pain in m' belly all night. I'm s'posed to be fetchin' the bread. Stopped 'ere, couldn't go nay further." The girl issued another scream. "What's wrong with me?" she cried. "Am I dyin'?"

"What is wrong? By the Deep, child, you are having a baby!"

The girl said nothing, her face blank, not understanding.

Do I know how to deal with this on my own? Tiola thought, doubting herself. *I am not many years older than this girl.*

~ *You are as old as the stars and the seas. You know what to do.* ~ The voice of her ancestors again; her creators and mentors. Their combined wisdom passed down through the generations to accumulate in Tiola.

The girl scrunched her face, began to strain, bearing down.

"No, do not push yet your baby is not ready."

"I've got to! It 'urts somethin' terrible!"

"Pant, short breaths - that's it, good girl." Again Tiola looked along the alley in hope of someone coming. No one. She would have to manage on her own. The child's head was beginning to emerge. "We are nearly there, dear-heart." She spoke calmly, hiding her anxiety. Working by instinct and what she had learnt on her maternal grandfather's farm, she felt around its neck, was relieved to find it unencumbered by the cord.

"*Ais,* alright my lovely, a big push now, as hard as you can."

Tiola eased the baby from the birth canal, tiny and sickly it lay limp and silent in her hands. She cleared its nose and mouth, and then tipped it upside down and with the ankles between her fingers, swung it sideways a few times as she would do with a lamb, smiled with elation as the infant filled its feeble lungs and emitted a thin, wailing cry.

"You have a daughter, a little girl." Tiola removed the ribbon that secured her hair in a single braid, tied the umbilical cord and with the knife she carried at her hip, cut it. Reaching for the sack intended for the cat - not clean but better than nothing - she wrapped the baby in it, gave her into her mother's arms.

The girl was bewildered, but smiling. "She'm beau'iful ain't she?"

"*Ais,* yes, that she is." The afterbirth, the lining of the womb, came away. Deftly, Tiola spread it, checked it was whole. Anything left behind would turn putrid, could cause death for the mother.

"What is this? What is going on here?"

From where she was squatting, Tiola stared up into the frowning face of a middle-aged, plump woman, dressed well, if gaudily.

"Thank the Lady someone has come," Tiola said, rising to her feet. "I found her in labour, she has delivered a girl. I am not certain if I did everything correct."

Immediately, the woman became concerned, took charge. Found to her surprise the makeshift midwife had been highly competent.

"She did not appear to know she was pregnant," Tiola explained as the woman removed her shawl and put it around the mother and child, already muzzling for her first essential milk.

"She'd not be dear, she's simple in the head poor lass. Don't often know her own name. I suggest we get her to my place, make her comfortable then go in search of her Pa. Though after this, I reckon he'll say he's had enough of her."

"Will he turn her on to the streets?"

"Probably, that's where most of them end up, dear. Or floating face down in the harbour." The woman handed the baby to Tiola, then lifted the girl into her own arms. "My place is around the corner, not far. I'm Bella Dubois. French mother, God knows who for a father."

Her "place" turned out to be a whore-house, brick built, two storeys high. Inside, it was clean and tidy, if vulgar in decor. On the ground floor larger, communal rooms where clients could play cards or dice, drink whatever their fancy before making use of the opulent bedchambers above.

Bella called two women in their mid twenties, who cooed and fussed and chattered, and took the mother and baby to private rooms at the rear, the proprietress's own as Tiola discovered when she was also invited through.

"You managed well, dear," Bella applauded as she poured herself a generous brandy. "Where did you learn your skill?"

Tiola offered a truthful answer. "I grew up on a farm."

A shrewd woman, Bella regarded her thoughtfully. This girl knew more than how to bring a few lambs or calves into the world. She came straight out with what was on her mind. "We have no midwife in this quarter of Cape Town, last one died two months back of fever. I care for my girls; in our line of work there are often babes born." Direct to the point, added, "You are young, dear, but you obviously have a talent. Do you know for instance, how to get a dead babe from its nest? How to deliver a child born backside first or upside down? How to stop a baby being made or be rid of one not wanted?"

Giving an enigmatic smile in response Tiola replied, "Should the answer be *ais*, yes, what would there be in it for myself and my guardian, Miss Pendeen?"

"There could be lodging for you both. At a cheap rent."

The offer was wonderful, but Tiola had no intention of sounding too eager too soon. "I intend no disrespect Ma'am, Jenna would not concede to live in a brothel. We are respectable people. My late father was a clergyman." She did not add what else he had been.

Bella Dubois ducked her head over her shoulder. "There are two spare rooms upstairs, with their own entrance out the back. You would be welcome to those. They need cleaning out mind, I have been using them as store rooms."

Tiola haggled. "The rent would be waived? In return, any fee for your girls will not be expected."

Knowing a good deal when she heard one, Bella nodded consent. "Fair enough, dear."

"Then *ais*," Tiola answered, offering her hand to seal the bargain, "I accept your offer. I know all those things you ask." Thought, *And more.*

- Nine -

The *Salvation,* hove to in the long Atlantic swell, three miles out from Nassau harbour, fell over yet another wave.

Christopher Columbus was a bloody fool to believe this was the eastern coast of Asia, Jesamiah thought to himself as the ship beneath his wide-spread feet rolled truculently again, and the island on the horizon disappeared from his vision. *His navigation was only out by several thousand miles. The daft sod.*

Only the name, *baja mar* - *Shallow Sea* - acted as a reminder of that brief, Spanish possession. Finding more lucrative land further west, Spain had soon relinquished their claim on these flat, often barren, islands. The present-day Spanish, however, had recently renewed their interest in the Bahama Islands.

Forget the fact that the Spanish had agreed and signed a treaty of peace with the British. Here in the Caribbean, documents signed in Europe held no sway. Spaniards continued to prey on English ships, while the English persisted in attacking treasure-laden Spanish galleons. And Nassau had become a haven for the pirates who needed somewhere to spend their hard won doubloons and pieces of eight. Rotting meat to buzzing flies. A safe, wide, beach on which to careen and carouse; a port to exchange plunder for silver coin to spend on women and drink. The few established landowners, tavern, and shop keepers being only too happy to milk those of the Sweet Trade of all they had.

Twice already in the past few months Spanish ships had raided Nassau, their intention, to deal the drunken English a lesson and retrieve what they considered to be rightfully theirs. The crew of the *Salvation,* not remotely averse to relieving the royal appointed governor of his hoarded baubles, had elected to make a third attempt. A short, sharp raid; take what they can and leave. The fact they were not Spanish seemed neither here nor there.

Jesamiah's luck had not deserted him. Two days out from Port Royal the severely listing sloop had almost been run down in thick mist by a brigantine. Glad to see the end of the leaking bucket, the men had climbed aboard and joined the crew, thankful to find the *Salvation* was a pirate craft. Had she been a Royal Navy vessel they would have either been pressed into service or hanged. Jesamiah had to relinquish his previous position as quartermaster and serve before the mast as able crew but he had no objection to hard work. Aboard a pirate ship they were brothers with a common cause; to hunt prey. Everything was shared equally, the work, the plunder. Unlike the Navy, they made their own rules and the few elected officers were there for practicality, nothing more.

Driven by the Trade Winds the Atlantic rolled beneath the keel as they waited for the moon to appear. The ship was wallowing, the almost non-existent breeze doing nothing to hold her steady as she lay in the star-studded darkness with her mizzen topsail backed. First, she lay right over until her gun tackles groaned with the strain of holding the cannon in position and it was hard for men to stay upright on the sloping deck. For a few heart-stopping seconds she remained there, not moving, then slowly, so very slowly, she righted herself, only to roll as steeply down on the other side. The blocks holding everything securely in place protested, taking the strain as she tipped over in the opposite direction, everything stretched to the limit. Men cursed and muttered prayers until the swell had finished moving under her and she swung upward again, to repeat the whole process. Jesamiah was hanging on to a secured belaying pin to stop himself from slipping down the deck and ignominiously landing on his backside in the scuppers.

From the quarterdeck the Captain, Jean de Cabo, a surly Frenchman, was watching the sky for the first hint of the rising moon. Only a fool would cross those sand bars into Nassau harbour in the dark. A full moon and a slow speed was chancy, but Jesamiah, Rue and this Captain had done it all before.

At last, a pale hint of silver on the horizon. De Cabo dipped his head once, an abrupt jerk. Said in French, "*Allez*, let us go."

The crew cheered.

Thank God, Jesamiah thought as he and other topmen scurried up the main mast to prepare to drop canvas. The helmsman turned the wheel and headed the ship into the waves, causing her to pitch rather than roll. Pitching, Jesamiah could handle, rolling, even after all these years at sea, brought the contents of his stomach up into his gullet.

Only a few miles to cover and they crossed them easily the *Salvation* hoisting through one oncoming wave after another. Heaving her bow up to the sky she rolled her keel slightly before the pitch was completed, the forward-pointing spar of the bowsprit continuing to rise higher and higher until she managed to toss free and slide down the opposite side. Then her bow started its downward arc, the sea swirling beneath her, pushing her stern upwards as the tail end of the roller passed behind, while for'ard, the bow almost immediately began the next rise as she completed the corkscrew movement. Pitch, roll. Heave, roll. Jesamiah, balancing in bare feet on the ratlines slung beneath the main topsail yard was blissfully happy.

With the moon risen they had no difficulty crossing the sandbar. Ahead, spread along the beach, were the dying embers of campfires and the slumbering scatter of bothies, tents and shacks that formed the pirate snake-pit of Nassau. Even the military fort, to the far side of the harbour was partially derelict. A succession of corrupt governors had taken poor care of the place.

One hundred yards from the beach, with the *Salvation* flying British colours in case anyone should be watching, the anchor was let go and the bow came around, jerked at the end of the cable and faced into the waves. Unhurried, the longboat was lowered over the side and those chosen for the first part of the raid were pulling for shore. Jesamiah, dressed in a looted best coat and clean, white breeches stood in the stern, his left hand holding the hilt of a cutlass, also a prize from a raided ship. He touched his earring for luck. This was going to be so easy!

Jean de Cabo had not been enthusiastic about the plan, but when challenged by his crew to come up with a better one than Jesamiah's, had reluctantly conceded. A short, skinny man with a permanent scowl on his wrinkled face, he sat apprehensive in the stern. If this went well, would the men decide Acorne would make for a better captain? Captains clung to the pride of their rank and title as determined as a drowning man grips a floating barrel. De Cabo shrugged, checked the two primed pistols thrust through his belt. There were ways of ensuring he kept his cherished position of authority.

Jesamiah stepped ashore, de Cabo, sullen, at his heels. Strolling together they sauntered along the wooden jetty towards the main street of the town. The first sign of life was a drunk, flat on his back, arms outstretched, mouth open, snoring. Jesamiah kicked him lightly with the toe of his boot. Kicked him harder. A snorted grunt, nothing more.

Nassau. The same as any other port. Ships at anchor, others heeled on their side, partially careened. Near the jetties a tramp of warehouses, chandlers' bothies, rope-makers, sail menders. Water barrels, hogsheads for flour, fruit, vegetables and salted meat. Kegs of gunpowder, piles of hemp. Pots of paint ... none of it tidy. This was a pirate haven, where all that mattered were the taverns and the brothels. There was one church which judging by the smell as Jesamiah walked past up the hill, housed pigs.

The hush of the wind rustled through the trees scattering the moonlight into dancing shadows. A dog barked somewhere, was abruptly silenced after a high-pitched yelp. A cat slunk from behind a heap of sacking, a dead rat clamped between its jaws, the head drooping, tail dragging in the dust. Jesamiah grimaced. He had no liking for rats, not since the night he had found one, a huge male, bloody and decapitated, left by his brother between the sheets of his bed. He had made the mistake of shrieking his fear -

well, he had been only five years old – and at least once a week after that there had been a dead rat left somewhere for him to find. Even on the day of his mother's funeral, when he was almost fifteen years old, Phillipe had slipped a severed head into his coat pocket. Jesamiah had found it, searching for a kerchief while standing there at the graveside. His hatred for Phillipe gorged into his throat as bile. One day he would take his revenge. One day he would stop thinking about it and actually do it. Abruptly, he pulled his mind back to the present.

At the main gate to the Governor's house, a solitary guard, asleep. Jesamiah stepped across the inner courtyard and hammered on the worn and scratched oak door. After a long while a bleary eyed servant, in need of a shave and a wash, shambled up from the kitchens to see who was making all the noise.

"I must see the Governor, I need immediate interview with him!" Jesamiah thrust past the sleep-muddled footman, striding into the gloom of what could have been an attractive hallway had it been cleaned occasionally of dust and cobwebs. One corner of the ceiling was mildewed, in another the plaster was cracked and peeling, everything looked and smelt shabby and neglected.

Fifteen minutes. Twenty, twenty-five. A man lumbered, yawning, down the stairs, Jesamiah noticing his stockings were silk and the buttons of his waistcoat were silver with a diamond inlay. Very pretty.

"M'dear fellow!" Jesamiah boomed heartily, affecting an upper class accent and bowing in extravagant formality. "Apologies for tipping ye from y'bed, I am in some grave dilemma and require urgent advice from someone of y'wisdom."

The Governor, suspicious, peered at him through sleep-tainted eyes. "And you are, sir?"

"Oake, Captain Jesamiah Oake of the vessel *Salvation*," Jesamiah lied, sweeping a second bow for all the world as if he were some dandy come straight from the coffee houses of London. "This," he indicated de Cabo, "is m'first officer; the fellow is

French, but of the Huguenot persuasion so has as much antipathy towards the Frogs as do we." He glanced around the hall, at the several official rooms leading from it. Lowering his voice he coughed and said, "Me enquiry don't warrant being imparted in the draught of a doorway."

From somewhere in the house a clock was chiming three. Made aware of his lack of manners the Governor reddened, ushered his guests up the stairs to his private quarters and shouted for breakfast to be brought.

"It is a little early, but once roused my stomach growls for sustenance. You will join me gentlemen?"

A free breakfast too? How delightful!

Seating himself at a scratched cherry-wood table Jesamiah explained his need. "As ye are aware, we sadly lost our dear Queen Anne some while ago, God rest her."

Gravely, the Governor shook his head. "A sorry thing indeed. She was a good woman. I was at Court twice, don't y'know?"

"Sixteen children she bore," Jesamiah continued, ignoring the boasting. "Or was it seventeen? And not one of them surviving longer than their dear lady mother. No direct line of succession to call upon, o'course, leaving one hell of an Anne's Fan between the Scots Stuarts who want their James as King, and the English Government who are in favour of George of Hanover. A man wholly devoid of charm and speaks only German I b'lieve. A King of England, who cannot utter a word in English, eh?" Jesamiah paused, allowing his inference to sink in. "When I sailed from Plymouth the Jacobites were about to rise in protest. I therefore need to know, Governor, whether their determination for civil war succeeded? Is King George overthrown?"

Spluttering indignation the Governor pushed his chair aside as he leapt to his feet. "If you are counselling I support rebellion, then you must think again! I am a loyal supporter of the Crown, and I beg you not to think otherwise!"

Placating him, Jesamiah patted the air with his hands. "Nay, nay sir, be seated, I merely ask because I have a gang of scrofulous Scotsmen on board who have been plaguing m'patience to drink the health of his Majesty King James, third of that name. Before I hang them for treason I need to know if they *are* treasonous. I'd look the fool were I t'set them decorating the yardarm only to discover Hanover had been plucked by the royal balls and sent back to Germany, would I not?" He chuckled, his fingers idly toying with the blue ribbon laced into his hair, his eyes lighting as the door opened. "Ah! Breakfast!"

Bacon, sausages, black pudding, kidneys - bread, churned butter and a jug of steaming, black coffee. It took barely fifteen minutes to empty the platters of the lot.

Patting his full belly, Jesamiah languidly stretched feeling the satisfying pull of muscles along his shoulders. "And now," he said, abandoning the ridiculous accent as he calmly removed a pistol from his belt, half cocking the hammer as he did so. "I have the second part of my business to complete. The first was interesting, but I confess I have no care whatsoever for which fat bastard sets his backside on the throne. One is, no doubt, as bad as the other." He pointed the pistol at the Governor and clicked the hammer full home.

De Cabo, who had barely uttered a word beyond a few grunts of response to Jesamiah's occasional translations, also rose and went to stand beside the door in case anyone should enter, his own pistols drawn and cocked.

"We require very little from you, my dear Governor," Jesamiah continued pleasantly. "Merely the contents of your treasury. The breakfast we thank you for, an unexpected bonus."

The Governor scrabbled to his feet with all affability gone. Jesamiah lowered the pistol and pointed it at his groin. "We will have what we came for, mate, with or without you in one piece to witness it. I can as easily shoot you now, as later." He smiled, menacingly, waved the weapon to emphasise his meaning. "Now what is it to be, eh? The cache of treasure you have accumulated, or your more personal package? Do I remove the private tool and tackle kept so snugly in your breeches?"

"Damned Jacobite! You will never get out of the harbour!" the Governor spluttered anger. His face suffused scarlet.

"Ah, you see, apart from ourselves and your few yawning servants who have undoubtedly already returned to their beds, I would be surprised to find a single man or woman on this Devil-spawned island who is awake and sober. Mid-day, mayhap, they will be stirring for another tot of rum to set them up for the afternoon ahead, but while the moon rides the sky? Come, come, sir, let us not be fanciful." Jesamiah smiled lazily, added, "And I am no papist Jacobite. Pirate will do."

As he had predicted, it was easy. Rue and the others were already at the fort. They loaded their own longboat until they were in danger of sinking, to speed the process, commandeered several more. The Governor's treasury was removed as easily as hauling in lobster pots. No fuss, no fighting. Just as Jesamiah preferred it. There was only one thing he had overlooked; the extent of Jean de Cabo's smouldering jealousy.

The last load had gone up from the strong room in the undercroft of the fort. In its place huddled the Governor - stripped of his fancy clothes, the silk stockings and the silver buttons.

"I am sure someone, eventually, will realise you are missing and find you incarcerated down here. In a day or two, perhaps?" Chuckling, Jesamiah fitted the key into the lock of the iron-studded door, made to shut it and felt the barrel of a pistol pressing into his back. He froze, all amusement gone, his stomach twisting in alarm. His muscles tensed as he fought down a lurch of fear. Phillipe had always come up behind him, to grab his hair, or thump him in the small of his back. Always the smaller, weaker, Jesamiah had never been able to get away. In adulthood he still hated people coming up behind him.

"Perhaps they may find you too, Acorne?" De Cabo said in his thick-accented English. He stank of garlic and body odour. "*Merci* for your ingenuity, monsieur, but I think the *Salvation* will be the better for it to not be repeated. My men are fickle, you understand, and I have a liking for the title Captain. I have no wish for them to be turning their loyalty in a wrong direction."

With the flat of his hand he gave Jesamiah a hefty push between the shoulder blades, sending him stumbling forward. Instantly recovering his balance Jesamiah spun on his heels, his hand, in the same movement, going to the knife tucked securely in his boot. Underestimating the speed of his reaction, De Cabo barely saw the flashing glint of Jesamiah's blade, but felt it go in diagonally upward under the ribs.

"*A knife needs an upward thrust, boy, for the ribs lie open to it going in from below, but they block a downward stab. From above you'll leave a bloody gash, also leave yer opponent alive to 'ave another go at ye. Go in low and upwards, boy. Always, low and upwards.*" One of the two efficient methods of killing that Malachias Taylor had taught to Jesamiah. It had saved his life on more than one occasion.

De Cabo was dead before he met the floor.

"I understand full well, Captain," Jesamiah said without a trace of compassion as he wiped the blade on the dead Frenchman's coat. "A pity you did not."

He re-sheathed his knife, stepped over the twitching corpse, shut the door and ignoring the terrified Governor cowering within, locked it. On turning, found Rue standing there, his own blade in his hand.

Jesamiah stood quite still. He had killed de Cabo with indifference, a contemptible man, but Rue? He had thought Rue was different, had thought of him as a friend. Ah, what was friendship among pirates? Loyalty only ran the length of a deck and lasted as long as the gold and the rum was available. Or until the hangman put a noose around your neck. Friends either got themselves hanged, or it seemed, decided to try to kill you.

Jesamiah's fingers went to his ribbons as their eyes met, held. And slowly Rue smiled, lowered the blade.

"'Ad you not moved so quick *mon ami*," he said as he flipped the knife upward, "I would 'ave dealt with 'im for you."

"I appreciate the gesture," Jesamiah said, releasing the tension from his muscles by resting his arm along Rue's shoulders. "But would it not have been a little late? I might have already been dead."

Rue rubbed at his chin, pursing his lips, holding his amusement. "You know, I 'ad not thought of that!"

Jesamiah barked his own laugh, slapped the flat of his hand between his friend's shoulders. "Remember it another time, eh? I have no difficulty with killing scum such as that bastard, but understand," he said, as they walked together companionably up the dank, slippery steps into the fresh, clean air, "had you decided to row in de Cabo's boat, I would have been obliged to kill you also. Savvy?"

No one aboard the longboat spoke of the absence of their French Captain, nor was anything said as Jesamiah stepped on to the deck of the *Salvation*. No one queried his right to set their course after the anchor cable had been cut with an axe – no time to haul at the capstan to bring it aboard. Dawn would soon be breaking and Jesamiah had no desire to be caught at anchorage in daylight. Efficient and capable he ordered the ship, under full sail, into the open swell of the Atlantic. Before he went below, he called the crew together.

"I take it you have no objection to my making free use of the Great Cabin?"

Only the Captain used that cabin. There came no uncomfortable shuffling of feet, no surreptitious glances. No one said a word.

"Nor, I assume, do you object to my preference of promoting Rue as my quartermaster?" Jesamiah gestured an apology to the previous incumbent. "You're a good man, but Rue is the better."

The man shrugged. He had not much cared for the job anyway. The quartermaster was always the first into a fight and the last to sample the rum.

And aside, anyone who was fast enough to kill de Cabo was not a man to argue with.

- Ten -

Concern etching her face, Tiola squatted on her haunches. "Your arm is broken, Kisty, here where the swelling is worst." She indicated but did not touch the girl's injured forearm. "It feels as though it is a clean fracture of the bone we call the ulna." Added with a compassionate smile, "Although I do not suppose the scientific words make it any less painful."

The fifteen year old African slave's face puckered into tears. She had been brave while Tiola examined the damage as gently as she could, but the courage was fading fast. "It hurts," she wailed, cradling the arm to her chest, the wrist and hand hanging limp, tears streaming. "Oh, it hurts so!"

It had been a silly accident, one that could happen to anyone. Kisty had slipped in the soapy residue of the slopped laundry water puddling Bella's rectangular courtyard, her foot skidding on the wet cobblestones that glistened in the sunlight like fish scales. She had tried to save herself from falling by putting out her arm, the sound of the bone fracturing distinctly audible as she came down.

Wet linen sheets and under-petticoats pegged along the washing lines strung to and fro, flapped in the boisterous wind. The yard, with its central well and seat of ease – a flimsy wooden hut containing nothing more than a board with a hole in it over the stink of the cess pit - was an almost unique amenity in this quarter of Cape Town. Bella was a wealthy woman who could afford the choice of luxuries. The southern end was dissected by a dark passage-way, three feet wide. It ran beneath the first floor of Bella's double-fronted property, which faced into Harbour Street. Although most people tended to call it Grope Lane.

Bella's personal apartment was to the left of the passage, the business side to the right, and at its courtyard end a flight of wooden stairs led steeply up to the two light, airy rooms of a first floor lodging. Tiola and Jenna had made them into a comfortable home.

Drawn by the noise, Bella appeared with two of her girls, Amber-Rose and Crystal towing behind. Kisty, purchased from the slave market as a housemaid, was aware she had a good place of employment, and Bella a fair woman to work for, although despite repeated assurances, remained dubious about not being required to work "upstairs." Frequently Bella told the girl she was unsuitable, not being in possession of the correct assets that were a prerequisite for entertaining gentlemen. Kisty's face was pretty but her bosoms were as flat as unleavened bread and had no prospect of filling out.

"Stop snivelling, child," Bella snapped. "Do you need to make such a caterwauling fuss?" All the same, she leant over Tiola's shoulder to inspect the injury for herself, her mouth making a small moue of concern. Bella Dubois was often blustering wind on the surface, underneath she valued her girls, from kitchen slave to prima prostitute.

"You had best send for Doctor Paterson," Tiola suggested, being practical. "I am no bone surgeon."

Both Amber-Rose and Crystal shrieked in unison, horrified. "Him? Oh no, not that charlatan! He is always drunk, and his breeches stink of piss."

"But this needs setting," Tiola protested.

"You can do it though dear, can you not?" Bella answered, confidently patting Tiola's arm. "You mended a dog's leg a few weeks past."

"That was a dog!"

"Is there a difference to bones then? Are those of a dog's softer, or harder or something?" Bella agreed with her girls, there would be no doubting the form of payment the useless drunkard of a doctor would be asking. And the better physicians, those who served the gentry residing on the other side of town, would never condescend to set foot in the brothel area to tend a black slave, for all Bella's pile of accumulated wealth.

Tiola protested again, adamant. "What does it matter if a stray cur runs lame? If I cannot set Kisty's arm straight, she will have a crooked limb all her life."

"I agree but will an oaf such as he do any better, dear?" Bella countered. "He is a drunken fool. His diagnosis would be to saw the arm off."

Kisty gave a quivering, alarmed cry, cradled her arm closer. "Oh no, no Ma'am! I do not want to be 'putated!"

"No one is going to amputate your arm, Kisty." Tiola reassured the girl. "It is merely a broken bone, a splint and firm bandaging, several weeks rest, and it should be as good as new."

"There you are then," Bella exclaimed, gesturing Amber-Rose and Crystal indoors, and then helping a shaking Kisty to her feet. "If you do not have the medications you require, as we have arranged, I shall obtain them."

Can I do this? Tiola thought. She glanced at Jenna, hanging the last dripping sheet on the line. The older woman merely shrugged.

"There was little your grandmother could not do," Jenna said pragmatically. "And what she could do, so can you."

Tiola took hold of Kisty's uninjured hand. "Do you want me to tend you, dear-heart?" The black girl nodded, her face grave, her front teeth biting into her lip.

"It will hurt."

"More than having my arm 'putated?"

Tiola smiled. "No, not as much as that."

"If you are a good girl and are very brave," Bella coaxed, "When it is all over I will buy you some sugar cane to suck."

Kisty's eyes widened. *Any* discomfort was worth enduring for such a rare treat.

*

Restless, Tethys wandered her vast domain of the oceans of the world, ill at ease. The winds, stirring and growling on the surface of the sea always agitated her. And when they billowed into the fury of a hurricane storm, her rage was also whipped into a savage ferocity.

In her churning discomfort she sought payment for the pain searing through her, and the vengeance of Tethys was never mild. Always, she demanded the taking of a ship and the claiming of life as compensation.

*

Kisty was feverish. She at last slept, helped along by the few drops of laudanum Tiola had administered. The tiny room at the rear of Bella's apartment was no more than the size of a large cupboard, but Kisty loved it because it was hers. She had brightened the cramped space by covering the cot with a quilt made from sewing scraps of material together, and on the wall, two pictures Bella had not wanted. One was of flowers. Round, yellow sun flowers and brilliant red poppies, The other was a ship. A Spanish Galleon, cleaving her way through a wild sea.

In between tending the injured girl Tiola had sat staring at the picture, seeing in her mind not a mediocre painting but a real ship. His ship. She felt the dip and rise of the deck, heard his voice calling frantic orders above the howl of the rising wind.

"Clew it up! For God's sake, get it clewed up!"

It was months since he had sailed away on the *Mermaid.* Had she really been here in Cape Town all this while? At times it felt as though she had lived here forever, at others as if she had arrived but yesterday. She had stopped feeling homesick for her own hills and the wild freedom of the moors, stopped grieving for her mother and brothers. Bella's was home now, the clack of her tongue when she shrilled about something amiss downstairs, the chatter of the girls; all had become familiar now, worn in and comfortable. This was home. These were people Tiola had learnt to love.

What had Jesamiah been doing all the while, she wondered? Up to no good, probably. How could a pirate be anything different? She barely knew him and yet, inside, she felt she had known him forever; every nuance of his tanned face was stamped indelibly on her brain. She thought about him every day recalling each subtlety: the way the white scar crinkled at the side of his eye when he laughed, the way he habitually fiddled with that gold earring or his ribbons. His voice, his smell. His cock-sure confidence. Only occasionally, when she was busy supervising a difficult birthing or doing something that required concentration, did he become nothing more than a passing thought, his face darting across her mind like the quick, come-and-gone shadow of a bird in flight. But he was always there, lingering somewhere in her consciousness.

He had another ship, for this one, the one she could see in the blur of the picture was not the *Mermaid*. This was larger, not so clean in her lines, not so agile. Where the *Mermaid* had been a sprightly maiden, this one was a portly matron.

Or was it the storm slowing her, making her timbers groan? For there was a storm, somewhere out there beneath an ink black sky that was not the sky of the African Coast or the Southern Atlantic. A sky and a sea being torn apart by the roar of a devil's wind. Jesamiah was facing into a storm and his ship was foundering.

As if in a dream, while Kisty slept, her arm splinted, her face contorted even in sleep, Tiola watched it unfolding, there in the blurring between the painting of a ship and the misted reality of the inner awareness of her Craft.

And as with any dream, she could do nothing but stand helpless and watch - unable to stop the nightmare from running its dreadful course.

- Eleven -

The last night of July looked like being the last night of Jesamiah's life. During the day there had been little indication of a storm coming, only a ripple in the spread of canvas and a churlish response from the *Salvation's* rudder.

The sky had been overcast since dawn with not the merest hint of where the sun might be. The crew were not particularly worried. The southern tip of the Florida Peninsula was a handful of miles ahead and providing they kept their bearing they would be able to run on up the coast to Charleston without a problem. Rough seas, hauling on wet halyards and wearing sodden clothing meant nothing to sailors. Here in the Caribbean it was never long before the sun shone again and they could dry out.

An hour before dusk Jesamiah had glanced with some concern at the spread of sail. The breeze began to veer and race beneath the leaden cover of cloud; blacker, more ominous weather was building. Then dusk crowded in, and the wind luffed right over, to scurry across the surface of the sea in a different direction to that of the current. As Jesamiah watched, standing beside Rue at the helm, the waves were growing bigger, white horses were starting to gallop, and as full darkness swarmed around them, the *Salvation* suddenly rolled heavily to starboard, lurching unsteadily like a drunk. Everyone aboard paused in what he was doing and apprehensively held his breath. She righted herself, an inaudible, collective sigh of relief.

"Best have topsails close reefed and storm trys'ls set ready," Jesamiah said quietly to Rue as he took the wheel from his quartermaster, folding his hands in a firm, determined grip around the spokes. "And get those tarpaulins secured over the hatches. Rig lifelines down the length of the deck. My bones tell me we're in for a rough night."

Grim, his older bones mumbling the same warning, Rue touched the red bandanna bound across his forehead, in a form of a salute. The first streak of lightning split the sky, followed by a cannon roar of thunder.

Another quarter hour and the *Salvation's* bow was pitching into deep troughs between waves rising higher with each successive onslaught. Her quarterdeck went up into the air, leaving Jesamiah's stomach behind as the stern hung for a second before hurtling downward again. The bow plunged and the ship slammed into the next oncoming wave, as if it had hit the solidity of a wall. She shuddered as the sea burst in a spume of foam over her fore rail, shook herself and forged valiantly on.

"Deck's secure, Cap'n," Rue shouted at Jesamiah, his voice raised to be heard above the roaring of the wind. "Shall I send men aloft to bring down t'gallants?"

"Aye, do so." The highest, thinnest, spar of the masts were the weakest, the topgallants. Better to strike them and stow them on deck rather than risk them breaking. "An' we'll have a couple o' reefs in the fore tops'l." As an afterthought Jesamiah added. "And get some men t'rig rolling tackles."

Rue nodded approval. Rolling tackles would stop the heavy spars from slamming from side to side when the ship really began to pitch and roll. Perhaps.

Twenty five minutes, thirty, and the sea was building bigger, a wild thing turned mad, rising up around the vessel to the level of the shuttered gunports, and within a further ten minutes to the quarterdeck rail. In between each massing wave as she dived into the next trough there was nothing to either side except a sheet of black water, as if they were wallowing in the open-jawed mouth of a sea monster. And then the *Salvation* would fight her way to the crest of another huge wave and hang there, suspended, before plunging downward to be gobbled up again. It was as if Tethys herself had been roused from her sleep. As if she was taking her temper out on any who dared to disturb her peace.

The topsail was reefed, half of it lashed tight to the yard, leaving only a token portion of the rigged stronger storm canvas exposed. Still the wind gained in ferocity; lightning split the sky in ragged tendrils spread against the blackness, followed almost immediately by the crashing anger of thunder. The rain fell, heavy, barely indistinguishable from the cascade of sea spray. Suddenly, within the drawing of a breath, any vessel running within the fury of the hurricane found she was at the mercy of nature. And of the terrible anger of Tethys herself.

With Isiah Roberts struggling to hold the wheel steady, Jesamiah seeing for himself that all was secured down in the waist, grabbed a belaying pin on the foremast and braced his body against the rage of the storm as it tried to bully him into toppling over. He peered up the mast, could not see much beyond shapes against a dark sky. His instinct and knowledge was enough however; even this meagre spread of canvas would not hold much longer.

"We'll take in and run on bare poles!" he yelled at Rue, also struggling to stand upright against the wind.

Then the devil that was the storm tried a different tactic; it gave a malicious shove, heaving itself against the *Salvation's* hull in one mighty effort, and the ship yawed sideways as if the sea was a monster trying to swallow her whole and had swiped out with a giant paw. She juddered and rolled hard, the waves boiling up around her higher than the rails, and with a rending crack, a bang as loud as the thunder, the fore topsail split up the centre. Where a moment before there had been half a sheet of wet, grey canvas there was now a ripped gash that as Jesamiah watched, horrified, tore further into a host of ragged strips. The *Salvation* slewed around as the balance of sail and hull drastically altered, and there was now nothing they could do to save themselves. Nothing except race before the wind. And pray.

Hauling himself hand over hand along the rail, Jesamiah ran, his hair sodden as he took the wind full in the face, the ribbons snapping as if in sympathy with the tattered sail. He needed to get to the wheel, to help Isiah keep her steady... but Rue was there before him, the both of them, grim faced hauling at the spokes of the bucking helm.

Jesamiah turned back to focus on the ruined sail. "Take in canvas!" he roared, cupping his hands around his mouth in an effort to send his voice further. "For fok sake, haul in sail!"

Combined with an angry sea, the wind was determined and vicious. Again the *Salvation* shuddered as the paw swiped at her, a tearing, scraping sound shivered, ominous and foreboding through her entire hull from fo'c'sle to rudder.

Tethys was full awake, and furious.

"We are too far west!" Rue shouted, although none could hear save for Roberts at his side, who with all his strength was desperately trying to hang on to the helm. "*Mon Dieu!* We 'ave 'it a reef!"

Jesamiah also yelled, his words torn from his mouth. The crew did not need to hear, they knew instantly. She was drifting against or over something. Coral? Rock? The clawing fingernails of Tethys herself?

"Drop anchor!" Jesamiah screamed.

The cable, thicker than a man's forearm was run out, the rattle and following splash of the anchor descending from the cathead masked by the gleeful howling of the storm. The anchor should hold them, should stop the ship from its sideways drift into disaster. Again the *Salvation* quivered and a muffled thumping pulsed through her keel.

"The fokken anchor's dragging!" Jesamiah cursed. If it did not find purchase because of flat rock there would be little more they could do. "Throw down the sheet-anchor," he shouted, and a moment later a second anchor and cable rattled out, another splash. But that also failed to grip as it too dragged across the unyielding ocean floor.

The scraping was heard again, echoing below deck, amplified through the wooden hull. Then, a terrible splitting noise and the *Salvation* groaned from bow to stern, her death rattle, as water began flooding in through two rents in her keel. They must have crossed one reef, dragged over shallows and hit another. She was heeling over, the water pouring in from below, surging across her rails as she fell, to lie on her side as if for careening, the deck pitching at an odd, impossible angle. Another final sigh as she settled onto the reef, and died.

A curling wave grasped Jesamiah and took him overboard as if it were a hand plucking from the sea. Everywhere, the saline smell of the ocean and decaying, rotting fish. Frantically, he tried to cling to a tangled mess of cordage, to shattered railing, to anything! But Tethys was for having her own way, and she wanted the man with the blue ribbons and the golden acorn. Wanted blood and life.

He heard a scream as he went under. It must have been his voice, although it was oddly higher in pitch, and it shrieked his name.

~ *Jes...a...mi...ah!* ~

Now why would he be shouting out his own name? Sounding like a desperate young woman?

What odd things a man thinks of, he pondered, *when he is about to drown.*

Twelve

Few of the crew made it to the lagoon and island beyond the reef, not alive. Swept along by the raging sea they were cut to pieces on coral as sharp as a razor's blade; the sharks, with no regard for the temper of the ocean and drawn by the pungent smell of blood, finished the rest. Some men, tangled in the rigging and shattered spars or trapped below deck, never made it from the ship. They were the lucky ones, for they died quickly; the handful who dragged their torn and mutilated bodies to the beach were beset by scavenging crabs. Some, too weak, too shocked or disorientated to brush them aside were eaten alive. Nature's way. Whether fish, mammal or man, the dead and dying providing food for the living. Kill or be killed. Eat or be eaten.

Eight men survived. Eight out of one hundred and sixteen.

Rue was an able man at sea. Middle aged, born on the Normandy Coast, he had spent virtually all his life aboard a boat of one kind or another. He believed himself to be a lucky man, so he also thought, was Jesamiah Acorne. Between them, by luck and chance, Rue and Isiah Roberts had somehow managed to launch one of the longboats. With his cutlass, Rue had slashed through rope and tackle, trusting the boat would fall keel down. Then he had jumped, Roberts following with several others. Some managed to climb aboard. Luck, Rue insisted, helped them fend her off the reef with the oars, barely making headway. Twice they were almost capsized. Half of the oars were broken, snapped off.

When they could, they hauled men aboard. A few they threw back. No use taking the dead. Rue, in the stern battling to hold the tiller, attempting to steer, saw a man struggling in the water, saw him go down beneath a sweeping wave that tossed the boat sideways, the same wave also lifting the man forward, slamming him against the wooden hull. Rue shouted for Roberts but he had already seen, was leaning over the side, others grabbing his legs to stop him from falling. Isiah plunged his black skinned hands into the sea, blindly grabbing, felt his fingers curl around hair and hauled.

They made a joke of it after, when they lay on their backs in the wet sand, gasping for breath, thankful, so thankful, to be alive.

"Just as well you have long hair Jesamiah, else Isiah would have had nothing to grab hold of."

"Lucky you'm not be one of they fancy cap'n's who wear them powder'd wigs."

"Lucky?" Jesamiah panted, his chest feeling as if someone had tied a band too tight around it, salt water still spewing from his lungs. "He damned near pulled half of it out!"

He hurt like hell, come morning would not be surprised to discover his whole body was bruised. His hands too, were agony, sticky with blood his palms and fingers ripped to shreds where he had tried to cling to the jagged coral. The salt water made the cuts sting abominably.

The hurricane wandered away to uproot trees and drive the tide to re-arrange the shore along the Mississippi delta. The survivors of the *Salvation* barely noticing its going. Exhausted, they slept where they had fallen.

Daylight. With scudding clouds and a weak sun the new day brought everything into devastating focus. They buried the dead, those corpses that had been washed ashore, in one grave, digging it with their bare hands and large shells, marking it with a cross Roberts fashioned from the flotsam. The island was small, two acres? No more than three. The four palm trees, bending before the wind, had survived the storm but were battered and ripped, the shade they gave, scanty. There was no water. Food aplenty, for the crabs were everywhere but with their weapons and powder sodden, they had no resource to strike a spark to make a fire. Wreckage spewed along the shore; sharks lurked beyond the reef.

The bloated bodies of the dead floated, macabre, with the swell of the tide.

They waited through the day and the night for the tail end of the tempest to fully blow itself out and then launched the boat, raised sail and limped towards the mainland of Florida. Rue took the tiller. Jesamiah sat hunched in the stern, his torn hands making it impossible for him to do anything useful. Looking over his shoulder as they carefully negotiated the shoals he stared at what was left of his ship. She lay keel up, the rent across her belly gaping like an open mouth pleading for help, the splintered wood her jagged teeth. She was a dead, lifeless hulk, to be haunted by men whose souls would remain washing in and out with the rise and fall of the tides forever. His ship, his first command. Gone.

He felt like weeping, but did not have the energy. He was beyond tears, his ship's loss as raw as the soreness of his hands.

"There was nothing more you could 'ave done," Rue assured him, setting his fingers on Jesamiah's shoulder and squeezing an offer of comfort. "When a storm blows, all you can do is pray God 'as the Grace to 'elp you survive it. We will not be the only ones in this situation." He shrugged, squeezed again. "We were the lucky ones, Captain, we 'ave a boat. Most of the poor souls either do not need one or will be facing a slow death without water, food or shelter."

"I could have taken in sail earlier."

"*Oui* or you could 'ave plotted a different course. You could 'ave suggested we 'ead for Africa not the Carolinas. You could 'ave taken us to where we caught the plague and died with our skin turning to boils and pus, our innards rotting, our brains roasting with fever. You could 'ave done lots of things *mon ami* but we are 'ere," he gestured towards their surroundings, "and we are alive. Let us just say *merci bien* to God and leave it there, *non?*"

"I think it was the Lady who saved us," Roberts said after a short while of silence. "The Holy Mother Mary." He crossed himself, muttering a liturgy under his breath, several of the men doing likewise.

"Why say you that?" Rue asked, intrigued. He had no holding with Papist views, did not particularly believe in God. Many pirates did not, although they were a superstitious lot. Nothing of the colour green, unless it was food, to be taken aboard. No whistling on deck, touching wood or scratching a stay for luck, tossing a pinch of spilt salt over the shoulder. Wearing a gold earring or having gold teeth to pay for passage into the next world.

"I heard a woman calling," Roberts explained as matter of factly as if he was saying the sun was shining in the sky. He tilted his head higher, his chin jutting out firm, knowing he would not be believed. "She hollered at me to look in the water."

"*Non, non!* That was me calling!" Rue corrected with gruff amusement.

"You changed your voice to a female's then?" Roberts challenged, defiant, casting a glower over his shoulder at the older man. "This was a young woman. Lovely voice she had, sort of sing-song. Bit like Mickey O'Hannagan's only different." He crossed himself again. Mickey O'Hannagan had been one of the victims to fall to the sharks.

Rue laughed outright. "That is the first time I 'ave 'eard the Mother of God to be Irish!"

Jesamiah said nothing. He sat staring at the empty ocean that was today so benign. The accent had not been Irish. He had heard it before, somewhere, he could not think where. But somehow, he knew it was Cornish.

*

Satisfied, Tethys subsided back into the darkness and the quiet of the deep, sated from her lust of devouring the dead. The one she had wanted had not been among her plunder; she had dragged him under, had held him in her watery embrace but had been forced to let him go. It did not matter. There was plenty of time to be claiming him. She was eternal, he was not.

The other one, though? She was a puzzle. Not of the sea nor of the earth, was she also beyond the restriction of mortality? One like Tethys herself, a Methuselah made from the stuff of the stars? One of power formed outside of time at the very dawn of being.

Tethys shrugged as she sank deeper, the movement rippling as waves upon the surface of the sea. There was no hurry to find out; she would unravel the secret of this female intruder one day, one millennium. The passage of time for Tethys had no concept, no meaning. Tethys was the spiritual manifestation of the sea. Time for her did not exist.

All the same, while she had held the one with the gold acorn and the blue ribbons, while he had almost been hers to keep, she had ensured he would not be remembering this other one's presence. Ensured his memory would forget who this witch-girl was.

- Thirteen -

Excited, Kisty ran up the stairs with an announcement which sent Jenna fluttering for her shawl and bonnet, and puzzled Tiola.

"Master van Overstratten has come to escort me up the Lion's Head mountain?" Tiola repeated, incredulous. "Is this one of Bella's jests?"

"I assure you, Miss Oldstagh, it is no jest, I am here to do precisely that!" Into the cluttered room walked a tall, slim man in his late twenties, fashionably dressed in a neat green velvet coat, white breeches, silver-buckled shoes. He bowed to Jenna, crossed immediately to Tiola, took up her hand and kissed it.

He was among the important men of Cape Town, Dutch, as all the important men were, a merchant trader specialising in fine wines, cotton and sugar; a man with rank and authority. They had met three days past when she had been requested to attend his sister's labour. Tiola had not expected to meet him again, most especially not here in the shabbier part of town. Stefan van Overstratten owned a fleet of ships and was one of the wealthiest men in the Peninsula. His house was an expensive three-storied structure on the elite location of Strand Street, overlooking Table Bay. Far different to the humble dwelling Tiola called home.

With her reputation as a midwife spreading beyond the vicinity of Grope Lane, Tiola had found herself to be popular among the women of Cape Town. Babies were always being born and her services were constantly in demand. There were days when she found herself hurrying from one side of Town to the other and back again almost without pause.

"How fares thy nephew, surr?" She enquired, hiding her consternation within the formality of a curtsey, the rolling burr of her Cornish accent unusually exaggerated. Why had he come here?

Why had he not sent a servant? Absently, she patted her hair, knowing it was a tangled mess beneath the mob cap; hoped her face was clean, smoothed her apron boasting more than a few stains. She had been clearing the ashes from the cooking fire, felt as grubby as the hearth. "He is thriving I trust?"

"I am amazed," van Overstratten admitted, setting his silver-topped cane and his feathered cocked hat on the table, and at Tiola's gesture seating himself. "I had no idea a child so small could guzzle so much milk and make so much noise!"

The boy was his sister's first. The birth uncomplicated, despite the mother, Berenice, hysterically screaming her way through its entirety. She was a pretty girl, delicate in build and in Tiola's opinion in mind also, for she appeared to be totally without intelligence. Spoilt from infancy by her father, and on his passing by her brother, she wanted for nothing. As for the husband, Tiola wondered how they had managed to re-produce, so lazy was he; but he was minor Dutch nobility, an attribute which as far as van Overstratten was concerned, negated any lack of charm or fault of character.

"I wish to personally repay your kindness towards my family, Ma'am," the Dutchman explained. "I recall, during one of our short conversations while waiting for my lusty nephew to arrive, you mentioned you have not completed the walk to the summit of the Lion's Head? It is most remiss of you. The view from the top is magnificent."

He spoke of the rock shaped like to a crouching lion that flanked Table Mountain as a smaller companion. With its lower slopes crowded by trees and flora, the outcrop provided a beckoning lure for an afternoon's tour, but Tiola had not found suitable opportunity to explore its charm. There were always so many more important things to be doing, and never enough daylight hours in which to be doing them.

"I have sent a picnic ahead," van Overstratten added, "and I will hear no refusal from you, *mijn beste* - my dear. I insist on this outing."

Delighted at the unexpected prospect Tiola answered in the only way she could. "Then it seems I must accept. Thank you." She was puzzled by his motive, but did a gentleman require one in order to impress a young lady?

Stefan van Overstratten's concept of a picnic would have done justice to a royal banquet. Everything had been thought of and provided, including a table and dining chairs. Tiola thought the slaves, who had lugged the stuff half way up the mountainside to the edge of the woods, were probably cursing her to Hell and back, but for once she did not care that another had toiled for her sake. She was enjoying herself. Stefan – he insisted on being called Stefan – was a charming host, regaling her and Jenna with such absurd stories Tiola was certain her sides would burst from laughter. It was good to find strangers were capable of offering kindness and friendship. Good to discover pleasure again after all the tears of the past.

Jenna, claiming her ageing years were unsuited for walking the last stretch along the upward path to the summit, elected to settle herself in the shade and await the return of the younger couple. Grateful for the opportunity to forge ahead, striding out with the wind from the ocean tugging through her hair, her petticoats and over-skirt billowing around her legs, Tiola confided to Stefan it was more probably Jenna's increasing girth that tired her, not her age.

"These hills do puff her so," she explained. "I am continually suggesting she ought not bustle about so urgently, for where can you walk in Cape Town that is not a hill?"

Stefan, offering his hand to help her over a tumble of rocks, his smile easy and pleasing, answered with his own amusement. "*Ja,* even the beach slopes, does it not? And with the wind constant from the south how often do you see the sea benign and flat?"

He was pleasant company. The air on the summit was fresh and clean, smelling of flowers and fruit, tasting of the sea. The August sun was warm, its radiance feeling good on her face. Yesterday and the day before it had been raining, more typical of a southern hemisphere winter.

At the top, everything was as he had promised. A panoramic view of the Cape Peninsula, spread green and lush with its dazzling carpet of woods, vineyards and plantations. The straggle of the settlement seeming not so squashed together from up here; the gleam of so many white walls, the star shape of the fort, even the ugly spread of the V.O.C. granary barns were attractive from this height. The sea, shimmering beneath the sun, stretched away until it fell over the edge of the world.

"It is truly beautiful," Tiola announced with a quick breath of awe. "I cannot believe I have been denying myself this wonder."

The Dutchman forged a congenial smile. He had wanted to impress; it appeared he had been successful. Seated on a rock, blowing hard and mopping at the sweat beading his forehead, he stemmed a gasp of horror when Tiola added, "How much more splendid it must be from the Table itself!"

Hastily he interjected, "The walk is not so pleasant, I believe, and the cloud often comes low, obliterating any expected view." Relieved when she did not press the idea further he added, "One evening soon we must make this climb again. To come up before dark and watch the sun set on this side and the full moon rise on this, is beautiful to behold."

Tiola turned her head to smile at him, the suggestion sounding interesting, a little romantic perhaps? She was fifteen years old, a young woman alone - apart from her guardian - in a new and strange world, and Stefan van Overstratten was not displeasing to look upon. Was there more than mere politeness behind his offer she wondered suddenly? He was a man of means, unmarried, and apart from his sister, her useless husband and this new born nephew, had no family. Such a man would be wanting a wife, and suitable wives were difficult to find here in Cape Town. The female population constituted native women, imported slaves, prostitutes or other men's wives. Men of van Overstratten's calibre usually applied to the marriage agencies in Holland and London. Unless there should be the rarity of someone suitable closer to home? Tiola blushed, flattered.

~ *Beware!* ~

The voice of her grandmother shouted in her mind and Tiola gasped as a tumble of rocks slid from beneath her feet to bounce down the sheer side of the drop below. Van Overstratten grabbed at her arm, pulled her away from the edge. She had not realised she was so close! Her breath quivering she clung to his shoulders, not daring to look down, all too vividly imagining the fall. He smelt of cinnamon and fine-blended tobacco; a hint of sweat from the walk.

"Come, come away from the edge Tiola," he said, guiding her to stand more safely. Embarrassed, she let go of him, smiled her gratitude. His purring Dutch accent blending into his perfectly spoken English was low and seductive, although he mispronounced her name. He made the emphasis on the 'o', Ti- *oh* -la. She said nothing, did not think it polite to correct his error.

Brushing his clean-shaven cheek close to hers, he pointed to a ship beating her way to windward, and casually slid his arm around her waist.

He was charming, handsome and wealthy. He possessed impeccable manners, and she knew he was everything Jenna had hoped to find for her and more. For all that, Tiola would not be taking a moonlit walk with him. She was flattered by his attention but she did not want him as a husband. There was something about him, something her inner sense was trying to tell her. To not trust him? Why would that be? Instinct was warning her of something, and a witch's instinct was never wrong.

Those rocks had been very solid when first she had set foot upon them. Had the warning not been for the danger of a steep drop, but for something else entirely? One day she may find the truth, but for the moment Jenna would be feeling abandoned.

Using her guardian as a convenient excuse, Tiola eased away from Stefan and began to descend the path. If the Dutchman realised her discomfort, he assumed it was because of her modesty. He made no mention of her reticence, indeed, admired her all the more for it.

He would have to make enquiry, of course, discover whether there was public scandal of any sordid misdemeanour he ought to know of. She was a delightful young creature, and so far his attempts to find a wife suitable to breed him sons had been unsuccessful. He was concerned for her background but she was obviously educated and intelligent. And beautiful women so rarely possessed these essential qualities as additions to their other, essential, attributes. He would need to search hard to find another as pleasing as Tiola Oldstagh.

Walking behind her, discreetly admiring the sway of her hips, her slender waist and trim ankle, van Overstratten decided that perhaps he would not make his search for information too diligent. What he did not know would not concern him.

- Fourteen -

Luck followed Jesamiah Acorne like gulls trailing behind a fishing boat. They found a settlement a few miles up the coast and were fed, cared for and made welcome. It was a poor place, reliant on what the sea could yield yet the five Spanish-descended families were willing to share what little they had. Those discarded by the sea were never turned aside by those who made a living from the sea.

Jesamiah was grateful for the food they offered, a warm fire to ward off the chill of the night and the mosquitoes, and a comfortable bed. A girl, pretty in her rough way, had helped her mother salve and bandage his hands. By the second night she was sharing that comfortable bed, which had been hers anyway.

Ten days and nights later, and he lay awake staring at where the low supporting beams of the roof would be if there was light to see them by. The dwellings along here were nothing beyond shacks, made mostly of mud bricks or woven sticks plastered with a mud-and-dung daub. Dark and smoky inside, but dry and not infested by too many cockroaches. The mosquitoes were a nuisance, they always were, wherever you went. Jesamiah as with many a sailor, nursed a theory that drinking rum kept them away. It was nonsense of course, but a good excuse to always keep a bottle to hand. Except the rum had gone with the *Salvation*. The gut-rot stuff these settlers brewed, although having the same blissfully numbing effect on the senses, tasted foul.

The flea-ridden bed was set in one of four alcoves. Beyond the shabby curtain a rectangular area provided a space where the family struggled through the daily misery of life. From the second alcove came Rue and Isiah's contented snoring; along the opposite wall, the girl's mother and wind-weathered father slept behind another thin and patched curtain. The girl's bundle of younger brothers were squashed into the fourth.

Her head was on Jesamiah's shoulder, asleep, a delicate smile tipping the corners of her mouth, her hair spilling across his skin. She had not been innocent of a man, and would doubtless expect a handful of coins for her attentiveness when it came time for him to leave. Lying there, sleep beyond reach, Jesamiah remembered the first woman he had looked at with aroused interest but, as a raw youth, had been too embarrassed to approach. A blonde with tight-curled ringlets; more bosom than bodice. In Port Royal, the night he had met Malachias Taylor, not long after he had been thrown out from the only home he had known by his bastard of a brother. With nowhere to go except the sea, to seek out his father's old friends and a life of piracy.

Phillipe had accused him of being baseborn, despite the wedding ring Jesamiah's mother had worn for more than a year before his birth. He was no illegitimate by-blow and she had not been a whore. Ah, leave it be! She was dead, his father with her. What sense in resurrecting the past after the distance of all these years? Except on occasion the past reared its ugly head and demanded attention. Still hurt.

He shrugged the mental image of Phillipe aside, refusing to entertain thoughts he would rather forget. Turned his mind to more pleasant recollections - how many women had he bedded since his first? But that thought too, turned sour. Beyond a few he could not recall their faces, let alone their names. Hermione, he remembered her, he had spent a month with her while they had careened the *Mermaid* at Nassau. Justine? Sal? Catrina. Arabella. Ah yes, the beautiful Arabella. Now *she* was a cat with sharpened claws! Had almost got him and the rest of the crew dancing a hemp-noose jig because of her lust for gold coins. His first woman? Oh he remembered her, though he had been three sheets into the wind from a surfeit of drink. Malachias had found her for him, said she was a friend; a prostitute of course. They always were.

Across in the Windward Islands that had been, after his first battle at sea; first Chase, first pirate attack. First woman. You always remember your first, Taylor had said as he had pushed Jesamiah into the welcome of Dolly's embrace and the apple-dumpling expanse of her chest.

"You always remember yer first encounter, Jes boy, so make sure it's worth rememberin'."

Yet he could not remember, when he was drowning, where he had heard that voice. *Jes...a...mi...ah!* The scream had rocked his mind, not his ears, had been *inside* his head, not outside. Where in damnation had he heard that accent before? Try as hard as he could the answer would not come. It was almost as if the memory of it had been erased, washed away. Memory was such a fickle thing. His brother he wanted to forget, that voice he wanted to remember.

Thinking back, he wondered how much Malachias had paid Dolly. She had initiated his eager, fumbling innocence into the secrets of manhood and then spent the rest of the night teaching him how to do it properly. How to give and get pleasure. Not love; there was never love from her kind. How could love be bought with a silver shilling? What use had a pirate for love, anyway?

Damn it all! Where had he heard that bloody voice before?

Lying there in the darkness he also recalled his first, terrifying, fight at sea. Would Dolly have been as terrifying, he wondered idly, if it had not been for the rum that had dulled his naive apprehension? He thought nothing of spending his sexual need with a woman now.

That first Chase, his first Prize, had been laden with sugar and timber. The *Mermaid* had cut in across her bow, firing a single warning shot, manoeuvred to larboard and taken all the wind, effectively crippling the poor blighters. Undermanned, underpaid, the crew had given a token resistance out of misplaced loyalty to their captain, but by then it had already been too late, the *Mermaid* was alongside throwing grappling lines and boarding, the pirates pouring over the rails cutlasses drawn, pistols firing, axes raised. All a reek of yelled shouts and swirling smoke. That was the point of attack, to make as much noise as possible, adding to the fear.

How many attacks since then? Jesamiah tried vaguely to count. *Alcide, Dinah, Vanessa. Resolve, Heliotrope, Cadiz, Cornelia, Topaz; La fleur de lis,* the *Rose.* Several with bird's names; *Cormorant, Gull, Sparrow, Flying Swan.* The *Wren.* He chuckled. An inappropriate name if ever there was one! *Wren* – she had been a huge, ungainly lump, wallowing close to the scuppers so badly was she leaking. *Pelican* would have suited her better. There had been a *Pelican.* Where? Ah yes, nor' nor ' west of the Bahamas.

So many more. So many. Odd that he could remember most of the vessels but only a few of the women. And that he had so forgotten Malachias Taylor these last weeks. He found grieving tears were dribbling down his cheeks, the hot salt taste stinging his chapped lips. Pretend to be fearless, to not have a care beyond where the next tot of rum and willing strumpet was to come from. Board a vessel kill those who resisted, take what you wanted including the virtue of a woman if it was available; destroy the rest. Laugh, hide the loneliness that continuously stabbed inside.

The girl stirred, her hand brushing against his stomach. She opened her eyes, smiled, expected him to make love to her again.

He obliged, but what was the point of that also? None whatsoever when he received so very little lasting pleasure from it for himself.

- Fifteen -

"Rue! Rue? Wake up!"

Had anyone been awake to witness Jesamiah's self-indulgent misery during the night they would not have believed the man urgently shaking his friend's shoulder to be the same person. Rue was stretched out beneath the shade of a palm, legs crossed at the ankles, the wide-brimmed grass hat he had fashioned pulled low over his eyes, arms folded across his chest. He shoved the hat from his eyes, stared at Jesamiah squatting beside him, closed his eyes again and resettled his hat.

"Go away." He added something crude and explicit in French.

"Listen! I have news! Bloody superb, gift from God news!" Jesamiah's excitement was unmistakable. Like a boy on his birthday.

"It 'ad better be," the older man growled, removing the hat and waving it ineffectually at the irritating buzz of insects. "I do not take kindly to being woken from my afternoon nap."

"Three more survivors have straggled ashore, down in the next village."

"Bravo for them! As long as they find their own shade I am most 'appy for them." Annoyed, Rue replaced his hat. Jesamiah snatched it, tossed it away.

"*Merde!*"

"Will you damned listen? They are Spanish."

The Frenchman was unimpressed. "Unless they are natives, so is everyone along this stretch of coast. Even you are 'alf Spanish, your mother was Spanish you are able to speak the language. In case you 'ad not noticed, we 'appen to be idling in Spanish territory."

"They were from a Spanish vessel. One of a fleet." Jesamiah ignored the sarcasm, had his hands on Rue's shoulders attempting to shake sense into him. "A convoy of galleons. *Galleons,* Rue. The entire fleet went down. Carrying gold from Mexico; packed to the fore-deck, bloody great, treasure carrying galleons!"

Interest was twitching. Rue uncrossed his legs. "You are serious?"

The grin swept over Jesamiah's mobile face. "As serious as a duck's arse, mate! Word is spreading as wild as fire in the hold; they were on their way to Spain from Havana, were hit by the same hurricane that did for us. All of them Rue, all laden with gold bullion and silver, precious gems and barrels of indigo. The wrecks are scattered along God-knows how many miles of reef." Hunkered on his heels he rested his forearms on his thighs, giving a moment of quiet silence for the implication to sink in.

The wind scurrying in from the Atlantic was strong on the far side of the dunes, among the scrub and vegetation its bluster dropped considerably. Here, it was more of a whispering breeze, its voice a very quiet, continuous, *sssss,* a muted harmony whispering with the muffled *whissh* of the ocean.

"A fortune's in the holds of those ships, Rue. A fortune run aground an' sitting there with only fish and crabs to shit on it."

Slowly the Frenchman smiled, a sweep that split his face from ear to ear. "Or for someone with enterprise and skill to salvage it, *non?*"

Scratching at his beard growth Jesamiah pondered the genesis of a plan. "No Rue, for someone with a fast ship and the savvy to go one better. I'd wager the Spanish are already running around like their arses are on fire. The stuff was destined for the King's treasury, wealth he cannot afford to lose. They'll be all over the Florida reefs these next few months, reclaiming what they can. Plenty of sharks too – and I am not talking of fish. Pirates 'ave as much a nose for the smell of gold as do our finned friends for blood."

Rue sat forward, his eyes gleaming, hooked. "So what is it you propose?"

Rising to his feet, Jesamiah strode a few paces to the top of the dunes, thinking. Unprotected, the wind hit him in the face and the sound of the surf churning on to the beach and roaring in his ears was startling. He stood there, legs wide-spread, hands on hips staring into the emptiness of the wild Atlantic. The air smelt heavy with salt, was humid, with an undertone of damp earth. He drank it all in, breathing it deep into his lungs the sight, sound and feel of the sea.

Turning his back to the ocean Jesamiah spoke his thoughts aloud, the wind streaming through his hair and ribbons. "They will have to store what they salvage somewhere. Build a warehouse along the coast? Somewhere easily accessible from the sea but with fresh water, and practical to defend. Probably near to where the main body of the fleet went down." Remembering the torn carcass of the *Salvation* added, "I'm not going to risk the hazard of shallows, reefs and the more deadly type of shark for nothing more than a few pieces of eight; not when all we have to do is let the Spanish do the collecting while we bide our time, learn where this storehouse is, then sail in and take what we want." There was no trace of the despondency of last night in his eyes. Nothing but an eager alertness.

"*Mon ami*, Captain, it is an excellent plan but are you not forgetting *un petit* matter?" Rue lifted his hand, held finger and thumb close together indicating something very small. "We are not in possession of a ship."

Jesamiah stood there, his bare feet sinking into the white sand. Stood there grinning. He spread his arms, palms uppermost. "So we get one."

"*D'ou* - from where?" Rue climbed the dune joined him on the top. With an extravagant sweep of his hand, he gestured towards the worm-riddled jetty that served the village. Pointed at the two leaking fishing boats and their own battered longboat.

"Are we to use one of those? What do we do? Beat a merchant crew to pulp with the oars?"

"Our longboat will take us to St. Augustine. From there we find a passage to Virginia, we can talk ourselves aboard something. Wouldn't be the first time I've had to do so."

"Virginia?" Rue spluttered, raising his arms in the air, exasperated. "'The sun 'as got at you? Why, in the name of God, do we wish to go to Virginia?"

"To get us a ship – keep close-hauled, man!"

Rue brushed sand from his bare legs. "I 'ave a feeling I do not wish to be knowing this but tell me anyway. Why do we need to go all the way to Virginia to get us a ship?"

Folding his arms Jesamiah smirked. "There are eight of us. Eight men to find and take a suitable vessel. We need to get something easily, something sleek and fast, and preferably something that has a cargo we can sell immediately to entice a full crew. We might strike lucky and find what we want in St Augustine, but we would have to get out past the fort. With that battery? We do not have the men or time to sit on our rumps and wait for something to come to us, therefore, we go to where I *know* there will be what we want."

"In Virginia?"

"In Virginia."

Suddenly, Rue realised what Jesamiah was alluding to. "You talking about somewhere in the Chesapeake Bay?"

Jesamiah smiled. "I'm talking about somewhere in the Chesapeake Bay. The Rappahannock River to be precise. When we get there they will have started loading the tobacco on to the convoy ships."

"One of which we commandeer?"

Jesamiah's easy smile faded and a different look came into his eye, one that was rigid and echoed the remnant of a long-buried lust for revenge.

Beneath a sky of pure crystal blue with the few clouds seeming as if they were just in reach, Jesamiah lost his familiar air of congeniality and the could-not-care-less attitude he normally portrayed. The bright sun was behind his head haloing his black hair into a shimmer of silver, shadowing his face so that Rue could not see the expression harden in his eyes. But he heard it. The hatred that had congealed in Jesamiah years ago was solid in his voice.

"No, not commandeer. Someone I know owes me a boat." Jesamiah paused, half turned and stared at Rue not seeing the Frenchman, seeing instead the contorted, mocking face of his half brother. A face that had delighted in the infliction of pain and fear.

The pause lengthened. He found it difficult to speak of his past, this part of it anyway. "My father, when he died, left me one of his three vessels. The smallest, a two masted sloop. She was nothing special, but I loved that boat." Another pause as he offered Rue a small, apologetic smile, embarrassed that perhaps it was not manly to be admitting such a thing. But the Frenchman raised his hand, a slight gesture of understanding. He too had known his share of special craft.

Jesamiah shrugged as if tossing aside the recollection of bad memories, gave an almost inaudible sigh. "She was called *Acorn*. I took my name from her so I would never forget what my brother, that bastard, owed me." Thought, *nor how he shamed me and what he made me do.*

Aloud, he said, "I had my father's name then, Mereno. Jesamiah Mereno. My half brother Phillipe hated me." He gave another, quick, smile. "Feeling was mutual."

The uncomfortable memories, now the box where he had locked away into was opened again, were flooding back. "He is almost seven years my senior. He made my childhood a misery. He was older, bigger, heavier than me." About to say more he stopped, then added with feigned indifference, "The names he called me, the words he used all hurt as much as the physical injuries he inflicted." Thought, keeping these particular memories private, *I could never run fast enough to get away.*

Apart from when he was safe with his mother or father, all of it, almost every day, had been one long existence of concealing his dread and hiding his tears. As a boy, he had been afraid of the night and had cringed from the coming dawn. As a man he had never completely forgotten the endless despair. Still, even now he flinched when anyone came up behind him.

Shooting Rue a wry smile Jesamiah snorted cynically. "Oh, he was a clever bugger, he made sure the bruises never showed." *Nor the blood. He did just enough to hurt and humiliate me. Never enough for anything to be noticed.*

The resentment and hatred surged within him, quickening his breath and heartbeat. He clenched his teeth, his fingernails dug into his palms. Lifting his eyes he stared direct at his friend, the words tumbling out of him. "My brother, when I was a sprog, would have made the Spanish Inquisition look like a doting aunt. His mother died when he was five and my father almost immediately went back to sea – he was a privateer. Made his first fortune as a young man sailing with Henry Morgan, his second on the Red Sea Coast. When he returned home two years later, he brought with him a new wife and a baby son – me! Phillipe resented my mother. Resented me even more. I suppose seven was a difficult age to accept a new baby as a brother, a new woman as a mother. To add insult, my mother was Spanish. To some eyes in the Colonies she might as well have been the Devil's spawn."

He turned his head to look at Rue, the pain evident in his eyes, his expression. "He hated us Rue. Hated me."

For a moment Jesamiah had to cease talking, the tightness was rising too high in his throat. He trod down the slope of the dune, half slithering, starting a small avalanche of sand, walked a few paces down the beach. A loggerhead turtle had lumbered ashore during the night to lay her eggs, the trail of her flippers gouged through the slope of the hot sand to end high above the tide line. Idly, Jesamiah kicked the trail askew with his feet, obliterating it. One nest of eggs that would not be gathered for food. One clutch of life that would stand a chance of survival.

Jesamiah finished kicking at the sand. "Father died within a week of my mother. On the day of his funeral Phillipe burnt my boat to a cinder and made me watch. She was all I had left." He turned his face away from Rue. There were other things that Phillipe had done, but he was not going to be admitting them, not even to the man he now regarded as his closest friend. "I was a boy, a few months short of fifteen. Phillipe was a grown man, almost two and twenty."

He did not bother to hide the bitterness, it was too raw to be hidden. "I changed that day, for some reason courage – a madness perhaps – took hold of me. Phillipe thought he had broken me but I turned on him. I had no idea how to fight I was all feet and elbows, fists bunched wrong, jabbing at the parts that would not hurt beyond a bruise. There was blood smothering his face. I had him down, me on top. God, but it felt good to be finally hitting him!"

Rue was no fool, he realised there was more here than Jesamiah was saying, but it was not his business to ask. Instead, he said, "So what 'appened? You did not kill him."

Jesamiah smoothed his moustache. "I was stopped. Old Halyard Calpin, my father's overseer pulled me off - for my sake not my brother's. There was blood pouring from his nose, I had broken it I think, and a couple of teeth were missing. Phillipe ordered the servants to throw me off the plantation, threatened to have me hanged if I returned. They did not have to do much throwing, I left willingly. Calpin managed to advise me where to go, what to do."

"To go to sea? To became a pirate?"

His face tipped towards the spread of the sky Jesamiah repeated, "To go to sea, to became a pirate." And his normal, carefree self-confidence returned. He grinned, said with a flourish, "A bloody good one as it happens. It was not too hard for me to find a few of my father's old shipmates, ask to crew with 'em."

"Malachias Taylor?"

"Malachias Taylor." Jesamiah stared out to sea. A few gulls were squabbling over something, a dead fish probably. Further out he caught the wicked glimpse of a shark's fin. Said, an uncertain question in his voice, "So we go to Virginia?"

Shrugging his agreement, Rue nodded. "A reckoning, *non?*"

His inner hardness returning Jesamiah, absentmindedly curled one of his ribbons around his finger. Answered, "Aye. A reckoning."

- Sixteen -

The plantation, *Sorenta,* looked much the same. The trees at the far end of the fields where the tobacco grew were further away than Jesamiah remembered; more ground would have been cleared for the cultivation of new young plants. There was a second storehouse built alongside the original one flanking the jetty, where the wide spread of the Rappahannock River meandered into a long, lazy, curve. The house and its gardens were unrecognisable. Phillipe had pulled most of the plain frontage down and rebuilt in a grander style. There were pillars and porticoes, carved statues and fancy lintels. An additional wing to the west, and what appeared to be an entire new stable block at the side. Business – profits - must be good to warrant such expansion, it must have cost a fortune. But then, their father had left a fortune, intending it for both sons. Jesamiah had not seen a shilling of it.

The gardens his mother had so lovingly tended had been informal and full of life. She had adored flowers; the grass slope running down to where the river wandered had been bordered by colour that had changed with each season, from the vibrant yellows of spring to the deep reds and mellow golds of autumn. They were all gone. A formal shorn and raked lawn had replaced the ramble of grass; there was hardly any colour, save for a few dour, circular flower-beds and a mass of shrubs and trees all lined up like soldiers on parade. The great oak beside the house had also gone. Not even its stump remained. Jesamiah had spent most of his childhood among the branches of that friendly old tree. Phillipe would have enjoyed destroying it.

"This," Rue said in a curt whisper at Jesamiah's side, interrupting the thoughts of the past that were crowding and shouting for attention, "is madness."

"No one said you had to come with me," Jesamiah growled tetchily back, ducking into an overhang of leafy shrubs as yet another laden wagon trundled past along the wide, formal sweep of the gravel drive. So far there had been several flaws in his proposed plan. The major one being the ship itself.

For several hours they had taken careful and discreet stock of the estate, the task unexpectedly made easier by all the people bustling about the place. It seemed a party was being prepared at the house. Carts and wagons had been coming and going with an army of tradesmen, slaves and bustling servants since dawn. With everything in turmoil, everyone busy, two more men would scarcely be noticed.

First, they had scouted the river itself and the ships. Not the expected *Querida* or *Sorenta*, the two vessels moored to the jetty were unfamiliar to Jesamiah - the *Fortune* and the *Alicia Galley*, a conventional square-rigged, three masted ship - her only difference, she was also fitted with oars. And she appeared to be falling to pieces.

The plantation was named after the original vessel, *Sorenta*, which Jesamiah's father had captured and claimed as his own. Ship and cargo – a hold full of Spanish doubloons and barrels of precious indigo.

"*Dieu* Jesamiah, these ships are worm-riddled 'ulks!" Rue had whispered, mindful of how voices carried near water. Jesamiah had not answered. There was not much he could add.

He had swallowed his disappointment, then brightened, ever the optimist. "The *Alicia Galley* looks in better repair than the other one and we only need her for a short while. As long as she holds together until we find us a crew and take what we want from the Spanish, so what if she then rots to pieces? We'll be rich after, can buy what we want."

"*Oui*, as long as she 'olds. 'Ave you got a few lengths of cordage to tie 'er together perhaps?"

"She cannot be that bad, Rue! She's already half loaded with hogsheads of tobacco for the voyage to England. Phillipe would not risk his precious cargo to an unseaworthy boat." Would he?

"I 'ope the fool 'as got 'er insured, that is all I can say."

Next, the house itself. Jesamiah had ached to go along the river bank to Halyard Calpin's cottage, walk in as bold as brass and ask what all the bustle was about. Except, he had already discovered the old man was no longer there, he was beneath a headstone in the plot designated as a cemetery. He had been a good man, a good friend. Old Calpin had never known all the sordid details of that last evening, Jesamiah had not the opportunity nor inclination to speak of it, and Phillipe himself would not be telling the truth. Jesamiah had found no sign of his mother's grave. No mound, no marker. He had not expected one.

Rue shrugged, decided he might as well make the best of a poor job. He stepped from the bushes fastening his breeches after relieving himself and waylaid a likely-looking trader dragging a mule burdened by packages and boxes up the long sweep of the drive.

"*Pardon monsieur,* what is it 'appening 'ere?" he asked, dipping his head at the distant house.

Sniffing, the trader wiped his cuff under his nose. "Christening ball. Mereno's wife gave birth to their first son, what two months ago, now."

Appearing behind Rue, Jesamiah raised his eyebrows. He was an uncle, then. "First child, eh?" he queried, wondering who the wife was.

Frowning suspiciously the trader hesitated, then touched his forelock in respect as Jesamiah casually slipped him payment of two silver coins.

"The first 'e's spawned with 'er, 'though there's prob'ly a scatter of others dropped along the way who don't warrant a fine christening. Only been married a year, long enough t'ensure the kid be 'is. She 'as another brat by a first 'usband. He left 'er sittin' well pretty when 'e died, so I 'ear tell."

Grateful for the information, Jesamiah touched his hat. "I'm indebted to you sir." He added another coin to the previous two, "And I'd be obliged for you to forget you met us?"

The trader walked on, whistling. It was none of his business who was on Mereno's property, or why.

"Let us find somewhere to squat our backsides for the rest of the day, Jes, then take the ship tonight. We will leave 'ere with no one the wiser, *n'est pas?*" Rue was still feeling apprehensive.

To sneak in and out again was not Jesamiah's intention. He had ghosts to lay; too many years of huddled fear to erase, too many childhood tears to wipe away. He wanted Phillipe to know he had been here, wanted him to know his brother had not forgotten or forgiven. And he needed to prove he was no longer afraid. Stealing a ship was not the demon Jesamiah had come here to face; the demon walked and talked and called himself Phillipe Mereno.

The vague plan was to arrive at the house unannounced as merchants, one Spanish, one French, with the offer of an enticing business proposition. Jesamiah was banking on the fact that after all these years his brother would not recognise him. Phillipe would not see beyond what he was supposed to see - a dark haired, bearded Spaniard who spoke very poor English. Men rarely noticed what was under their noses, not seeing what they did not expect to see. The easiest way to conceal something? Set it in plain sight. All it needed to make a man slide his eyes over you without seeing who he was looking at was nerve. And since leaving this place, Jesamiah had acquired nerve by the ship-load.

To Rue's mind the plan was the stupidest thing he had ever heard, outside of poking a sleeping cobra with a stick. He appreciated they could not take the ship straight away, for the jetty was busy with slaves loading tobacco. They would have to wait for nightfall when work finished, creep aboard, slip her moorings and quietly sail down river - with only eight of them , the last thing they wanted was a fight. To walk direct into the lion's den, though? Well, that fellow Daniel in the Bible might have tried it, but Rue would rather err on the side of caution. There again, Jesamiah was never a cautious man.

Dozing, hidden in a tumble-down barn, they waited until dark when the house became filled with light and noise and people. Carriages by the dozen, women dressed in satin and silk, the men as elaborate in powdered wigs and embroidered waistcoats. A lavish evening, where the opportunity to flaunt what you had, or purported to have, was displayed in full.

For all his bravado, the first person they met, aside from footmen and servants, was Phillipe. Jesamiah had not expected that, had assumed they would be shouldered aside into some unobtrusive corner and forgotten. He felt his palms go sticky with sweat, his throat run dry. His heart was leaping in his chest as if dancing a jig there. All the memories flooded back. All those endured cruelties. Mereno approached, a questioning expression on his face, he glanced at the Spaniard, swivelled his attention to the Frenchman who was making a courteous bow and relating the reason for the intrusion in an exaggerated French accent. Intrigued, the lure of wealth being dangled, Phillipe listened. Jesamiah relaxed, the first hurdle cleared, he had not been recognised. Now all he had to do was keep reminding himself he was a man grown and not a child who was afraid of his elder brother.

Beyond two false ivory teeth, there was no lingering sign of damage to Phillipe's face. That battering Jesamiah had finally found the courage to give him had been superficial then. Pity.

"*Monsieur*, my deepest apologies." Rue concluded, indicating Jesamiah who removed his three-cornered hat and swept an elaborate bow. "My partner, Señor José Menéndez de Avilés and I, 'ad we known of your preoccupation, we would not 'ave

- 115 -

interrupted such an occasion." For good measure Rue added a generous portion of flattery, and Phillipe preened to it.

"My dear fellow," he chortled, "what you outline is of interest to me. I am, as you rightly presume, heartily sick of my profits falling into some government official's pocket. Any venture that can retain the balance to my side of the account book I shall willingly listen to, but not this evening!" He slapped Rue's shoulder, cast another suspicious smile at Jesamiah. He did not trust Spaniards.

Sweeping his hand towards the crowd of invited guests Phillipe offered, "Please, take your fill of what you require and enjoy. You are welcome to remain the night, and on the morrow we will talk. What say you?"

Politely blustering a mild protest that they would not dare presume upon such generous hospitality - Rue eagerly accepted.

"What have you named the child?" Jesamiah asked in Spanish, doubting Phillipe would recognise his voice. When he had left it had barely broken, had still been high-pitched. Now, his vocal chords had a deep, husky tone that could resonate quietly in ordinary speech, or bellow at full roar when aboard ship. As for Spanish, his mother had taught him the language and to honour her memory he had never forgotten it.

Translating, Rue added, "My friend understands *Anglais*, but 'e finds it somewhat embarrassing to mispronounce many of your more difficult words."

Assuming this Spanish gentleman to be an imbecile, Phillipe regarded the tall, bearded man who stood casually with his left hand resting on the hilt of a cutlass. In deference to supposedly being a reputable sea-merchant Jesamiah had removed his ribbons and had tied his tumble of hair into a neat tail at the nape of his neck. All else was the same, except he had tucked his pistol beneath his coat. There were, after all, ladies present.

Answering disdainfully, speaking loud and slow, not liking this foreigner, Phillipe intoned, "My son is named for my father and myself, Charles Phillip."

Jesamiah's loathing peaked; he clenched his fists the need to lash out difficult to control. How dare this bastard soil the name of their father by linking it to his own? He turned away quickly, pretending interest in a group of ladies who were fluttering their fans and eye-lashes at him. A handsome man, he was already creating a stir. In faltering English he resorted to pricking his brother with insults. "Ah, Carlos, a fine Spanish name."

"As it is also a fine English name," Phillipe retaliated, offended.

One of the ladies caught Jesamiah's eye. She was staring at him. Blonde, a porcelain face, slender waist, generous bosom. As his stare met hers she coloured, looked quickly away and paid elaborate attention to what the woman beside her was saying.

Throwing his hands in the air Rue was laughing, easing the sudden flare of sparked tension. "And I claim it also, *un nom français, n'est pas?*"

Excusing herself from her companion, the blonde woman walked slowly towards the men, her fan fluttering, her body graceful in the rouched, close-fitting silk of her red and saffron gown.

"Ah! My wife!" Phillipe declared, glad of the interruption. He had a house full of important guests whom he needed desperately to impress, wanted nothing to go wrong this evening. "Allow me to introduce Mistress Alicia Mereno. My dear, monsieur Claude de la Rue and señor Menéndez de Avilés." He stumbled over the Spanish pronunciation. "They have come with a proposition to double the fortune I already possess."

The woman curtsied, demure and elegant. Much of the fortune was hers, generated by the profitable Barbados sugar plantation she had inherited from her first husband. Phillipe had already squandered half of his.

"So you have not come to sample the food spread along the buffet table?" she exclaimed. "I swear, there is sufficient to feed the entire Colony!"

Jesamiah thought her the prettiest thing he had ever seen, but then, he always had. As her eyes, with their long, curled lashes swept up to directly meet his she knew he had recognised her. As she had him.

Producing a Spanish doubloon from his waistcoat pocket, Jesamiah let its gold twinkle a moment in the flickering light of the many candles in wall sconces and candelabra. "Alas, nothing to offer I have upon me, for the child in a gift." Deliberately he spoke in very bad English, muddling the tenses and structure, keeping his voice low and deep. "Were I be honourable to place in his crib, this?" At Phillipe's frowned hesitation added, with a placating bow, "A son, my own, I have in Spain. Two years, soon, will he be."

"The child will be sleeping," Phillipe answered curtly, not attempting politeness, not caring for this black haired stranger to intrude.

"Phillipe," Alicia Mereno interjected, sliding her arm through her husband's, "this is the first gentleman who has expressed a wish to see my darling boy. I am flattered." She smiled alluringly at her husband who about to again say no, was distracted by a group of plantation owners seeking his immediate appearance at the card tables.

Her face flushing, Mrs Mereno conducted the Spanish gentleman up the stairs to the nursery, after Jesamiah had handed Rue his hat.

"Look after this for me," he had said amiably in Spanish, muttering, quieter in English. "and keep sharp."

Rue had frowned at him. Alright, they had awoken the snake, was that not enough? Ought they not be gone before the thing started spitting venom?

Seventeen

The child's nurse, dozing in a chair, started guiltily awake as they entered. With a reprimand Alicia sent her away on the pretext of fetching her mistress a shawl. It was a long walk from the nursery to her bedchamber - the length of the house and a flight of stairs – would take at least ten minutes; fifteen or even twenty if the woman dawdled as she was sure to. Alicia had not met a servant yet who hurried.

"Well, you have found a lucky landing for your feet Arabella, my dear." Jesamiah said, shedding the Spanish accent and folding his arms, leaning insolently against the closed door. "I wonder, does your husband know you were once a Port Royal harlot?"

"Of course he does not!" she snapped, hiding the anxiety that because of Jesamiah he may be about to find out. "And I would thank you to call me Alicia. I have not used Arabella these past many years."

"Not since you married your first rich conquest, eh?"

She tilted her head, chin defiant. "What of it? He was an old man, I gave him the son he longed for and I brought spring into his life."

"And his bed I warrant. Poor bugger. What did he die of? Exhaustion, or the pox?"

The insult stung. Alicia crossed the few yards between them and slapped his face. "As I recall," she said acidly, "you owe me for a night's pleasure. You left in a hurry when the militia came searching for the crew of a pirate ship anchored in the harbour."

He remembered it well. "We had to fight our way back aboard; escaped without our breeches." He tapped his fingernail against two gold-capped teeth. "I had to get these fitted, thanks to that brawl - and because of the interruption it was only half a night of pleasure." With his callused forefinger he stroked her cheek. "I suppose you would not be knowing who betrayed us?" He ran the finger lower, across the swell of her breasts, leaned closer, whispered, his voice huskier than usual, seductive, "Was it you, my pretty?"

Indignant, she slapped him again. "And why would I? Because you left in a hurry I never got paid!"

Smiling, Jesamiah produced a ribbon from his pocket, winding it around the gold coin he had kept in his hand, tucked both of them deep into her cleavage. "Will this settle the debt?" Stepping past her he walked to the inner room where the boy slept, gazed down at his nephew. Out of habit he fingered his earring, said over his shoulder in a lowered voice, "Do not get me wrong Sweetheart, I admire your enterprise. Good luck to you."

Behind him, holding an oil lamp high to illuminate the dim-lit room, Alicia answered in a curt whisper. "I do not need or require your patronising luck, Jesamiah Acorne."

"I am sure you do not. You seem to be managing quite well without it."

His father's grandson. Would Papa have been proud to know the name Mereno was to continue? Had he been proud of Phillipe? Of himself? Jesamiah did not know, it was his mother he had been close to not his father. Papa had spent his days supervising the plantation or the ships, had been away for months on end taking the tobacco to England. There had never been time for his boys. Jesamiah swallowed hard, his Adam's apple bobbing in his dry throat. If Papa had loved his sons he had never demonstrated it. Was it so surprising Phillipe had been such an evil child? Jesamiah at least had his mother. Phillipe, nothing. No one.

Then again, he could have chosen to love his younger brother, not torture him.

Delicately, Jesamiah folded aside the top cover hiding part of the baby's face. All babes looked the same, how women could declare they had a father's nose or a grandfather's chin was beyond his reasoning. To Jesamiah's mind, this boy looked, perhaps, a little like Phillipe, those same squint eyes? Nothing like Charles Mereno. The hair was fair, the chin square. He tried to picture him grown up with moustache and beard, gave up. Wondered, idly, whether the boy was Phillipe's.

Seeing his expression, guessing his thoughts Alicia hissed, "I'll thank you to know the child is Phillipe's, he is no cuckoo in the nest." Unable to hold her anxiety any longer, added, "Why are you here? To expose my past?" Her head tilted upward, only the rise and fall of her bosom betraying her agitation. "I can as easily endanger you, Sir. In these parts a pirate is treated with a deal more contempt than a one-time, now very rich, whore."

"I assure you I was unaware of your presence or your marriage. I came on business, nothing more." Jesamiah looked directly at her, "Ensure your son grows to be a good man, Alicia. One bully in the family is quite sufficient."

He walked past her into the stronger light of the outer room, the woman following, setting the lamp down on a table, her expression puzzled. "You know Phillipe?" she asked.

Interesting. She knew of whom he spoke when he talked of bullies.

"I know him. I've known him a long time. All my life in fact." From the far side of the room, Jesamiah shrugged, looked directly at her. "Although he has not realised he knows me." He spread his hands, apologetic, defiant. "I am his legitimate half brother. I'm a Mereno, we share the same father."

Her hand flying to her mouth, Alicia gasped. "I had no idea!"

"Nor would you." Jesamiah tossed an ironic laugh into the air. "That makes you my sister-in-law. How quaint."

She did not return his amusement. Did not truly know whether to believe him or not, but, yes, there was a similarity about the angle of the jaw, the slant of the eye. The same self-assured arrogance?

"He has never spoken of a brother."

"We were not exactly friends." In two strides Jesamiah crossed the room, stood before her his finger beneath her chin tipping it upward. Her eyes had the bluest sparkle. "You keep silent about my identity, Ma'am, and so shall I about yours. If not…" He shrugged, let the implication fall like a dropped cannon ball.

He smelt of the sea. Of tar and hemp; of leather, molassed rum and masculine sweat. Of the carefree life she used to know, and occasionally missed. "You promised me the moon, Jesamiah and I believed you would give it to me. I so loved you."

"I'm a pirate, pirates never speak the truth. I thought you knew that." His finger was still beneath her chin. She really was very beautiful. He tipped her head higher, dipped his own and put his lips to hers in an intimate kiss. One which she as passionately returned.

As he pressed his body against hers, she twined her arms around his neck, her breath quickening, needing him as much as he suddenly wanted her. Tugging at the lacings of her bodice he cursed beneath his breath to find tightly strapped, whalebone stays penning her breasts. Unbuttoning his breeches, he pushed her against the door and lifted her skirts, fumbling beneath the layers of lace-edged, under-petticoats, running his hand up the silk of her stocking, over the tie of the garter and along the smoothness of her inner thigh. Her urgency for him to enter her as demanding and insistent as his own he slid in easily, his hands on her buttocks, his mouth covering hers, silencing her gasp as he thrust, twice, hard. He was so ready it was done and finished quickly. The door rattled. Alicia squeaked, alarmed, her hands pushing him away to straighten her gown, her face flushing crimson.

Hastily making himself respectable, Jesamiah indicated she could move away from the door, said as the nurse entered, "You have a fine son señora." He fell back into his role of a Spaniard. "I wish him the same fortune in life as his grandfather had."

Smiling a polite goodnight at the nurse, he took the shawl and draping it around Alicia's shoulders, gestured with his hand for her to precede him from the room. Surreptitiously patted her backside as she swept by.

- Eighteen -

The temptation to dance with Alicia was too great, although the lady herself appeared to be having second thoughts about Jesamiah. What she had done upstairs was beginning to sink in, and frighten her. Mischief, however, was rising in Jesamiah; to his surprise, he was enjoying himself. He had come here to do what? To commandeer a ship or to prove to himself he was no longer afraid of his brother? To take long overdue revenge? For the latter he could not have planned a more fitting retribution. How delicious to know something about this woman Phillipe did not, something that could destroy his pompous arrogance were it to be shouted to the world. Except, unless pressed, Jesamiah would hold his tongue. For the sake of the baby upstairs, not for Alicia. He would not trust her further than he could toss a cannon ball.

The subtle vengeance of cuckolding a man in his own home he discovered, even though he must keep the fact of it to himself, was proving to be sweeter than anything he could have devised. All those years of shame swept clean aside by one quick tumble against a nursery wall!

After the first dance he felt Phillipe's glare growing hotter on his back. Danced a second.

"I believe sir, it would be appropriate to take a turn with my wife," Phillipe tapped Jesamiah sharply on the shoulder and drew Alicia aside. "You have embarrassed me sufficiently, woman," he hissed at her. "Do your duty to our guests."

Jesamiah raised an eyebrow. Phillipe had not altered then, was still obnoxious. Had he moved on from forcing his victim to eat live beetles and dog shit? From twisting his brother's arm so cruelly it had almost snapped? Wickedly, Jesamiah could not resist the opportunity to pour oil on Phillipe's burning jealousy. It had all been jealousy. Jealousy of a new wife, jealousy of a new son.

Feigning bad English Jesamiah observed, "You take your turn in your wife whenever you please, señor! I have only this one night to, how you say? Put my pleasure in her?" He almost roared aloud with laughter at Phillipe's outraged response to the innuendo. Masked the chuckle by coughing behind his shielding hand. A mistake.

Phillipe saw only his eyes and recognition partially dawned. "I know you?" he queried, his voice acid with poison.

Without thinking beyond the opportunity of instant spite Alicia blurted, "He is your brother, Phillipe!"

Lifting his head, Jesamiah narrowed his dark eyes and surveyed her look of triumph through half closed lashes. The bitch. He ought to have known.

Phillipe's nostrils flared, the fury rising. The connection had fallen into place a moment before Alicia had slammed out the information. How had he not seen it? "You cur!" he snarled, his hand going to the dress sword at his hip. "How dare you come back here?"

Jesamiah was quicker, his fingers lashed out caught Phillipe's wrist. "I would not suggest a confrontation, brother. Not in front of all these guests with whom you wish to retain your reputation. Would it not be embarrassing for them to discover not only has your annoying little brother returned, but he is now a notorious pirate come to sample the Chesapeake's riches?" He flicked his eyes towards the swell of Alicia's bosoms, smiled, his meaning plain.

"You dog!" Phillipe repeated, not missing the blush tinting his wife's cheeks.

"Aye, that I am, but not as accomplished a dog as you. Shall we step outside, brother? Finish this in private?"

"I have nothing to say to you, in private or public."

"Good. Then you will not object to these people taking an increasing interest in us." Jesamiah waved his hand towards the dancers swirling around them, their eyes and ears straining to hear the sharp exchange.

"One of them," Phillipe answered, the anger shuddering through his body, "Is the Governor of Virginia. He would be delighted to order your arrest."

Stepping back a pace to enact calm for the sake of the observers, Jesamiah bowed graciously. "And I wonder how he would react if, upon my arrest I were to inform him I use this estate as a convenient storehouse? As my brother you sell what I plunder."

"He would never believe you."

"Would he not? In or out of gaol I can organise stolen goods to be secreted here – not too deftly hidden. I know what blind dolts the local militia men are."

Aware several couples had ceased dancing, Alicia took her husband's arm, pleaded, "Phillipe, please."

He tossed her touch away but saw sense. Snapped, "Remain here. Instruct the servants no one is to follow." To Jesamiah, jeered, "You. Outside. With your sword."

"My pleasure," Jesamiah answered giving a slight, mocking bow of acceptance. He took Alicia's hand kissed the palm, a lover's token. "It was a delight to serve you again, I enjoyed coming."

Embarrassed at her indiscretion and his double meaning, she snatched her hand away. Glowering, Phillipe strode out through the wide-flung doors onto the lawns beyond, his elongated shadow leaping and dancing in flickering light of the many smoking torches set into iron sconces.

Rue sidled up to Jesamiah. "*Qu'est-ce qui s'passe ?* What's up?"

"Nothing I cannot handle. I would be obliged if you were to make your unobserved way to the jetty and make ready. We may need to leave here quick." Jesamiah took his hat from Rue, set it upon his head, sauntered lazily in Phillipe's wake.

"Thank God for that," Rue muttered as he turned aside and keeping to the shadows, darted away towards the river.

Phillipe was waiting on the far lawn, his coat and waistcoat slung carelessly across a low wall, exposing his loose cotton shirt. His sword was drawn; a thin bladed rapier, more for show than fighting.

"I will not have you make a fool of me, nor my wife."

Spreading his hands as if humbly agreeing, Jesamiah mocked, "You do adequately for yourself without my intrusion." Did not bother removing his hat or coat, languidly slid his cutlass from its sheath, the grating sound of deadly steel slowly withdrawing, malevolent and ominous. Twice the weapon Phillipe held.

Phillipe raised his rapier, assumed the formal stance for fencing. *"En garde!"* he snarled, oblivious to the superiority of a cutlass, his pride making him slow to understand that Jesamiah, now an adult, was the better man.

As a boy Jesamiah had not known how to defend himself or how to fight. As a pirate he had no interest in play-acting. He had experienced blood and battle, had stared the grinning leer of death in the face. The real thing, *real* fear and danger, things that had eclipsed most of Phillipe's petty jealousies into insignificance. Assessing the sharpness of the edge of his blade, Jesamiah contemptuously ran his thumb along it, scowled, sucked at the resulting ooze of blood. Raised his eyes, the memory of the terrors haunting him all these years had evaporated. The hurt would always remain as a scar that ached on an iced winter's night, but the fear accompanying it had gone.

And the ghosts? Standing here on the lawn with his cutlass drawn, Jesamiah realised suddenly there were no ghosts to lay, that beyond his own mortified guilt they had never been disturbed. Graves were nothing but earth covered holes in the ground. Nothing that happened to the corpse, a mere mouldering pile of flesh and bone, mattered. The important bit, the soul, once released from the shell of the body was answerable only to God. And as for the living, what more could Phillipe do to him beyond the humiliations he had once, long ago now, administered?

"Is this sensible?" Jesamiah drawled. "You can no longer make me do despicable things. I am not the child you used to taunt, a boy frightened of his older brother. I am no longer small and slow. I've grown bigger than you, Phillipe - all I see before me is a pitiful fop, about to piss his breeches."

"If you think to alarm me then think again. You are nothing. Nothing beyond a debased pirate."

A sneer lifted the side of Jesamiah's mouth. "Nothing, eh? Yet my men call me Captain. I sail in my own vessel and go where I please, when I please. What have you done, eh? Pulled down a house and rebuilt it. Married a whore. Well how accomplished is that?"

"I am a respected gentleman. You and your kind are naught but thieving scum. I say again, *en garde!*"

Raising his cutlass, the blade glinting in the shifting light, Jesamiah's leer was intimidating. "Oh, there's more to being a pirate than thieving, Brother. You are forgetting, we murder as well. Since we last met I have learnt how to kill. You've not seen the bloody brutality of death, not seen a man after he's been run through with a cutlass, trying to squeeze the gore of his guts back into his belly with his own hands, while his life blood seeps away between his fingers. I have Phillipe. I have." He leant forward bending from the waist, brushed the heavy blade along the more delicate. The sound and the action, menacing. "I've been the one with the cutlass. I'll show you how I do it if you like."

Whether he did not believe him or was too proud to take notice, Phillipe made no answer; he circled, light on his feet, then choosing his moment moved fast, his rapier snapping out, the tip aiming for the flesh of the face. Jesamiah was quicker. He tilted his head back and caught the whipping blade with his own, neatly turning it aside. This was foolishness; a cutlass was not designed for fancy footwork and delicate parrying, it was a fighting weapon capable of hewing through anything from an opponent's blade to flesh, muscle and bone. A killing weapon used by killers.

Backing away, Jesamiah lowered the tip of the blade to the ground. "It might surprise you, Phillipe, it certainly surprises me, I have no desire to fight you. I thought I had, I thought I wanted to kill you but I find I have nothing to prove to you, or myself. Nothing at all." And he actually meant it.

Phillipe spat into the grass. "You are a disgrace to the name Mereno!"

Jesamiah shrugged. "That privilege is for you to boast alone, I've not traded on the name Mereno for many years. I go by the name Jesamiah Acorne now." Added pedantically, "That's Acorne with an 'e'." He took several steps backwards in the direction of the wall and the river, sheathed his cutlass. "I've grown up. How about you? Or are you still the same stinking lump of shit you ever were?"

For answer Phillipe lunged a feint to the right, was appalled by the speed with which Jesamiah stepped aside and re-drew his cutlass, at the power in the blade as one handed, with no apparent effort, he shattered the flimsy rapier.

"Get yourself a real weapon if you want to fight me. But nothing about you is real, is it? You are a fop and a fool. I thank you for reminding me what an arse-hole you are and for the opportunity to renew my acquaintance with y'wife – Alicia you call her? I knew her in the whore houses of Port Royal as Arabella." He felt no pang of conscience, she had felt none when betraying him and he had warned her that confidences must be kept on both sides of the mast. It would not do for people to doubt the threat of a pirate.

Jesamiah gave a mocking nod of his head and kicking over the nearest torch, was gone, running into the sudden-shadowed darkness, jumping over the wall and across the lawn, ducking through the trees. Rue was waiting, anxious and impatient on the quarterdeck, topsails already set, the fore topsail aback to hold the ship steady. Jesamiah leapt aboard, yelled for the warps to be cut and the *Alicia Galley* was drifting into the current, gaining speed as the river claimed her. Jesamiah took the helm, Rue added his weight to hauling the heavy spars to bring the backed sail around, the men falling to the tasks with a will.

Phillipe was too far behind to do anything except stand on the jetty hurling abuse and bawling for men to come to his aid with muskets. Raising his hat in salute, Jesamiah called, "You've owed me a boat all these years now we're square. An' I'll square this with you an' all, I've not forgotten or forgiven what you did to me and what you made me do beside my mother's grave. So you can think on this you bastard, I've just enjoyed the pleasure of emptying my seed into your wife's belly. She's the whore, Phillipe! Now, don't that sound just grand?"

Rue said nothing. But his thoughts were of cobras.

Nineteen

The party was ruined. Embarrassment was his worst mortification and it was embarrassing, standing here on the jetty listening to all these commiserations that were as false as the smile he wore.

"Bloody pirates," the Governor of Virginia was saying. "How'd they get up this far? That's what I want to know." Amiably he patted Phillipe's arm. "Do not worry y'self lad, the Guardship will catch the buggers down river. Ye'll have your ship back by noon on the morrow, y'have m'word. Ye'll see 'em hang, ye'll see 'em hang. I'll not have pirates making the fools of us, no sir, I'll not have it."

The Governor's intention may have been well meaning but Phillipe knew the words for what they were; flatulence trumpeted in a silent room, quickly apologised for and hastily waved away. The Guardship hired and kept at great expense by the Colony was useless. She would be moored somewhere up river and her crew dead drunk. They always were. An entire fleet of pirates could invade before those useless ragamuffins were aware of it. And even if they were aware, they were inept and incapable of doing anything about it.

"D'ye know who he was, this blackguard masquerading as a Spaniard? Fooled us all eh? Don't blame y'self lad, fooled us all. Looked and spoke the part, some half-breed servant's brat, I've no doubt."

Reluctant to admit the truth, Phillipe hesitated. Yes, he knew the bastard, what had he to lose by being honest? "He was my half brother, the swab my father sired on the Spanish whore he lived with. You must remember her? I did not recognise him until it was too late."

Indeed, the Governor remembered the woman well, not least for the reason that she had refused his advances on several occasions. "Skinny, pale faced boy?" He queried. "Always mumbled if I recollect, scared of his own shadow. Wouldn't have had the courage to piss into a tin pot."

Phillipe nodded. That was him.

Slapping Mereno's shoulder the Governor declared with enthusiasm, his curled wig bouncing on his shoulders, "By Gad the fellow's changed then, eh? Has found out how t'use the prick in his package. Impudent bugger."

Phillipe merely glowered.

The servants managed to persuade everyone back into the house, the damp of a rising river mist helping them along, Phillipe feigning laughter made light of the affair, agreeing he could see the amusing side; damned fine entertainment, most unusual. Yes, the fellow had been his half brother, the one he had thrown off the plantation some years ago now, and yes, he would see him hang.

"Young Jesamiah? I always said he had a bad streak in him," someone said, one of the older men who had been a close friend to Charles Mereno. "To turn on you the way he did that night? Ah, a sorry business. A sorry business indeed. You did right to throw him out, the dog that bites the hand that feeds him is a dog that should be shot, I always say. Pity you did not hang the fellow there and then. Always said he was a bad 'un."

He had never said anything of the sort but Phillipe let it pass.

The orchestra made a valiant attempt to raise enthusiasm for dancing, a wasted effort, the party had been effectively ruined. A good two hours before expected, several of the guests were making their excuses to leave. The plantation owners with estates fronting the river, anxious to get home and ensure their houses had not been plundered or burnt by pirates. Damn fools. Did they think themselves so important? Only one ship had been stolen, one poxed, leaking ship! But it had been *his* ship and the bastard who had stolen it was the brother who had ruined his life all those years ago. And now here he was doing so all over again!

From across the room Phillipe's eyes met with Alicia as she happened to glance up while talking to some overdressed old biddy, and the rage already congealing in his stomach settled there like a solid lump of cold porridge. If he thought for one moment the words his brother had shouted were true...

Alicia saw the look on her husband's face, blanched. She had been a fool to marry him - had been swept up by his apparent charm and wealth, by his promises and declarations, only to discover soon after their wedding night it had all been lies. He had wanted her money, nothing more. Now he had it he did not care what happened to her or her eldest, three year old son. He treated them both with contempt and indifference. Jesamiah was a handsome bastard, his touch as it always had in the past, instantly firing her desire. He too had lied. In Port Royal where life as a prostitute had been a squalid hand-to-mouth existence he had taken her to the dizzy heights of hope for something better. Then casually dropped her back into the dung-heap. Yes! These two were certainly brothers! Her disappointment and the guilty realisation at what she, they, had so casually done upstairs now appalled her.

She said something, hoped it sounded sensible, to the foul old woman who smelt of mould and urine. Dreaded the moment she would find herself alone with her husband. Her mind returned to the room upstairs where she had allowed Jesamiah to - oh good God, what had she done?

Distracted by someone seeking conversation Phillipe moved out of the line of her vision. She breathed a sigh of relief. What was undoubtedly to come would not be the first beating she had received at his hands, he was a vindictive, jealous man. Fleetingly she wondered, if she saddled a horse and galloped it hard would she catch Jesamiah down river, could she plead to be taken aboard? A foolish idea. What would be her option then? To return to prostitution, give up both her sons? All this? The occasional beating she could endure, a lifetime of hopeless poverty she could not.

Playing the charming hostess another half hour passed, the stolen ship and Jesamiah's identity remaining the only topic of discussion, the same words going around and around like a spinning cartwheel. She squeaked alarm as a hand clamped on her arm, hauled her into a shadowed recess. Phillipe was not to wait for the guests to go then, was to say something now. She flinched, expecting a blow.

He did not hit her but came straight out with what he intended to say. "I have the impression you knew who he was all along."

Indignant, she countered, "Of course I did not! How could I? I assumed he was someone you knew, a friend of yours. I was shocked when he told me he was your brother! As shocked as you were."

"Oh, you knew who he was, my lady. I am not naive. And now I know who you were too. Who and what you were. I never thought I would be grateful to my brother for something."

Alicia tried to wrest her arm away from the grip hurting her. Her anger was real, fuelled by guilt. "I know not what you mean. I was the fool to be taken in by his charm, but he charmed you too, did he not? The foul man attempted to seduce me. I put him firmly in his place and returned to our guests. Had I accommodated him mayhap he would have been satisfied and not stirred muddied waters by revealing who he was. Had I lifted my skirts for him, perhaps he would have left your stupid ship alone!"

Her lie sounded plausible. Phillipe desperately wanted to believe her, for the alternative was sickening. From the day his father had returned home with the slut who claimed she was his wife and the son she had dropped, his life had been ruined. Father had been besotted with the woman, only had interest for her and that puking brat she cooed over. And when Papa came home from his sea voyages - he was often gone for months at a time – who was it he greeted first? Oh no, not his eldest, not his firstborn! It was always Jesamiah he swung into the air and played with!

Every time Phillipe had tried to attract Charles Mereno's attention to tell him things he thought his Papa ought to know, he had been ignored or shunted aside; passed over for that pretty boy with black curls and dark eyes.

How Phillipe hated Jesamiah!

"If ever I discover what my brother told me is true, Ma'am, before I have you thrown out I will see you publicly flogged and humiliated for the whore you may be. Do I make myself clear?"

She was an excellent actress. A good prostitute always was, for she had to pretend she was enjoying her client's attention, that he was special and well endowed in size and performance. Praise brought better payment. The truth of boredom and a man's inept clumsiness would have left a working woman penniless.

With dignity she pulled her arm free and took two steps away from her husband. She was frightened of him, but in this she held the upper hand. He was a spendthrift; he needed her money. He would never throw her out – and as for the other, to humiliate her was to disgrace himself. There was not a thing he could do were he to discover the truth, but, discretion and a few lies would by far be the better path to follow.

"I do not know what he told you, husband. I do know it was a lie. I am your wife, a very rich wife, and I remind you, I hold the Barbados plantation in trust for my firstborn son and if pressed I could decide his fortune would be better guarded outside of my marriage." She held her husband's scowl a moment, emphasising her point. "If you prefer to believe the word of a pirate – of a man who you obviously know to be a cheat and a liar - then I suggest you dissolve our marriage here and now. For I will not tolerate being so insulted."

It was a good performance and Phillipe believed it because he had to.

Alicia just hoped, prayed, Jesamiah had not left her with a child. Decided she had best take steps to assure her continuing status and safety. She walked a few yards, turned and said, "However, I must inform you of something I had been intending to tell you in the privacy of our bed, perhaps it might help you conclude whether you value me as wife or not." She put her hand on her stomach, not as flat as it had been before she had birthed her sons. "I believe I am with child again. My flux has not come."

As a lie it was perfect. If there was no child it would be easy to "lose" it within the next month or so. And if there was one, well, men were hopeless at counting and calculating women's dates.

Phillipe let her return to their guests. What choice had he? Make a scene here, add to the talk that would be buzzing and frothing through Virginia for months to come? He had wanted to be on the lips of every man and women, but as a superb host, as a respected man not as the idiot made a fool of by his own half brother.

Well intentioned, the Governor had said he would get his ship back, Phillipe doubted it, did not particularly want it back. All he wanted was Jesamiah Mereno or Acorne - with an 'e' - as he now called himself, to pay for this night's bad work. Oh he would be paying dearly! It might take a while to track him down, to capture him, but at some time in the future, whether it was months or years ahead, Jesamiah Acorne would make a mistake, and when he did, he, Phillipe Mereno, intended to be there to force him to his knees, make him beg for his life. Oh yes, the bastard would regret this day. Would regret he had ever been born.

What was it Jesamiah had said? That he was no longer frightened of his elder brother? Phillipe's lip curled in a small, humourless smile. Even if it took him years to do so, he would prove him wrong. Very, very, wrong.

- Twenty -

"Not fast enough!" Jesamiah roared. "Do it again!"

Gun practice. No use having a ship with ten, six pound guns, if the crew were so damned useless only one or two of them could be fired efficiently.

"Mr Rue, Mr Roberts," Jesamiah continued, ignoring the swathe of muttered grumbles and derogatory oaths, "I want you to time each side, starb'd against larb'd. Those gunners who finish first will get extra rum. Do it nearer one minute than two and I'll double the ration for a week. Losers swab the decks. We need these guns firing with speed and precision, lads – unless you want our new partner over there to get the pick of the plunder?"

Cat-calls, a few blasphemous remarks and gestures were directed at Captain Henry Jennings. It had not been in the original plan to team up with another vessel, but practicality had won the argument. As Jennings himself had said to Jesamiah in a Jamaican tavern to the western end of Kingston's main street, *"If you want to sweep up, lad, you are going to need a hefty broom."*

Jamaica had not been an ideal choice to find a crew and to re-fit the *Alicia Galley* – renamed *Inheritance*. She had needed guns and gun ports cut; extensive worm damage repairing, a new fore topmast and bowsprit, replacement sails. Kingston harbour had the best material and men, and as long as Jesamiah kept his face away from the fort, who was there to recognise him? Perfectly legal and innocent, he was a merchant selling his cargo of tobacco, re-fitting and having a decent bath and shave all at the one chance. He was glad to be rid of the excess of facial hair, preferring his more usual neat-trimmed moustache and jaw line beard.

Henry Jennings had been a friend of Malachias Taylor, naturally, he and Jesamiah had spent a few evenings yarning together. Jennings was a privateer, ostensibly, in the Caribbean at the commission of His Majesty King George to hunt pirates. A pity, he had declared, there did not appear to be any.

"They're loitering along the Florida reefs," he had complained as he poured another generous tot of rum for them both. "All turned salvage experts diving for treasure."

"Fools' errand." Jesamiah had responded. "Why put all the effort into collecting it, when the Spanish can do it for you?"

Jennings had looked at him quizzically, and Jesamiah, grinning, had outlined his plan. "The King of Spain is shitting his breeches to get his bloody fortune back. And the Florida reefs are crawling with Spanish divers to find the sodding stuff, which is then," he had paused, taken a long swallow of his drink, "Which is then shipped up the coast under heavy guard against us pirates." He had laughed derisively. The Spanish idea of efficient guardships did not match his own; there was not a Spaniard he could not take.

"The way to become rich, Cap'n Jennings me ol' mate, is simple." Jesamiah, rapidly becoming drunk, had banged the table with the flat of his hand, making the scatter of empty bottles and the sputtering candle leap. "I sail into wherever it is they've put this 'ere storehouse. I talk Spanish, I look Spanish, who's to say I ain't Shpanish? Least, not 'til I sail out again with as much in me 'old as m'ship can carry without sinkin'." Enthusiasm and an excess of rum made his eyes shine, and his speech degenerate into the lazy, ship-board pattern of talk.

Impressed with the idea, Jennings had suggested it would be even easier to dance to that piped tune if Jesamiah would accept him as partner.

The plan was simple, and as with most of Jesamiah's simple plans it should work as sweet as honey. Except, to make honey you required bees. And bees if annoyed, stung. Spanish bees in particular - hence the need to practise with the guns. Just in case.

Superiority in battle was obtained only by regular training, the raw energy of men, and team work. A second broadside of cannon fired simultaneously in under two minutes could be devastating, as Jesamiah to his cost had occasionally discovered. A cannon ball weighing six pounds, fired at close range, even if it did not penetrate through the thickness of a hull, could send up a cascade of splinters that maimed as effectively as the shot itself. Or rip down the rigging and tear holes in the sails – and men. But guns were only as good as the gunners who manned them.

Once fired, the heavy iron cannon had to be hauled in, the old wadding, muck and residue swabbed out and the whole process of re-loading started again. It was this routine Jesamiah wanted to perfect. The quicker it was done the better the chance of winning. And staying alive.

"You, lad," Jesamiah called to one of the younger crew, there were several under the age of fifteen. "Spread more sand on the deck behind number three gun. Look lively there, I ought not have had need to tell you!" Wooden decks became slippery when blood was running; sand helped men keep their footing.

"Make ready," Jesamiah shouted. "Run out the guns. Powder monkeys, on your toes!"

The youngest boys aboard had the task of bringing the gunpowder up from the magazine in the lower deck. Too dangerous to keep the stuff elsewhere, and even below the store was protected by curtains of wet canvas to stop sparks from flying in and sending the lot sky high, ship and crew with it. Raising his arm Jesamiah checked that the minute-timers were ready, paused, looked down the length of the deck.

"Do it for me lads," he thought, said aloud, "Let's show Jennings he has a partner to reckon with, eh?" He spread his fingers dropped his hand, shouted, "Starb'd battery - fire!"

The guns roared, the ship shuddered as the five cannon on the starboard side boomed out across the sea. The men worked hard, damned hard. They admired Jesamiah, a fair captain who never expected anything of any man that he could not do himself. Aside, he had promised a personal fortune at the end of this cruise.

Run in, swab, re-load, run out. The larboard battery went off, the gun captains yelling and cursing and urging their men on; the powder boys skittering about like the creatures they were named for. Men were sweating, the muscles in their arms and backs and legs aching from exertion.

"One minute and twenty, Captain!" Rue shouted, elated, as the last gun hurled its shot into the sea. "They 'ave done it!"

Jesamiah tossed his hat in the air, caught it, carolled his delight with the cheering crew. "Well done! Well done my lads! Rum all round I reckon, that was as near as damn it to being perfect!"

He leapt down from the quarterdeck, patting men on their backs, on their shoulders, shaking hands, his face a beam of genuine delight. Of course, they would have to do the same under enemy fire, which would be a different rig of sails entirely, but if they practised and practised again, the procedure would become second nature, whatever the foul conditions on deck. Many pirate ships did not care a cock's crow for practice, or discipline and order, but Jesamiah had made one thing clear. He was Captain and when there was work to be done, it would be done to the best of their combined ability. If anyone did not approve of his way of running things then they could bloody well clear off out of it. And forget the reward of Spanish treasure.

He walked the length of the deck, back again, sharing the achievement of his men, smiling as a keg of rum was broached. Starting to head for the privacy of his cabin he halted, swung slowly around on his heel and fixed the nearest man with his formidable stare; held the gaze until his victim submitted and lowered his head.

"One thing," Jesamiah said with rigid authority, staring, one by one, at every man present, his dark eyes briefly locking into and holding each returned gaze.

"The next time you grumble about my orders, if I hear any one of you scabrous dogs calling me a bloody bilge-sucker again you'll be shark bait." He snapped the last, loud and succinct. "Do I make m'self clear?"

Several men looked away, ashamed. The few who had deserted the Royal Navy saluted. A general embarrassed, mumbled, answer rolled along the lower deck.

"Aye Cap'n."

- Twenty One -

"By the deep, nine; by the mark, eight."

Isiah Robert's steady drone, in Spanish, and the regular splash of the lead-line sounding the rapidly decreasing depth of water as the *Inheritance* nosed her way through the sandbars, was the only sound - beyond the squeal of blocks, straining cordage and canvas, and the familiar groan of the hull. From the quarterdeck, Jesamiah surveyed his ship, the line of guns, idle on their unpainted wooden carriages; the length of white, scrubbed deck, the soaring masts and the reduced spread of sail. He could barely remember being so happy. Had he been younger than these two and twenty years – nearly three and twenty, it would be his birthday in nine weeks, come the fourth day of December - he may have been tempted to caper a jig. Except it would not be dignified for a captain to behave so childishly. He contented himself with a grin, instead.

The Atlantic Ocean, around the 27° north latitude. Half a mile or so to the north-east of the starboard beam, a wide, brackish river shimmered in the evening sunshine and snaked away into mangrove swamps, lush trees and vegetation. Southward, stretching down the coast, mile after mile, the froth of breakers scurried up the slope of the beach, or washed over the sandbars on which heron and pelicans, and a host of other wading birds were already beginning to forage for food as the tide fell away. The waves moved against the shore with a musical lilt, a rolling sing-song sound as it hushed in and out.

Dense vegetation covered the dunes beyond the sand, the shorter stuff of sea oats and palmetto, broadening into taller, thicker sea grapes and wax myrtle.

The current was very strong, the channel of deep water through the shallows no wider than two lengths of anchor cable. No captain in his right mind would risk bringing his boat in close along here without good reason. From the distance of a mile out Jesamiah had been tempted to shake out the reefs in his sails, loose the topgallants and stretch away for the open ocean. Were it not for the beckoning spirals of camp-fire smoke, the jutting, man-made jetty and the stone-built storehouse he would have done so.

This was the coast where some of the Spanish Fleet had perished; this was where the fortunate ones who had survived the hurricane had been swept ashore, and had endured those first few terrifying days and nights of shipwreck in this desolate, God-forgotten place. Alligators roamed the mangrove swamps and hostile natives hunted the land that spread westward.

As they nosed in, Isiah calling the depth, Rue careful at the helm, inching the *Inheritance* forward, Jesamiah used his telescope to observe the huts and bothies packed in along the far side of the dunes where the land dropped sharply away. Men were standing on the jetty, some with their arms folded, others fists on hips, many pointing - all of them with weary, annoyed expressions. They had not been expecting a second vessel to come in from the further salvage grounds many miles to the south, not on top of the one just leaving.

The Spaniard had pushed her way from her mooring and unladen, slid over the shallows with comfortable ease. Her sails were gathering the wind as she came about and tacked. Once clear of the sandbars she would be setting course to fetch another load from the forty mile stretch that was the graveyard of the lost treasure ships. Over one thousand men had perished with them.

"And a quarter five," Isiah's voice was sing-song in its chanting. Jesamiah had patiently taught him how to say the words in Spanish. Planned everything down to the last, precise, detail.

"Stand by fore and aft," he said, his voice low, "Bring her up Rue, if you will."

Rue nudged *Inheritance* into the wind, her foresail backing and Jesamiah dropped his hand for the signal to bring her to. The yards came around, the spread of canvas shrank, the rasping sound of halyards, bunt-lines, clew-lines and brails racing through their blocks. Again speaking in Spanish, knowing his voice would carry to those watching along the shore, Jesamiah gave the order to drop anchor.

The cable tumbled out, the fluked anchor splashed into the shallows. Neatly the *Inheritance* tugged at her anchor and they put the gig over the side. Jesamiah taking his place in the stern, directing his coxswain to take him ashore.

Somewhere out there, riding the swell, out of vision and lying on bare poles, was Henry Jennings. Half an hour until dark. There was much to do in the next half hour. The sweeps would be run out and the men would bring *Inheritance* to the jetty under oar. She appeared to be heavily laden - she was, but her cargo was nothing more valuable than rocks and barrels filled with sea water. A cargo which come nightfall would be dumped quietly overboard and, if all went well, replaced by something worth the carrying.

First, Jesamiah had to convince whoever was in command that he was a legitimate Spaniard making a maiden voyage to this storehouse, his hold full of salvaged coin. He climbed up the weed-slippery rungs to the jetty. Discreetly, the men in the boat settled their fingers around the butts of the pistols thrust through their belts, or loosened their cutlasses. If things did not go well for Captain Acorne they would be required to move fast.

As Jesamiah had hoped the day had been hot and long, the shore-men were weary and wanting their dinners and night entertainments. They were not best pleased at the prospect of having to unload another cargo. A short, rotund man of middle age, with curled moustache and pointed beard, ducked out from a mud and grass hut; from the braiding and style of his uniform, the man in charge. Disgruntled and gesticulating wildly, speaking in a torrent of abusive words as if there was no tomorrow, he stamped across the sand and on to the jetty.

Raising his hands in supplication Jesamiah strode forward to meet him, assuming a meek expression he apologised profusely, his Spanish fluent and perfect, and produced two bottles of best brandy from beneath his coat. One of which he slapped with a flourish into the Spaniard's hands.

Jesamiah had to admire the tenacity of the Spanish. All this, once the alarm had been raised, built and operational within a few weeks of the disaster. The Dons always were quick on their feet when it came to the matter of gold.

"My regrets, Admiral, the tide is ebbing and I am not familiar with this shore." Deliberately, Jesamiah promoted the man's rank, although it was doubtful he was anything above an ordinary captain. Playing to a man's vanity always established a quick, easy relationship. "You surely could not expect me to risk running aground?" He laughed at his own jest, an expansive belly-rumble of mirth. "All that gold on the seabed once-over already. Wouldn't do to have it snagged there again would it, señor?"

He slid his arm around the officer's shoulders, steered him towards the hut. "I am in no lather to return to those shoals, it's a devil of a job down there, you know – what with those scurvy pirates roaming on the edge of it all like basking sharks. Frankly, I do not know why I volunteered for the damned commission. If I had known it was to be like this I would have opted to go home and harass the British in Biscay instead."

Jesamiah laid his right finger alongside his nose, his gold acorn ring glinting in the brief, vivid glow of the sunset. "Now, a night ashore would be most welcome, especially if," he peered at the distant tents and shanty-town buildings, deliberately keeping his eyes from the storehouse. "Especially if there are any women here?" Of course there were. They would have been brought in along with the supplies.

He nudged the Spaniard with his elbow, whispered, "I have an itch needing a good scratch, if you get my meaning. What if I left my crew to lay the *Cariola* alongside and we unload at first light? She will be safe, no?" Jesamiah, spread his hands. "I am not going anywhere, you are not going anywhere and the gold as sure as the sun shines, isn't! Stand these good, tired, men of yours down, señor, mine will take care of my ship. What say you?"

Jesamiah handed over the ship's papers. They were authentic, with only the name of the vessel altered. Gun practice had paid dividend; the real carrier of the documents was at the bottom of the Atlantic with all hands, minus her load of gold, silver pieces of eight and casks of gems, which were now stacked snugly in the *Inheritance's* forward hold - the one portion of cargo that would not be jettisoned after dark.

The Spaniard frowned over every word written on the papers, Jesamiah prattling a continuous banter of nonsense. After a few moments he wavered, put the brandy bottle in his pocket, stretched across the table to reclaim the other one.

"Of course señor, if you would rather get on with the work now, it will not take us long to rig tackle..."

"*Està bien, no problemo,*" came the quick reply as the officer made a hasty grab for the brandy and unstoppered it, drank straight from the bottle. "This appears to be in order. You can leave everything to your crew?"

"*Claro.* Of course."

"*Bueno, bueno. Excelente!* Come, let me introduce you to a friend of mine, she has sharp nails, ideal for getting into those places difficult to reach."

With night settling and the stars showing bright against the darkening blue, Jesamiah rested his arm companionably along the duped officer's shoulders as they strolled, deep in conversation, to the encampment. He lifted his hat, waved it in a circle, clamped it back upon his head and disappeared over the crest of the dunes, his trailing ribbons fluttering as an off-shore breeze scuttled in with the night.

Nodding satisfaction at the received signal the men took the boat back to the *Inheritance* – the *Cariola* – and under Rue's direction added their weight to mooring her alongside the now deserted jetty. By the time Jennings brought his vessel silently into the cove, with no lights showing and the least amount of noise - warping her in, towing from the longboats - it was late and the Spanish salvage teams were either drunk or asleep. No moon, only the clear brilliance of stars studding the sky with silver light. Perfect.

Before they were even moored, Jennings' men were rigging hauling tackle to the main yard ready to sway the bullion aboard. Like a silent tidal wave men of both crews flooded ashore from the decks, knives and cutlasses drawn, bare feet padding. No pistols or muskets, there was to be as little sound as possible. The bray of drunken, boisterous pleasure-taking drifted from the encampment, drowning the choked-off grunts of the storehouse guards as their throats were cut, and the rustle of more than two hundred men working their way to raking in an easy-made fortune. The only misplaced sound, the sharp-bladed axe striking twice through the chain securing the doors. The only suggestion something was amiss, the steady flicker of moving shadows in the shrouded lantern light, as with organised efficiency the men transferred chests containing fantastic wealth from storehouse to ship.

Strolling into the almost emptied storehouse two and a half hours later, Jesamiah was well pleased with himself. Just as he liked things, clean and simple. He would not be admitting to Jennings he had employed his time ashore with a dark-skinned, slender-waisted beauty. What else could he have done? His new Spanish friend had insisted they share her, and afterwards it had taken both bottles of brandy to finally send the idiot to sleep.

They were almost done; both ships were set low but were riding the shallows well. The last chests were sent swinging into the *Inheritance's* hold and the lifting tackle brought down, the hatches secured. Jennings' quartermaster cut the lines holding them fast to the *Inheritance* and as the boat swung away Jesamiah himself took an axe and severed the warps. Her jib was already set and the mainsail half hoisted, she drifted free and the oarsmen began to row, the sweeps muffled, the men heaving in unison to take the boat out across the bar into the safety of deeper water. The advantage of a galley, it did not rely on sail alone. No calling aloud of the depth this time, no creaking of yards as they were braced around. Isiah spoke their passage softly, passing word back along the deck to Jesamiah who had taken the helm himself. No noise, save for the dip of the oars and the creak of timber, sounds which were hidden by the indifferent roll of the sea. Clean away. Simple, so damned simple.

Ten days on a secluded island to count the spoil and celebrate, and Jesamiah found he was personally the richer by a sum in excess of £30,000 sterling. When a senior Royal Navy captain earned less than £340 per annum, was it any wonder piracy was alluring and the Trade called sweet?

There was always a black cloud to stifle the sun, however.

They returned to Jamaica ready to crow their grand fortune only to find the Spanish were already there, loudly complaining at the audacity of British pirates. Jesamiah and Jennings pleaded the excuse of privateer, but the Governor was having none of their fluid interpretation of the word. Declaring them to be the pirates they were, he agreed the Spanish demand for justice and promised their property back. Fortunately, like most officials, he was also greedy. A generous donation into his personal funds and a turned blind eye would perhaps go in the pirates' favour? Providing they were gone from Kingston by sun up.

With a shrug, an obscene gesture and a hold full of wealth Jesamiah bid farewell to Jamaica. Jennings, who was to head for

Nassau, he saluted with a broadside of cannon fire and then set sail for Africa and Madagascar. A sensible precaution, Nassau and the Bahamas was too close to Phillipe who would probably not have taken the commandeering of a ship, and illicit intercourse with his wife, in the best of spirits.

Not that the now very rich Captain Jesamiah Acorne gave a cracked cannon for what his poxed half-brother thought.

Phillipe Mereno had not wasted time in setting revenge in motion. Backed by the shout of a handsome reward, word was already scuttling to the four winds along the sea lanes. Gold was there for the man responsible for the arrest and hanging of a pirate who called himself Jesamiah Acorne. Despite squandering much of his fortune Mereno was a wealthy man who could fund the payment of printed posters and the hiring of agents who specialised in hunting highwaymen, thieves, murderers and pirates.

There was one such agent lurking in the slums of Cape Town with nothing better to do than watch which ships anchored and who stepped ashore. Had Jesamiah known of Phillipe's new obsession, would he have given the South African harbour a miss?

Probably not.

- Twenty Two -

With the onset of dusk, all the miscreants of Cape Town made their way to the brothels and drinking houses - all those who had no decent home to go to, which in this flea-pit, was the majority. Jesamiah among them. It was the third day of December, tomorrow was his birthday he was entitled to celebrate.

The noise from the tavern below was increasing but he was too busily occupied with Aloette to notice the rowdiness. "That was good," he said, breathing hard and withdrawing from her, leant across the bed for the bottle he had left on the floor, the sweat gleaming on his naked body. He took a long swig, offered it to her. She shook her head.

"You have it my prince, you need to get your strength back for next time."

Jesamiah grinned, saluted her a toast. There was to be a next time then? Do anything for a handful of silver, these Cape Town strumpets.

From the room next door - the walls were only thin planks of cheap timber, plastered over and painted in pink-tinted lime-wash – came the rhythmic protest of a creaking bed, a girl's giggling and a man's grunting. Another couple doing what Jesamiah was doing, along with half the sailors ashore from their ships. Rue was somewhere down the corridor with a red-head.

"We have the entire night," Aloette said, her voice low and purring. "You have paid me, have you not?" she added with a coquettish smile, while trickling her fingers over his nakedness, her broken nails tracing the patterns of the acorn tattooed to the left of his chest and the mermaid on his left forearm. Doing as she suggested, he drank; with most of the bottle already consumed and his desire for a woman sated, was asleep before he had emptied it.

He awoke to find the candles had burnt low - several were out, the stubs a congealed mess of molten wax. The hubbub downstairs was less rowdy, the sounds in the street beyond the window quieter. The only noise from the room next door was a man's snoring. The early hours, then. He groaned, half pleasure, half headache and rolled across the bed his arm seeking the warmth and delight of the girl. Grunted, annoyed to find her gone. He opened his eyes properly, looking for her. The shabby room was empty, her side of the bed quite cold, her clothes missing.

"Bitch," he muttered as he lurched from the bed, fumbled for, and almost filled, the chamber pot and retrieved his shirt, breeches, stockings and boots. Most of his clothes were scattered over the floor; he vaguely remembered being in an eager hurry last night. He ensured his pistol and cutlass were where he had left them, looked for his coin purse in his coat pocket. The money was gone, he would have been surprised to find it had not, but his weapons were untouched. The coins did not matter there had only been five or six shillings anyway, and he kept a few gold doubloons sewn discreetly inside his waist sash. He could always filch some more silver when he had need of it.

Rather unsteadily he dressed, found his waistcoat under the bed; wound the sash around his waist, satisfying himself that the gold was where it should be, and fastened the leather belt from which hung a cartridge pouch containing shot and powder, and his knife. He pushed his pistol through his belt, checking it was loaded and buckled his baldric slantwise across from his right shoulder, more irritated to discover the girl had taken the second bottle of rum with her.

Grumbling at the dishonesty of women, he set his three-cornered hat firmly on his head, tossed his long coat over his arm and unlatched the door. Met face to face with the barrel of a pistol.

No time to draw and cock his own weapon; he swung aside, attempted to slam the door - the man fired, the acrid smell of powder and the sharp sound of the shot reverberating into the room.

Jesamiah reeled, somehow managed to ram the door shut with his boot, slapped the bolt home. Dropping his coat, breathing heavily, aware of a searing pain below his left shoulder and the sticky feel of trickling blood, he dragged a chair across the door, ramming it beneath the latch. He winced, slid his hand inside his shirt and pulled it away to discover blood on his fingers. He felt at the back, nothing; the lead had not gone clean through then. Damn.

He could not think about it now, there were more pressing matters to consider. He ran to the window, grabbing at the catch to the slatted wooden shutter. The thing was stuck, rusted solid. He pulled at it, swore again, spun around frantically looking for something he could use to smash his way out. The door was splintering as an axe struck through the flimsy panels, revealing more faces. He drew his pistol, cocked the hammer home, hearing the necessary double click and as the door burst open, aimed, fired. One shot. One dead man. He was looking at four more men with swords and pistols. Submitting, he stuffed his now useless pistol back into his belt and resigned to fate, held his hands up in surrender.

"You've got me fair and square, mates." Nodding at the rumpled bed, added, "You must have paid her more handsomely than I did."

"Jesamiah Acorne," the one with the fancy sword said, waving it uncomfortably close to Jesamiah's belly, his face crinkled into a leering snarl. "I am authorised to place you under arrest for acts of piracy committed against His Majesty King George and certain private parties. Crimes for which you shall hang."

"Oh aye? It is a long way between here and the gallows, lads." Jesamiah said with a tilt to his head and a calm smile. "Am I not entitled to a trial? The good citizens of Cape Town enjoy a good trial."

"As they enjoy a good hanging." One of the pistols was shoved nearer Jesamiah's chest. "Judge, jury and rope are ready and waiting for the pleasure of your company. As we await the pleasure of our reward." The pistol barrel prodded Jesamiah's sternum, none too gently.

He frowned. What reward?

The hammer cocked. One click. Two. "One hundred and fifty beautiful gold pieces to him who delivers you into his majesty's custody."

"We figured we'd split it a'tween us."

Only one hundred and fifty? Jesamiah was unsure whether to laugh or feel insulted.

A long blink of silence and a frozen stillness; a waiting for one man to move before the other.

"I am afraid you may have need to figure again, mates." Jesamiah finally said with a grin, "I'm not in the frame of mind to oblige helping you in your grand scheme of things." He kicked out, hard and sudden, catching the startled pistol holder in the crotch, sending him sinking, groaning and clutching at himself to the bare floor boards. Falling forward, Jesamiah rolled, grabbing for the dropped pistol as he rose, fired. The man nearest the door yelped, blood pouring from where an ear lobe had been. And within seconds the room had became a vicious brawl.

Ducking low Jesamiah drew his cutlass and slashed at the nearest pair of legs, avoided a punch, took a kick in his ribs. He felt something crack, a sharp hurt, crumpled, wincing, knocking the chamber pot over as he fell, but was up on his feet again, dodging another blow, taking a punch to the jaw that sent him staggering.

A man lunged, caught Jesamiah off balance. Almost at the same moment another pistol fired, the shot thumping into his midriff - the two blows combined sending him toppling backwards, hard and fast against the window shutter. Thin and rotten, the wooden frame gave way and with a yip of surprise, Jesamiah fell through, tumbling into the early morning quiet of the street below. He lay a moment, winded and disorientated. Gathering his wits, glancing upwards at the furious faces peering down at him, he was up on his feet and off, running into the night, darting and weaving along the narrow, dim-lit alleyway as if he were a hare with the Hounds of Hell chasing after him.

A musket shot whistled past his ear, he swerved, kept running, aware, with sharp curses rattling in his panting breath that he was being followed. Damn them! They had been expecting him to make a run for it, had posted men outside.

Dodging to the left behind some piled crates stinking of fish he flattened himself into the shadows, took the opportunity to get his bearings and breath back. He ran his left hand across his waist. Chuckled. No wonder the pistol ball had packed such a thump; it had met with one of his gold pieces! He would find a coin-shaped bruise there come daylight. Funny, the rest of the pain was not registering; he had a lead ball in his shoulder but could not feel it. Frowned, looked down at his right arm, saw a ragged shirt, sodden with blood dripping profusely from the torn skin beneath. He grimaced. Must have caught himself on the wood and glass as he crashed through the window, regretted looking. Now he had seen it his arm felt as though it were ablaze with searing fire.

Running footsteps, shouting voices and flickering torches coming towards him. He would have to move.

He tried to run, his legs feeling suddenly odd, his vision blurring. He stumbled, fell to one knee. Leaning on his cutlass - incredibly, still clasped in his right hand at the end of the bloody mess that was now his arm - he scrambled up, kept himself going by willpower alone, aware his blood was draining out of him like water leaking from a spout. He clamped his left hand across his forearm, ignoring the protest from the wound in his shoulder. If he did not find a safe hiding place soon, tend to this, he might well bleed to death. Could he reach the *Inheritance?* He cursed, realising he was running in the wrong direction, heading uphill away from the harbour. Aside, these were not fools; they would have had the savvy to put a watch on his ship.

"Fine bloody way to spend a birthday," he grumbled, stumbled again, leant against a wall, head back, breathing heavily. He closed his eyes, let the world of these dark, slum alleyways of Cape Town spin by a few times.

Feeling the first signs of consciousness beginning to ebb away, desperate, he murmured, "In the name of all that is good, someone help me!"

His vision blurring, walking – staggering, he no longer had the strength to run - he reached the end of the sewage-stinking alley, turned right then left, the agony of his arm and shoulder tearing through him. Men coming towards him. Where were they all appearing from? He side-stepped into a passageway, swore colourfully and explicitly as an arm caught at his waist, spiralling him inward towards the unlit darkness of a sheltering wall. He tried to kick out, to lift the cutlass clutched in his right hand but all strength was leaving him, seeping away with his pumping blood. He almost fell but a woman's arm was holding him upright. Her fragrant smell of summer, meadows and flowers filled his nostrils. Her voice, urgent, in his ear.

"I can help. Do not struggle." Deftly she turned him so his back was against the wall, her body pressing close into his to hold him upright as much as to shield him.

"Put your left arm around me - quick man! Do it!"

Bizarrely he still wore his hat. She reached up tipped it forward to hide his eyes, and then her lips were over his mouth kissing him, her palms flat against his chest as torches flared and the sound of heavy boots approached. With one hand she brought Jesamiah's head down burying his face in the mass of her black hair. She half turned, glowered at the two men who had paused to watch.

In a clipped uneducated accent, she snarled, "Go pay fer yer own pleasure, ye poxed curs! I be busy." And she turned her head, her mouth seeking for Jesamiah's again, her hand starting to hitch up her skirts.

Grinning, the men moved off, one of them lewdly fumbling at himself.

Bewildered, feeling wretched, Jesamiah moaned. This woman, a beautiful young woman, had come from nowhere, grabbed him, and was kissing him in a public alleyway. Yet when she had turned and bawled she was busy, her features had blurred, her immaculate appearance had become ragged, greasy and smutty. He shook his head confused, felt the dizziness churn through him. His legs buckling, blackness rushing in, he began to slide down the wall.

He was heavy. Attempting to hold him up, she eased her arm further around his waist and half pushing, half dragging him, she turned in through a low, unlit doorway. Inside, the passageway was dark, a feeble light showing from the head of a steep flight of wooden stairs. She let him sink to the floor in a crumpled heap, shut the door and slammed a bar across to secure it. Heaving him upright, pushed him up the stairs, his feet stumbling over most of them.

"Jenna!" she called, urgent, "Jenna, come help!"

From the top of the stairs the light increased as a curtain was drawn back, its rings scraping on the wooden pole, a frowning, sleep-mottled face appeared. "Now what scrawny misfit have you brought home, girl?" The woman, dressed in night apparel, her hair twisted and tied in strips of torn rags advanced downward. "Lord, child! Can you not learn to leave injured tomcats to their own devices?"

Nonetheless, she helped carry Jesamiah into the first floor room, the place filled with the pleasant aroma of herbs and fresh-brewed coffee.

"Put him on the table," Tiola gasped, nodding her head at Jenna who swept lengths of material and sewing paraphernalia to the floor. His face was drained of colour, a low moan escaped his lips and he slid into unconsciousness. Blood covered Tiola's bodice, was blotched on her skirt; his grubby linen shirt was sodden with it.

Without a word she eased the heavy pistol from his waist and holding it gingerly, not knowing if it was loaded or not, passed it to Jenna who placed it carefully on the top of a clothes chest. Tipping the hat from his head Tiola prised Jesamiah's fingers from the cutlass, unbuckled the scabbard and belt, tore open what remained of the shredded sleeve and sucked in her breath at the mangled, ragged flesh beneath. Plunging her hand over the ripped, blood-pulsing lacerations she clamped her fingers tight.

"We'll need the tourniquet," she said, but Jenna was already at a small cupboard, throwing wide its single door and reaching inside among the carefully stored medical things for a short length of leather strap which she deftly fastened around the upper muscles of Jesamiah's arm.

"Pull it tight," Tiola ordered, her anxiety making her brusque. "If we do not stop this flow of blood we will lose him." Keeping her hand over the head of the longest cut torn in a zigzag down through the flesh, Tiola's eye roved to where more blood was seeping through the shirt at the left shoulder. She flipped the linen away with her other hand, huffed a snort of dismay. A pistol shot.

"Damn fool. What have you been doing to yourself?" she whispered. The wound would have to wait, this arm was the more urgent to deal with.

"Stitching?" Jenna asked as securing the strap as tight as it would go, she went to fetch a box from the cupboard. Selecting lengths of a horse's tail hair she dropped them into a pewter bowl, and swinging out the steaming kettle suspended from the rakencrock, poured boiling water over them and fetched a needle from the sewing basket that had tumbled to the floor.

"Looks bad," she remarked to Tiola nodding at the mess of Jesamiah's arm.

"It is bad," Tiola answered. "I will be needing all my skills to save the limb, I am thinking."

"Well, he is in God's hands."

Tiola glanced at her, smiled affectionately. She had no belief in a specific religion, nor for any one particular God; as always she made no comment, except to say, "And my hands, Jenna. And mine."

The tourniquet was beginning to take effect, the blood loss was easing. Tiola worked quickly and efficiently, knowing exactly what she had to do and how to do it. The lack of confidence she had once possessed had left her long ago; she had the gift of Craft, she was a midwife and a healer. By instinct she knew the properties of herbs and medicines, how to mend a broken bone, stitch a wound or remove the lead shot of a pistol. And what she did not know by instinct, was there in her mind in the guiding voices of her ancestors.

Cleaning first with salted, hot water, she carefully and skilfully stitched the damage, easing the edges of ripped flesh together, making as neat a job as she could. Despite her care there was always going to be a pattern of livid scars - providing the wounds healed and did not fester, which would mean fetching in the saw-bones physician to remove the limb. That task, she could not do; she did not have the physique to wield a surgeon's amputation knives and saws. The job needed to be done quickly and efficiently. Sawing through flesh, muscle and bone in less than two minutes, while a patient screamed himself unconscious was beyond her. Physically and mentally. She hoped, in this instance, it would not be necessary. Finished, she unwound the tourniquet, satisfied to discover the blood now only seeped and oozed, not flooded.

"We will bandage it in a moment, let some of this congeal first." As she spoke she was cutting away the remains of the shirt, already inspecting the bloodied hole where the lead had penetrated.

"No exit wound," she commented as she delicately half lifted Jesamiah, thankful he had not regained consciousness. "I will have to remove the ball."

For all her light touch with fingers and forceps, the pain as she probed into the wound roused him. He gasped, jerked, his face contorting, the cry bitten back as she hastily withdrew.

"Fetch the laudanum please, Jenna, add a few drops to some rum." Tiola brushed back his sweat-damp hair. "Ssh, be still, Luvver, the discomfort will last but a moment."

He tried to say something, she put her fingers against his lips, hushed him again. "Save your strength there is no need to talk." And taking the pewter tankard from Jenna she held it to his mouth, her arm supporting his neck and shoulders. "Drink – ah, careful - sip it. Swallow slowly."

He gagged the liquid down, tried to croak something, again she quietened him, her hand spread lightly to the side of his face.

~ *You are safe. I am Tiola. Do you not remember me? None shall do you harm while you are in my care. Let the sleep take you. You are safe.* ~ She thought the words, smoothing them into his mind. Gave him a moment for the sedative to take effect, her fingers unlacing the ribbons from his hair, her eyes noting the two gold teeth, the acorn and mermaid tattoos, his ring and earring.

With a snort of scorn Jenna also saw the unmistakable signs. "Pirate!" she muttered. "Thieves and murderers, the lot of them."

"He could be the King's Navy," Tiola responded. "These items do not necessarily make him a pirate."

Jenna crossed her arms her expression stern. "A silver-inlaid pistol-butt, a fine crafted cutlass, an arm cut to pieces and a pistol-shot to the shoulder, however, do. Aside, my bones and my eyes tell me you are already aware of that fact and you know who he is."

"*Ais.* I know who he is." Tiola admitted.

She had known he was here in Cape Town. All afternoon and into the evening she had felt impatient and excited, her inner senses returning, again and again to the pull of the harbour as if it were a compass point and she the swinging needle aching to the north.

With nightfall she had been unable to sleep, had fiddled with items in the cosy, cluttered room, picking things up, putting them down. Had tried to read, to sew. Had wandered down into the quiet coolness of the courtyard an hour after midnight, back up the stairs again. Dozed, fully dressed on the bed for an hour or two... Brought suddenly awoke she had leapt, alert and already running down the stairs at the desperate sound of his voice pleading for help. Summoning her and her Craft.

"*In the name of all that is good!*"

The name Oldstagh was uniquely hers - fleeing from England she had rejected the surname of her father, nothing of his would she ever use again. Tiola was an inherited name, hers before she was born, a respected name to be proud of. Oldstagh, she had chosen for herself during those anxious days of waiting for the smugglers to get her away to safety. She had chosen well. Her new name commemorated her mother's courageous love and encompassed the wisdom and purpose of her White Craft, effectively countered the taint of evil lingering from her father's foul touch. Tiola Oldstagh. A summoning command. An anagram of *all that is good.*

Chance had guided Jesamiah to the street outside, to the passageway leading to her door. Chance? Or her thoughts? One or the other - perhaps both combined - had drawn him towards her. Did the compass needle not always point north? Where the one sailed the other always followed. Eternally inseparable.

She was ashamed to have doubted she would meet him again, that he would come back to her. Although she would not have wished it to be like this, for him to be suffering so.

Between them, she and Jenna stripped him of his clothes, noticing the bruise under the dented gold coin. With her healer's skill Tiola felt the broken ribs and bound them tight, salved the wounds with a soothing ointment of healing herbs, bandaging them with care. They moved him to the bed, made him as comfortable as they could, thankful he slept through all their pulling and prodding.

"He will bring trouble to us lass, mark my words," Jenna scolded several times over, with a meaningful, tight-lipped nod of her head.

Watching him sleep, holding his hand, the hurting evident even through his unconsciousness, Tiola merely smiled an enigmatic answer.

"Trouble, in some forms Jenna, can sometimes be most welcome."

Twenty Three

Jesamiah stirred, his eyes squinting against the early morning daylight of an unfamiliar room. A light that did not have the ripple of water-reflected patterns on the ceiling; a room that did not sway with the movement of a ship. He lay there disorientated for a confused moment, then became viciously aware of his body feeling as though he was being roasted on a spit and his arm apparently being crushed by a ton of rocks. His ribs were squashed against his lungs and in his brain, a battalion of drummers thundering in unison. He tried to move, found he could not. Tried again and gasped aloud as a burst of agony charged at full gallop through his entire being.

"Sweet Jesus!" He swore, sucking air in through his clenched teeth.

"That high an authority I cannot provide," a female voice said from the lingering shadows across the room. "You will have to make do with me I am afraid, Mr Acorne."

"I'm a Captain," he croaked pedantically as she opened the window to allow in full light and a waft of fresh air. The rumble of cart wheels, shouting voices, and a hen announcing she had just laid an egg, grew louder. The shriek of squabbling gulls drowned the more pleasant voice of song birds. Aimlessly, he flapped his left hand, asked, "How do you know me?" Added, desperately willing the thumping in his head to cease so he might have a moment to think clearly. "Have we met?"

Tiola crossed the room to lean over him, her hand going to feel his forehead; he was hot and feverish. She rested two fingers against the pulse beating in his neck beneath his jaw, frowned. The pump of blood was rushing there too fast. Much too fast.

"A captain you may be," she said with the smile wide in her voice as well as her eyes, "but you are also, so I understand, an infamous rogue known and wanted from the Chesapeake Bay to here in Cape Town." As he tried to move she put her hand to his shoulder pressing him back against the pillow. "Be still. The damage is extensive and raw, you will hurt for a while yet."

He regarded her through his muzzy senses, not remembering much beyond men bursting into a room intent on taking him prisoner or shooting him dead. Vaguely, he recalled falling through a window. Not much after that. Nothing really, except the touch of a woman's lips on his own and her fragrant scent of summer. He sought for the memory, to clutch at it tighter but it faded and then vanished completely. Despite her advice he moved, trying to relieve the aching stiffness in his body - yelled, his face screwing into a contortion of intense pain, his breath choking in his throat.

"Bloody, sodding hell," he gasped and then realised he was going to be violently sick. He tried to twist sideways, to not spew his vomit all over himself or the bed, half managed it. Tiola responded quickly, her arms going around him to help him lean forward, for the gush of liquid to cascade to the rag-rug on the wooden floor. His guts heaved again, the taste foul in his mouth, his stomach protesting. His head swam, his body was trembling.

She helped him to lie back, propping pillows behind his shoulders then whirled away to fetch a dampened cloth, wiped his mouth, his face, mopped up the mess on the edge of the sheets. Whisking away the soiled rug she dropped it into a bucket on the small landing at the top of the stairs.

"I'm sorry," he murmured, embarrassed, not sure whether there might be more to bring up.

"Not your fault, my luvver, do not worry on it." Tiola fetched the chamber pot from underneath the bed, placing it nearby. Just as well, he retched again but she had him in her arms, half sitting, the bowl beneath his mouth as he spewed up what little was left.

Carefully she laid him, weak and half conscious, on to the pillows. Sweat was streaking his ashen face.

"God, it bloody hurts," he grimaced, his jaw taut, the muscles in his face and neck twisting into rigid cords.

Reaching for a tankard, Tiola held it to his lips. "Drink this. You might vomit again but it will take away the worst of your discomfort." She persuaded him to sip, not gulp, was pleased he kept the herbal mixture of feverfew, white-oak bark, valerian and marigold down. Sat beside him, one hand covering his as he drifted into a restless sleep.

He awoke several times during the morning while the mid-summer sun climbed higher in the sky and the shadows shortened across the floor. Vaguely, he was aware of her reassuring voice and her cool hand soothing his hot skin. Saw her face, blurred, hovering over his own. He had no idea who she was but knew one thing - she was the most beautiful creature he had ever seen. Although she had no feathered wings and had black hair not spun gold, he assumed she must be an angel and felt easier, for if she was he must be in Heaven, not the other place.

When the red fog kept coming back more and more ferociously, and the heat in his body began to burn with the blaze of a furnace, he reckoned Hell had consumed him, after all.

The fire swarmed up and down his arm and tore into his burning shoulder with an insistent, never-ceasing thrumming. As daylight drifted into dusk and night sauntered in its wake, the bed linen was sodden with sweat. He plucked at the sheet covering him, thrusting it away, irritably pushing away, too, the arm holding a tankard that knocked against his teeth. Tiola persisted, gentle but firm, most of the liquid going down his throat more through reflex than co-operation. It brought sleep but could not fight the red-heat of fever consuming him, the fever slithering between his semi-aware consciousness and weird dreams, his body alternating between drenching sweat and uncontrollable shivering.

During the day and night Tiola battled with the demons that had overtaken his mind and body. Frequently he called out, nonsense words and slurred, rambling phrases of things haunting him; past fears, future worries. A man's name, Rue. Another, Phillipe, usually accompanied by agitation and vehement, explicit swearing. The names of ships. *Mermaid* was there, *Salvation, Inheritance.*

On the third day, she sent Jenna down to the harbour to enquire discreetly of any of them. Only the last, the one he muttered more often, was known.

"The *Inheritance,* Lady? Weighed anchor this morning."

Where bound? Unknown.

Through each sobbed breath of delirium Tiola eased Jesamiah's distress, washing the sweat from his skin, spooning cool, herbal mixtures into his mouth. Changing the sheets when they became too soiled and sodden with his sweat and urine. Often, holding him close and tight and safe. She talked to him and sang, rocking him as a mother hushes a child, encircling him within her arms through his pain, his head lowered against her shoulder. Her voice, calming and soporific. Spell-like.

Mid-morning the fifth day. Sunlight was streaming through the window, dust motes swirling and dancing in the slanting rays. Jesamiah realised, abruptly, he had been awake, watching them for some while. The burning was not as intense in his body and his mind was functioning again, albeit sluggishly, as if he were a ship drifting without a wind to hurry her along. He moved his arm, hissed breath in through his teeth, but the pain was not as unbearable as it had been, more of an aching discomfort beneath the restrictive bandaging. He felt light-headed, as weak as a new-born.

"Well, you are looking better at last," the face said as she came from somewhere beyond his vision and sat on the bed. Her hand, as ever, reaching out to touch his forehead and check the beating pulse in his neck. She nodded satisfaction.

"Let me look at you," Tiola said, opening his mouth to inspect the colour of his tongue and sniff his breath. Her voice had an accent he could not identify, a burr, Irish? Welsh? She also had a mass of dark hair and even darker eyes that sparkled and danced with merriment.

"Feel sick?" she asked.

He swallowed, considered, shook his head. "No."

"Good." Her smile was beautiful, a smile not just on her mouth, but one coming from somewhere within her. From the laughter of her soul, he guessed.

"I suppose I had better thank you," he offered. "You appear to have rescued me."

She smiled again, "From certain death, at least."

Returning the smile, showing his two gold teeth, he admitted with a half shrug, "I do not remember all of it."

"Not much to remember."

A huff sounded from across the room, Jesamiah swivelled his eyes to look at the other, older woman.

"She's one for bringing home unwanted and unwelcome strays." Jenna interjected grumpily. "Last time it was a mangy tom. We cut off its balls, tried to house train it, in the end I had to wring its neck."

On better judgement, Jesamiah decided to ignore the old bat. Instead, he held up his left hand one finger casually outstretched towards the girl. He grinned impishly. "I remember the nice bit, though."

Tiola took his other hand protruding from the bandaging, inspected the fingers. The nails were split and dirt encrusted, powder burns and tar had permanently blackened the skin around the base of his thumb and along his fingers.

"Is that so? And what bit would that be? Can you squeeze my hand?"

He tried, winced. "Ouch no, it hurts. The bit where someone very pretty was doing things which in other circumstances would have been extremely pleasant." He pouted, regretful. "I was not in a fit state to enjoy the attention though, was I?"

"If you were in the sort of state to have enjoyed whatever it was," she snorted back, peering into his eyes for sign of yellowing, "it would not have been necessary for it to have happened would it?" She sat back, rested her hands in her lap. "You will do. A couple of weeks rest and you will be back on your feet."

Moving sharply Jesamiah suppressed a yelp, attempting to ignore the protest from arm, shoulder and ribs as he tried to sit up. "A couple of weeks? I cannot stay here one week, woman, let alone two!"

Tiola rose from the bed, smoothed the sheet where she had been sitting. "Got something better to do Captain Acorne? Such as keeping an appointment with the men you cheated out of one hundred and fifty gold pieces?"

He cleared his throat, looked bashful.

"They are searching the whole of Cape Town for you, seem to want you very badly for some reason. Something to do with dancing a jig with Jack Ketch? I am not familiar with nautical terms but I believe that one refers to the hangman, does it not?" She paused, folded her arms her eyes were stern, accusing. "Would it not make sense to remain hidden for a while until whoever it is hunting you becomes convinced you are either long gone or dead? And as you will not be going anywhere until I say you have strength enough, you may as well remain here." She pointed at the floor, then swirled away across the room to fetch something from the cupboard.

Ignoring the advice he tossed the bed covers aside and grunted mild embarrassment to discover he was naked. Swinging his legs to the floor he pulled the sheet away and wound it around his lower half, his eyes searching for his clothes. "It is a generous offer to be sure, I thank you, but I have certain things demanding my immediate attention." Like finding his ship and Rue. He stood, swayed, the room spinning his head reeling.

He swallowed, took a breath to steady himself. "I will naturally pay what I owe, for I hold with settling my debts. If you would be so kind as to be fetching my clothes, I will…" he got no further; with a muted groan he crumpled to the floor sat there, sprawled, looking surprised.

Jenna gazed at him a moment, then returned her attention to a pot stewing over the hearth-fire; dipped in a spoon, tasted the contents. "Talks pretty for a pirate, does he not?" she observed, sarcastic.

"Oh, he is a Captain," Tiola said with a serious face, a gleam of amusement in her voice, as she squatted in front of him, a roll of clean bandaging in one hand, a pot of sweet-smelling salve in the other. "There is many a pirate captain with a silvered tongue. It goes with the gold teeth and the earring I assume. They do not tend to possess an inch of common sense, however. It must be all the salt-water rusting what little brain they have. Especially if your name happens to be Jesamiah Acorne."

She laughed out loud, then relented her teasing and putting the things in her hand on to the side table, thread her arms around Jesamiah, lifted him to the bed. Removing the sheet concealing his modesty, she straightened his legs, spread the linen and tucked its edges beneath the mattress. "When you can stand up without falling over, *Captain* Acorne, you can be on your way. The thanks are appreciated, payment is neither wanted nor expected."

Jenna snorted disapproval. "It is expected for us to live on thin air, however."

Glancing at her Jesamiah glowered. "I am not sure I wish to stay where I am not welcome." He paused, trying to think of a tactful thing to say. "Not with people I do not know. Us pirates tend to not trust strangers." He tried a faint smile. "A peculiarity that also goes with the gold teeth and the earring."

Removing the bandaging from his arm, Tiola flicked her gaze up to meet his. "Jenna is a dear but she is also a natural pessimist. If you were not welcome, surr, I would not have brought you here." She paused as she peeled away the final layer of the dressing. To purge the wound of impurity she had used a proven remedy, a mixture of marsh-mallow leaves and cayenne pepper steeped together in hot water and linseed oil. Set in place beneath a wool pad and changed regularly she rarely had problems with wounds turning putrid.

Her healing was different from that of the physicians and apothecaries. Contrary to what they believed, she knew for certain the four humours did nothing to affect the health of body and mind had nothing to do with the state of a wound or an ache in the belly. She insisted on meticulous cleanliness, thought the deliberate letting of more blood foolish. Ideas and practices she wisely kept to herself.

A faint staining of blood and pus clung to the old dressing, the wounds looking ugly, swollen and bruised but not smelling unpleasant and no longer fire-hot to the touch. "This is healing well despite the angry appearance." She met his eyes again. "I am not a stranger Jesamiah, my name is Tiola."

Jenna snorted indignation for the proprieties of correctness. "Miss Oldstagh to the likes of you."

Tiola's smile broadened, her dark eyes shining. "Tiola will do, I am well satisfied with my name."

Wincing as she set a fresh, hot poultice to his arm Jesamiah searched his memory. Where had they met? Surely he would have remembered her? She was too pretty to forget.

"I am a witch," Tiola stated blandly, riding over his silence. Finishing her bandaging she took the bowl Jenna proffered, dipped a wooden spoon into the broth and fed it to Jesamiah. "What you would call a white witch of course. I am not permitted to do harm, even to shameless pirates. A pirate in fact is probably more dangerous than am I." She talked as if she were speaking of something as ordinary as the direction of the wind, although he realised straight-way she was teasing him.

Swallowing the good-tasting broth Jesamiah grinned, playing along with her. "Too pretty to be a witch."

"I thank you for the compliment, though I am sure it is not deserved," Tiola responded still spooning. "White witches are not obliged to boast the appearance of hook-nosed hags and we use only helpful spells - even those we keep to a minimum. We perform on high days and holy days. The occasional Saturday."

Jesamiah responded to her absurdity, although beneath the frivolity he had an uncomfortable feeling, somewhere among all this nonsense, she was being serious. Where, *where* had he seen her before?

The broth was good but the tiredness was creeping up on him, he could manage no more than half the bowl. Understanding, Tiola did not press him to eat, left him to sleep. He lay a while, watching her move about the room, listening to the murmur of her voice talking to the other woman, Jenna. She, Jesamiah was not certain of, a harridan to be side-stepped where possible. Tiola though... Ah, he could get to like her. Get to like her a lot. Where had he heard her voice? He felt sleep overhauling him, blinked it aside, the puzzle annoying him.

She was talking to Jenna, recounting something that had happened: "Then the imp said, *'What fer ye b'wantin' t'take that blatherer's word 'afore mine surr? Tedn't fair, tedn't proper'* and hit him, square on the nose!"

He remembered! Cornish! Her accent was Cornish! Suddenly everything came flooding into his mind as if a great wave had creamed in across his senses and then washed out again taking all the clogging muck and debris with it, leaving the inside of his head clean and alert.

"My God!" he exclaimed, awkwardly shuffling to sit up. He was full awake again his heart beating fast, a mixture of excitement and lurching panic. "You were on the *Christina Giselle*. We met here, in Cape Town!"

From across the room Tiola dipped her head. "*Ais*."

"But," his face chiselled into a frown of bewilderment. "But the set-to with the horse? I assumed you were a child."

As he had been meant to assume. "I shall soon be sixteen," she stated. Indicating her short stature and flat bust, offered an easy explanation, "Perhaps you were confused because there is not much of me?"

"Hell's balls," he cursed again. Then a thought sent a second race of unease hurtling through him. "I heard you, you called out when the *Salvation* went down,"

He faltered, licked his lips, the uncertainty growing into alarm. "How did you do that?" Another thought which he instantly shoved aside. *Why did you do that?* Said, "And how did you know I was out there, bleeding to death."

Uneasily he answered his own question. *Witch.*

Logic told him it was all coincidence. Fate. Being in the right place at the right time. Witches were old women accused of making magic by people who were too stupid to understand sense, even if it leapt up and bit their backsides. Witches belonged with fairies, ogres, goblins and mermaids.

Ah. He *had* seen a mermaid. True, it had been a black, wrinkle-faced heavily whiskered crone, lolling on a mist-shrouded rock. Not the blonde-haired beauty that he had been led to believe were mermaids; he had clearly seen her tail as she had slid into the sea. Supposed even mermaids eventually grew old and tired-looking. Just his luck to see one of the decrepit ones.

Rue had insisted it had been a seal. What did Rue know? Frenchmen had nothing but lead for souls.

"You really are a witch?" he asked, uncertain, beginning to doze again.

Sleep, the natural healer, enfolding him as if it were a mist creeping in over the surface of the sea. Deadening all sound so that he did not hear her say, very quietly in her Cornish burr, *"Ais."*

- Twenty Four -

His back stiff, Jesamiah stretched, trying to ease cramped muscles and find a more comfortable position. From the angle of the sunlight he figured it must be the mid hours of the fore-noon, about five bells, ten-thirty. He had slept sound all night, then. His arm was throbbing, felt heavy, like a sodden anchor cable. His shoulder, his ribs, everything else ached too but he was healing, could put up with it. He shifted again, grimaced. He needed to relieve himself. The woman, the old besom Jenna, without glancing in his direction left the room, a shopping basket in her hand. Tiola was sitting by the window, reading, unaware he was awake.

This was embarrassing, would be more embarrassing to soak the bed. "Er, I'm sorry love I really need to er, pump ship. Visit the heads."

She looked up immediately her face lighting into a quick, comprehending smile. "I do not want you out of bed you are not strong yet, but there is no need to make things difficult. Here," she pulled the sheet back, "Swing your legs over – no do not get up, you will faint again as you did yesterday; sit on the edge." She retrieved the chamber pot from beneath the bed, placed it strategically and smiled at him. Jesamiah felt his stomach lurch. By God she was pretty.

"That alright? Can you manage?"

He nodded, "I think so."

"Call me when you are done." Flashing another smile she twirled away, her skirts swishing, leaving behind a cloud of her natural perfume. Disappearing into Jenna's bedchamber, the smaller room beyond the stairway curtain, Jesamiah was unaware she discretely listened to the sound his urine made, ensuring that he did indeed, manage. She waited a moment longer when he had finished, returned as she heard the bed creak and the mattress rustle. Amused, noticed he was modestly covering his nakedness with the sheet.

Without a word she retrieved the utensil and left the room, examining the urine when out of his sight to ensure it was the correct pale yellow colour not rusted brown or spotted with blood. She dipped a finger in, tasted to ensure no unnatural sweetness. As she crossed the courtyard to empty the pot down the stink of the cess-pit, she sang a jaunty tune learnt from Kisty. A song of Africa, full of life and rhythm, her voice floating upward as she ascended the stairs again, hitting the high long notes with perfect pitch, her fingers clicking the beat as the last few lines increased in tempo and key.

"You seem happy?" Jesamiah remarked, questioning.

"Why would I not be Luvver? You are on the mend. It is satisfying to know there will not be another grave in the churchyard just yet." She fell serious, "You lost a lot of blood, another handful of minutes and you may not have survived."

"Lucky you were there then, eh?"

"It was not luck."

He grinned. "Ah yes, you are a witch." He did not believe a word of it. He was a sailor, recognised a yarn when told one. Witches turned people into frogs, curdled the milk, that sort of thing.

The answering smile was enigmatic. Beautiful. But a witch? Yet... Yet, she was casting a spell on him. Not the sort which would turn his skin green and make him hop and croak, this was a more subtle magic. Something affecting his heart. Or his brain or - elsewhere. He shrugged. He was either falling in love or turning into a moon-mad fool. Perhaps both? The one did often go with the other or so he had heard tell.

Through the following days he watched her, sometimes openly, more often surreptitiously through half closed eyes, when she thought him asleep. Nothing showed him that she was anything more than a young, very pretty woman who knew what she was doing when it came to healing. But her presence was comforting, pleasant. He trusted her implicitly. Why was that? There was something so familiar, so *right* about her.

Was this love he was beginning to feel? Or desire? Hard to tell, he had never been in love before. Lust, he knew about. If nothing else, this prickle of wanting in his nether regions showed he was getting better.

She allowed him to get up now, to make his way down the stairs to the seat of ease when he needed it, going carefully for his head sometimes swam as if he were drunk. She did not exactly escort him there and back, but always watched, waiting, sitting at the bottom of the stairs at first, having to take his arm to help him return, exhausted, to bed. Another good thing, he had his breeches to wear now, no more covering himself with a sheet. That had amused him, he had not thought of himself as a man embarrassed about his own nakedness, but with her? Aye, he was glad to be wearing his breeches. Another confusing sign of this unfamiliar malady called love?

He did not sleep so often now the stitches were removed – in the name of all the Oceans, how that had hurt! Torture he could probably endure. Stitches buried beneath healing scabs being cut out, no. He had tried not to yell; half way through had given up the trying and screeched. Agreed with Tiola. Aye, he was a whimpering baby.

The scars on his arm were nasty, some of them stubbornly remaining red and angry. She continued to smear thick, sweet-smelling paste under the bandaging, insisted he rest. He tried reading; she had an interesting collection of books, among them Woodes Roger's new and arrogant publication of his circumnavigational expedition. The title page carried a dedication, *"To my admirer, mistress Jenna Pendeen, and her Young Ward."* Conceited ass.

Jesamiah could not concentrate, finding his thoughts insisted on returning to that night, desperately trying to remember. Aloette, who had betrayed him, was not worth remembering. The girl with her arms supporting him in the darkness of a passageway, her mouth over his? Who was she? He was certain it had been Tiola, although he could only recall the sour expression of a straggle-haired, street slut. Had he imagined it all? Embellished what had happened as unconsciousness had enveloped him? Tiola was not a prostitute - although he had briefly wondered when he first realised this room was situated above a brothel. In high indignation the black girl, Kisty, had put him right.

He had met her on one of his first independent journeys down the stairs into the courtyard. "You work here too?" he had asked, nudging his head towards the open back door to the ground floor, deliberately adding, "With Miss Oldstagh?"

"Miss Tiola? She don't work for Miss Bella, she'm special, she'm our healer. She done fixed my broke arm," and Kisty had proudly waggled the limb to prove it. "Hurt something bad it did, but she healed me. Like she'm healing you." Then she had realised what he had meant and her eyes had widened, her mouth rounding into outrage.

"You think I go with the men? And Miss Tiola too? For shame on you! She be a lady!" And Kisty had flounced away, her head high, shoulder's squared with pride.

The twenty first. Seventeen days since the fourth of December. He was healing well, no more bandages; the hurt was more of a persistent ache, a dragging uncomfortable pull with the muscles stiff and complaining, scabs itching. Tiola was sitting as she often did, beside the open window, her head bent over her sewing, finishing the making of a replacement shirt for him. The one he wore was old and a little tight across the shoulders, a shirt she had found him. He had been asleep, dozing in the lumpy, horsehair chair, but Tiola's quiet singing had awoken him. The disapproving Jenna, to his relief, was nowhere in sight.

He could not understand the words of the song for it was in a language he was unfamiliar with; it had a rhythmical lilt, similar to the swaying of a ship making way in a calm sea. The steady rise and fall of the deck beneath your feet, the wind sighing, friendly, among the rigging. He stood, stretched, found the ache in his shoulder and down his arm was receding. He scratched at one of the itching scabs as he walked across to stand behind her, watched her finish a cuff.

"It's a good song," he said reaching for a rum bottle on the shelf behind her. Holding it in the crook of his arm he unstoppered it, drank. The fire of the liquor tasting so very good after almost three weeks of doing without. "I do not recognise the language, although I have a good ear for foreign speaking." He took an inspired guess, "Cornish is it?"

"*Ais*. I was born in Cornwall, along the coast from Falmouth. My mother's people have lived there since time began."

"A long way from the heat and stink of Cape Town." He hooked a stool forward sat opposite her, took another large swallow. "When I was a boy my father offered to send me to England for an education. I agreed to go, to escape my brother, but my mother refused to allow it, saying English tutors were notorious drunkards and buggerers." He tipped the rum bottle to his mouth again. "I was too naive to know precisely what she meant." He chuckled, added, "I thought it a good word. I often called my brother a bugger after that. Although I had my backside whipped when mother heard me use it."

"And you are not a drunkard?" Tiola asked with a faint smile which broadened as he frowned. She lent forward, tapped the bottle meaningfully with her fingernail.

Understanding, he grinned at her, "Aye well, I might like m'rum, but I don't do the buggerin' bit!"

Obliging him with a laugh Tiola said, "Long way from an education in England to ending up on the Sweet Trade?"

He side-stepped the subject. "A long way and a long story. What was the song?" He grinned, half mischief, half mocking. "A spell?"

"No, just a song. I do not perform spells. It was about a sailor who loved his ship more than his wife."

"Ah." He drank again. "For some of us, wives do not come into it, we love our ships more than our life." When she made no answer added, "You do not approve. Of sailors? Or of pirates?"

She bit off a thread and began on the second cuff. "What you do is your business, for your conscience. Not mine."

"You disapprove." He snorted, derisive. "You sound like Jenna."

"I do not approve of killing for no reason, no."

"What if I was to tell you I kill only those trying to kill me first?"

"I would not believe you."

More rum. "My ship is my kingdom, my world. On a ship, as a pirate, I am master. She is my woman, my life, my love, everything. Unlike a woman you can trust a ship. You know what she's thinking, what she's going to do a moment before she does it. Ships do not betray or hurt you." There was bitterness there, squeezing from behind his words. "The sea, a ship, together they mean freedom. Freedom to do what I want, go where I want with no one to say I can or cannot do it. Land is commitment and rules and stupid laws. The only law at sea for a pirate is the swell of the ocean and the voice of the wind."

"And the fact that piracy is wrong? Does it not concern you? Stealing, murder, rape, are they not immoral?"

He was indignant. "I have never raped any woman!"

"I am glad to hear it," she responded tartly, although her tone implied she again did not believe him. "You might not have done so, there is many a pirate who has." Thought cynically, *Or a father.*

In hot defence he stated, "Not in my crew!" Relented, it was not true. There had recently been a man who did not follow orders. Jesamiah had tipped him overboard, not holding with his conduct regarding a female on a brigantine they had boarded. The man had stated she was a black slave, assumed he could do as he pleased with servants and slaves, black or white. Jesamiah had disagreed and when the sailor had pulled a knife, shark bait was the result.

"Laws are not always right, Sweetheart," Jesamiah said pragmatically. "Is it right to send a man to rot in gaol for poaching a rabbit to feed starving children? To send a child to the colonies as a slave for the stealing of a loaf of bread? Nor am I one of those men who believe in flogging a woman because she has committed adultery. Laws are made by rich men who sit on their fat backsides and have no idea what it is to feel hunger gnawing at their bellies. And who enjoy leering at a semi naked young woman as her skin is flayed from her back." He spoke with sincerity, the anger evident.

Conceding his point, Tiola thought, *Or to hang a woman for doing away with her husband because he was about to rape her daughter.*

"That does not make piracy acceptable, however."

He shrugged. "Life is not fair. I suppose I enjoy evening out the balance a little."

"By killing the innocent?"

"The captains of a Chase are to blame for any killing. If they were to heave to when first threatened no one would get hurt. All I want is what they carry, it serves no purpose to make a fight of it."

"How convenient. Their fault for being murdered, not yours."

For a moment he made no answer to the sarcasm then said, "If there was a way to be free without being a pirate," he shrugged one shoulder, "there is not and so I am on the Account and I sail under my black flag of a skull and crossed bones." He fiddled with the rum bottle in his left hand. Added, his voice and eyes lowered, "Or I did. Until I lost m'ship."

She recognised the anguish in his voice, a rawness he had been desperately suppressing these past days. The false bravado gone, he asked, "I suppose she has sailed? The *Inheritance*? I doubt she stayed in harbour."

Reaching forward Tiola laid her fingers sympathetically on his arm. "I am sorry. She sailed three days after I found you."

He scowled then philosophically toasted the air with the bottle, counterfeiting a grin to disguise the hurt. "Good luck to you Rue. Sail her well."

"Is there no loyalty among pirates?" she exclaimed, sorry for him, aware Jesamiah was a person who kept his feelings close to his chest and this glimpse of exposed emotion was an unintentional rarity. "Could he not have waited?"

"In a pirate ship? What, and risk his life and the entire crew? He did what's right, he had to. Aside I expect he assumes I'm dead. You say he sailed on the third day? He would have been looking for me, did not find me." He toasted the air again. "Good of him that was. He is a good friend." Added under his breath, "Was a good friend."

The rum was taking effect, damping the ache of loneliness, numbing the despair. Tiola leant across, removed the bottle from his hand and returned it to the shelf. His mouth turned down but he made no protest.

"So what will you do once you are able to go your way?" She motioned that he was to remove the old, tattered shirt and held the new one out for him, marvelled at the calm way in which she spoke of him leaving.

"Commandeer another vessel," he stated without hesitation as he pulled the garment over his head, the touch of her hand on his skin sending his stomach into knots.

"Steal one, you mean."

"Nautical term, commandeer."

"Land term. Steal."

Because of the rum he laughed more merrily than he would have done half an hour previously, tweaked one of the seams more comfortable. "If you insist, but piracy is what I do, Sweetheart. Would I not be damned useless at it if I did not steal?"

His eyes crinkled at the sides when he laughed, rippling the line of the faint white scar, bringing light and life into his mobile face. His eyes she had noticed, seemed darker than they really were because of the sun and wind-tanned skin, and because of his curled mass of dark hair, now free of lice. She had been vigorous with the comb those first few days while he slept. Pirates and ne'er-do-wells in need of help were welcome; not the crawlers they carried.

She began tidying her sewing things away into the basket. "And a wife? Is there one of those?" Again she spoke casually although her heart was hammering in case he spoilt everything and told her of one.

He guffawed outright. "Marriage and piracy don't make suitable companions."

"Not even if the wife was to sail with you?"

He was standing, tucking the shirt into his breeches. Answered with the simple truth. "It is not practical to have a woman aboard. Women produce children, children mean responsibility. They take away a man's freedom."

"A man is not forced to have intercourse with a woman," Tiola retorted sharply. "And he is well able to withdraw, to mind his pull back."

"What? Make a coffee house of her - go in and out and not spend anything?" Jesamiah stared at her, incredulous, and she had to smile at his astonishment. The common innuendo for *coitus interruptus* had reached even here, as far as Cape Town, made popular from the London coffee houses where men could sit and gossip all day without making a single purchase.

Used to bedding whores and loose women of the street, Jesamiah had not found it necessary to consider the consequences of his sexual pleasures. He scratched at his chin, asked, bemused, "What use is a woman like that?"

"I would say a woman is there to serve hot coffee when a man desires it, and entertain him while he savours its flavour, *neen?*"

Both Tiola and Jesamiah jumped, turned, startled to see a man standing at the head of the stairs chuckling at his own jest, elegantly dressed in a pale green coat and lavishly embroidered waistcoat. He removed his cocked hat, plumed with an ostrich feather. Swept Tiola an exaggerated bow.

"Stefan!" She squeaked, disconcerted. What was he doing here?

- Twenty Five -

Stepping into the room, Stefan van Overstratten directed his smile at Tiola; towards Jesamiah, an expression of solemn disapproval. He considered Miss Oldstagh to be the most beautiful woman in South Africa. He admired beauty, in all its forms. He was also conceited, vain and possessive, and resented those who had things he did not. If anyone was going to be Tiola's husband it would be himself. And no one, once Stefan made his mind to something, stepped in his path.

He offered a smaller, polite bow. "Pardon my intrusion, I met with Mistress Pendeen outside, she bade me enter." He strode forward, took the liberty of kissing her hand and then her cheek. With a flourish, produced a package from beneath his coat and announced, "Happy birthing day, *liefste.*"

Flustered at his endearment, her face tingeing pink, aware Jesamiah was staring at her, Tiola took the gift. Removing the ribbon and cloth, revealed an emerald bracelet; exclaimed, "Stefan *dank je.*" Solemnly, she handed it back. "Regrettably I cannot possibly accept this. You are more than generous towards Jenna and myself already." With a shy smile, added, "May I ask, how did you know this day is my birthday?"

The Dutchman ignored her protest and fastened the clasp around her wrist, the green stones sparkling in the sunlight, scattering flying motes of colour across the wooden floor. "Mistress Pendeen informed me of the date a few days past. Your modesty does you credit, my dear, but for the giving of gifts the pleasure is wholly mine. I must, therefore, insist you indulge me."

Leaning against the windowsill, his arms insolently folded, Jesamiah snorted. Who was this dandy? And why had Jenna not informed *him* it was Tiola's birthday?

The two men eyed each other, like circling dogs with their hackles raised.

Breaking the awkward silence, Stefan asked, "Are you not going to introduce us, Tiola?"

She smiled, benignly. "Jesamiah, this is master Stefan van Overstratten a kind and most generous friend. Stefan, may I introduce Captain Jesamiah..."

Jesamiah flashed her a startled warning not to betray his identity. Which she ignored. She was not a fool.

"...Oakwood. Mr Oakwood was attacked almost three weeks ago not far from here by cut-purse thieves who left him for dead. We have not troubled to report it, of course." She gave a dismissive gesture. "What use are soldiers in any matter not concerning the military?"

"Despite them being my own Countrymen, I agree, they are a useless bunch of layabouts." Stefan replied, critically assessing Jesamiah. So, this was the stranger Tiola had been tending? Jenna had indicated he was of a base class. She was correct, by the look of him, to have hinted concern at his low morals. This situation was not acceptable. Not acceptable at all. "It is unfortunate, Mr Oakwood, unless you are Dutch the law in Cape Town cannot assist you. It is a matter of resources, you understand."

Jesamiah understood very well. Dutch marines were lazy, cowardly, snivellers.

"Even for us Dutch, the local militias can keep the law only within the confine of the Peninsular. Anything beyond is outside their remit. As example, they could not even go after the pirates who ravished one of my ships some weeks ago."

Stefan set his hat and cane down on the table, seated himself, thought, *Who is this fellow? An hour before noon and not yet dressed? His shirt half hanging out; without stockings and shoes?* He brushed at his coat sleeve. Tutted to himself, the censure aimed at Jesamiah's state of undress, not the fluff.

"What ship was that?" Jesamiah asked offhand, finally remembering to shove the last of his shirt inside his breeches, and wondering whether the subject of pirates had been raised intentionally.

"The *Amsterdam*. Three mast, square rigged. She was carrying a cargo of finest wines destined for King George's own cellars." A chink showed in Stefan's charm. Anger puckered at the corner of his mouth.

"*Amsterdam?*" Jesamiah echoed as he stroked his thumb and finger down his moustache, frowning as if in thought. "Nope, can't say I've 'eard of her." He toed the stool nearer the window, lifted down the rum bottle again. Sitting, he stretched his bare legs out before him crossing them at the ankles. "I don't much care for wine. I find it often tastes more like cat's piss."

Scathing, Stefan quipped, "I would not be in the position to compare. I am unfamiliar with the taste of feline urine."

Ignoring the insult, Jesamiah almost retorted that the *Amsterdam's* cargo had tasted superb, and had fetched a handsome price from a merchant higher along the coast. That several bottles were stowed safely in his cabin aboard the *Inheritance*. But of course, he could not. Instead, glancing with one eyebrow raised towards Tiola, who was unnecessarily tidying things away, he asked, "Anyone killed aboard her?"

Stefan's answer was pinched with annoyance. "The Captain was most disgracefully terrorised."

"But not *killed?* Wouldn't tell where the specie was, I expect."

Removing Stefan's hat from the table and hanging it on a hook beside the doorway where it would not become soiled, Tiola asked the Dutchman, "What is specie?"

Amused that she was ignoring him, Jesamiah answered before Stefan had a chance to speak. "Money. Cash. The extra a captain carries for emergencies."

"He had thirty pounds sterling," van Overstratten grumbled. "More than the wretched man's monthly pay."

Jesamiah scowled. The dog! That captain had insisted he had only fifteen! Where in hell had he hidden the rest? Damn him - they had torn the ship apart searching for it! He took another swig of rum, said, without looking towards Tiola, "Anyone raped?"

Embarrassed at the indelicacy Stefan cleared his throat. "There were three female passengers aboard with their husbands."

"And?"

Indicating Tiola the Dutchman answered with disapproval. "This is not a suitable topic to speak of before a lady, but since you ask, *neen*, they were not touched. They were encouraged to donate their jewellery and were then permitted to remain in their cabins."

Turning his head to gaze square into Tiola's eyes which were blazing anger at him, Jesamiah mouthed, '*told you*" and winked at her, earning himself an indignant shrug and an audible snort of disdain. Grinning at her annoyance, he relaxed. If this buffoon had suspected him of being involved in piracy he would have shown the fact by now.

Tiola busied herself at the fire, noisily swinging out the kettle to make a pot of coffee, clattering her best china cups.

Stefan drummed his fingers on the table as the uncomfortable silence lengthened. He did not wish to make conversation, but manners dictated otherwise. Cordially he enquired, "What line are you in Mr Oakwood?"

None of your bloody business, Jesamiah thought. "I am a trader. I will consider taking anything if it is worth selling for a profit." He smiled mischievously at his double meaning.

An inkling of suspicion returning, Stefan flapped a hand in the general direction of the harbour. "Which is your ship? I do not recall seeing one I do not know riding at anchor?"

"She's sailed on to the Indies and the China Seas." Jesamiah indicated his injured arm, as if it explained everything; the lies came easily, he was well practised. "She will pick up a cargo of china, tea, silk and spices, that sort of thing, and will collect me on her return passage in a few months. I trust my first officer implicitly." The last was the truth, the rest? There was no certainty Claude de la Rue would ever come near Cape Town again. The *Inheritance* could be anywhere. Near any harbour, on any ocean.

Van Overstratten's dislike for this cocksure mariner was rapidly increasing, although he had nothing more to go on than appearance and prejudice. The fellow spoke as if he had received an education of sorts, was obviously familiar with matters of navigation and seamanship, but he was nothing more than an opportunist trader. What was his background? His position in society? Tiola ought not associate with this form of lowborn riffraff. Bad enough her insisting to live here in this squalid area of town among the layabouts and drunkards - to have taken one of them into her home! Stefan pursed his lips, his disapproval hardening. As well he had come today. This situation must be terminated as soon as possible.

"You have no concern for pirates then?" he queried, accepting coffee from Tiola with a nod of gratitude.

Again Jesamiah wondered whether this fop was on a fishing expedition for shrimps. He answered truthfully. "None whatsoever."

Glaring her displeasure at Jesamiah Tiola removed the rum bottle from his hand, exchanged it for a china cup. "And do not break it," she threatened under her breath. "I have only three left."

"*Liefste*, have you any of those delicious wheat cakes mistress Pendeen bakes?" Stefan enquired with a congenial smile, adding more frostily to Jesamiah, "She is a wonderful woman, devoted to her ward. She would not allow anything to upset her."

Retrieving the rum Jesamiah added a generous dose to his coffee. "Medicinal," he lied as the Dutchman raised a censoring eyebrow. For *anything*, he guessed the interfering busybody meant *anyone*. "I may be wrong," he drawled, "but my impression of Tiola is that she is more than capable of taking care of herself."

Van Overstratten's response was one of surprise. "Tiola is a woman. No woman is capable of caring for herself."

"Oh, I wouldn't say that, the women I've come across are capable of doing many things." Jesamiah grinned, toasted the air with the rum, took a swig and set it down on the floor.

"This woman has ears and is more than capable of speaking for herself, thank you." Tiola snapped, slamming the coffee pot down on to the table and marching over to retrieve the half empty bottle.

Into the following silence, a crash came from downstairs, then Kisty's piercing screech and Bella's scolding.

"I came," van Overstratten said to Tiola as he finished his coffee and placed the cup on the table, "to arrange a carriage for this evening. Will six of the clock suit?"

His head shooting up, Jesamiah's brows furrowed downward. What was this?

From where she sat on a stool at the far side of the table, Tiola thanked Stefan, replied that six would suit nicely.

Jesamiah, lasting a full minute of pretended disinterest, commented, "Going out are you?"

When Tiola made no answer Stefan felt obliged to explain. "This evening has been long arranged. The Governor holds a midsummer ball at the fort, Miss Tiola and Mistress Pendeen are to accompany my party as my guests." He smiled indulgently at Tiola who forced herself to respond graciously, and not scowl.

"That's nice for you," Jesamiah retorted, totally ungracious and scowling for both of them.

Another silence. The atmosphere was becoming as tense as the prelude to a lightning storm. Downstairs, Kisty was weeping;

- 188 -

outside, a pedlar was shouting he had ribbons and trinkets for sale. A group of children ran past, chattering and giggling, the sound of an iron hoop rattling over the cobblestones as they bowled it along.

Clearing his throat van Overstratten stood, fetched his hat. "You are of course welcome to join us, Mr Oakwood." His unfriendly tone firmly implied the opposite.

"I thank you, but I am not one for dancing and fancy to-do's, even when I am in fine fettle." Jesamiah waved his arm, showing the livid scars. "Do not mind me, you go off and enjoy yourselves. I am quite capable of finding my own entertainment. I can always toddle downstairs if I want company." *Ah,* he thought, as Tiola gave him a frosted stare. *That stirred her attention.*

"Then it is settled." Stefan said, relieved at this ruffian's refusal. He caught Tiola's hand and elegantly kissed it; smiled. "Until tonight then, Tiola my dear." And he produced another package from an inside coat pocket.

"I trust you will grant me the pleasure of wearing these also?" He unrolled the velvet, and drew out a necklace and matching earrings, sisters to the bracelet.

"Oh!" Tiola was taken aback, her expression dismayed for she had been annoyed at Jesamiah and had behaved so churlish towards Stefan – and now here he was offering her more gifts. She smiled up at him, genuinely delighted, murmured, "They are beautiful."

His response was predictable. "But not as beautiful as you, my dear." Stefan fastened the gems around her neck, declared with pride, "I thought these would look charming with the green silk gown I purchased for you. You are to wear it tonight, are you not?"

"Why, *ais,* of course," Tiola stammered.

Kissing her palm, van Overstratten nodded curtly at Jesamiah and took his leave. His thoughts as he entered his waiting carriage were less than complimentary. This Oakwood fellow, who was he? Where had he come from?

More important, when was he leaving?

- Twenty Six -

"*They will look charming with the green silk gown...?* Hell's bits Tiola, what slime-weeded depth did you haul that crowing cockerel from?"

Tiola was examining the emeralds against her skin, preening in the cracked looking glass above the cooking-fire. She ignored Jesamiah's sarcasm.

"Green is unlucky," He stated, petulant, when he received no answer. "Some sailors refuse to have anything green aboard."

"Just as well I am no sailor then," she countered, angry with him for a variety of reasons not all of them fair. Angry because she was not certain which of the two men she was more annoyed with; Jesamiah for being so deliberately reckless and annoying or Stefan for his blithe assumptions. Or with herself for allowing this silly anger to curdle in the first place.

Realising her displeasure Jesamiah remained prudently silent as she collected the cups, found a sudden interest in studying the books on the shelf again, although he knew every one of the dozen sitting there; Bartholomew Sharp's expedition, Sir Henry Mainwaring's nonsense about pirate hunting. Exquemelin's *Buccaneers of America* - none of them as remarkable as Mr William Dampier's publications of course.

"You going then, tonight?" he finally asked fully expecting her to answer no, she was not. Was startled when she declared of course she was.

"I am looking forward to it in fact."

"Wearing his dress and trinkets? I never had you hoisted as a woman who would jump to a fop's beck and call."

Her anger spilt over, she spun around threw the cup in her hand to the floor where it shattered into pieces. "Is this how you repay my hospitality? By being obnoxious about my friends?"

Jesamiah stared at the scatter of splintered china, thought, *Now you've only got two, you daft wench.* Said, "Good friend, is he?"

"He is an important man here in Cape Town and is no fool."

"Is he not? You surprise me."

"He will work out what you were alluding to, Jesamiah. What you are." Tiola closed her eyes and leant her arm on the beam of the mantel, sudden weariness sapping her energy. She did not want Jesamiah to go, did not know how she was to bear the sorrow of him leaving – and he would be leaving, soon, very soon. When he left, what would there be for her? A dull life as Stefan van Overstratten's cosseted wife? Was that why she was angry, because she wanted the amusing unpredictability of Jesamiah, not the proud arrogance of Stefan?

The fire crackled, steam rose in gentle spirals from the kettle. Sounds filtered from the street; a woman calling, children squealing. Kisty was crying. *Something has happened,* Tiola thought. *I will go down in a little while and see what is wrong.* Birds were hopping over the clay tiles of the roof, their claws scratching. The air was hot, the day dry and dusty.

"I think I ought to finish getting dressed," Jesamiah said cursing himself for being a fool. He had upset her, had not meant to. "My apologies, I did not intend to offend you. Nor him." The second was not true, van Overstratten could go rot.

"I know when you lie, so please do not patronise me." Tiola snapped, then sighed and accepted the inevitable. He would not be staying, and marrying Stefan was a sensible match. She fetched a broom and a hand shovel to clear the broken mess, pointed at a wooden clothes chest in the corner. "Your things are in there."

She had darned the hole in the toe of his stocking he discovered, and cleaned the blood from his waistcoat. His waist sash had been folded neatly. Ah! His ribbons! Surreptitiously, he poked at other folded garments, hers. Undergarments, petticoats, a shift, a lace-edged bodice.

"Your boots are in the corner behind the curtain," Tiola said tipping the broken shards of china into the fire, where they would eventually be removed along with the ash. Guiltily he pushed the bodice aside, lifted his hat and belt; the cutlass and scabbard were there with the leather baldric. No coat. Damn, it had been left in the brothel – his pistol! Lovingly, with a smile of pleasure, greeting an old friend, he brought it out. No man could be a pirate without a cutlass and pistol. Forgetting why he was standing there he began to load the weapon with wadding, shot and powder. An unprimed pistol was useless. Nor would a pirate captain be standing here in bare feet, half dressed. He chuckled, set the loaded weapon aside, pulled on his stockings fetched his boots.

Her anger lifting, Tiola realised it for the stupidity it was. This was her birthday she ought not be a cross-patch on this day. What would be was in the future so why waste the pleasure of the present?

"I'm sorry, Sweetheart, I truly did not intend to upset you." He repeated his apology as he thread the sash around his waist, buckled his belt over the top, wincing as his right arm protested. "Only," he paused, fiddled with his earring. He wanted to say, *"Only I am jealous of this Stefan van Overstratten. I do not know whether he is an intimate friend or a mere acquaintance."* Said instead, with a limp shrug, "He annoyed me."

"So I noticed." She fetched his waistcoat, held it for him to slip on.

The old hole made by a lead shot had been re-patched neatly, the new one also mended. A matching pair. Standing so close her fragrance was overpowering. Had he imagined her kissing him? It had seemed real at the time. Suddenly he realised there was only one certain way to answer so many questions. He dipped his head, his lips brushing lightly against hers his moustache and beard scratching against her skin. She yielded to his touch and he felt her eager response. Sliding his arm around her waist he pulled her closer, the kiss fiercer and more insistent, his tongue parting her lips to explore her mouth. As he would kiss any woman.

And she pushed violently at his chest, forcefully shoving him aside. He stepped back, at a loss, held his hands high, palms open, a gesture of reassurance and surrender combined. He had only kissed her - even for a girl who had never been kissed before she should not react like this! He moved more paces away, puzzled. What had frightened her? Had that bloody Dutchman tried something inappropriate?

"What is it? What have I done? I meant no harm."

She was fighting the urge to wipe away the feel of his mouth over hers with the back of her hand. Fighting it because the sensation had felt so nice, but his action had unexpectedly plunged her back into the sordid nightmare of those last days in Cornwall. The rekindled horror swept through her - her father's thick lips covering hers so she could hardly breath, his foul hands touching her body; her desperate struggles to get away from him. And the loathing on his face when instinct had allowed her to use Craft for the first time, thrusting him away with the strength of several men. His seething outrage that she should fight back, abruptly ended by his wife and the blade in her hand.

The repercussions, those dreadful following days. All of it coming back because Jesamiah had lowered his head and kissed her! And yet, when she had found him, bleeding and in trouble she had kissed him without a second thought. Had just done the most obvious and practical thing to hide his face and get rid of those two men, who would most certainly have finished him off.

Unaware of the cause of her distress Jesamiah was frantically searching for what else he could to do to salvage the situation. "If Stefan is your lover and I have offended you Tiola, then I beg pardon, I behaved inappropriate."

The curtain swished open, its rings rattling along the wooden pole. Jenna.

"Aye my lad, and if I catch you behaving inappropriate again you will find yourself tumbling down these stairs as a gelding." The woman swept into the room, her face suffused with rage. "Do I make myself understood?"

Royal Navy marines, soldiers – the gallows - all those Jesamiah could face with impunity. A middle-aged buxom woman with nothing beyond the sole interest of her young ward's well being? He cleared his throat, stated, "Perfectly, Ma'am."

Grunting as she pushed past, glowering at him, Jenna set her basket of purchases to the table. "Seeing as you obviously have your strength back, you can make yourself useful." She ducked her head towards the empty cooking pot hanging on its hook to one side of the fire. "I cannot manage without water. Pot needs filling, you know where the well is." She lifted one of the wooden buckets, thrust it into his right hand. He winced. "Four of these."

"Jenna dear, he is not well enough."

"If he can get half drunk and behave like the tomcat he is, then he is well enough to earn his keep." Jenna bobbed her head at Jesamiah who had opened his mouth to protest he was not drunk. "Do not deny you have been sampling the rum young man. I can smell it on your breath. Or are you grumbling that work is too grand a thing for a pirate to be doing?"

Jesamiah closed his open mouth, shifted the bucket into his left hand and touched the right to his forehead. "It will be my pleasure to be of service, Ma'am."

"Aye, it's your pleasure of servicing I am afeared of!" Jenna snapped at his departing heels.

- Twenty Seven -

"That was uncharitable and uncalled for," Tiola stated facing the older woman who stood with her arms folded, stern disapproval etched into her face.

"Was it? I think not, miss. You are an innocent where gentlemen are concerned and that one," Jenna pointed at the stairs, "is not a gentleman."

"I am not so innocent, Jenna. I am a midwife how can I be? I see the various results of what men do to women almost every day." In sudden affection, realising Jenna's reaction had been well-intentioned, Tiola stepped forward and hugged her. "I appreciate your concern but I am, after all, now sixteen. You must allow me to spread my wings one day."

"One day aye, and on that day I will give you my blessing. But not with the likes of him, a thieving pirate."

Jenna turned from Tiola, began busying herself with tidying away the new-bought provisions, making a start on preparing their midday meal. As well she had met Stefan yesterday and suggested he visit Tiola today, not wait until the evening. In her opinion, the sooner he made the girl his wife and this pirate returned to sea, the better.

Grumbling to himself, Jesamiah pulled at the well chain. Raising the bucket awkwardly with his left hand he swung it over the side, filled the house bucket and sent the other back down with an angry shove. Bloody fool! Stupid! Stupid! He should have taken more care, not leapt in as a drunken sot pouncing on the first woman available!

Tiola was a lady he ought to have treated her as one. He winced as he lifted the full bucket the movement pulling at the healing wound in his shoulder, set it down, sat on the edge of the well. What the hell was he doing staying here? Jenna despised him, she had made her opinion quite clear and now he had made a damn fool of himself with Tiola, she probably hated him too. Perhaps he ought not have drank so much? A man needed a tot or two once in a while, though. Needed a woman too.

Why did he not get his effects together and go? She was obviously fond of this Dutch peacock, van Overstratten would probably be better for her anyway.

Forgetting the bucket, he stamped back up the stairs, halted a short way from the top, heard Jenna say:

"Stay away from him girl, a pirate's no good. The only certain prospect he has is to dangle at the end of a rope."

"You would rather see me settled with Stefan?"

"Master van Overstratten is everything a sensible young woman would want in a husband."

Or what an interfering besom-broom wants, Jesamiah thought to himself. Listening intently he settled his shoulder against the wall.

"Stefan may not want me as wife, I have no dowry; nor does he know my background," Tiola said.

Jenna snorted. "Oh tosh child, he has wealth a'plenty, what interest has he in dowries? Suitable women as wives – educated, young women - are rarer than a snow storm in a desert. Aside, he knows all he needs to know. You are the daughter of a gentleman, and both your parents are dead. We came to Cape Town because there was no future for us in England. The man has heard nought but the truth."

"With which we have been economical," Tiola answered wryly.

Jesamiah raised his eyebrows. Interesting. There was something to hide then, was there?

"Van Overstratten wants a wife who can give him sons – above that, none of the rest matters. After he has given you those, can you not see?

She would be pointing to the emeralds, Jesamiah guessed. He knew about gems, these emeralds were exquisite. Nor, unlike anything he would have given, had they been stolen.

And the next he heard, Jesamiah could picture Jenna standing as she often did, fists on hips, her brows furrowed.

"You risk ruining a secure future young lady by encouraging this vagrant of a pirate. You have done the best you can for him, now he has to go before he is discovered for the miscreant he is, and drags us into the dirt along with him."

That hurt. Hurt because it was the truth. Jesamiah sat on the fourth stair down, his chin cupped in his left hand his breath puffing out through his cheeks. It was not often he did some serious thinking. What was he going to do with himself? He would have to find a new crew, find a new vessel. With one arm stiff and sore? He flexed the fingers, the resulting tremor of discomfort bringing a grimace to his face, waited for the ache shambling up and down his right arm to ease. He knew only piracy. What else could he do? Become a legitimate trader? Possibly.

He snorted grim laughter. If nothing else he knew how to keep pirates away, any cargo he carried would be safe! Did he want to settle down to a life as a land-lubber? Have a sedentary life? No, but he wanted Tiola - or did she want Stefan? He could not believe that. Emeralds or no emeralds.

"Not even if the wife was to sail with you?" She had said. How much had she meant it?

Slamming to his feet, he stormed down the stairs. This was nonsense! He was a pirate God-damn it! As Jenna had stated, his only certain prospect was the noose, he was a no-good nothing. Someone such as Tiola needed a man who could care for her. Love her above all else.

"Sod it," he growled to himself. "I can do that. Better than any over-dressed jay can."

Tiola's reaction to his kiss had been a natural one, he supposed. Damn fool, the women he usually passed his time ashore with were all, there was no delicate way of putting it, were all sluts. Women who would do anything a man paid her to do, the more skilled the woman the more shillings she demanded. The advantage, they rarely wanted anything more, only the money. No promises, no ties. No commitment. He had never kissed a woman for love, and he would wager, Tiola had never been kissed by a man at all. Except for his clumsy, stupid attempt - and that night in the alley. Which, now he thought of it had been through her desperation to do something to help him, pure impulse to save his life.

A kiss for passion was something entirely different and he, stupid fool, had waded in like a clumsy, inexperienced youth! That did not explain the other puzzle of how she had changed her appearance. He shook his head, he must have imagined it. Problem sorted. His kiss had alarmed her, taken her by surprise. Next time he would move more slowly, be more considerate. And there would be a next time, he would make sure of it.

Next problem, Jenna. She was a trained guard dog, always on the prowl, teeth bared, ready to sink them in down to the bone. And she had a preference for this cock-robin, Stefan van Overstratten. Fair enough, she had Tiola's future at heart. Could he try getting round her? Show her he was just as worthy? He would have to start by being nice to her. Might work.

Four buckets, she had said.

"Bet the old basket thinks I'll not manage it," he muttered.

"One," he counted cheerily as he emptied the first into the cooking pot. "You use this as your cauldron, Sweetheart?" he said to Tiola, with a grin making a pretence that all was right with the world. "On those midnights when you make a new batch of potion, remember who fetched the water up before you go casting the next lot of spells, eh?"

Before she had chance to answer he disappeared down the stairs, whistling. Bad luck to whistle on board. He shrugged, what about on land? He switched to humming instead, breaking into song as he visited the privy to relieve himself. Chanties were sailors' songs, designed to keep rhythm and pace while the heavy anchor cable was hauled in, or sails hoisted. As with most nautical songs, the one Jesamiah was singing inclined towards the bawdy; he thought it best to la-la the more indelicate words, *"The Captain's a bugger, di da, da, di da, da,"* he improvised.

Emptying the second bucket he leaned close to Jenna as she stood at the table, mixing flour and eggs. For Stefan's bloody cakes he assumed. Sang the next line softly, with a grin, into her ear. *"The bosun's a daisy, we know 'e's 'alf crazy..."* He pinched her backside and swung quickly away, disappearing to fetch the third bucketful, finishing the verse as he went. *"So swab out yer gun and we'll get the job done. Heave ho, heave ho, heave ho, m'lads."*

"You impudent flea!" Jenna called after him. "I know your game!"

Jesamiah jumped the last two stairs, crowing his mirth, returned within a minute. *"The bilges are stinkin' – who cares we're a'drinkin! We'll sit in the sun an' might get the job done..."*

His shoulder and arm were hurting like the pain of all the damned, but he ignored the discomfort. Emptying the bucket he put it down and as Jenna moved from the table to wipe flour from her hands, caught hold of her waist and twirled her around the room, singing. *"Then I'll do yours, while you do mine; and we'll do 'alf the crew of a ship o' the line!"*

Although sounding lewd the song was innocent – nearly every chanty had a double meaning – the line alluded to men helping each other plait and tar their long hair into the single braid of a queue, so favoured by many sailors.

Jenna batted at him with the cloth in her hand, he ducked beneath it and planted a kiss on her lips. "You're pretty when you smile, love," he said. "Do it more often, an' I'll give you another kiss."

From across the room, Tiola laughed, her head back, delighted. He was so absurd!

Lifting the bucket, swinging it in his left hand he set off again to fetch the last. *"The lieutenant's a baby, 'e's got two - well maybe; so I'll 'old yours while you 'old mine and we'll do all the crew of a ship o' the line!"*

It was shadowed in the stairwell, lit only by the daylight filtering up from below, the sun bright, as Jesamiah stepped out into it. Grinning, he filled the fourth bucket returned to the stairs. About to step on to the first, out of the corner of his eye he caught movement in the deeper shadow beside the street-side door. He paused, Kisty? One of Bella's girls? Heard the very familiar double click of a flintlock hammer, at the same instant saw a man coming forward - and the glint of a pistol barrel.

Suddenly sober, Jesamiah yelled, dropped the bucket and ran, taking the stairs two at a time. The pistol fired, the sound booming loud in the confined space, the lead shot plunging past Jesamiah's ear to embed in the wall a few inches from his head. He hurtled on up, his only thought to get to his own pistol, heard feet pounding after him, the ominous click of a second weapon. Whoever he was, he would not be missing again.

Tiola was there, at the top of the stairs. Jenna peering, anxious, behind her.

"Out the way! Move!" Jesamiah barked.

If he had to fight, God alone knew how effective his right arm would be. He was not even sure he could hold his cutlass for long, let alone use it. The pistol he could fire left handed. Thank God, through old habit he had loaded it!

"Where's my weapon?" he bellowed as he swept past Tiola and pushed Jenna aside. He skidded across the room, found the pistol, cocked it, relieved to hear the satisfying click, click, of the hammer as it locked into place.

Back to the top of the stairs - everything happening so quickly, a matter of seconds - and Tiola was standing there, two stairs down, blocking the way, the man's second pistol raised pointing straight at her. Jenna caught hold of Jesamiah, swung him to a halt.

"Leave this to Tiola boy. Put the pistol down. She knows what she is doing."

Jesamiah swore, struggled to free his arm, almost going to strike her, but Jenna's grip was strong, her voice commanding. "Do as I say!"

He stood, breathing hard, a mixture of anxiety, exertion and anger surging through him; did not lower the pistol, recognised the man on the stairs. The one who had pushed him through the window. "What? I wait for him to shoot her first, do I?"

Calm, Jenna folded her hand over of the barrel. "Just wait."

"Wot be 'ee 'bout yur?" Tiola said, her accent a strong rolling Cornish, quite different to the mild, soft lilt Jesamiah had become accustomed to. *"Tiddn the whorehouze by yur, tiz oop auver to there you'm wantin', vine gentry folk like ee be."* She cackled like a crone. *"Or bist ee vancying an aua dummun? Show me yer zilver my bura, an I'll pool un var ee. Doan't make a bit av odds, you'm that 'ansum bay."* Wheezing into a paroxysm of mirth, she reached out her hand suggestively, squeezing and releasing her gnarled, misshapen fingers, her meaning clear.

Jesamiah's brows furrowed, gasped as she half turned, moved up a step. He knew the woman on the stairs to be Tiola, he had pushed past her - but this woman, the one speaking, this was not her! This one was a hunched and deformed old hag with wrinkled skin and squint eyes.

The attacker was unsure, hesitant. Tiola lifted her right hand, gestured a sort of beckoning, figure of eight sign with what appeared to be gnarled and misshapen fingers. The air shimmered, as if there were a haze of heat, except the stairs were in shadow. *"Be no one 'ere, beyon' me'sel' boy."*

Jesamiah was stunned, stood rigid, open mouthed. He was standing clearly in sight at the top of the stairs, so was Jenna, how could Tiola say she was alone?

Gesturing with her hand again, Tiola's unblinking stare never left the man's eyes. She spoke again, commanding, in her own, sweet voice, and from her own, familiar face. *"This is not the place to be looking for pirates! You will not be remembering coming here - be gone with you, and leave us in peace!"*

The man turned, unlocked the hammer and slid his pistol into his pocket, began to walk away. Tiola made a sound, a breath mixed with a hiss, *"Hie-asssh"*, and the air quivered again with a high, long note of sound, barely audible, perfectly pitched. He opened the street-side door, went through, closed it behind him.

Tiola nodded satisfaction. It was done. *"Ais."* Yes. Turning, looking up the stairs she was the normal, familiar, Tiola. "I would be obliged if you would follow him a while, Jenna dear, to ensure he has no friends lurking outside."

Jenna grunted, grumbled something under her breath but fetched her shawl and bonnet. "Do it for you, lass," she said as she began to descend the stairs, jerked her thumb over her shoulder at Jesamiah. "Not for him though. I said he would be trouble. He has to go."

As she passed, Tiola kissed Jenna's cheek. "Thank you, my friend." She looked up the stairs, Jesamiah was standing there the pistol lowered, staring, pale-faced. His arm was aching abominably and he was shaking.

She had said she was a witch, he had not seriously believed her.

Twenty Eight

His legs buckling, Jesamiah slithered into an untidy heap; Tiola was there, kneeling beside him, not touching, her eyes searching his ashen face, his gaze stubbornly not meeting hers. Tentative, she reached out, touched his cheek.

"Are you alright?"

His eyes closed, he took several breaths to steady himself. Not trusting his voice, managed only a nod. When he looked up at last Tiola's heart lurched for he was not alright. Terror was bolting through him at full gallop.

She smiled, apologetic. "I did tell you I was a witch."

"I did not believe you, " he whispered.

"It is perhaps as hard for you to accept I am what I am, as it is for me to accept you are a pirate. I heal. I bring life into the world, you think nothing of killing and torturing and stealing for no reason except the satisfaction of your own greed."

"You missed out rape."

She raised one eyebrow. "Do I add it to the list?"

One hand steadying himself against the wall he pushed himself upright. "Alright, aye, I've killed. I lie, I cheat, I steal," He flinched, finally speaking the truth. "And yes, I've raped." He ran his hand through his hair; he was sweating, he could feel it trickling down his back.

"I've joined with men stripping terrified women naked, abusing them. Aye, I'm part of all that, and you know what?" He backed away from her into the room. "I bloody enjoy it!"

For the last, he was lying again, she could see the false bravado clearly in his anxious expression, in the rigid way he held his body. Lying to appear strong, to convince himself - her - he was not afraid, that he was dangerous. A regular pirate trick; make as much noise as possible when attacking, make them think you are the very Devil come to claim their souls and they will give up without a fight. Anger was mixing with fear, and the two together were as volatile as a barrel of gunpowder left open where sparks were flying. She would have to stop this flooding panic before it erupted.

Best to do it now, make him forget, get it done, although she was reluctant for she had wanted to be able to trust him. Beyond Jenna, no one else knew of her Craft – even Tiola herself was uncertain of what she could or could not do, for her power had not yet reached its maturity. It would come, but not until it was ready to reveal itself. Like a tree in the late days of winter, it had lain lay dormant until awakened, but as yet the branches bore only buds and a few bright catkins. Soon, very soon, the leaves would burst open and the tree would come to vivid life. So it was with the power of the White Craft.

Jenna had known Tiola's grandmother, and what the old lady once did, so could the young woman do now, but Jesamiah was a stranger, Tiola's telling him what she was, even disguised as teasing jest, had always been a risk. One she had not taken lightly – it had been the only way she had known of conveying, albeit obliquely, that by trusting him with her identity he could trust her with his. It was not to be.

She raised her right hand made a small gesture with her fingers, breathed the same sound as before, *"Hie-asssh..."*

Jesamiah moved quickly, with agile speed caught her wrist in his injured right hand, ignoring the pain he pushed the barrel of his pistol, in his left hand, against her throat.

"Not on me," he said, furious, the words spitting like venom. "You will not be using bloody witchcraft on me!"

She held the blaze of hatred in his eyes a long, long, moment, then blinked slowly. "You can only stop me by silencing my Voice. If you are intending to kill me, then do it now, Jesamiah."

Silent, she waited, standing very still barely breathing. Her dark, stare holding his, then dropping his gaze he lowered the pistol, unlocked the hammer. Released her wrist. He walked into the room, put the pistol on the flour covered table, set his hands to either side and lowered his head, breathing heavily.

She did not move beyond the curtain. "I was only intending to cause you to forget what happened here, nothing more," she said. "For my benefit, not yours. I shall continue trusting you with the memory of what you saw, what I am and what I can do if that is what you want."

"Want?" he shouted as he lurched around. "What I want?"

He wanted to cross the room, push her to the bed and take her. That was what he wanted. Wanted to show he was not frightened of her, could dominate her. He was a pirate he could do whatever he pleased! He took two steps, his face contorted and ugly - stopped abruptly when he saw the sudden fear flood her expression. He had seen such a look before God help him, on the faces of terrified women aboard a prize.

"I am so sorry," he whispered, his shoulders slumping. "Sweetheart, I'm sorry. I did not mean to frighten you." He held his left hand out, his Adam's apple bobbing, swallowed hard. Admitted, "Actually..." swallowed again, looked away, talked quickly, confessing. "Actually, I've not forced myself on any woman since I reached seventeen years old. That last time? She was about your age, barely a woman." He cupped his hands near his chest, expressing what he meant. "She had nothing much up here. She was a maid, only I hadn't realised that until I.." He faltered, the shame making it difficult to continue. "Until I'd entered her. I wasn't careful. I was drunk, I was rough. She lay there so quiet, she just... as I..." He took a deep, inhaling breath, "She didn't make a sound, didn't move, nothing, and I suddenly thought, why am I doing this? There was no pleasure in it, no satisfaction. The opposite in fact. I realised I was no better than..." His voice choked, the words, *my brother,* caught in his throat. He looked down at his boots, the incident as clear in his mind as if it were yesterday.

"I've not regretted anything so much, nor been with a woman who didn't want me, since." Shrugged, conceded, "Well, not with one who didn't want m'silver, that is."

Raising his hands he offered a gesture of surrender. "I'm dishonest and I've done some bad, stupid, things in my life. I have killed men and thought nothing of it. I am a pirate. I pretend I am a rough, hard bastard. I rarely have to do anything more than draw my cutlass, wave it about and make threats like a black-hearted devil with no capacity for mercy. Makes sense to not disillusion anyone." He shrugged again. "I'll kill a man who is as capable of killing me first without a qualm, but I'll not hurt a woman or a child." Said, very quietly, "I ain't like my brother. I don't hurt those who can't fight back. Those who, because they are too weak or too small can't run away. I know what its like, you see. I couldn't run either." He held her eyes. He had never told anyone about that. Never.

"I'll leave. I got angry with you because I thought you were going to do something," he attempted a laugh to hide the fact he was hurting inside, that he did not want to leave. "I thought you were going to turn me into a toad."

"Now why would I be wanting to do that?" Tiola asked, "When you already are one?"

He smiled, appreciating her attempt at a jest. "Forgiven?"

Running her hands through her hair she turned slightly away from him. What was she to do? Here was this man in front of her, a man she had been attracted to since she had first seen him from the quarterdeck of the *Christina Giselle*, but he was a man who frightened her because of the emotions he was awakening. Because of her Craft she was ageless; in experience she was a sixteen year old. The woman that her body was becoming, wanted to grow up. The child within her wanted to stay innocent. But children should not be always having their own way. Too many who looked like grown men and women on the outside, behaved like spoilt children on the inside. She was sixteen, a child. She was sixteen, a woman.

She wanted him to kiss her, to hold her, to do – other - things, but was too scared to let him. Her mind kept seeing her father's face, remembering the panic and revulsion of his mouth on hers. Surely, that was because it had been wrong – against the law of nature and the balance of the White Craft? Jesamiah was not her father, he was not tainted by the influence of the Dark Power; he did not mean her harm, he only wanted to give her love.

The past was finished and must be left there; the now, the future, was all that mattered. And to walk confident into the future she must abandon the uncertainty. The child must become the woman. And the past must be forgotten.

"Forgiven." She walked across the room, touched her hand to his chest. "You have no need to be afraid me, Jesamiah. I will never use Craft on you. Not on you."

Bravado made him answer, "I am not afraid of you, I'm a pirate!" He bit his lip, took several breaths before blurting out the truth, "How can I be sure? How do I know you have not already made me forget everything?" He pointed towards the stairs. "As you did to that poor beggar?"

"You would rather have him remember then? So he can slink back and put a pistol to your brain later?"

"That's not what I meant."

Patiently, Tiola reassured him. "I cannot physically harm anyone. To do so would be to destroy myself. You know I am telling the truth because you *can* remember. You remember the Crafting that made those men chasing you believe I was a street hustler – the same skill as I used just now. The only thing you are not aware of, I took the worst of the pain from you, those first few days when your fever raged. That is all the Craft I have used on you, and will ever use. You have my word."

He was not convinced.

She looked into his eyes, her hand still resting on his chest, feeling his quick breathing beneath her palm. "If you cannot trust me Jesamiah, then as sure as a ship floats, neither can I trust you. How can I be certain the moment you walk out of here you will not betray me?"

Tilting her head she said with force, not quite the command she used with Voice, but near to it. "Think on this. They hang pirates, sometimes they hang witches, more often they do far worse to those of my kind."

The accusation horrified him, instinctive, he curled her hand within his own. "Sweetheart, I promise I would never betray you! Never!"

"Promises are so easily given. So easily broken." Jenna declared coming into the room, swinging her shawl from her shoulders and untying her bonnet ribbons. "The intruder has gone. I left him drinking ale in a tavern." In the same breath said to Tiola, "Bella wants you, Kisty has managed to scald her hand. I swear the girl is more trouble than she is worth."

Ah, so that was all the noise and fuss a while ago.

Collecting a few things from the cupboard Tiola gave Jesamiah an eye-sparkling, assuring smile, then whisked away down the stairs. Jenna began clearing the mess abandoned from her cooking.

"If I thought, for one moment, Captain Acorne, you in any way have hurt that girl, you will regret the day your mother let your father come anywhere near her."

He countered with his own vehement accusation. "I wonder who it was who sent that man here? Eh? If it was van Overstratten he moved pretty damned quick. You have had plenty of opportunity to set them on to me though, have you not?"

She gave him the withering look he deserved. "Had I wanted to betray you, boy, I would have done so a week past, when you were unable to run or defend yourself."

- 209 -

He hesitated, about to say something else caustic, asked instead, "Why do you not like me, Jenna?"

"Why do you think?"

"If it is money, I have plenty. Probably more than van Overstratten. It is all safe in various banks. Dutch, mostly, a fair bit is secured in this new-formed Bank of England."

"It is not about money. It is about reliability and honour. Two qualities you will never possess. I can trust master van Overstratten to take good care of Tiola. Could I so trust you?"

She pushed him out of her way to reach the other side of the table, pointed at his pistol. "You live by that," she said with scorn. "Stefan lives by good manners and courtesy. When he proposes marriage to Tiola tonight, I am expecting her to accept."

Jesamiah looked up, sharp. "How do you know he will?"

"Because he has already asked my permission and I have seen the betrothal ring. An emerald, to complete the set."

- Twenty Nine -

Jesamiah wandered down the stairs soon after they had gone. He had peered from the window to watch Tiola and Jenna enter the carriage sent for them by van Overstratten, watched them being driven away. He hated green. Whether it was unlucky or not, he did not care, not now, just knew he hated it. She had looked beautiful with her hair piled high and falling in a cascade of curls. Looked beautiful in the gown van Overstratten had given her. In the emeralds.

And what had he given for her birthday? Nothing. Absolutely nothing.

The rum was gone, he had finished it the moment they had left. He needed another bottle. Needed something else, too. Finding Tiola's scissors Jesamiah unpicked one of the gold coins sewn into his sash. Went downstairs to spend it.

Bella's was plush, richly decorated and furnished. This was no seaman's cheap-house brothel but a place for men of affluence to spend an evening of pleasurable entertainment, either at the gaming tables, or upstairs in private company. Jesamiah felt as though he were walking into the luxury of an English nobleman's house. He stood inside the door more lost and lonely than he had ever been in his entire life. Bella herself rose from a couch to greet him, waving Crystal and Amber-Rose aside.

"I'm from upstairs," he said lamely, indicating his lack of coat and hat.

"I know dear. Come in, you are welcome. As you see we are quiet tonight. My usual clientele are all hob-nobbing with the Governor I expect. He is holding some fancy do at the fort."

Aye, he knew.

"Crystal, a drink for the Captain." Bella had caught the smell of Jesamiah's breath. "Rum, dear, I think? How are the wounds? Healing, I assume, or you would not be here."

"How do you know me?" he asked, suspicious, his mind darting to the intruder.

"I sat with you once, dear, while your fever raged. Tiola was urgently required elsewhere. You do not have exclusive rights to her gift you know."

"I do not have rights at all, apparently," he mumbled as he handed her a single gold coin. "Rum and a woman."

She took his arm, his left, seated him on a couch in a discreet corner and sat with him. Shrewdly, she said, "A drink, certainly, dear, but a woman? We will see."

She watched him toss back a generous tot of rum, refilled his glass, then aimed straight for what she guessed to be the problem. "It troubles you that Tiola has gone to this ball with the Dutch fop?"

He drank the rum in one gulp. "Jenna says she is to marry him."

Bella Dubois, slapped her hands on her thighs, tossed back her head and guffawed a great belly gust of mirth. She wiped at the amused tears in her eyes, "I very much doubt it, dear!"

"He is to ask her tonight, at this bloody ball."

"He might ask. She will not accept."

Frowning, Jesamiah glanced at her. "Jenna says she will."

"Damn Jenna, the fusty old cow! Do not get me wrong she can show a heart of gold when it suits, but she wants the best for Tiola's – and her own - future, and Jenna's ideas of the best, and our Tiola's, are not one and the same."

"This van Overstratten, he could provide…"

"What?" Bella interrupted sharply, "A grand house? Carriages, servants by the dozen? Do you think Tiola wants all that? A life of day-by-day dreariness, being naught but a dutiful wife with the sole purpose of producing an heir?" Bella lowered her voice, although there was no one to hear. "Tiola can no more give up her midwifery and healing, Captain Acorne, than you can give up piracy."

He winced. "You know I am a pirate?"

Bella chuckled, put her hand on his arm. "I run a brothel. There is not much I do not know. I also know you are wasting your time down here my lad. What you need is to sober up and sort yourself out. Decide what you want, the sea, or Tiola - or both."

His turn to laugh, scornfully. "What in damnation could I offer her? I have money, but what has that to do with it? It's in here that counts," he tapped his chest. "I am a no good, lying, cheating, thief of a pirate."

"Who is very much in love, I think."

"Love?" He ran his hand through his hair, tears of despairing loneliness filling his eyes. "I do not know what love is. I've never experienced it before. I do know I can't tally all the ways I would willingly die for her though, if I had to."

- Thirty -

Jesamiah awoke with a throbbing headache to hear a grim sound on the stairs. He had collapsed across the bed and fallen instantly asleep, how long ago he had no idea. Only one lamp was burning, the others had guttered out. He groaned, eased cramped muscles, tried to shake the muzziness away from his spinning brain. Froze as the sound came again.

Alert, instantly awake and sobering fast, he crossed the room, lifted his pistol from the table; carefully, quietly, cocked it. Shielding the lamp with his hand he blew the flame out, leaving only the faint glow from the dying embers of the fire to light the room with a dim redness. Treading with care he slipped through the curtain and waited at the top of the stairs for his eyes to adjust.

The stairs creaked, the third from the bottom, it always did. Someone was there.

"I have a pistol," Jesamiah announced into the darkness his muscles tensed, ready to fling himself sideways at the sound of a hammer striking flint, igniting gunpowder, firing a shot. He was ready to shoot at the flash. "It is loaded and cocked. Who are you? What do you want?"

A moan. A woman. "Help me!"

Dear God! Tiola?

He swung back into the room, grabbed the lamp, a spill from above the fire; with trembling fingers lit the wick, barely controlling his patience to encourage the flame to burn. Was down the stairs again, sat midway, his head in his hands trying to stop his heart from thumping, his body from shaking. It was not Tiola.

The woman moaned again, a bitten-off scream clamped between her teeth.

What do I do? Jesamiah thought. "What's wrong, love?" No answer. Get her upstairs? Good idea.

He lifted her, his own hurts grumbling. At the top the woman pleaded to be put down, crouched on hands and knees, gasping. From the pain she was in he assumed she was dying. Her skirts were stained with filth and blood; had she been attacked? Her face contorted and she grabbed his hand, screeched. He yelled too, for she nigh on broke his fingers.

"Come on, I cannot leave you here." Somehow, with difficulty, he got her into the room, although not as far as the bed. She stood at the table clutching it, her knuckles white. He lit two more lamps.

"I'll go fetch help." Would Bella come? Would she know what to do?

"No! No! Do not leave me! Please?"

What to do? Oh, God, what should he do?

The stair creaked again, someone coming? A knot of panic grovelled in Jesamiah's stomach. He ran to look down into the shadows, closed his eyes, puffed exhaled air through his cheeks.

"Tiola! Am I bloody glad to see you!"

Weary, she stared up at him. "Jesamiah? Are you alright? Is there something wrong?" Her hair was dishevelled, the hem of her gown and her shoes were soiled with wet sand. Her face was flushed.

He jumped down the stairs to meet her, took her arm and hurried her upward. "There's a woman here in trouble." As they reached the top tilted his head, questioning. "You been on the beach? Been running?"

"*Ais,*" was all she said as she pushed him aside and flung her mantle carelessly into a corner of the room, followed by the wet shoes. "My dear how long have you been like this?" She was beside the groaning woman, stroking back her hair, her hand going to her swollen belly.

"I found her on the stairs."

"Ssh," Tiola waved Jesamiah to silence, indicating she was counting. "Fetch me linen towels from the chest over there, Jesamiah. Is there hot water?"

He peered into the pot. "Quarter full."

"Pour some into a bowl. Fetch me the brown glass bottle, too, if you please." She was rubbing the woman's back; the woman hunched into herself and screamed as if she was being torn in two.

Uncertain – a little afraid - Jesamiah half turned towards the stairs. "Er, should I fetch Bella?"

"No. Sit on the floor, dear-heart. What is your name?"

"Rosa," the woman gasped, clutching wildly at her abdomen as Tiola helped her to sit.

"What's wrong with her?" he asked, bewildered, as he fetched what he had been asked.

Tiola looked up at him, her eyes crinkling with amusement. "By the Deep, the innocence of men! She is in the advanced stages of labour you fool." To Rosa, as she lifted the woman's petticoats and peered beneath then felt with her hand. she said, "Is this your first, my dear?"

Rosa shook her head, biting back her agony. "My fifth."

"Ah, you know what we are about then. Jesamiah, you will have to help there is something wrong here. Sit behind her, brace her."

"I'm not sure about this Tiola."

"Shut up and just bloody do it!"

Amazed to hear her swear, he did it.

Screeching like a banshee, Rosa arched against him and he gasped, the strength she had was incredible, almost pushing him over.

"Help her, Jesamiah."

He shuffled on his buttocks to make himself more comfortable, his bent legs to either side of the woman's shuddering body, his arms encircling beneath her breasts; braced, as straining, she again thrust her weight into him.

"When this contraction ends I am going to find out what is wrong," Tiola said to both him and Rosa, while swabbing her hand and arm with the glistening oil from the bottle and folding back the woman's petticoats to expose her lower half. With her hand, Tiola briefly made the gesture Jesamiah had seen before, saw her lips breath the sighing sound, *"Hie-asssh..."*

The woman relaxed, her head folding on to Jesamiah's shoulder, the torment for a moment seeping from her. The quiet was noticeable, now she had stopped yelling.

He shut his eyes, to protect Rosa's modesty or his own squeamishness he was not sure. Opened them again when she threw herself back into him with a long, piercing shriek, as another contraction poured through her. This was like holding a bucking helm in a storm; needed strength and concentration to keep on a steady course.

"Your waters have not broken, Rosa." Tiola said, cleaning her soiled hand in the water and sitting back on her heels. "Until they do, the babe cannot be born."

Dripping with sweat, breathless, unable to speak, Rosa lifted her hand, indicating she understood. Jesamiah merely looked blank.

"I am going to pierce the babe's bed, there will be a lot of fluid, so do not be concerned, it will be nothing amiss." Tiola said to Jesamiah.

He bit his lip, uncertain. "Then what?"

Tiola smiled at him as she padded towels beneath Rosa. "Then we deliver this good lady of her son or daughter."

Despite the warning Jesamiah was not prepared for the mess. A gush of bloodied water flooding everywhere. "You ought to have taken that gown off," he admonished Tiola. "You've ruined the silk."

"Damn the gown ... *ais,* we have it... I can see the head. A few more pushes, dear heart... one more... it is coming... Careful, ah careful, gain your breath."

With the waters broken the pain had eased, for Rosa was now pushing with the steady contractions, not against. She no longer screamed but bore down, her face red and contorted, her head flung back on to Jesamiah's shoulder, her teeth bared,

Tiola took her hand, guided her fingers to where the crown of the babe's head was emerging.

"I want a son," Rosa said, panting and laughing both together, before the next wave of labouring spasm overwhelmed her. Her shriek became a shout, "I have daughters – I want a son!"

Jesamiah leant into her next contraction taking her weight, his arms supporting. He looked down, also elated, caught so unexpectedly within this woman's world usually held secret from men. "By God, I can see it!"

"One more big push now, Rosa," Tiola said, gathering up a clean linen towel.

Excited, Jesamiah urged, at the top of his voice to match Rosa's own shout, "Come on woman, you heard what she said!"

And they were howling laughter and crying tears, together, all three of them, Tiola kneeling there, holding the new born, unlacing Rosa's bodice, lifting the wailing child to her breast. "Your son!"

"Look at him!" Jesamiah exclaimed in wonder, hardly daring to believe this miracle of a perfect new life. "So small! Look at his hands! His toes – his tackle! Hell's balls, he's going to please the ladies when he's grown!" He spoke with elated pride, as if the boy was his own son. Looked up, caught Tiola smiling at him. "Blimey Sweetheart, that was wonderful!"

His face fell serious, gazed at her in respectful awe. "You were wonderful."

She laughed, knotted thread around the cord and offered him her knife. "Cut it, here. Once this is done he will have to make his own way in life. I was nothing of the sort. Women go into labour every day, midwives such as myself help them everyday, in every country of the world."

Jesamiah cut, was happy to help Rosa begin cleaning the babe with the warm water Tiola brought them. "Tell he's a boy," he grinned. "Covered in muck and filth. Had he been a girl I'd have expected the hair to be curled in neat little ringlets and tied in pink ribbon." He repeated what he had said. "You were wonderful, Tiola. Bella said your gift of healing was to be cherished, not feared. I see what she means."

Ah, so he has been downstairs. Tiola thought.

"She also said I was a damned fool."

"Oh yes? Look away, Luvver," Tiola said as she pushed down on Rosa's abdomen. "There are some things, the babe's nest, even a pirate would not care to see."

He did look, briefly, but turned his head quickly away as something foul and bloody was expelled.

"And what else did Bella say?" Tiola jibed, tempted to spread the afterbirth out in front of him to check it was intact. Subtle revenge?

"Nothing much," Jesamiah admitted wrinkling his nose, disgusted, as she lifted the bloodied thing and carried it to a bucket. "I came back here. Fell asleep."

Passed out was nearer the truth, but he was not going to be admitting that. Nor was he going to admit Bella had kept the gold coin.

Half an hour later, dropping the last of the soiled towels onto the heap he had made, Jesamiah grinned at Tiola as she emerged from the smaller room.

"Rosa is asleep. The poor dear is exhausted," she said, wiping her sleeve over her forehead. She had removed the ruined silk of her best, her only, formal gown, to dress more comfortably in bodice, petticoat and overskirt. She draped her sodden stockings beside the hearth to dry and sank into the chair beside the fire which he had chivvied into life, spread her bare toes to its warmth. Was pleased to note the kettle was beginning to sing.

Jesamiah thought she looked exhausted also, but there was no point in stating the obvious. "I have washed the floor where it was stained. Anything else I can do for you, Sweetheart?"

"Thank you for helping. A lot of men would not have done what you did." She smiled, her beautiful, enigmatic smile. "Especially not a pirate."

He shrugged. "Didn't have much choice did I? Where is Jenna?"

Leaning forward Tiola swung the kettle off the rakencrock. "Do you want coffee? I can make some."

"No. Where's Jenna?"

The baby, settled in a drawer for a makeshift crib, whimpered.

"She is not here."

"I can see that. Where is she?" Jesamiah collected the boy up, wrapping one of Tiola's shawls around him, jiggled him tenderly in his arms. "And where are those rather lovely emeralds you were wearing when you left here some hours ago?"

He had noticed their disappearance almost from the first moment she had walked in. A sudden thought. Alarmed, he said, "You are unharmed? Nothing has happened?" Pirates were not the only thieves in Cape Town.

Tiola gazed at the crackling flames. Her Craft had alerted her to come home, if it had not she would be on the beach still, walking and thinking. But Craft had its own way of working these things which other people would call fate. She had been so relieved to discover her summoning had not been because of Jesamiah himself. She sighed, studied her hands. "Jenna is disgusted with me. She remained at the ball, it ends at dawn. I walked home."

"Oh? And why would that be?" The baby stopped his whimpering; snuffling, contented in Jesamiah's strong arms he drifted asleep.

"Because I returned Stefan's gifts. He asked me to become his wife and I refused."

"Ah." Jesamiah made a half-hearted attempt not to grin.

"Jenna said I was a fool, and she would have nothing more to do with me."

"Ah," Jesamiah said again. "I think you are a fool too. That makes both of us fools don't it?"

"Do you really want to hold the babe?" Tiola said rising and offering to take the child. Amused, added as he shook his head and settled the baby himself. "I declare, Jesamiah Acorne, you have gone quite broody!"

"*Oakwood*. I am now the respectable Captain Jesamiah Oakwood. It appears the acorn has matured and is no longer a sapling. Or a pirate." How his mother would have approved! "*Great oak trees from little acorns grow*." He could almost hear her saying it.

Tiola tipped her head on one side, quizzical.

"I've decided to make an honest man of m'self."

"Oh? And what brought this on?"

Jesamiah tucked the shawl around the tiny body, satisfied himself the baby was content. Stood, put his hands on Tiola's shoulders.

"You did," he said. "It goes with this, your birthday present."

Tiola glanced out of the partially shuttered window, it was still dark but midnight was long past. "That was yesterday."

"So, I am a day late." He removed the signet ring from his finger, slipped it on to hers. "As soon as I can I will purchase something of a better fit. A diamond if you want it." He grinned cheekily. "Anything except an emerald."

She stared at the gold band swamping her marriage finger. "I do not want a diamond," she said, lifting her eyes to capture his. "I want only you."

Very gently he kissed her, nothing intrusive, nothing demanding. Her arms encircled his neck as she kissed him back.

"And I want to make love to you," he said, moving very slightly away from her so he did not appear threatening or intrusive. "If you will let me."

For answer, Tiola also stepped back, her hands going to the pins in her hair. She pulled them out, dropped them to the floor letting her black mane tumble from its formal confinement. Then she unlaced her bodice and pushing it from her shoulders exposed her breasts.

Jesamiah's callused hands, rough against her smooth skin, spanned her waist, slid up her back and then fondled their soft swell. He bent, ran his tongue over her nipples, his breath coming faster, needing her. Aware he must not do anything stupid, not again, he moved upward to nuzzle her neck, delighting in her smell and feel.

She gave a small moan of pleasure, gently put his head back to a breast. And he knew he could not wait. Hooking his thumbs into the waist band of her skirt he skilfully undressed her, savoured her beauty for a moment - pulled off his shirt, dragged the belt and sash from his waist and removed boots, breeches and stockings almost in the same movement. Lifted her, carried her to the bed.

"I won't hurt you," he promised, lying beside her and holding her lovely warm body against his nakedness. "I'll go slow, gentle."

Tiola shook her head, that was not what she wanted. She needed his roughness, needed him to possess her so she could lose the stifling arrogance of Stefan van Overstratten's assumptions and the patronising disdain of his friends. Wanted to play the harlot for this one night. If it hurt, what was a moment of passing discomfort compared to a lifetime of love?

Still unwilling to inflict pain he hesitated, but she curved her hand around his erect penis and guided him in; enjoying the sensation of feeling him slide into her, his erotic kisses on her mouth, neck and breasts easing aside the small involuntary intake of breath as he took her from girl to woman.

He murmured an apology. "Sorry love, I tried to be careful."

Her own kiss, lingering on his mouth was her response, and tightening her arms around his waist she rolled her hips as his breathing quickened and his rhythmic movements became more demanding. His lovemaking was never selfish though. Moving his hand lower, he used his fingers to heighten her pleasure and she arched her back to take him in deeper. He groaned something about not being able to belay it any longer, and as she ran her hand down his spine he gasped, pushed harder, shuddered.

At some time in the past, the full when and the where of it's happening not yet revealed, their souls had briefly met and touched but had not become bound together. This joining, this linking through their intimate coupling was forever. The act of love uniting soul with soul, her Craft absorbing a part of him into herself as he emptied his seed within her. Soul mates mated. Through love become inseparable, unless some future force of malevolence should attempt to shatter their unity and leave them bereft.

When Jenna returned an hour after sun up, her angry disappointment had mellowed. Stefan had convinced her he was not offended by the rebuttal, that indeed his admiration for Miss Tiola had increased threefold with the display of her charming modesty and lack of desire for wealth and luxury. Had assured Jenna he would ask again in a week or two, after Miss Oldstagh had become accustomed to the idea.

But there would be no asking again. Jenna found a strange woman asleep in her bed, a new-born babe snuggled in a drawer before the embers of the fire, and Tiola and Jesamiah curled together, smiling and contented in sleep.

Thirty One

A wind howled along the Rappahannock River and whipped across the cemetery on the open part of the hillside above the house. It was only a small graveyard with a handful of grass-covered mounds. Considering it was late April in Virginia, the sun ought to be shining and the dull earth bursting with life. Winter had been long and tedious however, and spring seemed to be dawdling like a woman before her mirror, reluctant to show herself in public until she looked her best.

Three-day old dead babies did not need elaborate caskets. The grave was small, no larger than two feet or so. If Phillipe had had his way even the plain wooden box would not have been necessary. Wrap the disgusting thing in a sack and fling it into a hole. He stared across the grave at Alicia, swathed in the black of mourning, tears speckling her cheeks. Stupid woman. If she so wanted brats he could easily give her more. And the next one he would ensure to be his. This one, the sickly, puking girl, might not have been. Phillipe was not a fool, he could count to nine. Alicia had insisted the babe was full term, had come late. But why, then, did it not have hair or fingernails? Why was the thing so small and weak? They could have dressed it in a poppet doll's clothes, for goodness sake! Oh, he had no doubt who had fathered the child, but he had no proof of it and he could not risk losing face before his neighbours, or losing Alicia's fortune, so he stood here in the cold wind feigning grief.

Phillipe shut his ears to the monotonous bumble of the parson droning on, let his mind drift to the sea voyage he was to undertake next week. He was to go to Alicia's Barbados plantation – normally he would have made the trip already but her condition of pregnancy had prevented it. Not that her breeding concerned him, but it would have looked bad in the eyes of the community were he to leave her for a month or so at such a time. Aside, the delay had been providential. A Dutchman wanted to increase his trade options, Phillipe was to meet him in the Caribbean to discuss terms.

The trade would be useful but his overseer could have handled the negotiations. It was master van Overstratten Phillipe wanted to meet. He came from Cape Town where Jesamiah Acorne had been seen, and disappeared, last December. The letter sent by Phillipe's hired agent had informed him that Acorne was believed dead. But no corpse had been found and until he was convinced of it, he was determined to keep looking. Maybe, just maybe, this Dutchman knew something about him? Or could find out?

Jesamiah's arrival here at the plantation all those years ago had been the final ruin of Phillipe's life. Aged only five he had been unable to understand why his mother had suddenly gone away. And then, within a few days, his father had gone too, sailing away in his ship, leaving his son in the indifferent, abusive care of servants. The slaps, the withheld food – the hours locked in the cellar – all because he cried or wet the bed, wanting his mother, aching for his father. And when one of the men, a stable hand, had befriended him? Huh! The innocence of childhood!

Two years later when Papa at last came home he had expected everything to be alright again, except his father had not been alone. He was damned if he would accept a new, replacement mother! He was supposed to be overjoyed? Well he wasn't. When he was rude to her, shouted or showed off, he was punished for it. His backside whipped or sent to his room. And then, when the brat who was his brother began to grow and his irritating presence became unbearable, Phillipe had made the pleasing discovery that Jesamiah was the one person he could pinch and poke and dominate. As the child's fear grew, so Phillipe's spite swelled with it. His one regret? Those years later when they had buried Papa here in this graveyard, he ought to have burned that damned boat with his bastard brother in it.

As for her, that second wife, the day after he had thrown Jesamiah off the plantation he had ordered her bones disinterred and thrown into the midden.

One day, and one day soon he promised himself, Jesamiah's bones would also moulder there.

~ *Tiola* ~

"The shell that is my body is new,
but not the knowledge I carry and use within it.
In that, I am as ageless as you."

- One -

Tethys stirred, her presence swirling the currents as she travelled the vast loneliness of the bottom of the oceans. And as she passed, her shadow churned the debris of her accumulated trophies; the decomposing bone and flesh of once living things, lifting the rotting carcass of a whale, moving the mouldering flukes which were once its tail as if the creature were still alive. Rocking the hull of a ship torn in half, its single remaining mast pointing forlornly towards the far distant light as if imploring the sun to beat down upon the splintered and jagged decks once more. The tattered sails waved like swaying weed, and the empty eyes of the dead, her crew, stared, unburied and forsaken.

Tethys was alone among the dead. Her many daughters had gone and there was no other like her. She was the sea, she was the ocean, and only in places did she touch her sister the land or her brother the air, but they all despised her greed and were indifferent to her loneliness.

She did not mind her solitude, but sometimes, sometimes, the desolation overwhelmed her and she had the urge to rise to the surface and make her presence felt among the humans who dwelt within the sight and the sound of the sea. She was searching for him, for one man in particular, the one she wanted as her own.

And where she reached with her senses, the winds of the world captured her scent and filled the night air with the smell of the sea and the sound of her desolation as she touched the shore and called to him.

~ Jessh..a..miah? Jessh..a..miah? ~

*

Leaning on the wall at the end of Grope Lane, watching the passageway intersecting the frontage of Bella Dubois' property, Jesamiah wondered how in Heaven he was going to tell Tiola what he had done. Drop a few hints? Wait, let her find out for herself? Walk in, come straight out with it? "*Tiola. You are not going to like this; I have something to tell you.*"

A squeal of Amber-Rose's high-pitched laughter swept through the open front door opposite, followed by a man's deeper guffaw and Bella's barked amusement.

Jesamiah smoothed his moustache and fiddled with his earring. Gone were the ribbons, the shabby seaman's clothes. He still wore a sash but it was of expensive silk not rough-dyed cotton. His coat and the clothes beneath were new-made of fine material, he had even taken to wearing cotton drawers beneath his breeches. The only old, familiar, things were his pistol and cutlass. And the earring.

With his money he and Tiola could easily have afforded better lodgings but both were content to remain above Bella's, although there had been concessions. Jesamiah had bought a larger bed and a comfortable chair in which he could happily sprawl, with Tiola curled on his lap.

She had made him have a bath. At the time, seven months ago in late December, he had not remembered when he had last had one. He shaved and washed his face, usually daily, but for more than that a sluice with a bucket of seawater had sufficed twice a week, or a swim if they were ashore and careening, every two or three months or so.

That first morning together he had made leisurely love to her again; she, awakening to the new pleasures and sensations he conjured from her body with his hands and tongue, he, delighting in her response. And for the first time, ever, not having to pay someone to appreciate his acquired skills. His euphoria deflated, later in the day, when she told him he stank.

Ignoring his protests Tiola had appropriated Bella's copper-lined tub, while Bella herself had sailed in and out to exchange various tattled gossip, calling him dear, and seeming not to notice his nakedness, which had foolishly disconcerted him slightly. Tiola had giggled, unabashed had stripped to join him in the hot water. From then on the novelty of bathing had become a more regular - and interesting - occurrence.

His hands tucked beneath his armpits for warmth, he smiled at the sensuous delight of sharing a bath with a beautiful young lady. Bella, coming in with towels had said, "*Never yet seen a man and a woman take a bath together without more water ending up on the floor than in the tub.*" The smile broadened as he felt a twinge of arousal at the erotic memory. He and Tiola had not wasted his upright eagerness.

Tiola. How did he tell her?

He had been ashore these many months and he was aching for the sea. He was trying not to, desperately trying to enjoy this new life on land. Tiola he loved, but wherever he went in Cape Town he could hear the roll of the surf driven in by the wind, smell it, see it. He missed the roll of a deck beneath his feet, missed the familiar rumble of an anchor cable, the creak of timbers, the booming crack of unfurling canvas. Awake or asleep a need of the sea was pulling him as strongly as drink or laudanum whined at a dependent.

He hunched his coat tighter, the wind, hurtling northward from the southern polar region of Antarctica sent icy gusts swirling along the cobbles and shivering down his back. As a seaman he appreciated a lively wind, as a man standing ten minutes before midnight in a windblown street trying to decide what to do, he did not.

Tiola did not agree with his gambling. She did not like him going into the taverns either, but he did so most evenings when she was out delivering a child or nursing someone sick, or setting a broken arm, or whatever she did when called hurriedly away.

Usually, he would escort her to where she had to go, ensure there was always someone to see her home again and pursue his own entertainment. Trying to suppress the increasing boredom he drank rum, played cards.

This July night had started out as nothing unusual, except for the person he had played against. Jesamiah was not expert at cards, played because he enjoyed it, because it did not matter if he won or lost. What he lost one day he usually won back the next; his strategy was to never go out with too much silver in his pocket and never to bet more than what he carried. This game had been different; his opponent had been the Dutchman, Stefan van Overstratten and the modest stakes had risen higher than either of them could afford to lose.

Jesamiah sighed again, his thoughts returning to what had happened. Hoping that something would inspire him to find the courage he needed to tell her...

The suspicion that van Overstratten had not walked into the *Golden Hind* tavern by coincidence alone, was uppermost in Jesamiah's mind as he watched the Dutchman remove his cloak and absently hand it to a servant. He shook the spatter of rain from his hat and turned to speak to a group of people he obviously knew well. With about thirty men present, some sitting quiet contemplating their cards in the gaming room, others, like Jesamiah, propping up the bar, the place was not as busy as usual. Perhaps because of the rain and the biting chill of the wind, or did most men have nagging wives or pretty mistresses to keep them within-doors?

Tossing a few coins on to the counter, Jesamiah picked up his drink and sauntered across the room to one of the empty card tables, grinned as a loud cheer from the far corner announced a delighted win for someone. The wood panelling and low beamed ceiling made the place dark, with each table a separate island of yellow light. As he sat, the potboy brought a new candle, removed the sagging old one with its grotesque trail of wax. This was the only room where there were no mirrors to enhance the glow of candle and lantern. Mirrors in a card room were not popular.

With a half smile Jesamiah watched van Overstratten surreptitiously preen before one of the several full-length looking glasses in the outer room. Knew the Dutchman would come to join him. There had been something in the way he had looked around as he stood a step or two inside the door, a pretence at casually observing who was there, his gaze lingering a fraction too long on Jesamiah. In return Jesamiah's gaze did not leave the Dutchman, following his every move for twenty minutes or so as he accepted wine, made polite conversation.

Waving aside one man well into his cups who wanted to play, Jesamiah waited, patient.

"I hear you have been away for a few months," he said laconically as Stefan finally wandered over, and feigned surprise at seeing him sitting there. "I cannot say we have particularly missed you."

"A business venture," Stefan answered, indicating with his hand whether he may take the empty seat.

"Successful?"

"I think so. Most profitable. How fares Miss Oldstagh? She is well I trust?" Stefan clicked his fingers, called for new cards and wine, rum for Jesamiah.

"She is very well."

"Breeding yet?"

"Not yet."

Van Overstratten made no answer, lit a cheroot from the candle flame, the blue, aromatic smoke drifting into Jesamiah's face, then he shuffled the cards, dealt. They played three hands Jesamiah winning two, the little pile of silver on the table accumulating.

After the fourth, a win for van Overstratten making the evening equal, the Dutchman said, "Would you consider playing for something more worthy of a wager?"

"Such as?"

Blowing a perfect smoke ring van Overstratten answered glibly, "Name it. Ask for anything you would have of me. I am a rich man; if it is mine to give then it will be my stake."

Aware he was being manipulated, that Stefan was too easygoing with this air of congenial charm, Jesamiah called his bluff. "I'll have the fine three masted, square-rigged in the harbour. The one you brought back from Antigua."

The Dutchman blanched, the muscle at the corner of his eye beginning to tick in agitation. To his credit he recovered quickly, protesting with a false chuckle, "She is new, sir, built in London only last year."

Folding his arms on the card table and leaning forward, Jesamiah leered, "I know. I inspected her from mast-head to bilge day before yesterday."

Stefan's nostrils flared. Whoever had been responsible for allowing this wretch aboard would be flogged and dismissed from service, the entire crew, from captain to cabin boy if necessary. Massaging his clean-shaven chin to hide his annoyance the Dutchman considered the request. It was unreasonable, of course, which was why this scoundrel had suggested it. He lit another cheroot, came to a decision.

"Very well. On condition you agree my choice."

Jesamiah shrugged, had expected such a reply. "Name it."

Stretching the anticipation Stefan called for the pot boy to replenish their drinks, waited until it was served then also folded his arms and said, quiet and ominous, "I know who you are Jesamiah Oakwood, or should I call you Acorne? I also know what you are. I have known these past weeks. Since I returned home however, I have said nothing out of respect for Miss Oldstagh, whom I greatly admire."

Ah, so that is the game we are playing, Jesamiah thought. *Hangman's Noose.* A sardonic smile tilted the side of his mouth, "You have said nothing before now because you have suspicion but no proof. Even here in Cape Town a man must be tried and convicted before he hangs, and for that you require evidence I b'lieve."

He could not be certain this weasel did not have the evidence, although it was unlikely. Not unless van Overstratten had discovered several reputable people who could swear before God to his identity as a pirate - and if he had, he would not have waited. Once they had careened and provisioned, most captains and ships' officers did not linger in foreign harbours while a fresh wind was blowing and a tide was running. To a merchantman time and tide was money.

"I do not require evidence. It would be a simple thing to be rid of you, but I am not a murderer who thinks nothing of spilling another man's blood. Unlike you, I am a man of honour."

Bullshit, Jesamiah thought, sitting passive, with no outward reaction. *You do not want me murdered because you want to crow the glory of capturing a notorious pirate.* He sipped his rum, had another thought. *Or is it that you do not want to lose Tiola's favour? As you surely would were you to be the man responsible for my hanging.*

"And as a man of honour I shall give you fair chance to avoid the gallows." Van Overstratten picked up the playing cards, his eyes returning to Jesamiah's face. "I shall speak plain. I want you gone. I therefore name as my stake," he paused, shuffled the cards, and feigned the impression of giving the matter some thought, although it was obvious he had planned much of this days ago. "If you lose, you leave Cape Town. There is a brig in harbour, she sails on the morrow's noontide for England. You will leave alone. If you do not leave I shall instruct the Governor to have you arrested and once within the fort's rat-infested dungeons I shall make certain you do not see daylight until the day you hang. And hang, Captain Acorne, you shall."

Expression unconcerned, thoughts racing, Jesamiah ignored the cards the Dutchman was dealing. He tipped his chair, balancing on the two rear legs. "You still want Tiola for yourself then? I admire your fortitude. She'll not have you though, even if I am not here." Curiosity getting the better of him, added. "Why her? Why not have any loose-in-the-rump doxy to bed with? I've seen a few who would wash up pretty enough."

Several of Bella's girls for instance, were handsome, although they did not possess a degree of intelligence between them. Amber-Rose was lovely to look at, useless to talk to. But then, men did not pay whores for the pleasure of intellectual conversation.

Dealing the last card and placing the excess of the pack in the centre of the table, Stefan waved his hand in a flippant attitude, a ring on his finger sparkling in the light of the candles. "I require a legitimate son to inherit my fortune I therefore need a wife to provide me with one. Were I to send to Holland I risk getting a hag or a simpleton." He visibly shuddered. Van Overstratten was a man who took pleasure from possessing beautiful things; his apparel, his house, his ships. He would not contemplate a wife who did not have a striking beauty, and Tiola Oldstagh, although she scampered around the town clad like a street urchin on occasion, was undeniably beautiful now she had matured into womanhood.

Dropping his chair on to all four legs Jesamiah said crudely, "And you want Tiola, even though she has been fornicating with a pirate?"

Stefan picked up his cards. "I have no objection to making use of soiled goods, Mr Acorne, if they are the goods I desire. She suits my purpose, providing she does not carry the pox or drop a bastard, which you have apparently in all these months not managed to sire. I am certain I can perform where you have been limp and lacking."

Reacting against the insult Jesamiah's hand fell towards where his cutlass should be, but weapons were not permitted within the gentleman's clubrooms of the *Golden Hind*. He took several calming breaths, reminding himself van Overstratten was deliberately goading him. Why Tiola? Because the Dutchman could not tolerate someone having something he wanted. He was like Phillipe, obsessed with getting his own way and caring nothing for who or what he crushed beneath his boot in the process.

"And if I win?"

Studying his cards, Stefan did not answer immediately, when he did he spoke in a tone implying the suggestion was absurd. "If you win?" He looked up, "Then you sail away on my ship, again, apart from a scratch crew, alone, and on the morrow's noontide. I shall make no attempt to stop you."

Smiling, his expression displaying no hint of friendship, Jesamiah answered, "Win or lose you are asking me to leave?"

Stefan blew another perfect smoke ring. "No, Captain Acorne. I am not asking. I am *telling*."

Jesamiah picked up his cards, did not look at them, his steadfast gaze not leaving the Dutchman's face for perhaps half of a minute. Saying nothing he looked at the cards in his hands, began arranging them into suits, said at last, "And how do I trust you?"

"You trust me because you have no choice. I am a man of my word and my word can be taken either way." Stefan shrugged one shoulder. "Win or lose you will be gone; cross me, you will hang."

"And does Tiola not have a say in all this?" Jesamiah asked, considering which card to play. He set the deuce down.

Van Overstratten laid his first card, the tres. "She is a woman several years short of the age of mature independence. She is not entitled to a say."

Jesamiah did not agree, but held his silence. Played.

- Two -

Puffing air through his cheeks, Jesamiah again glanced up at the window to their room. The shutters were closed, a flicker of light showing through. It could be Jenna there of course, Tiola may still be at that birthing although she had expected to return before midnight.

How to tell her?

~ *If you stand here much longer my luvver, you will find lichen growing on your boots come morning.* ~ Tiola's voice clear and resonant, unspoken, sounded in his thoughts not his ears.

He yelped, spun around his hand automatically going to his cutlass. "Hell's tits woman do not come up behind me like that! You nigh on frightened the shite out of me!" He rammed the cutlass back into its scabbard and scowled. Even Tiola coming up, silent, behind him evoked echoes of his childhood. "I have only been here a few minutes."

"Over an hour. I have been watching you," she spoke aloud this time, a soft smile on her face. It was useful to be able to put words direct into his mind like a lovers secretive and intimate touch. "What's wrong?" Sensing his brooding disquiet she slid her arms around his waist. His breath smelt of rum, his clothes of tobacco smoke.

Pulling her close into the warmth of his coat Jesamiah said nothing, held her, his chin resting on her head. He might have guessed she would know.

"I think I have done something foolish, Sweetheart," he admitted after a moment of quiet. "Well, damned stupid, actually."

"You lost at cards? You have gambled away your entire fortune?"

"No love, the fortune is safe." Who gave a damn about fortunes? Where one came from there was always another. On impulse he took her hand, started walking. "Come with me, I cannot tell you here. Not like this."

On occasion Tiola regretted not having the ability to eavesdrop on another's thoughts but secretive intrusion was not permitted. With one of her own kind, communicating by thought alone was natural and usual, but there were few who held the Craft. She smiled to herself as they walked. She often knew what Jesamiah was thinking anyway. It did not always require skill; the lust in his eye and the bulge in his breeches, anyone could interpret!

His fingers locked around hers, he said nothing. He walked her to the harbour, a sickle moon rode between the rushing clouds, the wind stinging their faces made their eyes water. Took her on to the jetty near the tree-lined canal, stood holding her close gazing at the vessels moving restlessly against the restraint of their anchors. A brig, a sloop and two Dutch East Indiamen – he snorted ironically, one was the *Christina Giselle* on her way home from the far China Seas. Had her captain been van Overstratten's source of information? Possible, but unlikely.

The air was heavy with the smell of the sea, the aroma of wet canvas and fresh tar, the odour of decaying seaweed and rotting fish.

"You are missing the sea aren't you?" Tiola said, nestling deeper into his warmth. "It calls to you; a lost child whimpering for its mother."

He did not have the courage to answer immediately but his fingers tightened around hers. "I come down here most nights to see what ships are at anchor. Who is here."

"Watching for Rue and the *Inheritance?*"

"Not really." Jesamiah sighed, there was no headway in lies. "Aye. Watching for Rue, hoping he might one day pass by." He pointed to a dark-hulled sloop anchored to the edge of all the others. "That one is a pirate craft."

"How can you tell?" She peered up at him, at the wistful longing etched in his face, aching in his voice. "Looks the same as any ship to me."

"Boat. She ain't a ship."

"There is a difference?" Tiola frowned at him, astonished.

Giving her a quick, affectionate kiss Jesamiah answered. "As a rough rule any vessel that don't have three masts is a boat."

Tiola asked again when he said nothing more. "So? How do you know that *boat* is a pirate?"

He shrugged. To him it was obvious. "Small things, details. The name across her stern has been re-painted, her anchor cable is rotten; few merchant captains allow slovenliness. Pirates are not concerned if cordage and cables rot, we can always get more."

She noted the use of the word '*we*'.

"See her sails? Not neatly furled are they? Decks are probably a disgrace too. I'd wager her keel is full of teredo worm, most of the planking eaten away as they bore inward. Her crew's here to find a replacement vessel."

Tiola tugged playfully at his short beard, laughed. "The rest I grant you have deduced from experience, but how can you possibly know they are looking for another boat?"

He chuckled, lifted her hand kissed each individual finger. "I don't, not for certain; it's what I would do were she mine."

"I suppose you would commandeer the *Christina Giselle*?"

"Good grief Sweetheart, no! Far too big! The best pirate craft are fast and manoeuvrable, shallow on the draught. The brig, for instance, or the three masted square-rigged warped alongside the far jetty."

"The ship – she has three masts, that makes her a ship? The one with the bosomed lady as a figurehead?"

"Aye. Grand ain't she?"

Tiola was uncertain whether he referred to the ship or the figurehead with her bold, bare chest. Jesamiah had a fondness for a plump bosom, although her breasts were small and almost insignificant. She smiled to herself, what she lacked in size she more than made up for in enthusiasm.

"Ain't she?" he queried again, giving Tiola a nudge with his elbow.

"*Ais.*" She was.

"She's mine." There. He had said it.

Silence.

Quickly he said, "All above board, all legal. I'll have her papers signed to me by noon on the morrow." He glanced up at the sky to where the moon sailed, corrected himself. "Noon today."

"You bought her?" A chill in her tone as iced as the blowing wind.

"Er, no. I won her. Playing cards."

Suddenly wary, angry, Tiola released her hold of him. "Against whom?"

"Does it matter? Is it relevant?" This was not going well.

To stop herself from slapping him, Tiola moved further away. Did it matter? No it did not. He had a ship, he wanted to go back to sea. He had every right to do as he pleased. Furious she retorted, "Yes it bloody does matter!"

When in the wrong, shout. Lose your temper. Jesamiah shouted back at her. "Stefan van bloody Overstratten, if you must know!"

"Tethys! You can be such an idiot at times Jesamiah!"

"What? Me? He wanted to raise the stakes, not me! Not my soddin' fault if he is as useless at cards as he is at everything else!"

"He is not useless at cards, he is an excellent player. You think of him as a dull-witted fop because that is how you want to see him, but he is not. He is a clever man, one of the most competent and agile-minded in Cape Town." Her agitation was rising. "He is setting a trap Jesamiah, a trap which will end with a noose around your neck - and you have stupidly stepped right into it! Do you seriously think he will stand aside and let you take his ship?"

No, he did not think that. He knew Van Overstratten had deliberately let him win. The Dutchman had known the pirate in him would not resist the challenge of setting sail. Jesamiah would never have left Cape Town had he lost, not on the back of a mere threat - but the lure of a beautiful ship? Tiola was right. Van Overstratten was a clever man.

"Traps are only traps when you do not know they are there, Tiola."

"He will *not* honour a game of cards, *nor* will he hand papers over to you Jesamiah."

Jesamiah was well aware van Overstratten would not honour any of it. He had no proof of his winnings, no witnesses. Even if he did, who would believe him, a pirate, over the word of a respected and wealthy merchant? Opening his mouth to shout at her, to jibe she was being unreasonable he shut it abruptly, spread his hands, tried again; swallowed, took another breath and said quietly. "I do not need papers, Sweetheart. I've never had any before."

Tiola stared at him, disappointment and despair clouding her face. She turned on her heel and walked away without looking back.

- Three -

Through what was left of the night he held her, so very tight, her face buried in his shoulder. He had followed her home, apologised, taken her to bed and made love to her. Praying it would not be for the last time. And afterwards, she had wrapped her arms around him and wept.

"Come with me," he finally said, stroking her hair. "Come with me? Please?"

"I cannot."

"You can. We can go anywhere you want, Tiola. Anywhere. That is the freedom a ship gives you. You choose we will go there. The East Indies, the West - Cornwall. I will take you home to see your brothers."

Tempting but unwise.

During their first breathless days of being together she had told him of her past; of her grandfather's farm and her eight brothers. Jesamiah's arms fiercely protective as she had found the courage to admit things she had tried to forget. What her father had attempted to do to her, and how her mother had died. Listening in silence, he had comforted her while she grieved, realising why his first intrusive kiss had so frightened her. Swallowing down the sickness curdling in his stomach, he had held her close – oh he knew what it was to fear someone! And hanging? Slow strangulation was a bad end for a man, but for a woman? No woman, whatever she had done, deserved such a death.

In return he had talked of his parents and the Virginia tobacco plantation. Told her of Phillipe, making light of the misery his brother had made of his childhood. Beyond speaking of Rue and Malachias Taylor, his friends, had said nothing of his life as a pirate and she had not asked. Had not wanted to hear of the men he had killed or the women he had bedded.

After the sharing of her secret Tiola had never cried again, not even after the disagreements they occasionally had, when Jesamiah lost his temper and shouted. Went banging out of the door and thundering down the stairs in search of a tavern and a drink. Always coming home again before midnight with an apology and a loving kiss.

He wondered now, here with her in their bed and watching the dawn mature, whether Phillipe had some connection with van Overstratten. The Dutchman was principally a merchant trader, although he had fingers dipped into many pies. Partially he dismissed the idea. Phillipe sold tobacco to England. Ah, but what of the sugar plantation belonging to Alicia? Stefan had just returned from the Caribbean. Coincidence? Either way, perhaps it was the right time to be moving on from Cape Town.

"Sail with me," he said, pressing his body closer, his hands smoothing over her skin. "I want you to be with me aboard the *Sea Witch*."

"*Sea Witch*?"

"I'm renaming her. For you."

She snuggled her head into the cradle of his neck, her mass of black hair draping over the red scar that had been the pistol shot. "You are a pirate and I am a healer. How can the two mix Jesamiah? Our lives are as opposite as salt and sweet."

Cape Town was her home the only sanctuary she knew, the world out there frightened her. How could she leave? "And what of Jenna? And my work?"

"Jenna is capable of caring for herself. I will leave her an endowment. As for the other, I remember you once said, '*Women go into labour every day, midwives such as myself help them every day, in every country of the world*'."

"Did I say that?"

"You did."

He kissed her, long and lingering. "You will come? I do not have to be a pirate, I can do other things." He could not think what, would worry on it later.

"*Ais,*" she answered, making her decision, Cape Town was her home but Jesamiah was her life. "Yes, I will come with you."

Aroused, he made love to her again, more urgent this time, more possessive. Then he left the warm hollow of the bed and dressed. He had made his plans leaning against the wall in Grope lane, knew exactly how he was going to outwit Stefan van bloody Overstratten.

"You must be on the jetty by noon Tiola," he said, draping his baldric across his shoulder, settling the cutlass comfortable into place at his hip. "Once I have gone aboard I will not be able to wait. If I do I'll be a dead man." He emphasised the point. "By noon."

"I will be there."

He thrust his pistol through his sash. Going to the clothes chest, rummaged for his ribbons, laced two into his hair. He had not worn them for these seven months ashore. "Bring nothing, only what you stand in."

She balked. "My books, my things..."

"I will buy you new books and better things in Madagascar."

"Madagascar?"

"Aye, we'll be there a month or so, refitting her."

"As a pirate ship?"

Not wanting to lie he ducked the question, walked to the bed, kissed her. "Be there. Noon."

Four

Jenna stood with her fists bunched, knuckles pressed into her hips. She had never been so angry with the Tiola before. "You leave here with that good-for-nothing wastrel over my dead body young lady!"

Tiola folded the shawl around the small bundle on her bed, knotted it securely. Despite what Jesamiah had said there were some things she had to take with her. Her personal needs for instance. Men did not think of these things; the necessities for dealing with her monthly flux; a block of soap. She doubted he would have any of *that* on board!

"You are to be provided for. There is money in the bank for you, Jesamiah is to have arranged it this morning. I am sorry, I am going. I am fond of you and I am grateful for all you have done, but it is Jesamiah I love."

"Do you seriously think van Overstratten will permit him to leave?"

No, Tiola did not think that, neither did Jesamiah. He had not told her his plan but he had one, and until now his schemes usually worked. And if she was to admit the truth? The thought of stealing away beneath Stefan's nose excited her.

"I would rather go with your blessing than without it, Jenna," Tiola spread her hands, fighting back her tears. "There is nothing you can do to stop me, though."

Defeated, Jenna slumped into the chair before the fire, her face in her hands, her shoulders shaking from where she wept.

Tiola ran to her, enfolded her dear friend in her arms, wept with her for a moment. "I would that you could come with me, but you do so hate the sea," she said, wiping at her tears with the back of her hand.

Jenna snorted. "The sea I can tolerate, pirates I cannot."

There was no use in attempting to explain that Jesamiah had given up piracy. Jenna would not believe it. Neither did Tiola, for that matter.

Taking a deep breath, resigned – all fledglings had to leave the nest - the older woman composed herself. "Very well, if your mind is set then go with my blessing." Fabricating a smile she busied herself putting the kettle to boil, then unfolding the bundle, tutted at all the things Tiola had left out. Picked up the little glass bottle nestled among a cushioning bundle of herbs.

"You'll need more than these few meagre items, my lass. Go fetch the valise from beneath my bed. Oh, and you had best take the blue shawl from behind the door; it was your mother's, you ought to have it."

Tiola hugged her, whisked away and Jenna took the bottle of laudanum, unstoppered it and poured a generous dose into a cup.

In a moment Tiola was back and Jenna was packing the bag with neat care. "You will have a cup of hot chocolate and something to eat? I will not be permitting you to go from here with nothing in your belly. And you sort some warmer clothes, too. It will be cold come nightfall at sea." Jenna indicated the clothes chest as she bustled to the kettle. "You will need wool stockings, another layer of petticoats. Drink this first."

Obedient, Tiola sat at the table, sipped at the chocolate. It was strong, how Jenna preferred it, tasted bitter.

"All of it mind," the older woman admonished, wagging her finger. "Lord knows when you shall see decent food and something hot to drink again."

Jenna placed bread and cheese on the table, seated herself opposite her ward, sipped her own cup of chocolate. Watched, impassive, as Tiola drank – and realised, too late, what she had swallowed.

Tiola stared at her, appalled. Laudanum. The drug that brought sleep and numbed the senses, that could claim the soul and destroy it. For Tiola, a poison which could obliterate her ability of Craft.

She dropped the china cup which shattered on the floor, the stain of the tainted chocolate spreading in a pool, her hand going to her mouth, her eyes wide, tears of betrayal beginning to fall.

"Oh Jenna, what have you done?" she whispered.

The guiding voices of her ancestors fled from her mind, screaming in terror, and the giggling, insipid chuckle of a Malevolent crept in to replace them.

To all things there was a balance. Hot and cold, gay or sad. Salt, sweet, rough, smooth. Day. Night. The White Craft and the Dark Power. Without the balance of strict, disciplined awareness, the Dark was always eager to penetrate and control. Terror, doubt and fear were always there, hovering outside the white shield wall of protection, ready to rush in when the barricade fell. Devouring all sense, ability and confidence in one quick gobble of greed.

Tiola stood, the room swirling, the rush of demons possessing her. Stared at Jenna, horrified. "What have you done?" she whispered. "Oh Jenna, what have you done to me?"

She tried to call Jesamiah, to send her thoughts to his mind but it was too late, her gift of Craft had been plundered. It had gone, fled, leaving her totally alone within the Darkness.

- Five -

A few minutes to noon - and she was not here!

Official papers authorising ownership, promised by the Dutchman had not arrived; the surprise, nor had the militia. Van Overstratten was expecting some move towards the ship, did he really think Jesamiah was stupid? He had a strong suspicion if he went anywhere near, set one foot on her deck he would be riddled with lead shot. To get aboard in one piece there had to be a diversion. Jesamiah was not certain what van Overstratten was expecting, hoped it was not for his precious warehouse on the far side of the harbour to blow up.

As with all his ideas this one was simple, but it would require exact timing and expert help. The hard part had been locating the captain of the decrepit pirate ship anchored in Table Bay. Eventually, Jesamiah had discovered the man in the arms of a plump-breasted brunette; gained his immediate attention by tipping the naked doxy from the bed.

Offering a placating smile and a diamond the size of a thumb nail, which effectively diverted the intensely annoyed captain from shooting him in the balls, Jesamiah had said, "I need a crew and gunpowder. You can either resume your carnal pleasures or come and help me."

"What do I get in return?"

"The position of quartermaster aboard a ship that won't sink the moment it hits rough water, passage to Madagascar where I intend to refurbish, and another diamond as big as that one."

"Although I don't suppose its going t'be quite so simple?" the man had answered, pulling on his breeches and boots.

"Well, no, I grant there are a few barrels I want your men to move first, and there might be a bit of a scrap before we sail."

Grinning, Jesamiah's new quartermaster had pocketed the diamond and gone in search of his men.

The *Anchor*, a tavern, squeezed between a chandler's and a cooper's bothy, gave a decent view of the harbour. Since eleven of the clock Captain Acorne had sat in the front window, the place busy with sailors and dock-side workers; the inevitable whore displaying her wares and touting for business. Observed by van Overstratten's lackeys, he sat engrossed in a book and drinking coffee, apparently oblivious to the comings and goings of the world outside.

Tiola was not here! He could not wait, she knew that. *Knew* he could not wait!

Tentative, he tried locating her, thinking her name, speaking to her through thought as she did to him. *Tiola?*

Nothing happened.

As the cannon announced midday he innocently dropped his book to the floor, bent to retrieve it from beneath the table and stayed there as the blast of a second explosion, dwarfing that of the signal gun, hurled through the town. A shower of glass, wood and dust burst through the shattering window, women were screaming, children crying. Dogs barked. Chaos and confusion as a cloud of debris-choked smoke rolled through the streets; everything knocked sideways by the aftermath of the shockwave of the blast. People were running, milling, uncertain what to do, where to go. Inside the tavern men were scrabbling to their feet, darting outside, tables being knocked over, glasses of ale and drink, cups of coffee, plates of food all scattered to the floor. Jesamiah hurried with them.

Shouting and confusion. Were they under attack? At war? All eyes along the wide curve of Table Bay were turning to the awesome spectacle of destruction. Where there had been Stefan Van Overstratten's warehouse, filled with silks and cottons, china, pewter, spices and tea, there was now only a reek of smoke pluming into the sky and gushing flames roaring upward in its wake,

The gunpowder had been easy to set in position; pirates knew all about its volatile properties, how to stack it for maximum effect, how to lay a fuse. At Jesamiah's suggestion the captain of the Pirate had chivvied his crew into unloading the barrels from the leaking hold of their ship, placing them instead along the frontage of the warehouse with the green-painted woodwork. The dock-master had complained, but happily accepted the bag of gold slipped into his pocket and then, with only a little encouragement, had gone in search of a tavern in which to spend a portion of it.

Shops, bothies, ale-houses, all buildings emptying as people ran to gawp. From the brothels, whores tumbled, clutching sheets to hide their assets, men pulling on breeches, hopping into boots or shoes.

Tiola was not here!

No one in the melee noticed Jesamiah walking quickly in the opposite direction from the destruction, towards the far jetty.

The fools who were Stefan's crewmen were gathered along the seaward rail of the moored ship, pointing excitedly at the spectacle of the burning building, orders and weapons entirely forgotten as Jesamiah had known they would be. Without a shot, without one of them knowing what was happening, they were being tipped over the side, heel over head, splashing helpless into the sea their places taken by a ragged-dressed pirate crew.

Equally lack-witted, the men who manned the fort were standing gaping at the spreading fire, some of the officers at last mustering the sense to hurry and organise bucket chains.

With her aft cable cut by three blows of an axe, the south-easterly wind began to nudge *Sea Witch* from her moorings.

Tiola had not come!

Jesamiah could not wait. He stood on the quarterdeck staring anxiously towards the upward climb of the sprawling town, at the flat stretch of the beach. Where the damn was she? The pirate captain was frowning at him, impatient to be gone; arson was as much a hanging offence as piracy. Any moment now someone on the bastions of that star-shaped fort might come to their senses and remember the reason for cannons to be pointing down into the harbour.

Gulls, disturbed by the great boom of the warehouse disintegrating into smoke and fire swooped and mewed their displeasure, circling and wheeling around the height of the masts as Jesamiah stared upward.

"Away aloft!" he called waving his arm, and instantly men were scurrying into the shrouds, racing up the rigging. Still he waited, his eyes darting between the streets feeding the foreshore and the sails tumbling from the yards.

Then, "Jenna!" He sprinted across the deck, jumped down the ladder into the waist, was out over the entry port, bellowing the woman's name, leaping ashore across a widening gap of sea between the stern and the jetty. "Jenna!"

Shambling at a waddling, jog-trot run, her bust heaving, her bonnet ribbons flying, face red, Jenna was shouting something at him. Something he could not hear above the shriek of the gulls, the crack of sails.

The fear he should come searching for Tiola had prompted Jenna to walk to the dockside. She had to ensure he had gone – either to sea, or to Hell.

His hand outstretched, intending to grasp her arm, Jesamiah met a torrent of fury. Jenna flung his touch away and pointed towards the burning warehouse.

"Are you responsible for that? Did you order this carnage? Are you not concerned for those many you may have maimed or killed?"

Ignoring her he shouted back. "Where is Tiola? She said she would be here!"

"There will be people dead in there! Who knows how far such a fire shall spread? Do you not care, you despicable malignant."

"Where is Tiola?" he repeated, not hearing her.

Folding her arms Jenna took a step away from him, certain she had done the right thing, her head bobbing to emphasise her words. "She is not coming. She has realised her life here is more important than running off with ne'r-do-well scum. She bids you be gone and stay gone."

Jesamiah stared at her, the hurt and hatred running through him like the primed fuse laid to those barrels of gunpowder.

"She knows you for what you are, a liar, cheat and murderer. Do you seriously believe a young woman such as Tiola would commit herself to a man who as soon as his eye settled on a suitable ship, is off sailing away in it and damn the consequences?"

The fuse ignited the powder, exploded. He screamed at her, drawing his pistol aimed, arm outstretched thumb pressing on the hammer to click it home. "You lie you bitch! You bloody lie! She loves me! She said she would come with me!"

Jenna's contemptuous scorn seared across her face. "Then why is she not here?"

Men were racing along the foreshore from the fort, men in the militia uniform of the Dutch Guard, with pistols and muskets. Among them Stefan van Overstratten. The pop, pop of small arms fire, the whistle of shot slicing through the air.

Automatically Jesamiah ducked his head. "You lie Jenna, I know you lie! You tell her I'll be waiting for her in Madagascar!" He rammed his pistol into his belt, leapt for the ship swinging further from her moorings. Clinging to the cordage draped along the bows, he scrambled upwards, willing hands coming down to haul at his coat, to help him. One of the crew brought his axe down on the final warp and the ship was free, Jesamiah still only half way over the forward rail.

"Tell her I'll be waiting, you hear me?" Jesamiah screeched flinging his arm out, finger pointing, accusing, as he ran aft, dipping his head as musket shot whined through the rigging. "You fokken tell her, Jenna!"

He bellowed for more sail to be spilled off the yards, issued a stream of urgent orders as he ran; "Let fall... Sheet home. T'gan's'l sheets... Hands to braces – look lively there... Belay!"

"Shoot him! Shoot the bastard!" Van Overstratten was ordering.

His concentration flickering between the need to get *Sea Witch* under way and Jenna, Jesamiah did not see the Dutchman. A gust from the wind sent the ship bounding forward, sail trimmers ready to meet her, to send her skimming out onto the ocean.

"Tell Tiola, Jenna, or by God I'll come back and rip your bloody heart out with my bare hands! You hear me, woman? Tell her or I'll see you burn in Hell!" Jenna was not listening, was walking away.

Van Overstratten saw the woman. What she was doing here? Alarmed that the lack-wits he had hired to ensure Miss Oldstagh did not leave her premises had failed as miserably as these along the jetty, he darted through the smoke of inadequate musket fire. Clasping Jenna's arm he spun her around, demanding to know what was happening. Where was Tiola?

"She is safe at home," Jenna reassured him. "I gave her laudanum to make her sleep. I will not be having her running off with that reprobate."

He smiled, his hands on her arms rewarding her with an approving squeeze. Half a victory perhaps?

Leaping on to the quarterdeck, nodding at the helmsman to bring the ship up into the wind, anger flooded into a torrent of frustrated rage as Jesamiah glanced over the rail and saw the Dutchman talking with Jenna. He grabbed a musket from one of the men, checked it was primed, aimed at van Overstratten, fired, and turned immediately away. He had always been a good shot but he doubted he would hit his target; the aim was careless and the distance widening too rapidly. He did not wait to see if the shot struck home, word on the wind would tell him soon enough.

Horrified, Stefan saw Jesamiah raise the gun, put it to his shoulder. He was not a brave man. His hands were on Jenna's arms - he had been leaning forward wondering whether to plant a grateful kiss on her cheek - saw the flash and the puff of smoke. He reacted instinctively, without thought or consideration - swung Jenna in front of him, using her as a shield, ducking his head as he did so. And she gave a small, surprised gasp. Fell, limp, against him.

Sea Witch was moving, the ebbing tide taking her; another gust of wind caught the sails that flapped once, uncooperatively, then another and another. The canvas filled, the wind merged into one steady thrust and the ship was gathering speed, skimming cleanly through the surf, sleek and fast. Belatedly, the fort fired two cannon, the first shot whistling between the main and mizzen topmasts to splash in a plumed spout of water several yards beyond the hull, the second dropping hopelessly short in the ship's lengthening wake. They were too late, *Sea Witch* was gone, was free.

The bow wave foamed to either side of her, the rigging beginning to sing, the sound exultant as *Sea Witch* flew before the wind, her sails mithering, wooden keel and decks griping as she came to life.

With the wind strengthening, tangling his hair and whipping his ribbons forward over his shoulder, Jesamiah took the wheel and headed his ship into the open water of the Atlantic, spindrift foaming high over her lee rail. He let her pay off until a particularly exuberant flurry had scuttled by and then took her up a point, his strong hands gripping the spokes, the feel of her, alert and beautifully responsive beneath his fingers. The vibration of her rudder flowed upward direct through the deck and into his feet, into his body and soul, her very existence becoming a part of him. Captain and ship, lover and mistress. A bond so intense that for a short moment Jesamiah forgot everything except this feeling, like that of sexual release, of utter consuming exhilaration.

The ship was enjoying the elation of forging into each oncoming wave, shouldering her way through the ocean as if it were of no more consequence than a sedate village pond. Nothing could catch her now!

Watching for the telltale shudder on the fore topsail that would tell him he had pushed the spars to the limit of endurance, Jesamiah brought his ship closer and closer into the wind. There! She was racing as fast as she could, any more and a sail would split or a spar crack under the immense strain of pressure. He eased her off a point, let her settle into her full-gallop pace.

Glancing at the binnacle, at the steadying of the swinging compass, he nodded, pleased.

"We'll run on this bearing for now," he said to his new quartermaster who had said not a word but had watched, with critical admiration, a true seaman sail a ship.

"Keep 'er so until we're beyond sight of eyes studyin' our course," Jesamiah added, handing him the helm and slipping, already, into the clipped, lazy, speech of a pirate. "Then we'll turn south down the coast, round the Cape and head east'd to the Indian Ocean. In this wind we'll 'ave to work 'er 'ard."

With some gusts reaching seventy-five miles an hour, almost hurricane strength, there would be some delicate tacking to do to reach around the promontory of the Cape of Good Hope, and beyond to the most southerly tip of Africa, Cape Agulhas - the Sea of Storms as it was called by those sailors who understood the uncertain temper of these waters.

"Welcome aboard, friends." Jesamiah called, grinning, to the men of his new crew gathering, euphoric at their success, down in the waist. "I promised excitement did I not? I trust you'll find *Sea Witch* a more superior ship than the worm-pocked, bilge wreck you left abandoned in Cape Town 'arbour?"

They laughed, cheered. There was no comparison between the two vessels; may as well compare a hawk with a turkey. Fixing a smile Jesamiah added an acknowledgement of thanks and made the additional promise of rum all round once well clear of danger.

He went to stand at the stern, his fingernails digging into the varnished wood, staring back at the rapidly diminishing settlement, at the white walls of the fort, the straggle of the houses and taverns and shops. The people were too small to see with any distinction. A knot of them were gathered on the jetty, the bright coloured coats of the Dutch militia standing out, huddled in a group. On the far side of the harbour, the pillar of smoke reached up to the sky. If Tiola was there he would not have been able to see her -if he was to fetch the telescope, look closer? He stood where he was, Jenna's words echoing in his mind. "*Do you seriously believe Tiola would commit herself to a man who as soon as his eye settled on a suitable ship, is off, sailing away in it?*"

If she loved him, if she had intended to come – if something had delayed her – she would have spoken into his mind. Wouldn't she?

Tiola? Please Tiola, answer me! Nothing. No response to his thoughts. But why would there be? It was not he who held the Craft.

The wind was buffeting his face, the salt from the sea stinging his cheeks and eyes. As well it did. It would not have been fitting for his crew to discover the moisture on the face of their new captain was not from the spray, but from spilling tears.

- Six -

The voices cackled and giggled in her head.

~ Jenna is dead. Jesamiah is gone! ~

Tiola tried to concentrate on what Bella was saying, but her brain was a fog, stuffed with bundled cotton. There was more than one voice now, chuntering spiteful laughter inside her; the voices of the Malevolents, the creatures of the Dark, disorientating and confusing her.

~ Jenna is dead. Jesamiah is gone. ~ The liturgy was whirling around and around and around like a spinning top, never ceasing, tormenting and torturing her. Baiting her, as vicious boys would bait a cowering, chained dog with sticks.

"Jesamiah would not shoot Jenna," she said, desperately trying to force herself to think clearly. They were saying he had killed her? Bella and Stefan, the both of them bending over her, their faces blurred, alternately receding and enlarging, their words drifting away into the mist, then coming closer. Jesamiah would never have done that. Never!

Never?

"Over my dead body" Jenna had said.

Jesamiah?

~ Jenna is dead! Jesamiah is gone! ~

Jesamiah!

She tried to stand but the room was swirling, her legs feeling as if they did not belong to her. "I have to meet him," she mumbled. "At noon on the jetty. He is waiting for me."

Stefan whirled away across the room, throwing his hands, exasperated, in the air. Could the silly bitch not understand?

"He has gone dear," Bella said more patient, kneeling in front of Tiola, rubbing her hands, anxious because the girl did look so dreadfully pale. "He has already sailed."

"But I was to go with him." None of this was making sense! Oh, if only these wretched voices in her head would stop their silly chattering!

"He had no intention of taking you, *liefste*," van Overstratten said pushing past Bella, and bending nearer grasped Tiola's arms. "He felt nothing for you. If he did, would he have shot your guardian and dear friend? He shot her in the back. Took careful aim, fired and killed her." Blood was on Stefan's shirt and white breeches. Jenna's blood from where she had fallen, dead, against him. From where he had used her as a shield, but already his mind had twisted the fact, had dismissed his cowardice. Acorne had shot her deliberately, that now was the believed truth.

Tiola's tongue felt thick, her lips numb. Her mind as unfocused as their distorted faces. The Dark Power was smothering her. With effort she fought back, fought against the malicious sniggering. "But I was to meet him at noon." Still the muddle; still she did not understand.

"Noon? He was already under way come noon, girl! Was heeling out to sea with a following wind."

Bella looked sharply at the Dutchman. That was not what she had heard. Stefan frowned at her, shook his head and put his finger to his lips. Said in a hoarse whisper, "Is it not kinder for her to think the scoundrel has lied all along? That he had no intention of waiting for her?"

Reluctant to distort the truth, Bella hesitated, found herself agreeing; what good would it do for Tiola to know the precise sequence of events? Acorne was gone and it was unlikely he would come back. With an audible sigh she nodded, justified the lie by saying, "I liked him. I am sorely disappointed he has turned out to be no better than any other rogue on the look out for nothing more than the quick tumble of a pretty girl."

Stefan felt no remorse for Acorne at all, but retained his silence, held Tiola's arms, his grip tight. "*Liefste,* it is imperative you answer me this. The man is a murderer, a liar and a thief. He must be punished for his crimes. You owe him nothing for he thought nothing of you." The grip tightened. He had to know, had to get his property back! "My dear, to where has he sailed? Do you know where he has taken my ship?"

"Gone? Jesamiah has gone?" Tears streamed down Tiola's face and the Darkness filled her.

~ He thought nothing of you ~

The chortle of the demons consumed her, possessing her, and submitting to their will, she believed the lies.

- Seven -

It often rained during the winter months in Cape Town, June to August. Rarely did the rainy season linger into September, certainly not as heavily as this. The streets were sticky with mud that lifted poorly-laid cobblestones, leaving gaping, ankle-wrenching, puddled holes. The shacks along the coast, slave quarters mostly, had washed away, the poor wretches left to shelter as best they could beneath tarpaulins or dripping trees.

Tiola had ploughed through the rain and mess two days ago to deliver a dead child, now she had trekked the same three miles to lay out its dead mother. A midwife's responsibility, to bring life into the world and to tend the life gone from it, to bring the new born into the light from the womb and to prepare the departed for the dark of the grave. It was not a task she enjoyed, this cleansing of the husk that was the body, the sewing of it into a shroud or dressing it in finest wear. Nothing was enjoyable about death, but this was a compassionate duty, a final completion of the circle of life. The sadness was when the death was a healthy woman who had not survived the ordeal of birth.

Bone tired and wet through, the sole of her boot was leaking, her foot and woollen stocking saturated. She would have been no wetter had she jumped full clad into the sea. The giggling voices continued to snigger in her head, making her temples throb and her patience wear thin. Midnight was approaching; good folk were abed the boisterous only halfway through their carousing. Her head drooping, feet stumbling, she made her way along the side-streets, avoiding the attention of men by huddling into her mantle, the hood pulled forward. They left her alone. No one was interested in a timid drab.

As usual, Bella's Place was crowded. She held a reputation for clean girls and offered an entertaining evening. Tiola leant against the wall in Grope Lane reluctant to enter the passage and go up the stairs. To go home. Kisty had lit a lamp for her, she could see the glow behind the closed shutters.

Jesamiah had stood here in this exact spot. That night. That last night.

She tipped her head against the wall, closed her eyes. She was so tired, but when she slept the dreams haunted her. She was weary of surviving through one bereft day after another. Her Craft had deserted her, she could do nothing to ease what was eating away inside her. Not the gangrene which had rotted that young mother, but something as malignant. Grief.

She was tired of the tears she could not shed, of the ache tearing her apart, and the hole within her that would not be filled. Drained by emotion and memories refusing to be silenced and stilled. The voices kept giggling and whispering, reminding her he had abandoned her; had never loved her.

And the rain fell, despair flooding in its wake.

Stefan had protested when she insisted on returning here to Bella's, but Tiola had found his patronising condolence overbearing. She did not resent being cosseted and cared for, but she would not be told what to do, and Stefan was persistently attempting to advise her. Constantly watching her.

She trudged up the stairs, an effort to put one foot in front of the other, pushed into the room where only two months ago she had been happy. Kisty had also lit the fire, had been unable to do much about the leaking roof.

Jesamiah was supposed to have mended it. *"I'll climb up there, patch it up,"* he had promised. But he was a pirate, and pirates were known for not keeping their promises.

She emptied the buckets, set to catch the drips, out of the window. Stepped from her wet petticoats and stockings, laid them to dry before the fire. Added more charcoal, hooked the kettle on the rakencrock. Routine chores.

The Malevolents, the Demons. Always there, always whispering.

~ He shot Jenna! ~

~ He never loved you. He only loves the sea. ~

Where was he now? Perhaps he had returned to the Caribbean, he had talked often of the islands with their beaches washed by the surf of turquoise seas. She had tried to use her Craft to call him but she had lost the ability to send words into his mind, and even if she had not, she knew she would only meet with a wall of silence. He had shut her from his thoughts, had, as the voices said, abandoned her.

Huddled beneath the blankets of her bed she lay shivering. The bed where she had lain in his arms, his warm, strong body entwined with hers. The bed where he had possessed her, had made love to her.

The roof creaked. She tried to sleep but feared the dreams, for even in sleep demons mocked her, caused her to dream of the sea, of a ship and a man standing at the helm. She knew it was him, Jesamiah, although he always had his back to her. When she shouted out to him, trying to attract his attention, she would wake to find herself tangled in the sheets and alone in the darkness.

Another creak and the bulge in the ceiling burst, the rain cascading through bringing down a waterfall of coldness, plaster and broken tiles drenching both her and the bed.

And then the tears fell, the tears she had so desperately suppressed through these long weeks of loss. Tears, once they started would not stop.

"You should have fetched me earlier, Madam Dubois," Stefan scolded as he disdainfully surveyed the wreckage; the saturated floor, the gaping hole in the ceiling. "Nor should you have neglected this roof."

His chiding stung but Bella did not protest, for he was right she should have done both things. At least it had ceased raining, although the clouds were louring moodily, threatening more misery. Table Mountain, brooding behind the grey covering of mist had become invisible.

"I have been saying it would be best for her to live within my household," van Overstratten continued to rail. "Well, now she is ill and I remove choice from her. She requires nursing and comfort."

Statements which, although she searched for reasons, Bella could not oppose. It was well known van Overstratten wanted a wife to give him a son. As well known, Tiola had refused his offer of marriage several times over. Bella did not care for the Dutchman, he was pompous and opinionated, but he had wealth and as he said, Tiola required nursing and comfort, for she was a very sick young lady.

- Eight -

"She is not coming *mon ami*, it 'as been three months. Your ship is refitted, she is ready to sail. It is senseless to wait 'ere much longer." Rue meant well. He put his hand in friendship on Jesamiah's shoulder, did not expect the response of a snarl and a raised fist.

"Bugger you. When I want y'bloody opinion I'll soddin' ask for it." Jesamiah was drunk. He usually was these days.

"Let me get you to bed. Sleep it off, *non?*"

The fist swinging into a left-handed punch was not co-ordinated. Rue ducked with ease and deftly caught Jesamiah as he over-balanced, toppled forward.

Dishevelled, stinking of spilt rum and sweat; in need of a shave, a wash and clean clothes Jesamiah knelt in the short, dry grass which never stopped its muttered conversations with the wind. There was always a wind here in Madagascar, blowing in from the sea or down from the forested hills. He hated that damned, mumbling wind.

He looked at the rum bottle clutched in his right hand as if surprised to find it there. Looked too, at the scars zigzagging in a crazy pattern against the sun-tanned skin of his right arm. A reminder he would carry to his last day. Not for the first time this week the thought occurred that with one quick slice of his cutlass he could get rid of the reminder. And if he was lucky, the rest of this miserable life into the bargain.

He had thought she would come. Those first few weeks, when they had been busy refitting, he had laughed with the men as they worked, had been there, on the beach waiting to greet every ship dropping anchor, expecting her to be aboard. And gradually he came to realise Jenna had spoken the truth, Tiola did not want a skunk of a pirate. From there, what was the point of staying sober?

Tipping the bottle to his mouth, Jesamiah fell backwards, unconscious.

Carrying him into the hut at the edge of the clearing Rue covered his friend with a light blanket; in these hot climates the nights turned cold. Near the door, a rectangular opening covered by a ragged deer-skin, he kicked an empty bottle sending it spinning across the earth floor. He picked it up, collected two more.

This had to stop.

The day Jesamiah had arrived was one of the best Rue could remember. Seeing a perfect ship glide into harbour and drop anchor close to the rotting carcass of the *Inheritance* had been a joy, and to discover Jesamiah stepping ashore, there had been celebration in this corner of Madagascar that night! Aye, and for the entire week after!

The pirate settlement had its compensations, a life of ease and black-skinned women by the dozen, an endless supply of provisions; anyone who wanted to make a secretive profit on a cargo called in at Saint Mary's Anchorage. Legal merchantmen alongside buccaneers. Even the occasional Royal Navy ship if she carried a captain who had a prize to sell and knew he would not personally obtain its full worth in England.

The township - more of a clutter of dilapidated huts and bothies than a town - ambled along the shore and boasted four taverns, three brothels and not much else. Several hundred men lived there with a variety of women and a gaggle of lice-riddled children, who could name any one of the men as their father. The trading was operated by a group of self-styled Company Men, literate ex-pirates with the savvy for business. They had the sense to build on the higher hills in better style and comfort, and kept themselves to themselves, emerging for their share of the cargo only when a ship dropped anchor.

Rue and Isiah Roberts, soon wearied of the constant round of senseless carousal, had followed the Company's example by moving further down the coast. They chose a spot where the forested hills overlooked the sweep of the sea and the harbour entrance, then traded with the natives for food and friendship. The huts they built within a day, mud for the walls, grass thatching for the roof, earth for the floor. By the second day they each had a woman sharing their lodging, willing to cook, fetch fresh water, wash their shirts and keep them content during the night. An idyllic life without worry or threat. A life that, when Jesamiah had sailed into the harbour, Rue had realised with sudden clarity was repetitively dull and mind-numbingly boring. Two months on, apart from the brief spell of activity when they had enthusiastically altered the *Sea Witch* from a merchant trader into a pirate craft – cutting gun ports and fitting guns, re-stepping her mizzen mast and removing the high, poop deck - things had not changed.

Collecting stained clothing abandoned on the floor, Rue hung his captain's hat on a nail in the wall, touched the hardened and cracked leather of Jesamiah's cutlass strap. Shaking his head and with a sigh of despondency he partially drew the weapon. The metal needed rubbing with sand to stop it rusting, then oiling. A whetstone running down its blade to sharpen its edge.

From his bed Jesamiah groaned, belched.

Slamming the cutlass back into its sheath Rue strode with great paces from the hut, swept across the clearing and ducked into Isiah's dwelling.

He was sitting cross-legged on the floor eating an evening meal of roasted chicken, his woman indicated Rue could sit, eat. Waving her away the Frenchman refused both offers. "Isiah, I 'ave 'ad enough of this. I am going back to the sea."

Isiah Roberts stopped chewing, his eyes beginning to gleam. "When?"

"Right now. No more excuses. It is September, the 'urricane season is almost finished in the Caribbean. I am going 'ome."

Spluttering half-chewed bits of chicken from his mouth Roberts leapt to his feet. "Are you serious? Can I come? Will you have me, a black man as crew?"

Flinging his head back Rue crowed. "The colour of your skin 'as nothing to do with ability aboard ship *mon ami!* You are eager to come then?"

"Sod it Rue, I'll cut my own throat if I sit here doing damn all much longer!"

"*Oui.* I think there is a perfectly fine ship idling down in the 'arbour. One which will be 'ard to match in the waters of the Spanish Main. I also think I would rather 'ang after a few months of excitement, than sit 'ere waiting for the next, God-alone knows 'ow many years, going grey and rotting to dust, bored out of my skull."

"You thinking of taking the *Sea Witch?*" the younger man asked dubiously, his heavy brows frowning down over his eyes.

"*Oui.*"

"Jesamiah ready to sail?" Added quickly, "I'll not commandeer her, I'll not steal from him."

"*Non.* Nor would I, nor would I," Rue placated, patting the air with his large hands. "I intend to tell 'im tomorrow. No use now, 'e is dead to the world. 'E can come with us or stay 'ere."

"Or," Isiah suggested, speaking slowly as he mulled over an idea, "we could carry him aboard and hope he pulls himself together once we get to sea?"

Rue frowned; that was possible. "Our first chase, first prize? *Oui,* action might snap 'im out of the melancholy 'e is wallowing in."

"We had best get word out for a crew, get her careened and provisioned." Roberts said tossing his unfinished meal into the fire and wiping his greasy hands on the seat of his breeches. "She's been bobbing idle these weeks, bound to have barnacles sucking at her. Bit of worm too no doubt, although she has a right good copper-clad keel to protect her. It'll not take long to see her ready." He was grinning, excited at the prospect. Rue slapped his friend's shoulder. Already he felt he was coming alive again.

Waking several hours into the fore noon to a thundering headache, Jesamiah staggered to his feet. He tottered to the door, peered out, squinting at the brightness of the morning sun. He dipped a wooden cup into the bucket beside the door, the water warm and brackish, but sufficient to slake his thirst. Not bothering to go into the bushes, directed his urine against the outside wall.

"You would 'ave threatened us with a flogging if we 'ad been so lazy as to do that aboard ship," Rue observed wryly from where he stood some yards away.

"Well we ain't aboard." Jesamiah grunted adjusting his breeches. Wished the fellow would not shout so loud.

Rue stepped forward offering a pewter tankard. "Drink this."

Hesitant, Jesamiah took it wrinkled his nose at the foul looking liquid. "What is it?"

"Old French recipe. Brandy, ground garlic with 'alf a pint of ale. *Deux œufs* - fresh-laid is that cackle fruit - a pinch of gunpowder and a generous lump of melted pork lard."

Jesamiah sniffed again at the concoction, gagged at the stench. He poked a finger into it and picked out a piece of floating egg shell. "I don't care for raw eggs."

"Just drink it."

Doubtful, Jesamiah raised it to his mouth. Changing his mind, offered it back. "Later perhaps."

Folding his arms, Rue ignored the tankard. "Isiah and me we are getting the *Sea Witch* ready to sail. You 'ad 'er refitted when first you came, she 'as cannon and swivel guns, all of it wasted with 'er sitting there in the 'arbour. Isiah 'as beached 'er this morning and is already scraping 'er keel. We 'ave got a crew volunteered as well. Good men." He encouraged the tankard upwards. Jesamiah was staring at him, his expression blank. *Sea Witch*? To set sail?

" *Écoute mon gars,*" Rue said finally losing patience. "Look, my friend, you 'ave a choice. You lead us like the brilliant captain you are or we leave you in this God-forgotten emptiness, with as many bottles of rum as you please. You can drink yourself into oblivion, with only this wind for company."

Jesamiah looked from Rue to the tankard. He hated the wind. Hesitant, he raised it to his lips. "It smells foul."

" The fouler the medicine, the quicker the cure, or so *ma mère* used to say."

"What was she? The village poisoner?"

"One gulp. Straight down," Rue advised.

Taking a deep breath Jesamiah drank, much of it trickling down his chin into his scruffy, untrimmed beard. Rue held a finger against the bottom forcing him to finish it.

Swearing as he pulled away, Jesamiah wiped his hand over his mouth, grimacing, gave Rue the empty tankard then swallowed hard. One hand went to his belly the other to his mouth. "You sodding..." He doubled over sinking to his hands and knees, retching and vomiting up the contents of his stomach. When nothing more was heaving from him, rolled on to his back, eyes closed, his hands covering his face. Managed to croak, "That was bloody disgusting."

"Cured your 'eadache though, *non*?"

Opening one eye Jesamiah glowered. "And how d'you figure that mate? It's still thumping away as if three 'undred crew of buccaneers are bouncing about in there, vaporing after a Chase."

Rue offered his hand to pull him to his feet. Jesamiah accepted and stood, unsteady, the world wheeling past.

"You will be so busy puking your guts up this next 'alf 'our, you will forget about your sore 'ead." He guffawed heartily at Jesamiah's murderous expression.

Nine

Sunrise. *Sea Witch* had run under easy canvas during the night and with nothing to slow her below the water line she bowled along under fore and main topsail.

Jesamiah ducked from his cabin, a cup of steaming coffee in his hand. He wore a clean shirt and breeches, had tidied his moustache and beard, shaved the rest of his face, a nick of blood spotting his cheek from where the ship had heeled at an unexpected moment.

The whisper went around, "Cap'n's on deck!" They were a pirate crew but respected their captain. While Jesamiah listened and watched from the rail of the quarterdeck, language became cleaner and tasks were completed more efficiently.

"Aloft there!" Jesamiah called, his dark eyes squinting up the height of the main mast. "Make anything more of that ship yet?"

"She's hull up, Cap'n, just sheeted full canvas an' veering sou' sou' west. Reckon she's spotted us."

Finishing his coffee and sending the dregs over the side, Jesamiah glanced at the compass. South south west. Noted the sand trickling through the half hour-glass, the trim of the sails. Isiah Roberts handed him the bring-it-close. "She's over there, two points off starb'd."

Extending the brass telescope Jesamiah put it to his eye. Smiled. So she was.

Sea Witch was a fine ship. During their long voyage across the Atlantic, running before the Westerlies, they had put her through her paces pushing her up to her limit and almost beyond, to see exactly what she was capable of doing. Discovered she was capable of doing a lot.

They had not sailed from Madagascar, in the end, for another two weeks for with the return of enthusiasm, Jesamiah had decided to fit a bow-chaser gun to her forward rails and purchase two more nine pound cannons. Which meant two more ports to be cut and the other guns re-arranged to balance the weight. He then had her hull painted royal blue. Blue, the colour of his ribbons. Jesamiah Blue, as the crew called it.

One hundred and twenty-five feet from stem to stern. *Sea Witch*. Three masts and twenty guns, two of them twelve pounders. After these many weeks back in the Caribbean she was the talk of the Islands. Not all of it, from the merchants' point of view, complimentary.

By keeping an experienced eye on the set of her sail and the angle of the wind, Jesamiah could manage to squeeze that last, vital knot of speed when it was necessary. He had pushed himself as hard to learn all he could about her during the Atlantic crossing, taking the helm himself for hours on end, climbing the masts, setting and trimming canvas. Exploring every inch of the below deck world, even to crawling through the vileness of the cable tier, where the hemp coils of the anchor cable were stored on slatted platforms in order for them to dry and not rot. A place where the rats scurried in the pitch black humidity of stinking bilge water, the very lowest part of the ship in both senses of the word. Methodically, Jesamiah had become familiar with every inch of her, observing and caressing as if he were investigating the intimate contours of a woman's body while making slow, passionate love to her. Which in a way, he was.

Sea Witch swayed with the tide and the wind; she sang or she moaned depending on her mood. Was mother, sister, wife and whore to the men aboard, but most especially to her captain, who by the very nature of his position of command served as her consort. And as with any capricious woman, to keep her sweet her chosen lover must indulge all her whims and fancies.

Equally, Jesamiah was as meticulous about his crew. He wanted able men who knew their job and would do it with a will. Shirkers or mitherers he would not tolerate. The men were to work together as brothers and he insisted on a modified version of the Articles of the Pirate Code. *Sea Witch* was *his*, *he* was the law while aboard. There would be no electing a new captain, no voting for destination or enterprise. Rue was quartermaster, Isiah Roberts first mate. The rest of the Code he honoured; the scrupulously equal share of plunder, the sensible rules stating weapons must be kept in good condition, no smoking below deck and safe lanterns used, not an open flame. Gambling and fighting were entertainments to be kept for when ashore.

The only extra rule, no woman aboard a Chase was to be harmed. And as a concession to his belligerence in running his ship his way, he promised whoever crewed with the *Sea Witch* under Captain Jesamiah Acorne, would never be sorry for it.

A promise he rigidly adhered to.

Only once had he been tempted to give it all away, the twist of pain contorting his stomach into knots, and that had been at the very start as they had sailed by night past Cape Town. How he had wanted to give the order to bring *Sea Witch* around, ease her quietly into the harbour and steal ashore.

To do what? To carry out his threat to Jenna? To find Tiola? Why? She was gone from him, had rejected him. If she had wanted him she would have come on the day he had commandeered his ship, or as soon as possible after. She had known where to find him.

He did not know Jenna was dead. Neither he nor Tiola realised the lies they had been told. Both thought the one had abandoned the other, put blame where it should not be seated. Both suffering an ache that was eating them alive.

With Cape Town's distant lights on their starboard beam and Table Mountain a shadow against a star-emblazoned sky, Jesamiah had shut himself in his cabin and given temporary command to Rue. As they beat past the Bay and headed out into the Atlantic he had swallowed down an entire bottle of rum. By the time he was capable of standing again Africa, and its inhabitants, had been left far astern.

Shutting the telescope with a snap and handing it back to Isiah, Jesamiah announced. "Full sail and then breakfast." He grinned at the men waiting, watching him from the waist. "I doubt we'll 'ave chance to fill our bellies in an 'our or two, eh lads?" The crew cheered, more canvas tumbled from the yards as willing hands hurried to backstays and sheets, while others hauled the topgallant halyards. With all sail set and drawing well *Sea Witch* leapt to life as eager to be about her business as her crew.

Two hours later the other ship tried to make a race of it, to reach the safety of Antigua only fifteen miles ahead. She had no hope of succeeding, not against *Sea Witch* running steadily at more than ten knots. Straining to put distance between herself and the suspicious sail bearing down upon them, the Chase hoisted her colours. Dutch.

"Humour 'er Isiah. Run up a British ensign if you please," Jesamiah was happy to follow the tradition of this charade. The Chase knew full well *Sea Witch* was a pirate.

He was fully dressed now; buckram coat, three corner hat settled comfortably on his head, his cutlass at his hip, his left hand resting lightly on the hilt, his right fiddling with his ribbons. A breakfast of pork chop, sliced ham, eggs and fresh coffee digesting in his stomach.

Sea Witch was ready too, cleared for action everything not required on deck stowed away below or tossed as jetsam overboard. The bulkheads in Jesamiah's cabin were unbolted and removed, his mahogany table dismantled hoisted to the ceiling, out of the way to give more floor space for the gunners to run out the two stern cannons.

Jesamiah drove his victim hard, as if he were a cat playing with a mouse – until tiring of the game, and her bowsprit creeping towards the merchant's stern. he ordered the final burst of speed, clewed up into fighting sail and brought *Sea Witch* level with her prize. She edged forward, the two vessels soon flying along on parallel courses two hundred yards apart and closing, their bow waves mingling in crazy swirls of foam.

The Chase fired a feeble defence of her four guns, but her aim was poor and delivered in haste. Spumes of water fluted in the space between them as the shot fell short, only one ball striking along the *Sea Witch's* rails amidships. Beyond gouging a few splinters, did no serious damage.

"Run out the guns if you please," Jesamiah ordered, unhurried. "And make sure your firing is better done than theirs! One shot across her bow on my command."

From his position on the quarterdeck he watched with satisfaction as immediately the gun ports were hauled open and the great weapons were run out. Each man, his heart racing with the build of blood-heat excitement, waiting in position for the word to fire.

"Our correct colours, if you will Isiah," Jesamiah indicated the superfluous British flag.

With a wide grin, Isiah brought down the ensign, hoisted Jesamiah's own pirate emblem of a lurid skull and two crossed bones white painted on a black background. Lifting his arm, Jesamiah waited, his experienced eye watching the rise and dip of his ship's bow.

"Number one gun, on the up-roll," paused, dropped his hand. "Fire!"

And *Sea Witch* roared into a hell of smoke and noise as her larboard cannon belched its hideous power and slammed into the bowsprit of the Chase, ripping away spars, sail and shrouds all in the one shot. The gun crew were already running in, swabbing and loading as the powder monkey boy scurried forward with fresh powder. If the Chase did not see sense and heave to, surrender, there would be a another shot and a third. Even the dread of a broadside.

No pirate wanted to destroy a ship if it could be taken by insistent persuasion. Unfortunately, not all merchant captains held the same view of passive domination.

The second gun was ready, loaded with chain shot. Fired at maximum elevation it brought down shrouds and rigging, the air choked with the thick drift of smoke. The *Chase's* fore topmast shattered, toppled. She slewed to larboard and then her foresail ripped away in a great tear of sound.

With a nod of his head, Rue acknowledged Jesamiah's next order and put the helm hard over, *Sea Witch* responding by inclining her bow towards the panicking merchant. The pirates were chanting the regular, haunting sound that would bring terror into the very Devil himself.

"Oi, oi, oi, oi!" Beating their pistols and cutlasses, belaying pins, anything which came to hand on the rails, keeping the rhythm of their shout steady. Their bare feet pounding on the deck. *"Oi, oi, oi, oi!"*

A wolf pack, Jesamiah thought, watching them with detached approval. *A wolf pack running in full cry on the scent of its floundering prey.* And he was the leader of the pack. The wolf king, it was for him to call them off or send them into the kill. He did not know, long ago now, that Tiola had stood on the shore of Table Bay with Mr William Dampier comparing him to a sleek-pelted wolf.

The gap between them closing to less than one hundred feet, Jesamiah gave the last order to fire once more, grape shot - small cast iron balls bound together in a canvas bag, and langrage, jagged pieces that spread and scattered tearing through rigging, sails and men alike. Foul stuff if you were on the receiving end of it.

Sea Witch rocked as the gun sent this next taste of death into the merchant, her crew of twenty or so men foolishly beginning to mass along the rails to defend their ship against boarding. Lead shot tore through them. Two of their guns were now useless and the ship had holes gaping in her side; her torn shrouds dangled like a marionette's severed strings, her canvas was shred to pieces. And the chant from the foredeck of the *Sea Witch* was joined by the gun crews in the waist, the pace and words altering to something more sinister as the distance between them closed to fifty yards. To twenty five.

Caught in its intoxicating excitement, Jesamiah pulled out his pistol and used the butt to thump on the quarterdeck rail, adding to the chanted rhythm. Joined his voice with the sound all merchantmen feared.

"Death! Death! Death!"

Bow first, *Sea Witch* smashed into the Chase and the men on the foredeck were going over the rails, yodelling their murderous intent, the *pop, pop* of pistols firing; the cries of the wounded and dying.

Isiah Roberts took over the helm, Rue leapt atop the quarterdeck rail, ready to jump across to the mizzen shrouds, waiting beside Jesamiah as the *Sea Witch's* stern swung inwards.

"With care *mon ami?*" Rue said, setting one hand momentarily on Jesamiah's arm. "You have been taking too many risks of late, when we board."

"If I was to take care, Rue," Jesamiah answered having to shout as he grabbed for the shrouds, the Dutch hull grinding against *Sea Witch*, "there would be no sense in my being here or doing this."

He had no intention of being careful. The quicker someone shot him through the heart or the head, the better. That was all he wanted, to end it all, to end the long nights of loneliness when only a rum bottle offered comfort. Rum was not the same as Tiola's smile, or her laugh or her love. Or her intimate response beneath his touch. Nothing made up for the loss of Tiola.

Aboard the Chase the fight was bloody and over in five minutes. Both his pistols fired, one after the other and meeting their mark, Jesamiah had soon drawn his cutlass and was working his way steadily towards the quarterdeck where he found the officers making a last stand of defiance. Damn fools!

Rue was beside him, his cutlass swinging almost in unison. He saw the Dutch captain take careful aim and fire his pistol; heard Jesamiah gasp, saw him falter and stumble to one knee. Rue stopped and bent down, alarmed, ducking his head as another shot whistled past his ear. All around him, the frenzied sounds of fighting, the bang of firearms the clash of steel.

"Get on Rue! You're turnin' into a mother 'en, don't bloody fuss!" Jesamiah swore at him. "It's nothin'." Investigating beneath his waistcoat he found his fingers came away from his shoulder sticky with blood. He cursed, heaved himself to his feet and shifted his cutlass to his left hand, shoved the right, useless, through his baldric. Angry, he marched to the quarterdeck where the officers, finally seeing sense, had lowered their weapons.

"Can you not even sodding shoot straight, mister? This will bloody soddin' 'urt by tonight!" Jesamiah was swearing, furious, direct into the frightened captain's face. "You'll be damned sorry for this, I promise you!"

Already the ship was being ransacked of what she carried. A trader, her hold was full of sugar, molasses and - oh glory! Rum!

Her crew, the few left alive, were secured below in the fore-hold once it was emptied, the officers stripped and tied naked to the mainmast. They would provide an evening of entertainment once the necessary work was completed. If they had wanted decent treatment then they ought not have made a fight of it.

Jesamiah left his crew to their gleeful pleasure to make a search of the captain's cabin for anything of use. Awkwardly reloading a pistol with powder and shot, his shoulder already starting to ache abominably, he fired through the lock of the crude safe and pocketed the specie he found. Everything of value above a piece of eight would go into a common pile to be sold ashore somewhere, the profit equally divided. Only the maps, charts and the Ship's Log were Jesamiah's prerogative to retain. And the several bottles of French brandy.

He called for men to come and roll up the carpet from the deck. "It'll look fine in my cabin, better than in here. I'll pay its value into the fund." He took himself back aboard the *Sea Witch* to search out Jackson, their surgeon. A good doctor when he was sober, who grunted and peered at Jesamiah's shoulder, satisfied the shot had gone straight through, concerned it had taken shreds of coat and shirt with it.

"It will probably fester; you're damned lucky it missed the bone. Could have shattered your shoulder."

Jesamiah did not reply. He lay back on to the narrow bed in the surgeon's cramped cabin, occupied with consuming a bottle of brandy. A little lower and to the left and he would have been dead. Was he charmed or cursed or something? What kept saving him - it was not for want of trying to make an end of it all! He closed his eyes, clenched his teeth against Jackson's none too gentle probing. This nightmare existence? It was a curse, it had to be. And the spell to break it? Ah, only a witch could do that.

He always allowed the crew their fun with a captured ship that had put up resistance – those who surrendered were relieved of their cargo and otherwise left in peace. With this ship he let his lads do as they please, as long as he was not expected to take part.

Tossing in his captain's box-bed he slept fitfully, his shoulder on fire, his dreams disturbing him as the two ships lay alongside each other and the crew caroused on deck. He dreamt of a woman tending a pistol shot in his shoulder. Her dear face swimming before his eyes, that well before dawn were swollen and red-rimmed from self-pitying tears.

He missed her. God's truth, he missed Tiola so much!

For the audacity of wounding Jesamiah, the crew had stripped the Dutch captain naked and made him run up and down his own deck between two howling and mocking lines of pirates each with a sailing needle in his hand, pricking at the poor man's buttocks, back and shoulders as he hobbled past. Again and again they made him run, and when there were enough pockmarked spots of blood they put him bleeding and miserable into an emptied sugar-cane cask swarming with cockroaches. They thought it hilarious. If he was lucky someone might eventually remember to release him.

Come morning not a single man of the *Sea Witch* was sober enough to witness the sunrise. The two ships, warped together, rocked gently and drifted with the tide and the wind, while the men slept where they had fallen.

The only thing different about this captured Chase, her name. *Berenice.*

Jesamiah would not realise the significance until many days later, after the crew had lost interest, turned the few survivors free and cast off in search of new prey; after the fever that had raked his body faded, and the wound in his shoulder finally began to heal. When a rain squall sent the sun behind dismal clouds, for want of something to do, Jesamiah thought to read the captured ship's log.

He sat in his cabin, his new carpet spread over the wooden floor hiding the gouges the heavy cannons made whenever they were manoeuvred into position. His arm in a sling, he sipped fine brandy his feet propped on his desk. Idly, he flipped through the pages of the meticulously accurate record of the log. Glanced at the vessel's registration and jerked to full attention, spilling brandy over his breeches. The crew would bait him for that. *"Can't get to the 'eads quick enough, Cap'n?"*

"Bloody hell," he murmured as he stared at the written words. "She's one of van Overstratten's fleet!"

The wry smile that lifted the corner of his mouth was one of deep satisfaction.

- Ten -

Endless days blended into weeks, the weeks into months and months into eternity. Tiola had nothing to do and no reason to be doing it.

Fever had raged to the point where Stefan had called in the priest, sending him away again when she had become agitated at seeing him standing, muttering his prayers at the foot of her bed. After that, Tiola slowly recovered but the tiredness and weakness lingered. Beyond the windows of Stefan's grand home, the hot African summer matured and faded into a mellow autumn. February and March, the threshold of April.

Cosseted, her every need pampered by servants, Tiola's only escape was to walk, and fortunately Stefan's physician believed exercise would do her well. Walking took energy, tired her enough so she slept at night. She walked along the shore, listening to the murmur of the sea. Walked into the heights of the Table Mountain where only the wind whispered a distraction. Never alone, for always there was someone with her, watching, guarding. A servant trailing behind or occasionally van Overstratten himself determined to be cheerful as they strolled through the market or the Company Gardens.

Did he think she would run? A young woman, fragile and afraid without money, with nowhere to go? Did he expect her to steal aboard a ship and follow Jesamiah - after he had made it quite plain he did not want her? She had no idea where Jesamiah was, nor even if he was alive. Again and again, she tried to convince herself she did not want to know.

She wore fancy silk garments, fine brocades and French lace. Shoes with silver buckles. She ate a little, talked a little, slept a little. Walked. And still the demons taunted her.

She stood at the edge of existence looking into the depth of her misery. Came very close to stepping over the edge into oblivion, except, one small part of her Craft must have remained. A fragile thread left behind, holding on to the sanity that hid itself, unseen and almost forgotten inside her grieving heart.

And then she found the letter, a letter to Stefan from a man regarding an arranged business venture. Saw it, read it.

As always, she had been walking, returned to Stefan's house – she could never think of it as home - tired and dishevelled. He came striding from his study, brows furrowed hiding his irritation, an expansive, false, smile tipping the corners of his mouth.

"Ah, there you are Tiola!" As always he pronounced her name incorrectly, the emphasis on the middle vowel. "I was beginning to worry, it is almost dusk." Hurrying across the entrance hall he took Tiola's arm, tutting, ushered her into his private domain to where the last of the day's sunshine slanted into the room.

Her hair was damp from the spindrift of the sea, and her gown edged by a rime of wet sand and salt. The sound of the ocean, the voice of Tethys roaring up on to the land was still buffeting her ears. Removing her cloak and bonnet Stefan handed them to a maid, instructed tea, hot and sweet to be fetched. He sat Tiola in the chair he had pushed back from his desk, removed her sea-sodden shoes, quite ruined, rubbed at her feet and hands.

"*Mijn beste*, you are cold. I do so wish you would not walk along the shore, the wind can be bitter." He knelt before her, folded her hands within his own, paternal.

"Dearest, this cannot continue. Please reconsider my repeated request and consent to be my wife?" He forced a jest, "It is inconvenient to always be requiring a chaperone to watch over us whenever I wish to talk with you." He patted her hand again. "Perhaps if you are settled in marriage this debilitating melancholy will ease? And when sons come along..." He spread his arms as if he had no need to say more. "Look how fulfilled my sister is with her babies. You could find contentment in children, I am sure."

Perhaps she could. But not with children sired by him. She wanted Jesamiah. Oh, she so wanted Jesamiah!

Stefan had not pressed for marriage when first she had begun to recover, for he did not desire a sickly woman as wife, but she was stronger now, and beside, despite frequent enquiries, the marriage agencies had found no suitable alternative. Add to that, it was safe to take her now; no child had been planted in her belly by a pirate's tainted seed.

Receiving no response beyond a polite murmur that she was well and he need not concern himself, Stefan hissed his disapproval and swept from the room. Tiola heard him running up the stairs, taking them two at a time, talking briskly to the servants, issuing orders for bath water to be heated, dry clothes to be produced. Soon he would come and usher her upstairs to be fussed over. She so hated it all!

He had been sitting at his desk, reading correspondence delivered from the Caribbean. In his haste to play the concerned gentleman, the ardent lover, a letter had fallen to the floor. Absently Tiola retrieved it - knew instantly without seeing any of the writing or the flourished signature who had sent it. And her ability of Craft roared into her with the full force of a broadside of cannon.

The room lurched as if the earth had shrugged. The hole, the pit of despair entrapping her these long months collapsed in upon itself, the emptiness imploding like a giant star in the heavens. A star that when the debris settled and the dust cleared, might not appear so large, but contained, instead, a limitless and immortal power. Gasping, breathless, she fell to her knees her head spinning, elation shouting inside her as the gift of Craft returned, its power renewed threefold.

The demons fled, replaced by an inrush of joyful greeting.

~ *Welcome home, my dear!* ~

~ Good greet you, Tiola Oldstagh! ~

Beyond the window she heard the birds singing their evening cadence of glory, the chirrup of insects and the friendly murmur of the wind. Heard also, the hush of the sea as it washed the shore and heard the Earth itself, gently breathing. Could feel the pulse of the Universe, all time and existence encircling and embracing her. The final transition from child to woman all completed and made whole as her gift of Craft matured into its full potency, and with it came the complete knowledge and wisdom of all life and existence. If it could be spoken, Tiola now knew the words to say it; if it could be seen, she had the sight to recognise it. If it could be done, she had the ability to do it.

~ You were strong before, ~ her grandmother said with pride *~ and now you are stronger still. You have endured desolation and have conquered fear. You have stood at the edge of despair and found the strength to turn away from the depth of darkness. Nothing now can harm you, Tiola, for there is none more powerful than those who know they can survive. ~*

Tiola looked at the letter in her hand, read it, taking in certain words above others. Nassau. New governor. Amnesty. She could see the writer's face, the dark eyes, black hair tied at the nape of his neck by a silk bow. Similar height, similar build. So similar to Jesamiah - but not quite the same. They had different mothers but shared the same father.

Phillipe Mereno. Stefan was corresponding with Jesamiah's half brother. And there could be only one reason why.

Because of Jesamiah himself.

- Eleven -

The noise on deck was so loud it could have roused the dead, what with the cheering and shouting and the squawking of flustered chickens. Hen racing was a favoured pastime, although Finch, the galley-cook and Jesamiah's self-appointed personal steward, grumbled that making them run up and down the deck tainted the eggs and addled the yolks.

Jesamiah had his bet – five black pebbles – on the hen with one white feather in her tail. He did not permit gambling for money on board, it led too easily into vicious fights. Her opponent, the fat one with short legs, reminded him of Jenna. Perhaps it was the way she stood, head cocked to one side her beady eyes staring at him disapprovingly, or the width of her broad backside? Aside, young Jasper had been diligently training White Flash these last few days. She had a good chance of winning.

Two lines of sand marked the start and finish on the deck, the track between covering five yards. This was the final race, the two best contenders left from a series of exciting heats. The loser faced the threat of becoming the prime ingredient in tomorrow's stew. Jesamiah stroked the soft feathers along White Flash's back, crooning to her as he held her beneath his arm.

"Now then, m'beauty, you know what you have to do. Look, there's our Jasper with your reward." He held her up showing her the lad at the far end of the track, Jasper's tin mug held provocatively in his hand.

"You ready?" Rue asked. He lifted his hand, paused, dropped it, and the two hens were set down with a hefty shove forwards. The crew, spread each side, roared encouragement.

Jasper rattled his mug, shouting. "*Chuck, chuck, chuck!*"

"Go girl!" Jesamiah yelled clapping his hands, itching to give her a prodding kick up her feathered arse.

As a race it was not exactly exhilarating. Both chickens strutted about two feet then stopped to put their heads on one side and then peck at insects crawling on the wooden planking. White Flash's opposition even turning around to amble back towards the start – against the rules to touch the runners once they were released!

Then White Flash heard the rattle of Jaspers mug; she hitched her wings like a little fat lady lifting her skirts and scurried at a waddling comical run towards him, her bright black eyes fixed on the glint of the tin and the sound it made. She was across the line and Jasper tipped out the contents for her to gobble as a mixture of dismal groans from the losers and the exultant cheers of winners leapt towards the Caribbean sky. Some of the winners hurled their hats into the air and then cried out in dismay as an unexpected gust of wind took the lot of them overboard. The two sails on the fore and main mast, the one a-back with the wind full on its face, and the other counter-balancing to hold *Sea Witch* hove to, flapped, cracking, as the gust rippled through the canvas.

Jesamiah patted Jasper's shoulder well pleased. Grinned as the lad confessed his secret.

"I've been collectin' the weevils from the food barrels – trainin' her to recognise the sound they make rattlin' around in the mug 'ere!"

Several of the men were leaning over the rail waving boat hooks, trying to fish the lost hats out of the sea. One glanced up stared a moment, blinked, yelled; "Sail ho!"

"Where away?" Jesamiah queried rushing to the binnacle where the telescope had been left. He extended its length brought it up to his eye, a smile of satisfaction spreading across his face.

"Leave those hats lads, we'll get us a new haul from that fine-looking British East Indiaman over there!" In the heat of the day every man needed something to cover his head, to stop his brains roasting. Hats and bandannas were not an accessory, they were essential.

When she eventually limped in to Kingston harbour, the captain of a merchant vessel carrying hatless passengers and crew angrily assailed the Governor, demanded he do something about these pirates prowling like basking sharks in the sea lanes off the Jamaican coast.

The Governor shrugged, was uncertain as to exactly where the man's indignation was directed. Because he had been chased and boarded by the crew of a blue-hulled pirate named *Sea Witch*? Or was it because of the embarrassment that his loss, aside from the specie, was nothing more than a haul of hats?

Jesamiah was pleased with the better quality three cornered hat he had taken from a wealthy lawyer, or perhaps he was one of these new bankers? It was good to know there were opportunities for light-hearted camaraderie aboard his ship, the sound of laughter to balance the killing and the lurking claw of death. Good too, to ease the residue of discomfort left after the decision taken yesterday.

Jesamiah wanted no part of it, but the others had voted and he had been outnumbered.

Piracy they had said, was all well and good but the English Government was waking up to the fact that something had to be done about it. Until now, the one or two Ships of the Line had been next to useless in the Caribbean, their captains untried and untested. The Navy sent men who knew nothing of these waters or the shoals. Consequently, the pirates sailed rings around them. But it was all changing. Someone with sense was now the Lord High Admiral in London, and England was starting to send better men and faster ships. While anyone on the Account had a fair chance of staying free and untroubled, the easy life suited - it was the other side of the coin when a hangman's noose dangled too near for comfort.

"We have a hold full of wealth," the crew had said. "Let us divide it and see what this new Governor has to say when he comes to Nassau. See what he intends to do with this amnesty of pardon on offer."

Rue too, apologising to Jesamiah with spread hands, had voted for Nassau.

Jesamiah did not trust pardons, governors, politicians or governments. The only cheering thought, he did know this particular Governor. Perhaps he would turn out to be better than the rest of them? Woodes Rogers. The man he had met in Cape Town. He had appeared to be a man who liked the sound of his own voice and listened only to his personal opinion; but he was also scrupulously honest. In Jesamiah's view, to the point of rabid stupidity.

That was all a while ahead yet. Rogers would not be coming to Nassau until the tail end of July. Until then, Jesamiah intended to put the fear of the Devil into anyone who glimpsed the *Sea Witch's* topgallant sails appear over the horizon.

- Twelve -

From across the churchyard, Stefan watched Tiola tidying Jenna's grave, a task she did every Sunday after the service of worship he insisted his household attend. He wished she would let go of the past and concentrate on the future.

This Sunday, however, things were different. Tiola had her ability of Craft returned and she intended to use it to seek the truth. While her body undertook the menial task Tiola ignored the Dutchman's close proximity and skilfully directed her mind to a different plain and a different time.

Looking down through a time-shifting haze of mist, she saw herself kneeling beside the grave, seemingly engrossed in what she was doing. Saw the spread of the churchyard, Stefan impatiently watching her. As she drifted higher, her view widened: Table Mountain, Cape Town, the beach and the pound of the surf. The harbour.

And the scene wavered, changed into the past. Black smoke spiralled into the sky, a warehouse was ablaze, people standing, pointing. Across the bay a ship was about to make sail, her hawser cut, her stern swinging outward. Rough-dressed sailors were swarming up the rigging – and a man was running along her deck, leaping to the jetty, shouting.

Her heart lurched. Jesamiah! The moment when he had shattered her heart!

From a great height and distance Tiola observed Jesamiah confronting Jenna. Saw him draw his pistol – she caught her breath. Had she been wrong?

She closed her eyes in relief when he tucked the weapon away and sprinted for his ship. She had never believed, had never accepted that Jesamiah had dispassionately shot Jenna.

No sound, save for the singing of the drifting winds of Time weaving together the past and the present. She could see the puffs of smoke as muskets were fired from the jetty, the spatters of dust and splinters of wood as lead shot found a target. Her heart was beating fast as Jesamiah scrabbled aboard his ship. There was Stefan agitated, talking to Jenna and then his face broke into a smile, pleased at something she had told him.

Then Jesamiah took a musket into his hand, he levelled it, fired at Stefan - and Stefan was swirling Jenna around to duck behind her.

Tears streamed Tiola's face. All they had told her had been lies! Jesamiah's bullet had killed Jenna, but his aim had been for Stefan – and at that distance, he would not have expected the shot to do damage; the killing had not been intentional. And he had not sailed without her. He had waited as long as he possibly could; had been distraught when she had not come. Tiola's watching spirit followed behind the *Sea Witch* as she heeled out to sea. She saw him at the taffrail, his knuckles clenched white, the distress contorting his face. And her heart broke all over again. She tried to call out to him, her voice shouting his name - but the shifting of Time was a fickle thing, and the scene shimmered and faded.

Was his pain still there, these months on? Or had he now forgotten her, set her aside as just another whore bedded and pleasured? Until she found him again, in the present time, in the present world, Tiola had no way of knowing the answer.

Other scenes were shimmering in her vision as if they were illusions created by a haze of heat across a barren desert. She was to be shown something more then.

Jesamiah. Ten years old with his mother, admiring a boat moored to a jetty. The father, looking so much like his younger son, proudly showing off her sleek lines. A second boy, older, stood scowling in the background. Another blur of movement, a rapid change of time and location; the elder son kneeling on the younger's back, painfully twisting his arm - holding his head in a barrel of rain water – kicking him where it hurt most. She was watching Jesamiah's childhood. His daily misery.

Another shift of scene: a few years later and that same boat was now burning. It was night, the sky pocked with silver stars, and early autumn, for the trees were turning to russet, gold, and red. The *Acorn*. Her hull and deck were soaked with scattered pitch, the flames were licking up her masts, devouring the canvas of her sails. In the reflected light Tiola could see him clearly, Jesamiah, not quite fifteen years old, kneeling on the jetty, weeping for the thing he loved being destroyed so callously.

And again the scene moved on, the time-shift a mere flicker, like the blinking of an eye. Half an hour ahead? Perhaps less.

I do not want to see this, Tiola thought, recognising the malevolent presence of the Dark Power swirling around the two figures a way below her hovering spirit. The stars had gone. The black, enshrouding cloud of evil had stalked in to swallow everything, to play its nasty game of mischief.

She was about to discover what Phillipe had done to so hurt Jesamiah – and what had given him the strength and courage to finally turn on his brother. To claim his right of freedom.

Two graves. One, their father's, new-dug. Phillipe, grown to a man now, was dragging the brother he hated by the hair, the boy kicking out, screaming, pleading to be left alone. Phillipe made Jesamiah stand by his mother's grave and forced him to urinate on the mound, her resting place not yet a week old. Steeped in misery by years of intimidation and torment, the boy's submission was indoctrinated by fear. And then Phillipe kicked at his brother's knee, sending him sprawling with a cry of pain across the grave. Appalled sickness gorged into Tiola's throat. She shut her eyes, turned her head away, could not watch what happened next. Could not so blatantly pry into the sordid privacy of Jesamiah's defilement.

When she opened them again, Mereno was leering as he straddled the boy and pushed his face into the muddied puddle of piss.

"Tell me she was a whore. Let me hear you say it!"

With tears of pity wetting her cheeks, Tiola heard Jesamiah's answering sob of despair. "She was a whore, my mother was a whore."

"A fokken whore!"

"A fokken whore."

Mereno moved away crowing his triumph. Turned his back on a boy, who with shaking fingers was buttoning his breeches, trying to make himself descent; mortified at the abuse, and because he had so insulted and betrayed his mother. The misery was breaking him apart. His spirit, his weeping soul, was on the very edge of being shattered beyond repair.

With compassion flowing through her, Tiola stretched a hand through the barrier of time. Rested her palm between the boy's shoulder blades. A friend, a lover's, touch.

~ *Jesamiah. This is not your shame, but his. Words are only words; saying things you do not mean cannot harm your mother. It is what is in your heart that matters. And you have a good heart.* ~

The boy looked up, confused, puzzled. Clearly he had heard her voice in his mind.

Was it wrong of her to interfere? Perhaps. But those who brutalised the weak or the afraid had no right to remain unchallenged. Evil fed upon itself to mutate and grow beyond control. It was not interfering for one of the White Craft to put an end to the harm of the Dark Power.

~ *Fight him Jesamiah!* ~ she ordered, sending her courage into him through that touch of love. ~ *I give you my strength. Get up! Fight back!* ~

As her spirit re-entered her body, Tiola brushed earth from her hands. So now she knew when and how her soul had first brushed against his. When he had desperately needed help to survive, a subtle manipulation of existence had allowed her to be there in his past, her presence igniting the anger he had needed to fight for his dignity, freedom and his life. If he had stayed there on his knees, drowning in his shame? Then the good man Jesamiah was, beneath his rough exterior, would never have come into being. His life would probably have ended there, that night, the deed commissioned by his own hand.

Jesamiah is a part of me, as I am a part of him, she thought, as her fingers slipped into the pocket-bag at her waist to withdraw something small and gold. *Our souls are love and lover, and we have been torn apart. An arm ripped from its socket, the Sun made into forever night. And this little death that is forced between us, is become unbearable to endure.*

Helping Tiola to her feet, Stefan frowned as he glimpsed something shining in her hand. A ring. That damned pirate's ring!

He said with disapproval, pointing at it, "I thought you had discarded the thing the day Acorne committed murder."

Tiola put the ring away, stepped a pace from him, rejecting his touch. "But he did not, as you implied, deliberately shoot Jenna did he Stefan? It was not as you told me. All of it was lies." What she had learned filled her with anger. She wanted to strike him, shout at him – shout to the world his deceit and defamation of Jesamiah. But she could do none of it for she had to know where her pirate was now. Had to get to him.

She raised her hand, gracefully wove her fingers into a figure of eight pattern. *"Hie...sssh; you will tell me all I wish to know of your acquaintance with Phillipe Mereno. And then you will forget I asked, as you will also forget we stood here beside this grave of the woman who took the shot meant for you."*

There was much she could do with her power, but as much she could not. Some things required Craft, for others the natural wit of a woman's charm would need to suffice instead. She could not risk exposing her abilities - she would not be helping Jesamiah were she to get herself hanged as a witch. A woman of her young age would attract questions and suspicion were she to travel alone. Yet to stop Stefan or Mereno from killing Jesamiah she *had* to get to Nassau for the arrival of this new Governor and his offer of unconditional amnesty to all pirates.

The solution was the only one she could think of that would not compromise her safety or draw undue attention. It was perhaps dramatic, but simple.

When next he asked, Tiola agreed to become Stefan's wife.

*

While she was incapable of fear, Tethys felt a disturbance, a tremor of concern, which trickled through her transparent, fluid, mass. An unbalance distorted the equilibrium of her world, her anxiety caused through the not knowing of from whence it came. Tethys knew everything but this. This was new and as yet unrecognised. A capability which, while not a threat was ambiguous in its intent.

Diligent, she searched for the source of the intrusion.

It came, she eventually discovered, from one of the ships gliding upon the surface of her domain. Not one of those pirate ships with their loud ways and roaring cannon - although she kept a part of her awareness on the blue-hulled one. No, this was from a ship that had sailed from the hot, dry lands of Africa to the turquoise, crystal waters of the Caribbean and the scattered islands of the Bahamas.

Not that Tethys cared for the quaint names these humans gave the land forms. All that concerned her was the potential capability surging from a female aboard that ship. A capability which intrigued, and a little - just a little - unnerved her.

Thirteen

Captain Woodes Rogers' arrival at Nassau on New Providence Island was to be five days later than expected. With capricious winds, the flux of the tides and a voyage length from England of something near two months, this was entirely understandable. Stefan van Overstratten, however, was not a man who contemplated the virtues of patience. He fretted and fussed, his temper raw and his disappointment in his wife increasing daily.

They had been wed on the first day of May. Tiola had wanted a private ceremony, Stefan a grand affair. As always, he had his way. These three months on, he well understood women took time to begin breeding, but as yet there was not a sign of her womb quickening. His doubts were rising about his wife; that perhaps she would be unable to produce children had never occurred to him. Her barrenness with the pirate he had assumed to be Acorne's lack, not hers. He would not be knowing that through her Craft Tiola had control over the working of her body. It was for her to decide when she would be nurturing a child within her womb. Nor would he know she regretted not giving Jesamiah the son he would have been proud of, or that she had no intention of permitting Stefan's seed to impregnate her.

For the week they had been here, Tiola had spent most of the daylight hours observing the jumble of ships resting at anchor in the harbour, looking for one particular ship. As had Stefan, for a different reason. Nassau was busy, the harbour filled with vessels of all sizes and states of sea-worthiness. Close on three thousand men, scavengers of the sea as Stefan called them, had descended here - from curiosity more than pursuing a government-granted pardon. They took the opportunity of freedom from harassment by the authorities to careen, and to enjoy the available women and plentiful supply of rum and ale. The taverns and brothels, delighted with the glut of trade, made the most of it while it lasted.

Lodging at the Governor's official residence, empty and echoing with only servants and themselves to rattle around the private quarters on the first and second floors, Tiola felt the days of anxious waiting crawl by. Life, even if it was only that of degenerates, was stretched in a ragged uproarious muddle along the beach, straggling between the camp fires and whore-tents. It was not in this pink-and-white painted, bleak house. Was most certainly not in her marriage, although she had not expected it to be. Stefan demanded everything for himself. Unlike Jesamiah's fire of lovemaking, he had no tenderness and no understanding of her passion or her needs; his act of sex was impersonal and devoid of emotion, completed in a matter of minutes. He used her as was his right and for his own satisfaction; treated her as if she were an object devoid of feeling.

The temptation to use Voice and send him from her had pushed her self-restraint to the limit on several occasions, yet she had to wait, had to maintain this pretence. An ear soon became deaf to familiar sounds. The repetitive use of Voice would diminish its strength, Stefan would become immune to its command and she could not risk that, in case Jesamiah came. Use Craft unnecessarily and the illusion was at risk of wearing transparent thin and then ripping apart. She could suffer Stefan's tedious attentions for they were merely inconvenient and irritating, were not life threatening. But how she missed the sensuous touch of Jesamiah's hands! His tongue and lips exploring her body, his skill of love making which could conjure such prolonged delights of intimate pleasure! How she missed the sensation of his own release, exploding inside her as, together, they reached the height of a dizzy crescendo. She wanted him. Oh, how she wanted him!

Tiola sighed, thrust away erotic thoughts of Jesamiah and concentrated on the ships in the harbour. The one advantage to the Governor's house: the view from this first floor front window gave out over the bay. A ship was carefully nudging her way over the sandbar, a Royal Navy frigate, flying the Great Union Flag from her stern ensign staff, the Jack from her bow. Not one of those vessels at anchor even remotely resembled *Sea Witch*.

Would she look the same as when Tiola had last seen her? Jesamiah would have altered and refitted her, made her into a pirate ship with cannon and gun ports. He had re-painted her hull, that fact appeared to be wide-spread knowledge, for every indignant statement of his attacks had reported a blue-painted hull. Did *Sea Witch* still have the figurehead? The lady with the generous bust? Tiola smiled at the thought. Knowing Jesamiah, she would still be there in all her fine glory.

If only she knew where Jesamiah was and what he intended to do! Was he on his way to Nassau or was he somewhere else, on the far side of the world, perhaps? The idea of remaining Stefan's wife and tolerating his dull and arrogant presence for no reason filled her with dread. All this could be such a waste of time - but if Jesamiah *was* coming, if he was even now just beyond the horizon... To see him again she would suffer a thousand indifferent nights with Stefan grunting on top of her. If only Jesamiah would lower the barrier he had erected against her and allow her to enter his mind!

On the long voyage across the Atlantic she had persistently called to him. Leaning on the lee rail, pretending to be mesmerised by the churn of the sea, she had slowed her heartbeat, set her mind to think only of Jesamiah; the memory of his face, his voice, his smell. Had met nothing beyond a blackness that would not yield to her probing. Subconsciously – he would not have been aware to do so deliberately - he had created a shielding wall, blocking her thoughts from connecting with his, and until she physically saw him there was nothing she could do to tear it down. But if he came, Stefan was also waiting.

Exasperated, Tiola whirled away from the window, an explicit and crude sailor's cuss Jesamiah had occasionally muttered leaving her lips. Found her husband leaning against the door frame, watching her intently with a disapproving stare.

"So disappointed to see me?" he commented as he crossed the room. "And a sailor's oath as greeting? I was unaware a gentlewoman would know of such filth."

How long had he been standing there? Spying on her? She made light of the expletive. "I must have heard it aboard your ship. I have no idea what it means."

"Or perhaps your pirate used it?" Stefan walked towards her, took her hands in his own, his thumbs rubbing the soft skin across her knuckles. His own hands were smooth, unlike Jesamiah's there were no calluses across the palms, no stains of tar or gunpowder ingrained beneath the nails. "It sounded the sort of lewdness an immoral felon such as he would utter."

"If he did, I cannot recall it. Indeed I remember little of those months. I was a naive young girl, Stefan, blinded by the lure of adventure. Those childish days are behind me, I am your wife and I have matured into sensibility."

He shifted his fingers to encircle her wrists, his breath, tainted with tobacco and brandy, unpleasant on her face. "Oh I think not. I think you remember very well. I think you remember *him*, very well."

Tiola attempted to pull away. "You are hurting me."

"Do you think me a fool?" he snapped, tightening the grip. "Since our first night you have lain beneath me as a frozen block of ice. It is him you think of; his touch, his kisses. His prick poking into you!" Abruptly he jerked her close against him, the feel of his arousal hard beneath his breeches pressing through her gown.

"He has nothing I have not got, Madam!" His mouth covered hers, the kiss dominating, devoid of love or passion.

She made no response, movement or sound. He pulled away, annoyance puckering his nose. "You have no regard for me at all, have you?"

Restraining an instinctive urge to unleash her power Tiola said, as calm as she could, "If that is so, then why did I marry you?"

Releasing her, Stefan turned away to quietly close the door. "Why? Because you knew I would never have permitted you to leave Cape Town, and you wanted so desperately to come here, did you not *liefste*? Wanted to be here in Nassau because you hope *he* will be coming."

There was no point in the telling of lies. "Had I wished it, Stefan, you could not have stopped me. It is the other way around, I would not have allowed you to leave without me, but being your wife was the easiest way of travelling without drawing undue attention or comment from others."

As Madame van Overstratten, who had queried her presence aboard his ship? Had she been alone, ah, the Craft she would have had to use to ensure her privacy and safety! Day after day, hour after hour concealing herself, blending illusion, bending the truth; always afraid someone would be immune or the Dark Power, delighting in creating mischief, would expose her for what she was. A witch. Women were permitted so little freedom, were treated as chattels and servants; a means to ease a man's sexual need. Unlike Stefan, Jesamiah had treated her with respect. Another reason to so love him.

Stefan regarded her with distaste, his feelings for her beginning to turn to hatred. Wrongly, he had assumed once a married woman with responsibility – and children on the way - she would behave as did his sister, dutiful, obedient and attentive. He had not expected Tiola to continue with this stubborn streak of wayward independence. He had wanted her because she was beautiful: a woman he could parade before others and watch the envy in their eyes. Now he feared those same men would soon be openly mocking him for taking a wife who was empty-bellied, as useless as a broken piss-pot. And he knew well the snide comments of men. How many of them were sniggering that the fault rested with the stallion not the mare?

"I promised you once that you would see Acorne hang. Cheat on me, woman, and I can promise you this also; you will hang beside him." He turned the key in the lock, the sound of the slight click small, but ominous. "Unless, of course, you begin breeding." His hand went to the buttons of his breeches. "I think now is as good an opportunity as any to try again? Do you not agree?"

He was a fool if he thought he could make her fear him. Tiola raised her hand, her eyes, blazing contempt, staring into his own – and a great blast of gunpowder roared from the harbour, rattling the glass in the windows and startling birds, sending them squawking and cawing into the early evening air. Then cannon fire, two, three, guns booming and echoing across the entire island.

Stefan darted to the window. A single masted sloop was adrift and full ablaze, her powder magazine evidently exploded. A second vessel, sails tumbling from the yards, anchor cable cut, was racing for the harbour entrance, while a third, the inbound frigate, slewed wildly to starboard to avoid collision with the one afire. Half her crew were running to fend her off with boat hooks, the other half manning the guns to make a retaliatory volley at the ship that had fired at them. But they were too slow and too late. The fleeing vessel was over the bar and away.

Someone was rattling the door handle; Captain Henry Jennings voice cursing explicitly. Tiola crossed to the door, snapped open the lock and Jennings, pushing heavily from the far side, almost fell through into the room.

The same Jennings who had sailed with Jesamiah Acorne to acquire for himself a fortune in gold. Labelled a pirate by the Spanish, he vehemently opposed the slur to his character, protesting he was a legitimate privateer. With an estate a few miles from Nassau, the ability to read, write and tally numbers, and respected by pirates, the Royal Navy and the British Government alike, he was an ideal candidate to become adviser, mediator and personal aide to Governor Rogers; effectively, an unofficial Vice Governor.

"Bloody doors are all warped!" he cursed as he hurried to peer out of the window. "Half of them don't close properly, the other half get stuck! What was that explosion? What has happened?"

"One of your damned pirates appears to be making a run for it. Vane's brig, I believe," Stefan announced with a disdainful flourish of his hand. "I heard rumour he had fallen out with you over who is to be appointed second in command to your authority. From the disruption he is causing out there, I take it the rumour is true?"

Jennings regarded the Dutchman with distaste; thought him an arrogant fop. But then, he thought the same of most wealthy merchantmen. "I must correct you sir, rumour is most certainly not true. Below the Governor I hold sole commission for legal jurisdiction, my position of authority has not been in the least gainsaid. It is correct, however, that Vane and I did exchange harsh words. He requested a letter of marque in order to hunt down those on the Account who do not respond to this amnesty. I refused him on the grounds he is unreliable."

Retrieving a telescope from a small table beside the window, Jennings extended it and peered down into the harbour. Commented after a moment's study, "The fellow appears to have confirmed my objections." He swung the telescope slightly, assessing the situation. Vane was a fool if he thought flouncing off in a temper was the best option because he could not get his own way. As a dramatic gesture, setting that old hulk afire achieved his aim of seeking attention, but Jennings doubted the British captain coming into harbour would be impressed by the little tirade. He shut the telescope with a clatter, opined, "I would wager this Navy fellow has been sent ahead to inform us of our new Governor's imminent arrival."

Van Overstratten had withdrawn to stand beside Tiola, his hand gripping her arm, leaving a bruise to mark her skin. In her ear he hissed a warning. "You are my wife, I expect you to behave as such. You belong to me, not that pretty pirate." He shook her, a rough expression of annoyance. "I brought you here because I want you to watch him hang. Once he is dead you will forget him. Do you understand me?"

Tiola understood him all too well. How could a man so apparently charming alter so abruptly after the exchange of marriage vows? What had happened to the wooing? The congenial concern? With distaste she removed his fingers from her arm and moved towards the door, from where she said, not caring that Captain Jennings would hear, "He may not come. Unlike Charles Vane, my Jesamiah is not a fool."

Van Overstratten smiled, lazily presumptive. "Oh he will come. He will not wish to be left outside of all that is happening here. Do you not agree, Captain?"

Belatedly realising he had walked in upon a marital squabble, Jennings tactfully made no answer.

Stefan laughed, a cynical sound. "If he does not come, it is no matter. As the good Captain Jennings has indicated, there is adequate provision being made for the hunting down of those who choose to disregard the law."

- Fourteen -

Pirates were considered the dregs of the earth, detritus floating as scum on the surface of the sea - they also had a flair for parade and ostentation. As Governor Woodes Rogers stepped ashore in the early morning of the twenty sixth day of July the pirates were waiting for him. Wearing their finest and their best, all decorated with ribbons and bows, beads and buckles, they trooped into George Street to line its shabby length of ill-built taverns, crammed stores, ordinaries and hotch-potch of houses. From the harbour to the Governor's residence each man stood and cheered, cutlass drawn to form an arch for Rogers to walk beneath, his timid wife clinging nervously to his arm. There were huzzahs of welcome and enthusiastic applause, all of it sodden with the distinctive, sweet waft of rum.

Rogers took their welcome in the spirit it was intended: as good will and good fortune. Aware the congenial atmosphere would last only as long as the rum did.

He had arrived aboard a Royal Navy man o'war, escorted by three companies of red-coated marines scattered through three frigates, three more vessels of his own and a former East Indiaman, the *Delicia* of thirty six guns. She was to become a Guardship, her purpose to patrol the waters of the Bahamas against rogue pirates who refused to accept amnesty. The men ashore were impressed by his show of strength. As Rogers had intended them to be.

Flanking the door of the Governor's residence, waiting to greet him with ceremony and formality, were two impeccably dressed men. On one side, Captain Henry Jennings, on the other, a man Rogers remembered from Cape Town. A Dutchman of wealth and influence who had personal experience of the lusting greed of pirates - and who had partially funded the cost of commissioning the *Delicia*. Master Stefan van Overstratten had honoured Nassau's new Governor by expressing his desire to offer practical aid in ridding the sea-routes of the blackguard devils. Trade - cotton, sugar, tobacco - was suffering because of piracy and unlike many who were making heavy losses, here was someone who had not confined himself to belly-aching and whining. Rogers was indebted to the man for his generous foresight and greeted him warmly.

Jennings, slightly irritated that van Overstratten had been greeted first, removed his hat and swept the Governor an elaborate bow. He took Mrs Rogers' hand and elegantly kissed it.

"Welcome Sir. Madam. We bid you long life, peace and prosperity."

"Aye, with many a sleepless night thrown in while trying to fathom how to keep the upper hand over yon bunch of swabs, eh? Ha! Ha!" Rogers guffawed, taking Jennings offered hand and vigorously pumping it up and down as if it were a rusted spout. Despite the unfortunate incident of Vane's act of insult yesterday, this appeared to be a good start. A very good start indeed.

There was much to do, much to discuss and implement. The detail of the pardon issued by His Majesty's Government stated any man who, with his hand on the Bible, swore to relinquish piracy and then signed his name, or made his mark in the leather-bound book Rogers reverently carried beneath his arm, would be pardoned of all crime, including murder. That might sit well with the pirates and the Government in England, but it rankled with those ship owners who had been plundered and would not see a glimmer of their stolen property again.

Among them, van Overstratten and Phillipe Mereno. Rogers treated the Dutchman with respect and friendship, aware he and his partner expected something in return for their generosity. Something in the line of waiving taxes or turning a blind eye to a venture not quite legal, he assumed. Providing whatever it was they desired was not too outrageous, he could probably accommodate them.

When Phillipe Mereno's fine new schooner moored alongside the jetty, eight and forty hours later, Rogers discovered the blind eye to be turned was somewhat distasteful to a man of his high morals. Did it matter? The rogue they wanted him to hang was not in Nassau, and until he was, their asking was mere mist on the sea. And if he came? The Governor shrugged, said he would consider their petition and left it at that.

But between the last night of July and the first dawn of August, another ship on reefed topsails slid across the sandbar, the phosphorus of her bow wave rippling under the impartial gaze of a sickle moon and a serene, star-studded sky.

Reluctant, wary, and with many misgivings, Captain Jesamiah Acorne had brought the *Sea Witch* into anchorage within Nassau harbour.

- Fifteen -

Rue had wanted the amnesty, or at least had wanted to find out more about it. So had Isiah Roberts, although as an African he had expressed concern over the attitude towards his black skin.

"I smell a rat," Jesamiah had protested. "A big one with a nest of smaller rats waiting to do their mischief."

"There are rats in the bilges," Rue had answered philosophically, "but we still go down into the 'old."

"Aye, but when we do we take a damned big stick with us." Jesamiah hated rats.

Slapping his captain's shoulder Rue had chuckled, "And I 'ave no objection to taking the same precaution with the rats in Nassau, *mon ami!* None at all!"

Crossing the sandbar, Jesamiah luffed *Sea Witch* up into an anchorage, insisting the hands set her fair before disappearing ashore, probably never to be seen again. He took pride in his ship and would not have her dishevelled as if she were a drunken slut with her petticoats draped around her ankles, her shoes scuffed and her stockings torn. As he pointed out to the few who bellyached, they would be glad of it should they need to take their leave in a hurry. Within thirty minutes *Sea Witch* rested, neat and tidy, as close to the harbour exit as Jesamiah could safely trail an anchor cable. Rocking gently, her furled sails glistened as the pale moon caught the rime of salt which always covered everything, turning her into a shimmer of silver.

The town lay off her larboard beam, the torches outside buildings flared and the campfires burnt and crackled, sending sparks high into the darkness. The merriment of carousing drifted across the water, the excited shriek of a drunken harlot, a barking dog. Wandering in from starboard, the north-easterly wind was pushing *Sea Witch's* stern around as she tugged against her restraining cable, as apprehensive at being here as was her master.

The boats were lowered to ferry the crew ashore, the men keen to be away, their mood jubilant at the prospect of enjoyment. Nassau's fort reflected the moon off its white-limed walls and Jesamiah could all too easily imagine the muzzles of loaded cannon pointing straight at him. Would not have been at all surprised had one of them erupted to spit grape shot into the rigging. His last visit here had been profitable; he could only hope no one in authority up behind those bastions recollected it. Or him.

Rue swaggered on deck from his small cabin, sited forward of the captain's grand luxury running across the entire width of the stern.

Slapping his thighs, Jesamiah guffawed amusement. "Well and are you not dressed for the ladies! Look at this!" He fingered the gay canary-coloured waistcoat, the white breeches; pointed at the buckled shoes. "Are we the dandy then!"

Embarrassed, Rue scowled at him. "If I am to be a man of 'onest leisure from now on, I intend to find myself a wife. I will not be doing so dressed as a tar-smutted, deck-swab."

Tears of laughter were pricking Jesamiah's eyes. "Listen mate, the harlot's ashore over there'll be too damned pickled in rum t'notice your paunch of a belly, whatever fancy dress its covered in!"

"It ain't his belly he wants noticed!" Isiah Roberts called his two shillings' worth of banter as he stepped down in the gig. "The bit he wants rubbed hangs below his sagging gut! He ain't been able t'see it for himself these last few years!"

Saluting the both of them a crude gesture, Rue prepared to descend down the cleats,

"You not coming, Captain?" Roberts called as he took his seat near the stern. Rue paused, his head level with the rail.

"Come on Jes, we will watch your back for you."

"Aye, until you get too drunk to know which is back and which is front - or you find someone prettier than me to be watchin'!"

Those in the boat chorused their good humour. "That should not be too difficult!"

"Prettier than your ugly mug, Cap'n? No chance!"

Rue shrugged. From experience he knew it was futile to argue with Jesamiah when he was wallowing in one of his black moods. "Isiah and me we will 'ave a look around, ask a few questions, do a bit of listening. One of us will come back in a couple of 'ours, tell you 'ow the wind blows. Does that settle your stomach?"

"Nay, I'll be alright. You enjoy yourselves. Go on, stop your chantering and clear off out of it."

"I would enjoy myself more if I knew you were not being so maudlin," Rue countered. "As I said, one of us will be back in a while."

"As long as you don't make it a couple of days; I'm not wantin' to be stuck here on me own from now 'til eternity. If I do change me mind, aside o' swimming or a bum-boat pulling over 'ere, I've got no means of getting ashore." Jesamiah waved them off, watched them pull for the nearest quay, his hands resting on the rail, his eyes roaming over the shapes of buildings straggling up the hill towards the governor's house. Some of them had only a faint light showing from behind closed shutters; others with all windows open and ablaze. Rue had marvelled at the speculation that this appointed Governor was incorruptible. Having met the man, Jesamiah had set his quartermaster straight.

"Think of the most corrupted man you know, then turn him inside out - you are left with Captain Rogers. He would sell his grandmother into slavery rather than take a bribe. The man is a trusting fool."

Jesamiah stroked his fingers down his moustache. So what was it turning his bowels to water? He stared again at the town.

Something was wrong. Some warning was shouting at him from out of the watching shadows. The moon was bright on the church, on the sea - all seemed as it should, nothing amiss. When was the last time he had felt something like this? This prickle across the nape of his neck, down his spine? He brushed the unease aside, made for his cabin and poured himself a generous measure of rum; stretched out on his bed not bothering to remove his boots, the cot rocking gently with the mild motion of the ship as *Sea Witch* turned with the tide. He balanced the empty glass on his chest, put one arm behind his head and stared at the beams on the underside of the quarterdeck.

How many bumps and bruises had he sported from moving clumsy and careless below deck those first few months as a boy at sea! After all these years he ducked by instinct, thinking nothing of low door-lintels, beams and cramped spaces. And then he remembered! As he drifted into sleep the memory flooded back as clear as the moonlight peering through the curve of the stern windows beyond the open door of his sleeping quarters. He had felt these same misgivings when the *Mermaid* had given chase to an East Indiaman off the African coast. When the *Christina Giselle* had gotten the better of them, and a girl – a child as he had thought - had stood in the stern watching him. He had felt a presence, *her* presence, when he had seen Tiola that first time.

~ *Jesamiah! Do not come! Do not come!* ~

The shout of his name leapt into his brain as if someone were in the room yelling into his ear. He sat up, wiped at the sweat beading his top lip. The words reverberated in his head, shunting around like a capstan being turned. His hand was shaking as he walked into his day cabin. He did not bother pouring into the glass, but drank straight from the bottle.

What was the term for delusion? For hearing voices? Insane? Aye, that was it. Insanity.

Sixteen

The shielding wall disintegrated, shattering as if a pane of glass had been broken by a tossed brick. The darkness erupted into a splintering of fragmented rainbow colours, shooting out in all directions like exploding gunpowder. Tiola gasped as the door opened - and she shrieked her warning.

~ *Jesamiah! Do not come!* ~

No one who had been about to seat themselves at the Governor's dining table would have noticed anything different about her. Why should they? Woodes Rogers was too full of his own self importance, Henry Jennings too much the gentleman and Stefan would not see because he did not know what to look for. He was unaware of her Craft - unaware of anything concerning Tiola beyond his disappointment in her. And Phillipe Mereno? Of them all, perhaps only he would be suspicious; he was a man suspicious of his own shadow. He was not here, however, was rarely away from the harbour or his ship.

~ *Do not come!* ~ Tiola shouted in her mind, but the wall had immediately solidified again, the splintered glass merging together to become whole, as impenetrable as before. At least she now knew Jesamiah had been blocking her thoughts, he had built a screen to shelter behind, shutting her out because of his loneliness and hurt. Something had jostled him into allowing the door to open though – admittedly, to slam it shut again – but it *had* opened and she *had* touched him. Her concern, had he heard or listened?

Mrs Rogers hissed, gritting back a cry of pain, trying to control both her dignity and her tears. Tiola swung her attention away from Jesamiah to the immediacy of the Governor's hallway, the curve of the stairs and the lady sprawled, undignified, at the bottom of them having fallen most of the way down. Everyone was talking at once, offering advice, making suggestions with not a single practical idea between them. The servants in the background anxious because dinner was served and the Governor was known for his tempers if the soup was cold. With light care Tiola moved her hands over the rapidly swelling ankle, explored the damage. Part of her mind concentrated on the injury, the other, desperate to reach Jesamiah again.

"It is only sprained I think," she commented, certain there was no fracture. "You will be needing rest for some while though, Ma'am. And something for your discomfort?"

Rogers himself lifted his wife, carried her to their bedchamber. She buried her head in his shoulder choking down a whimper of pain. Tiola followed, making a mental inventory of the remedies she had brought with her. Not many, for Stefan had destroyed most of her stock, assuming as his wife she would have no necessity for potions and cure-alls. Where the banisters curved in a wide sweep and would have looked elegant were it not for the peeled paint and the gouged wood, she glanced into the hallway below. Mereno had hurried in, his coat flapping, hat awry. He almost ran to Stefan talking with animated, excited gestures.

Dread infused Tiola. She loathed that man! He reminded her of a weasel. Sharp eyes that missed nothing, always watching and waiting its opportunity to dart out and destroy its victim. Too clearly could she remember what he had done to Jesamiah as a boy. The man had succumbed to the clutch of evil – and her husband called him friend? She shuddered, felt the press of the Dark huddling closer, heard its low chuckle of conquest. Whatever was causing it, she could do nothing at this moment, for Mrs Rogers needed her skills as a healer. Tiola hurried on up the stairs in Governor Rogers' wake. She did not like the pallor of the woman's face or the racing of her heart and perspiring skin. If she was not tended with skill and care, there could well be worse than a sprained ankle come morning.

Engrossed with concerned thoughts for her patient, she did not, therefore, witness the slow smile of triumph spread over Phillipe Mereno's face as he spoke to her husband. Did not see Stefan eagerly collect his hat and coat. Did not see the both of them hurry away, gleefully, out into the night.

Seventeen

A heavily built man in seaman's boots climbed silently up the ship's cleats and dropped over the rail to the deck. He whispered down to the boat alongside, beckoning the others waiting there to follow. Agitated, *Sea Witch* bobbed very slightly as several men came aboard.

Vaguely, Jesamiah was aware someone stood outside his cabin door; a sixth sense instinct. He knew every nuance of his ship, all her moods, all her manners. Every creak and complaint and sigh she made. Something was upsetting her.

"Rue?" he mumbled, his speech slurred, not bothering to glance over his shoulder as the cabin door opened letting in a movement of air to rustle at the papers scattered on his desk. A shaft of light from a held lantern slanted across the floor. His own light had guttered some forty minutes past. Jesamiah stood at the stern windows, five panes spreading the entire four and twenty feet across the rear of the ship; stood staring into the night at the anchored vessels, at the town. At nothing. More than a little drunk, he had stood there for over an hour.

"Took your bloody time, Rue? Couple of hours you said, been more like four." Then he caught the illuminated reflections in the glass, two men standing sixteen feet away at the door. He stared a moment, registering their presence, felt his throat run dry and swallowed down the sickening jolt of horror scrambling up from his stomach into his gullet. Felt sweat trickle down his spine. He thought the fear of his brother had gone. It hadn't.

When he turned, slowly, to face them he was cold, stone sober.

"Hello Brother," Phillipe Mereno drawled from where he leant against the door frame, his arms folded. "We have been waiting for your arrival. We almost thought you were going to pass up the invitation to come to Nassau, which would be most remiss of you, given your predilection for attending parties." He gestured towards the man beside him, the one holding the lantern. "I believe you know my business partner, master Stefan van Overstratten?"

"*De goede avond* - good evening," Stefan acknowledged as he hooked the lamp to a nail on the nearest beam ahead of him. Removing his feathered hat he offered Jesamiah a sweeping, formal bow. "I see you have taken a few liberties with my ship. She did not carry those ugly gun ports when last I saw her."

Stepping further in as if seeing it for the first time, van Overstratten gazed around the cabin. A lovely room, even when not lit by the magic of snail-trail silver from the moon. Barely a right-angle in sight, the design of the interior mirrored the shape of the outer hull; the curved deck-head, the cushioned lockers curving below the stern windows. the desk built into the inclined sides. *Sea Witch* could have been made for Jesamiah, for the panelling was of light oak, some of it carved with a detail of oak leaves and acorns. This cabin, as a crowning glory, had made Jesamiah so want the ship for his own when he had first inspected her, those months ago in Cape Town. An easy done thing - take a bottle or two of rum aboard at an hour when the watch was growing bored; sweet talk an invitation to look round.

Stefan walked towards the desk, poked through the scatter of papers and rolled charts, tossing those of no interest to the floor. When he found a ship's log book he smiled. The false leer of the alligator.

"Ah," he said, thumbing through it. "The *Berenice.* You ought not keep trophies, my friend. This is evidence. I have the sworn statements of the few wretches who survived the indecencies you inflicted on them, of course, but it is always better to be having irrefutable proof, is it not?"

Jesamiah said nothing.

Lazily pushing himself away from the door Phillipe waved in three men, broad shouldered, mean mouthed. As mean minded. He pulled a chair from beneath the table, settled himself comfortably onto it.

"Master van Overstratten and I share a common interest," he explained superfluously. "We are recently established in the excitement of pirate hunting."

"Of punishing the scum who are thieves and murderers. Who steal ships," van Overstratten added as he too found a seat.

"And what about cheats and liars and bullies?" Jesamiah answered. "I won this ship fair in a game of cards, yet you conveniently forgot that small fact, master Dutchman, did you not? And you Phillipe? What did I ever do as a child to make you hate me so?"

Phillipe crossed his legs. "What did you do brother? Why, you were born!" Raising his right hand he beckoned with his fingers for the men to come forward. "You may proceed."

They made a thorough job of beating Jesamiah senseless. Not Mereno or van Overstratten, they were not prepared to soil their hands, not when it was more interesting to watch while others, professionals, undertook the kicking and punching. Jesamiah did not have a chance to defend himself for they twisted his arms behind his back and while one held him, the other two laid into his ribs and the soft parts of his belly and groin with their fists and a length of chain wrapped around the knuckles.

When he was down, blood streaming from his face, nose and mouth, gasping for air, gagging against the pain, they used their knees and boots instead.

Eighteen

Strangely empty of occupants Tiola paused as she entered the east-facing breakfast room with its large, and in her opinion, ugly, Tudor-style furniture. Normally, Governor Rogers filled the small room with his wide-bellied, loud-voiced presence; nor were Stefan or Phillipe Mereno at the table breaking their fast. Not that she missed Mereno. Beyond acknowledging the basics of politeness she had deliberately avoided him as much as possible, although she knew he constantly watched her with those suspicious, soulless eyes.

Only once had he arrogantly questioned her about Jesamiah.

"You were my brother's whore, I believe."

The insult had stung, but Tiola had answered with proud dignity. "I was no whore, surr. Your brother used me ill. I am here to see him hang for it." She had despised denying Jesamiah but for as long as it was necessary, had to pretend she had no care or feeling for him beyond that of hatred.

Henry Jennings was seated alone at the table. He greeted her with courtesy and enquired after Mrs Rogers' progress. "You have a compress placed on the ankle, I trust? And keeping it tight strapped?" Bowed an apology. "Forgive me, I was forgetting you have somewhat of a reputation as a healer."

Of all the men, Tiola liked Captain Jennings, a considerate and affable gentleman. She could understand why Jesamiah had so admired him.

"Do you know to where my husband has gone?" she asked, attempting to restrain her anxiety. "He was absent for much of the night. I have an urgent necessity to ask something particular of him."

Something had occurred last night, Tiola had sensed its imbalance, but she had been unable to pursue it for Mrs Rogers' distress had required her full attention. At least now the woman was sleeping, the palpitations of her heart ceased.

"I believe your husband had reason to accompany the Governor and Mr Mereno to the fort this morning," Jennings said casually as he spread honey on fresh-baked bread.

Tiola's face remained passive, not a muscle moved.

Monitoring her reaction he continued, "Last night, your husband and Mereno claim they were in the fortunate position of apprehending another vessel from leaving in a similar despicable fashion to Charles Vane." He took a bite of bread, chewed, swallowed. "As you must be aware, any pirate who refuses the King's amnesty will be subject to hanging without clemency."

He finished the bread, poured tea for himself and Tiola; observed, "Although it seems strange to me, as a seaman, that a man should attempt to sail his ship out of harbour barely four hours after he has dropped anchor. Especially while his crew are ashore sampling the delights Nassau has to offer. Curious, do you not think?"

While busy with the tea his attention had glanced away from Tiola, now he observed her closely. "As much as I admire him - he is, I concede, an excellent mariner - I doubt even Captain Acorne could take the *Sea Witch* out of harbour on his own."

He had sat here, anxious, for more than half an hour waiting for her and received the reward he had been hoping for. Tiola's cheeks drained pale, a muted gasp left her lips and she was thrusting back her chair, scrambling to her feet.

"Jesamiah is here?"

"The *Sea Witch* dropped anchor half an hour after moonrise last night, but her captain, because of this fabricated nonsense, has been a guest of His Majesty's Governor for most of the hours of darkness. He is reclining with the rats and the filth of the dungeons of Nassau's dilapidated fort."

She was off, running like a rabbit up a bolt hole escaping from hunting ferrets.

Jennings drank his tea. So, the rumours about Jesamiah's lost love were true then? Van Overstratten's wife had indeed been Jesamiah's woman, she was the one he had been pining for all these months. Jennings could quite see why. The only thing he could not understand – the tongue wagging had not extended that far - was why Acorne had left her behind in Cape Town in the first place. The damned fool. Women as attractive as she had no right to be abandoned, nor did they deserve to have mean-minded toad spawn such as van Overstratten as a husband.

Jennings was fond of Acorne; he had already tried reasoning, unsuccessfully, with Governor Rogers against this disgraceful imprisonment. Mereno and van Overstratten were men who assumed they could get whatever they wanted by paying enough money and damn the cost in human terms. Men like these were building personal empires and making their fortune from the miserable labour of others throughout the Colonies.

Fervently, Jennings hoped this pretty young woman would have more persuasion over Rogers than he so far had managed. If the Governor chose to continue turning a deaf ear and blind eye to what was happening in the dungeons of his fort, then, God help him, Acorne would be dead by the morrow morning.

- Nineteen -

Jesamiah moaned, attempted to move, thought better of it. Stayed where he was on his back in the cell they had dragged him to, somewhere in the bowels of the fort. His eyes were closed. He would open them soon, when the spinning stopped. Something warm and wet was dribbling down his face from his temple, from his cheek and mouth too. He tried moving his arms, gasped as an angry shout from protesting muscles shot up and down his body. His muzzy brain registered several sluggish facts; he could not move his arms, they were tied together at the wrists behind him. Tied too tight, the rope was biting into the flesh. Cramp was swarming from fingertip to shoulder.

He squeezed open his eyes and the early morning sun streaming in through the high, narrow bars of the cell's single window hit him smartly in the face. Another mean blow from another bully.

He shut his eyes again. Concentrated. He was bleeding. Loss of blood was not desirable but he was still alive – he thought – therefore he had not bled to death. Not yet anyway.

Slowly, very slowly, he built the courage to alter position. It was going to hurt he knew but he had to move, had to roll to his side because if he did not the vomit churning in his gullet would choke him. He took a breath, released it in a sudden gush as the pain from several broken ribs lunged into his torso. Tried again.

He rolled, half pushing half squirming. Passed out.

Groaning into the bloodied dirt beneath his face, Jesamiah felt even more wretched than he had before. He had no idea how long he had been unconscious, some while he assumed, for the sun was no longer directly on him, slanting instead to his left. He had been sick, the stink of it was beside him, spewed down his clothes, dribbled into his beard.

Pushing himself to his knees with his elbow and sheer brute force, ignoring the discomfort and another wave of nausea, he attempted to rise to his feet. Abandoned the idea as the wall swam by in a series of dizzying circles. Decided he preferred to be lying down. At least the floor kept still.

He stared up at the window, at the clear blue sky beyond. Why had they not simply killed him? Strung him up from the yardarm and left him dangling? He laughed, a mocking sound that echoed against the damp walls and was instantly bitten back into a blood-frothed cough. He knew the answer to that riddle.

Because they had not finished with him. There was more of this to come.

He dozed, slipping in and out of consciousness. When he awoke again the sun had moved another inch and van Overstratten, his brother and Governor Rogers had come to gloat.

Go on kick me as well, Jesamiah thought through gritted teeth, peering at Woodes Rogers, one eye half blinded by congealed blood.

By design prison cells were disgusting places. Covering his nose and mouth with a linen kerchief, his expression wrinkling in distaste at the assault by a variety of obnoxious odours, Rogers bent over Jesamiah and tipped his chin upward, examining him.

To van Overstratten he said, "Jesamiah Acorne y'say? I met him in Cape Town? I do not recall him." He straightened, wiped the blood smeared across his fingers on the square of linen then dropped it to the floor. He tutted, shook his head, uncertain about all this. It had a bad smell as foetid as this cell. "He has as much right to the offer of pardon as anyone. I cannot have one law for one pirate and one for another."

"With respect, Governor, he has no intention of seeking a pardon," Phillipe argued, keeping his patience with difficulty. They had discussed this subject, up and down and in endless circles for the past hour.

"We caught him in the act of preparing to make sail," Stefan added, refusing to come further than the doorway because of the filth. "If he were to leave and continue with piracy, think of the havoc he would cause. Vane is already making himself a damned nuisance out there. With Acorne joining him..." He let the implication trail off.

It was true. Charles Vane was becoming a thorn in the backside even after these few days, but there were several inconsistencies in all this. Henry Jennings had flatly stated there was no crew aboard the *Sea Witch*, that Acorne had been alone. And these two, van Overstratten and Mereno, clearly had a personal goal of revenge to achieve.

"You must understand," Phillipe said, from where he leant against the wall beside the open cell door, his voice slick with enticement, "my aim is to see an end to the pirates who are decimating our tobacco and sugar convoys." He stepped forward to toe his boot into Jesamiah's side. "This sorry specimen is one of the worst of the rogues. I am ashamed to admit he is my kinsman, although the fact he *is* my brother has not deterred him from attempting to ruin *me*."

He spread one hand. "If you deny my request Governor, then I may be forced to divert my portion of finances. You will need to seek alternative funding for your guardship." He let the threat hang, poignant.

For his own contribution van Overstratten expanded the threat. "To secure our generosity, all we ask is what we have already pleaded; while we are available to state our personal evidence you convene a trial and find Acorne guilty. He can hang this evening and our honour will be satisfied. A quick end to this sorry matter."

Mulling his thoughts Rogers ambled from the cell, his hands clasped behind his back, unsure. He did desperately require the money. This was going to be an expensive business harnessing these rogues into lawful behaviour - and the British Government had not been over generous with their aid.

There again, Captain Jennings had put a significant counter argument. Many of these pirates had come to Nassau on trust. *"Hang one while under your word of unconditional amnesty, Governor,"* Jennings had pointed out, *"and the rest will weigh anchor and leave. You will never entice them back and that will be an end to law and order - and profitable trade - here in the West Indies."*

He was right of course. Rogers chewed his lip, sighed, stroked his grey-grizzled moustache.

"Or I could consider *increasing* my aid," Phillipe coaxed, sensing Rogers' doubt. "Between us, van Overstratten and I could, with the right incentive, perhaps see our way to financing your guardship for two years instead of the one?"

From where he lay on the floor Jesamiah coughed his mockery. "And I thought you were beyond corruption, Governor. How bloody naive of me."

Woodes Rogers chose not to hear. He did not consider payment intended for the general good of the community to be bribery. If the gold was for personal gain it would be different – but he had given his word; every pirate who came into harbour before the close of August would be offered a pardon. It had to include this fellow.

Unconditional terms meant the slate was to be wiped clean of everything - of stolen goods and ships, of committing rape and murder. Which was why they were here in this stinking cell; Van Overstratten and Mereno were not interested in justice or pardons. They wanted vengeance against Acorne. This brutal treatment of the fellow, proved it.

"Let me think on it," Rogers said, making a partial decision. "I will let you know by noon." He nodded curtly, the matter temporarily dismissed and hurried up into the fresh, clean air pleased to be leaving the stink behind. A stink that was not the odour of human discomfort alone; a lack of personal honour and a lust for deliberate cruelty always harboured its own, foul stench.

Phillipe kicked Jesamiah's broken ribs and his victim bit back a scream. "Rogers is not going to accommodate us, van Overstratten. He is going to allow this bag of scum to get away with all he has done to us." Maliciously he kicked again and when his brother gasped, kicked a third time.

Ruefully the Dutchman agreed with Mereno's observation, answered, annoyed, "We ought to have hanged him last night as I suggested. We would have got what we wanted, quickly and quietly."

"What? A few minutes squirming at the end of a rope, pissing and shitting himself as his tongue swells and then it's all over? I think not, sir! I think not!" Phillipe squatted beside Jesamiah's head, whispered very quietly. "For humiliating me in front of my friends and, I suspect, for making a whore of my wife, I intend for you to suffer. Really suffer. You will end your life begging me to let you die."

"What more can we do?" van Overstratten protested, not hearing and reluctant to step forward on to the filth that squelched and stank and crunched on the floor. He glanced up at the low ceiling at one of the supporting roof beams. "Do we ignore Rogers and string him up ourselves? Here?"

"It wasn't my fault we had a lousy father," Jesamiah gasped, surreptitiously trying to curl into a more protective position. Thought, *It wasn't my bloody fault he preferred me to you when he was at home.*

Leaning closer, Phillipe's spittle dribbled on to Jesamiah's cheek. "Are you suggesting the fault was mine?"

Jesamiah returned the iced stare as best he could through the blood and bruising. "No... but we are grown men... we ought not squabble over the failures... of our parents." He spoke slowly, taking several shallow breaths to fight the pain. "Let me go. Let's talk sensibly about this."

- 324 -

"You're pathetic," Mereno jeered.

Jesamiah closed his eyes, remembered all the hurts he had endured. All that he had suffered. Dreaded the thought that he was about to suffer them again.

He had asked his mother once, when he was eight years old, why his father spent so little time with Phillipe, why he disliked him. As a child on the receiving end of the torments and the brutalities he could understand why *he* hated him, but not Father. Mama had smiled indulgently and ruffled his hair. Had told him not to be silly: "*Tal insensatez, mi nino..* Your father thinks the world of you both."

But she had then added something else, something that as a child Jesamiah had not absorbed. Only now, remembering, crumpled here in this stink, with blood on his face and pain in his ribs and balls did he realise its significance. "*He cannot look at Phillipe, he is too much like his mother,*" she had said. "*Your father's first wife. He did so adore her.*"

Very quietly Jesamiah said, "I pity you Phillipe. You were so full of hatred, you never gave anything else a chance. You never will."

"Save your pity for yourself, I have no need of it." Making a pretence at appearing thoughtful, Mereno stood, crossed the cell to join the Dutchman,. "Rogers Governs New Providence, he holds no jurisdiction elsewhere." He spoke slowly as if he were only now thinking of an alternative solution. Had in fact been calculating this for many months - and now it was all falling sweetly and effortlessly into place, aided by the stroke of fortune of trading with this Dutchman. He would not have persuaded Rogers even thus far on his own. But with van Overstratten as partner? He smiled, sated with pleasure.

"What if I were to take this bastard to Virginia for trial instead? We do not hold with the fool idea of amnesties and pardons for pirates along the Chesapeake."

Jesamiah closed his eyes, through his split lip said, "If you give me to my brother, Stefan, I shall not reach Virginia alive."

The Dutchman carefully stepped over the debris, stood looking down at Jesamiah then hunkered to his heels and leant forward. He reached out a hand to peel one of the pirate's soiled and bloodied ribbons from where it had stuck to a congealed clot of blood.

"Do you know something, Acorne?" he said. "If that is so, what makes you think I care?"

- Twenty -

Tiola sprinted down the hill ignoring the stares of curiosity following behind. A woman without cloak or coat, bonnet or outdoor shoes? Running? Even among pirates and their doxies she drew attention. Slithering to a halt on the rough boards of the jetty she saw *Sea Witch* across the harbour dozing peacefully at her anchor, as Jennings had said. She was as graceful and as beautiful as a slender thoroughbred against feather-heeled, cobs. The sails on all three masts, fore, main and mizzen were neatly furled with the yards set square, as if she had the discipline of a Royal Navy crew. The shrouds and stays were taut and freshly tarred, her rails gleaming from a recent coat of linseed oil. Her hull, blue painted, was clean, without dribbles of bird lime or trails of clinging weed. Twenty cannon, ten a side, sited with thought and care, their weight spread evenly along the waist and lower deck, their presence hidden behind closed ports. Two lanterns sat high on the taffrail at the stern, polished and gleaming. The busty figurehead, blonde-haired, pink fleshed.

Chiding herself with reprimands at her stupidity, Tiola raked a hand through her hair, scattering pins and combs, sending the coiffured curls into a dishevelled tangle. Why had she not felt Jesamiah's presence? Why had she not walked down here last night, as she had every other night to see if he had come? Why!

Why? Because of the barricade he had built against her – the barricade he had needed to survive the chill of his own despair. Believing she did not care for him, he had blended into his surroundings and shut her out.

It had not been her fault, but yet again she had failed him. She could not do harm to another living person, but at this moment Tiola was tempted to turn aside from the honour binding her to her Craft and hurl her power into the four winds. To destroy the whole, damned, lot of the human race for daring to hurt the man she so desperately loved.

      The spinning blackness of unconsciousness alternated with a red agony as Jesamiah felt himself being half lifted, half dragged. His legs and heels bumped up the steps slimed with slugs and snails, the double crunch of shells breaking beneath his captors' boots. Outside, the sunlight dazzled his eyes. He tried to struggle as he became aware of what was happening and where they were taking him; the attempt was futile. His arms were trussed like a chicken ready for the spit and he was as weak as a kitten, helpless to do anything to stop them trundling him along the jetty and hauling him aboard a ship as if he were a barrel of cargo. As he would be helpless to prevent Phillipe doing whatever he wanted once they were at sea.

      Oh God, he thought, knowing what his brother was capable of. Then, resurrected out of desperation, hope suddenly sprang alive. There was something van Overstratten had said last night after they had bound his wrists and ankles and were dragging him, half conscious, from his cabin.

      Tiola was here in Nassau. In between the beatings they had delighted in telling him how she hated him, how she was here to see him hang. Van Overstratten had added his own crudity, explaining every intimate detail of his marriage to her. Jesamiah had schooled his face to reflect nothing, but the inner hurt at discovering she had turned from him and married this louse was as agonising as the broken ribs and the bleeding cuts. He was sorry to learn of Jenna's death, bloody mad this bastard had blamed it on him – had Tiola thought so little of him to believe he would deliberately shoot a woman in the back? Had their months together meant nothing? And then, after the last beating, the Dutchman had said something. Jesamiah struggled to remember it – they had been pulling him along by his ankles. The Dutchman had spoken to Phillipe, had not intended Jesamiah to hear. A gull flew low, screeching - and the words came back to him!

"Her indifference is all pretence of course. Why she still loves this bastard I cannot understand."

The barrier disintegrated, the shield his weeping soul had erected shattered, and in his mind he screamed the words he needed.

~ *By all that is good, help me, Tiola!* ~ And he felt her instant presence filling him, heard her wonderful, beautiful, comforting voice answer him!

~ *Jesamiah?* ~

~ *Thank God! Oh thank God! Please Tiola, please help me, I'm in big trouble here!* ~

~ *Where are you?* ~

They were pulling him along the deck towards an open hatch. He guessed where they were going to stow him, down in the cable tier above the bilge, along with the rats. He had put his own prisoners down there in the cramped stench and blackness, although they had never been half beaten to death beforehand.

Ignoring the protesting muscles he summoned the strength to shrug his captors aside, stumbled to his feet and lurched to the larboard rail; had some vague thought of throwing himself overboard. Better to drown now, quickly, than endure what Phillipe had in mind. He looked up, looking as well he could across the bay at his beloved *Sea Witch*. Probably the last time he would see her. And then he glanced at the jetty on the far side of the harbour.

She was standing there, Tiola, her image as clear and close as if she were right here on this very deck in front of him. Her beautiful eyes meeting directly with his, her soul reaching out as it had when first he had seen her aboard the *Christina Giselle* - and all those years ago beside his mother's grave! The realisation slammed into him with the same force as those kicks and punches. It had been her, Tiola! *Her* voice telling him to get up, to fight back. Bloody Hell! Why had he not seen it before? She had been there, with him, right from the start. That was why she knew everything – everything – about him.

Her overwhelming love flooded into and through him, shunting aside the dread in the pit of his stomach.

~ *They lied to us Jesamiah.. I have never stopped loving you. I never will.* ~

He had only a moment before they grappled him again and thudded their fists into his stomach, sending him to his knees gasping for air. He didn't care, it had been long enough for him to find her again and he screamed her name aloud across the harbour.

"Tio... la!"

He was still in trouble, but Jesamiah was smiling as they chained him into the darkness. There was one thing van Overstratten and Phillipe had not counted on, one thing they had missed. They did not know Tiola Oldstagh was a witch.

She saw them hit him, felt his agony, watched them drag him away, and she forgot every law of her Craft. She screamed. The high octave of her voice piercing and unnatural, the sound splitting the heavens as lightning ripping from thunder clouds. The wind rose to meet the keening sound and the sea lifted in anger as the witch howled her fury, and his name, across the harbour that separated them.

"Jesamiah! "

*

Anger consumed Tethys, her immense power exploding in a response of outraged protest to the furious sound that boomed and shouted and then fled away out to sea, carried by the rush of a gusting wind. The sky shuddered as that terrible scream tore across Nassau and swept over the entire island of New Providence.

Summoned by the call made by one who had no right to enter into her realm and give impertinent command, Tethys echoed the shrilled, shouted name in her own, sea-song voice, the sound of a white-foamed breaker crashing against rocks.

~ Jessh..a..miah...! ~

Birds, squawking and flapping their alarm swirled from their mast-head roosts, and as agitated as they, the sea rolled. A single great wave churned beneath the keels of anchored ships, sending them leaping and prancing, tugging at their cables; it slapped at the jetties and hurtled against the shore, the swirl of froth spewing up the steps and washing on to the sand of the beach. It swamped the tents and bothies, doused bonfires and the ardour of sailors coupling roughly and drunkenly with their whores.

And still the residue of that distraught sound boomed with the shout of the wind and the crash of the sea.

Twenty One

Mereno grimaced at the sudden squall scurrying across the harbour, the disturbed birds, the whipping pennants and ensigns on the ships. Were they in for a storm? August was the hurricane season, not the best of months to be in these waters. He usually came earlier in the year, January and February, to ensure all was well on his wife's inherited plantation. A good excuse to be away from the winter fogs that could plague the Rappahannock. Alicia usually accompanied him, but he had not thought it suitable for her to be involved in this particular venture. A wise decision as it turned out, with his brother now chained like an animal down in the bilge.

Despite giving her several beatings, Alicia had not changed her story. He was certain she lied. He intended to ask Jesamiah about it, see if, under his present circumstances, he still wanted to crow that she was a whore. Phillipe's lips turned up into an unpleasant smile. Somehow, once he got started on what he intended to inflict upon his brother, he doubted Jesamiah would be crowing about anything.

Courteously he spoke to the vessel's sailing master, asking whether it was possible to make way immediately in view of a storm possibly brewing. Was satisfied to hear the opinion that it was wiser to be on the open ocean where a ship could run, rather than be trapped at anchorage. The quicker they left this island behind the better, before Woodes Rogers learnt of what they had done. Van Overstratten was to cover Phillipe's back by ensuring a sufficient amount of gold found its way into the Governor's pocket but confident the Governor would be only too pleased to have the dilemma quietly solved, Phillipe had not been as sure of the Dutchman. He had expected him to protest against the plan, was surprised at van Overstratten's delight; his only concern was the disappointment at not personally seeing Acorne hang, at not seeing for himself he was quite dead. Mereno had been able to reassure him on that.

"He will be dead, Stefan, I promise you. If you wish I am happy to send proof; would his head suffice?"

It was no idle boast. Standing on the quarterdeck watching the crew haul in the warping lines Phillipe was already planning what type of container to use. A pottery urn? A large, glass bottle? Vinegar, he assumed, was best as pickling brine. Brandy would be a waste of good liquor. Or would it be wiser to coat the thing in tar? Preserve it that way? He thought he might keep the hands for himself, give another, intimate, part as a present to Alicia. He grinned maliciously, eager to see the look on her face when he presented her with her lover's pickled prick and balls. The only lie Phillipe had made to Stefan; he no intention of permitting Jesamiah to die easily.

The wind was pushing the ship from the jetty, once across the sandbar they would make full sail and put water between themselves and Nassau. It was only here within the harbour someone might decide to stop them – but then, why would they try? Mereno was no scoundrel reverting to a degenerate life, he was a respected plantation owner, entitled to come and go as he pleased.

Phillipe Mereno went below. He had questions to ask. Things to do.

The pain Jesamiah was enduring fused through Tiola with such violence she stumbled to her hands and knees, sobbing for breath. This world and the next spun around her in a vortex of red and blazing white, in shards of iridescent glass and spears of shining iron. His scream pierced her mind, more primeval than the first sound made by the first creature to experience agony. Mercifully, it lasted a few moments only. Oblivion crowded behind the torture delivered and suffered in the darkness of the below-deck world of Mereno's ship. Jesamiah sank into unconsciousness, releasing both himself and Tiola.

She knelt on the wooden jetty, her hair dishevelled her stockings torn, the frills and fancy lace edging her petticoats were splashed and dirtied; knelt and helplessly watched Mereno's ship with its red-painted hull clear the sandbar and tack to larboard as the wheel was put hard over. Hands were scurrying to draw the foresail sheets, bringing her bow round. Heeling over a degree or two the vessel caught the wind and picked up speed. Leaving. Taking Jesamiah, bruised and bloody, away.

Tiola could snap a halyard or a brace, could cause the sails to rip into shreds that would shriek and flog in the wind. Could even tear a great gash in the keel – but what if in stopping the ship someone should be hurt or killed by cause of her command? For Mereno she had no sympathy, but were his faults and cruelties to be paid for by his crew? Or Jesamiah? It could as easily be him who drowned because of her action.

Her grandmother's voice whispered in her mind, gently consoling and guiding; ~ *You are right to be careful what you wish for child.* ~

Struggling to her feet, forcing aside the aftermath of disorientation and sickness had caused by Jesamiah's plea for help, Tiola accepted there were things she could not do. Unless it was imperative for her own protection, to deliberately do harm would bring upon her a permanent curse. There had to be balance in everything. Good countering evil, light revoking dark. Right contradicting wrong and hope outweighing despair. Her Craft could do nothing to change the rigidity of the laws of Existence, and in this instance, could do nothing to cause Mereno's ship to heave to.

And then two cannon were fired in quick succession, their urgent sound, *whoomph, whoomph,* booming startling and unmistakable across the harbour. Tiola raised her head, stared towards the cause of the glorious noise - *Sea Witch!* Men were aboard, hurrying about the decks. A blue ensign was raised as she watched, to flutter in the tug of the breeze at the very top of the foremast, another in almost the same instant was set to the mizzen. Everything had its opposite - despondency replaced by elation!

At the blast of those cannon several heads bobbed up above the parapet of the semi-ruinous fort. Heads all along the jetty and the shore were swivelling towards the ship, all curious, some, those few not of the pirate persuasion, momentarily alarmed. Scrambling to her feet Tiola dusted the grime from her skirts, tucked a strand of loose hair behind her ear, a smile as wide as the Atlantic ocean spreading across her lips. Someone aboard *Sea Witch* was aware her captain needed help.

Once – long ago it seemed – Tiola had asked Jesamiah how he gathered his men together should there be the necessity of hurry. His answer had been precise and practical.

"A blue signal is raised on the foremast and we fire two rapid shots of our largest cannon. Men know the sound of their ship's guns, they're as distinctive as voices. Anyone not aboard within one half turn of the half-hour glass, fifteen minutes, forfeits his place in the crew and we sail without him. A second blue signal at the mizzen gives them half that time to get their arses aboard. A lot of them do not make it, although a good man always stays close to his ship when in hostile waters." He had grinned, she clearly remembered the glint of his gold teeth, the matching sparkle in his eye. *"That's why most brothels and taverns are built along the shore. I've had to scuttle aboard without m'breeches many a time!"*

Tiola had laughed with him, her arms going around his neck, his lips finding hers. His hands, strong and firm on her body as he had made love to her.

"And a third flag?" she had asked later, when they lay quiet, the sweat of passion cooling on their skin. She could so vividly recall his taste and his smell. The feel of his hands

caressing her breasts. The wonderful feel of his hardness inside her.

"A third signal on the mainmast, Sweetheart? Shift your arse we've cut the anchor cable."

Two blue flags. In seven minutes *Sea Witch's* sails would unfurl, the sleeping vessel would rouse to life. Tiola could do no deliberate harm to a ship, but others could. Pirates could.

"Madam!"

She whirled at the sound of the disapproving, appalled voice, her skirts flying out like the flutter of a pigeon's wings; gasped as her husband's broad hand clamped possessively around her forearm.

His demand for explanation slapped as vicious as any blow. "What are you doing here? And in this disgraceful state? Look at you!" Disgusted, Stefan indicated her ragged appearance, his face contorting into blazing anger.

Blankly, she stared back at him.

"You have the appearance of a harlot, woman! Do you want the filth that are these sea-scum to think you are the sort of slut they can offer a penny for a poke beneath your petticoats?" The Dutchman snatched at her other wrist, shook her as if she were a pebble trapped in a bottle. Oh, it was obvious now where her feelings rested! The tear stains streaking her cheeks? The way she had been staring at Mereno's ship? He would tolerate no more of it, she was his wife and Acorne was gone. Would soon be gone for good.

He was certain Phillipe Mereno's obsession for wanting to make an end of Acorne was the trait of a mad man, but there again, he was not privy to the full circumstances behind the seething hatred. If Acorne had, as he suspected, cuckolded Phillipe at some time – in addition to commandeering his ship and making a public fool of him   - Stefan could well sympathise with Mereno's determination to see the fellow hang. Mereno's lust for excessive brutality unsettled him somewhat, but there were men who received satisfaction from inflicting pain on others. Was it for Stefan to judge another man's private pleasures?

Almost, he could feel sorry for Acorne. Almost, but not quite enough to feel remorse. After all, he too wanted an end of him; and he had, even if he would never admit it, enjoyed watching him suffer. The thing was ended. Done. It was time to pick up the pieces and salvage his marriage as best he could.

"I will not have you behaving in this demeaning manner, Madam. I will not have you publicly embarrassing me."

Very slowly Tiola blinked her eyes; said, ominously low, "What have you done to Jesamiah?"

Stefan shifted the grip on her arms with the intention of ushering her back to the privacy of the Governor's house, away from the curiosity of prying eyes, where he would deal thoroughly and finally with this intolerable behaviour.

Tiola shook him off as if he were nothing more than a sand fly. "I said, what have you done to Jesamiah?"

"Enough of this nonsense, people are staring. We will discuss this in private."

Low, dangerous. "I will not ask thrice, Stefan."

"Acorne? He is to die." Impatient, van Overstratten indicated Mereno's ship, the sails that had tumbled in a crackling cloud of canvas from her masts, her blood red hull. "He will be as insane as his brother by the time they reach Virginia I would wager. Once there, what is left of him is to hang." He chuckled his delight, a sudden, unexpected petty feeling of triumph over her.

Again he took Tiola's arm, managed to drag her two paces, jerked his hand away, his palm stinging. He rubbed at the skin, stared at the reddening mark. She must have a pin or something caught in the material of her gown. He grabbed again, firmer, and yelped as he staggered backwards, almost fell to one knee.

He caught his balance, stood, angry, raised his hand, "You bitch!"

Someone caught his arm that was rising to strike, hauled it forcefully aside. Captain Henry Jennings.

"I do not hold with violence towards women, sir. I believe it to be a coward's act, for a woman is not in a position to return the blow. Odd, is it not, how a man can beat his wife to death, yet if she so much as strikes him in self-defence she has every chance of being flogged or sent to the gallows." Contemptuously he released van Overstratten's arm. "Odd too, how a man can be dragged aboard a ship and taken to sea while under the protection of amnesty."

Stefan shrugged, dismissive. "Odd it may be Jennings, but there is now nothing anyone can do about it."

A half smile tipped the corners of Tiola's mouth. Nothing? Ah, but there was! Stefan and Mereno had not taken *Sea Witch* and her crew into account, had not calculated the loyalty of Jesamiah's men. Or her own love.

Holding her husband's sneering gaze, her eyes ,narrowed, reflecting the contempt she had for him she said, "You would be surprised, probably horrified Stefan, were you to discover exactly what I can, or cannot do." She gestured her appreciation to Jennings. "I desire to go aboard the *Sea Witch*, Captain. I would be most grateful for your assistance."

Van Overstratten snorted disdain. "You are thinking to persuade them to go after your pimp? Think again Madam. If that crew leaves this harbour without authorisation to do so they will be branded as pirates who have refused amnesty."

Jennings was at the jetty edge, beckoning one of the bumboats plying for trade between the anchored ships.

"Ah, but I am empowered to issue such authorisation," he stated as he caught the line the ferryman tossed him. "I am, after all, deputy to Governor Rogers in everything concerning this offer of pardon."

He handed Tiola down into the boat, delighted she had outmanoeuvred this pompous oaf. "Go save your lover, my dear. He will be a better man for you above this stuffed peacock. Tell Rue he has official permission to fetch back whatever cargo he can salvage from that red-hulled schooner. He must return here before the end of August, however, when the application for amnesty ceases. And remind him I have no jurisdiction to protect the crew from any commissioned ship of the Royal Navy or the Colonies. Mark that mistress Tiola, you have four weeks no longer, I cannot extend authorisation beyond then but should you meet with difficulties, you are on your own."

"Thank you. Thank you Captain Jennings," Tiola called as the little boat was pushed off. "Go back to Cape Town Stefan," she advised. "Forget about me. As I shall forget about you." She glanced over her shoulder, urged the ferryman to hurry.

Shading his eyes against the glare of the sun, Henry Jennings endorsed her suggestion. "Aiding and abetting a prisoner to escape from goal, sir, is not well thought of here in Nassau."

The Dutchman spluttered a protest. "You know damned well I did no such thing!"

Abrupt, Jennings cut him short. "I know nothing of the sort. All I saw was your conspiracy in smuggling Captain Acorne aboard that ship currently heeling out to sea. To my mind it looks very much as if you were aiding his escape."

Dismissing the subject, Jennings began to stroll from the jetty. "Do as your ex-wife suggests," he said over his shoulder. "Go back to Cape Town. And stay there."

Twenty Two

"Women are not permitted aboard ship." Rue stood, arms folded his face set grim, blocking the entry port. "Rules of Articles."

"Sod the bloody Articles." Giving a fair mimicry of Jesamiah's voice Tiola stepped over the rail from where she had climbed up the hull cleats, and swept Rue aside with her arm. He was a large man, in his mid-forties, tall and heavily built, she, half his size less than a third his weight. Tiola ignored him, marched towards the quarterdeck and swung herself easily up the narrow, companion way.

"I have seen Jesamiah set sail in a matter of minutes," she announced, tartly. "Why are we still in harbour? Would it not be best to cut the anchor cable now?"

"Now, belay a minute *mademoiselle!*" Rue blustered, astounded, hurrying up behind her. "Just who in 'ell do you think you are? Throwing your weight about - what there is of it - aboard my ship?" He scanned her slender figure, reckoned he could lift her with one finger and toss her overboard.

Tiola cocked her head to one side, her eyes sparking. She was at least two hand-spans shorter than he but her confidence made her appear twice as tall. "I am Tiola Oldstagh and this is *my* ship."

Rue put his fists to his hips, legs straddled and laughed outright at her audacity, a great bull roar rumbling from deep within his belly. "And 'ow, by 'ell, do you figure that one?"

She copied his pose. "Because Captain Jesamiah Acorne named her after me and because I wear this." She lifted her hand, showed her marriage finger and the acorn signet ring she had slid from a pocket while in the bum-boat, exchanging it for the one Stefan had put there as proof of ownership. That ring, she had disdainfully dropped into the sea without a second thought. "Because also, I am his woman and he is my mate. And because twice now you have referred to Hell. We are not there, Rue – it is Rue, is it not? – Jesamiah is. He has been taken into its burning pit and I intend to fetch him out, preferably while he is still alive and sane. I cannot do so without this ship, however. I would therefore appreciate your help, although I do not need it."

Again Rue guffawed. So this was the wench Tiola? Looking at her he could well see why Jesamiah had plunged full scale in love with her, aye and broken his heart over losing her. Several scathing answers rumbled into his mind to belay her arguments; about to launch them at her he paused, reconsidered. Henry Jennings had sent word that Jesamiah required urgent assistance, he had seen for himself his captain being dragged aboard that red-hulled ship. Had seen the blood on him, and the stains on the floor of the great cabin aboard this ship.

To go to this length? Phillipe Mereno must want revenge very badly. Rue had always thought it unwise to have confronted him on his own turf. He frowned at Tiola standing there before him, her dark eyes fixed, unwavering on his. Not a sign of doubt in her. She reminded him of a pet dog he had been given as a boy. Damned thing had a mind of its own and once it got hold of something in its teeth, brute force would not have made it let go. Damned loyal little thing. Best friend he had ever had.

And then he had a sudden suspicion that trying to remove this young woman would not be such a good idea. "Short of physically tossing you over the side, you are not going to leave are you?" he asked shrewdly.

She shook her head. "I am not."

Rubbing at his chin he flung a questioning look at Isiah Roberts who had come up behind him. Roberts shrugged. Across the harbour came the last of the men, pulling hard at the oars.

"Cut the cable as soon as those laggards are aboard Isiah," Rue ordered, making a sudden decision, which he hoped to God was the right one.

"Aye, sir!" Roberts grinned, proffered an imitation of a Navy salute, fingers to his fore-crown palm innermost. Soldiers of the army, marines - everyone except a sailor - saluted with the palm faced outward, but then their hands were not permanently grimed from the stain of tar.

"And you, er, *Madame*," Rue pointed his stubby finger, as tar and gunpowder-marked as Isiah's, at Tiola. "Remove yourself from this quarterdeck. Jesamiah's cabin is below, I will expect you to remain there."

Tiola acknowledged his acceptance of her presence with a polite, feminine curtsey. "Thank you."

"You are welcome," Rue answered as he began loosening off halyards to raise the gaff of the mizzen sail. "Away aloft! Trice up and lay out!" he shouted to the crew. Instantly men ran, eager to obey orders.

As she stepped down from the quarterdeck he remarked casually, "By the way, I am surprised you 'ave not learnt from Jesamiah; one person alone cannot sail a ship of this size. Especially not a woman - a slip of a girl such as yourself." He laughed aloud at the ridiculous thought.

Tiola smiled pleasantly up at him, thought perhaps this was not the appropriate moment to disillusion him. Indeed, one person alone could not. One witch, however, were she to put her mind to it, certainly could.

The last of the men, blowing hard from their rowing, scrabbled aboard and hauled in the longboat. Others were hurrying aloft, their bodies ascending the shrouds dark against the brilliant blue of the sky, and running out along the yards to cast off the gaskets and wait there, poised, holding the sails.

Roberts was hurrying forward with two other men – Mr Janson and Toby Turner, Tiola was to learn later – axes over their shoulders. As requested she left the quarterdeck, but had no intention of going below. Instead, she followed behind Mr Roberts, made her way to where the bowsprit soared outward above the sea and the figurehead. As she progressed forward she felt the crew staring at her with mistrust and hostility; there were some men who thought it unlucky t have a woman aboard ship. Curt, and with authority Rue stowed the muttering with one bark of explanation. "She is the Captain's women. She 'as as much right to go after 'im, as do we."

That as all that was needed.

"Might not be sensible to stand there miss," one of the crew offered respectfully, a young man with the first fuzz of a blond beard grazing his chin.

"If the sea blows up rough the spray can be uncomfortable up 'ere," the lad advised, knuckling his forehead in respectful salute. As with many a pirate, disillusioned with the harsh discipline and sordid conditions, she guessed him to be ex-Navy. Piracy was as harsh and sordid, but there was an ocean of difference between being your own man or being at the mercy of a Navy captain's rule of brutal flogging with the lash of a cat o' nine tails.

She offered him a generous smile. "And you are?"

"Jasper miss. Jasper Hicks."

"I thank you for your concern, Jasper, but I prefer to remain here. The more for'ard I am the closer I am to your captain. I wish I could stand out on the bowsprit to be closer still."

The lad swept her a startled expression of alarm. "It be dangerous, ma'am! We call the 'sprit the Widow Maker; many a good man has fallen to his death from there." Wondering at the daftness of females, he knuckled his forehead again and scurried up the foremast as agile as a monkey. Half way up he cast one quick glance down to ensure the woman had not done anything foolish.

Rue watched as Isiah, Jansy and Toby, with a will, set their axe blades to the cable, then put his two hands to the helm, his fingers firm around the spokes. "Let fall" Sheet 'ome, sheet 'ome!"

he cried in a voice that could stretch half a mile. "*Allez, allez, vite, vite* you laggards, get to it! Man the 'alyards: 'aul, 'aul! Belay. *Merde!* Shift your arses - we 'ave a wind to find and our captain to fetch!"

The ship's timbers creaked in protest as she was held in check while crossing the sandbar and eased with a stately elegance out to sea. Once clear, more canvas was spread: the maintop and foretop fell away, then fore and main course, ballooning wildly at first, before being tamed into a fine, taut curve. With each wind-shivered spread of sail and rumble of canvas, *Sea Witch* moved faster, eager for her mission, until ten minutes from Nassau she was flying. A hawk seeking its prey, her sails, a majestic eagle-spread of wings.

The ocean foamed to each side of her bow, boiling over the figurehead, dousing the forerail in a cascade of spray that shimmered with dancing rainbows of colour. The wind sang through the rigging and blustered about the crews' ears, whipping Tiola's hair into a tangle.

Sea Witch heeled over, her larboard cathead and lee rail dipping beneath the smother of white foam, and Tiola grabbed for a backstay to stop herself from sliding down the wild angle of the deck. For a moment – a moment only – she felt fear, but it fled as elation swarmed into her. The utter exhilaration of moving at speed under full sail; the power, strength, courage and gaiety of the ship as she ran before the wind - and suddenly Tiola realised why Jesamiah did love this life so! This was freedom, this was being truly, wholly alive!

Filled with wonder and delight she laughed aloud, would have clapped her hands had she not been holding on so tight. With her fingers curled around the backstay for support she leant backwards, looked up and up and up, past the fill of the sails, and beyond, to the race of the clouds passing by on a scudding blue sky. Heard, in her mind, a distant very faint response to her euphoria. A feeling only, the awareness of a presence, nothing more. A presence that was almost childlike in its innocence, one filled with the same unbridled ecstasy.

The voice of the ship herself, of *Sea Witch*. As eager as Tiola to find Jesamiah. She too wanted her beloved captain back.

Twenty Three

"I'm in Hell. I'm in Hell. I'm in Hell..."

The mantra mumbled from Jesamiah's split, bruised lips, repeated over and over as he lay curled within himself, not caring that his ribs were aching, not caring that rats were running over him. Not caring about anything at all except the horror of his misery. His eyes were closed, the left one partially crusted with dried blood. No point in opening them anyway, the cable tier down here in the bilge was as black as pitch. He would not be able to see his hand in front of his face, even if he had been able to raise it high enough.

To bring ultimate humiliation, they had stripped him, and chained his wrists and ankles to bolt rings too tight for him to be able to move more than an inch or two. All he could manage was lying or sitting, except it hurt his back and ribs to sit. He had tried. The ship was tacking to larboard again; she had been rolling slightly through the Atlantic swells, but the motion now they were altering course was easing. It would start again next time they tacked. As the ship heeled, the slop in the bilge washed around, slapping against the timber bulwark exacerbating the foetid stench of stagnant water. Jesamiah could no longer smell it; his own stink was as bad.

How long he had been down here, he did not know. He had fallen unconscious soon after they had set sail, after Phillipe had come to ask questions that first time, which he had refused to answer, and paid the penalty for. For all he knew, since then he could have been blessedly unaware of everything for a few years. The ship had been running smoothly when he had regained his senses, had only started rolling when, he guessed, they had cleared the shelter of the Bahama Islands and run out into the open Atlantic. After that? Two, three days? No, he was not hungry, his body was not craving food, he felt light headed because of the beating not lack of nourishment. From that alone he guessed less than a day had slid past. A while ago they had brought him half a tankard of stale water to drink, pouring it into him so that he gagged and spluttered, most of it wasted, dribbling down his chin and chest. The water was not for nicety or care and attention. The water was to keep him alive.

The men had not spoken and neither had he, Jesamiah had not trusted himself. The only way to ensure he did not break down before ordinary hands into the disgrace of pitiful begging was to keep his mouth shut.

Food and water had not been his worry. Soon after waking he had felt the need to piss. That was when he had tried to sit, to wriggle on his backside as far as he could from where he lay. He had considered shouting, yelling he needed to use the heads. Knew, even if there had been anyone to listen they would have ignored his pleas. That was the idea of chaining him down here, to humiliate him, to treat him as less than one of these rats. To let him lay, naked, in his own urine and then his own filth. To put him in the purgatory of Hell and leave him here.

The sound of the sea was tearing past on the far side of the hull only a few inches away. He could hear feet above, hurrying about on the lower deck, hear the occasional faint shout of command as they braced and sheeted home. Familiar sounds that in his misery he only dimly registered.

A rat scurried over his face, its paws and tail slimy, wet and cold. He shuddered, continued his repeated litany. The words drowned out their squeaking. He hated rats. Both the animal and human kind.

He figured he was right, they could not have been at sea long, for apart from when they had first brought him down here as they had prepared to make sail in Nassau harbour, Phillipe had left him alone. And that, Jesamiah knew in the pit of his aching, bruised stomach, was not going to be his brother's intention for long.

When Phillipe did come again Jesamiah realised he had not been in Hell after all, but only set on course to it. He abandoned pride and begged.

It made no difference. On deck, the crew still heard his cries of agony.

Twenty Four

The storm Phillipe had expected never came, instead, the wind had dropped and a fog rolled in - and *Sea Witch* lost her Chase during the night.

Stefan had told Tiola that Mereno was taking Jesamiah to Virginia – Rue guessed he had meant the plantation along the Rappahannock River - a voyage of five or six days if wind and weather held fair, twice that if not. By then, Jesamiah could be dead. There were guardships in the Chesapeake Bay, narrow channels, sandbars and rocks – as a rendezvous point to hang around and wait, it was impractical. Better to intercept Mereno in the open sea, but first he had to be found.

From the way he had run up through the scatter of Bahama cays and islands with *Sea Witch* stretching in pursuit, Rue was convinced he was aiming to head out along the shortest route, diagonally across the open Atlantic, not following along the safer, slower, Florida and Carolina coastline. And then the fog had come down like a shrouding blanket. Of all the damned days for wind and visibility to fail!

Mindful, from bitter experience, of the Florida reefs, Rue chose to swing out to meet the sullen rollers of the Atlantic, hoping the winds there might disperse the grey soup of fog and allow a clearer view of the horizon hoping Mereno would be sensible and do the same. Most seamen, where fog was concerned, if they knew shoals were close by would either heave to or head for open space.

For a full two days none of his hopes were met. The wind had gone and the fog obstinately stayed. As another evening crawled in from the east, *Sea Witch* crept along on topgallants only, with barely a whisper of a breeze to make headway. Now, the only hope was that Mereno was also trapped in this frustration of making less than a mile in an hour.

With night approaching Tiola felt her frustration building into anger. Unreasonable she knew, for fog was not Rue's fault; all the same, as the grey murk turned into nighttime blackness she confronted him on the quarterdeck. The men, as anxious, concealed their grins at this half-pint lass fearlessly standing up to a man who had been known to haul in an anchor cable with his bare hands. That the cable had not been attached to an anchor, was not so wide known; a small truth Rue kept firmly to himself.

"We need to find him!" she demanded, stamping her foot. A futile, childish gesture she knew, but one which relieved her tension. Standing for long hours up in the fo'c'sle, she had tried shifting the fog, but it was stubborn, a thing, she guessed, deliberately manipulated by the Dark to hinder them. "He is suffering. We must get to him!"

"And 'ow do we do that?" Rue shouted back, as disheartened and irritated as she was. "I 'ave been up to the tops myself more than once, even with the bring-it-close there is nothing to see except fog banks and patches of open – empty - ocean. *Dieu!* I am not a sorcerer, I cannot see what is not there, nor can I conjure a wind!"

His bellow blasted along the length of the deck, causing glances and raised eyebrows to be exchanged. Rue was a placid man who rarely lost his temper; they were all agitated and on edge. *Sea Witch* was a fast ship, they should have had the Chase found and dealt with by now. No one said it - were all thinking it - they should not have lost her in the first place. Jesamiah would not have done so.

Rue was a good seaman, knew how to handle a vessel and keep a crew in order but he was not Jesamiah. Which was perhaps why, in addition to the loyalty they felt towards their captain, the crew were so determined to have him back where he belonged – growling at them from the quarterdeck.

Tiola had also attempted to reach him with her mind, although she assumed he would not be knowing the ship's position. There might have been something, sounds or the feel of how the ship was running, something, anything, to help them find him. But for the few fragmentary connections she had managed he had not been lucid enough to convey anything of sense, even after she had sat through the night cross-legged in his cabin, his personal possessions strewn around her. His cutlass across her lap, his hat, too big, tipped to the back of her head. One of his ribbons woven through her fingers which were splayed across the stains of his blood on the floor.

Jesamiah's misery was too great for her to hear anything beyond his whimpering; those few connected moments unbearable for her to listen to. Reluctant, she had decided to pull back. If he was being tortured and she continued to try and feel into his mind she too could break into brittle shards of insanity, which would be of no use to him.

Her worry, if he had been aware of her mental presence, he did not now assume she had abandoned him.

~ *I am coming! I am following!* ~ Her last words sent to him. ~ *Cling to that, Jesamiah. I am coming for you and I will find you! I will!* ~

The pointless belligerence against Rue sapped from her, she was being unfair and unrealistic. As anxious as herself the man was doing his best. *"I am not a sorcerer,"* he had said. Neither was she, but she did have her Craft. *"Nor can I conjure up a wind!"*

No, Rue could not, but she could.

Without knowing where Jesamiah was, however, even a wind was of no use.

"I need to eat," she said, decisive. "I also need to speak to you in private, for what I intend to do is for you to know alone."

Rue shrugged, politely indicated the way to Jesamiah's cabin and handed the helm to Isiah. "Stay on this course, call me if a wind shifts its arse." On his way below following behind Tiola, he called for dinner.

"The lady is 'ungry and so am I," he growled to Finch in his bear voice. "Fetch us something worth eating."

The stores were not low, the chickens in their crates laid well, there was salt pork and beef in sealed barrels and someone had thought to bring fresh-butchered joints aboard.

"It's cooking!" Finch's irritated shout came back. "I can only char the bloody stuff as fast as the bloody stove will burn it!" Those in hearing, Rue included, grinned. Finch was an excellent galley cook but he would never admit to it. He had appointed himself as Jesamiah's personal steward, and on discovering Tiola was his captain's chosen woman had instantly taken her under his wing as well. Finch, however, Rue had quietly warned her, was inclined on occasion to be a curmudgeonly old mother hen.

In the great cabin Rue sat at Jesamiah's desk shuffling aside a few of the papers scattered there. Tiola was at the table, a fine piece of furniture. He noticed she had not tidied the place; the papers and charts were where they had been strewn, a chair still lay on its side, the red velvet cushions scattered, one torn, its stuffing spewing over the carpet. A broken bottle, its thick glass shattered. Jesamiah's blood staining the floor. He did not know if there was anything missing, nothing obvious had gone. Except for their captain. Beyond the curve of the stern windows, the fog spread in a solid, depressing bank.

"Well?" he said after a long pause.

Her fingers were twirling her ring. Not looking at him she spoke low, very quiet, in almost a whisper. "How much has Jesamiah told you about me, Rue?"

"Ah, 'e said you were *tres belle*, that you were smart – Jesamiah is known for 'is tendency to exaggerate, but in this, rare for 'im, 'e told us the truth."

Tiola acknowledged the compliment with a smile. "He did not tell you of my talent?"

"That you were clever with potions and salves, and a midwife? *Oui,* 'e told us of the birthing 'e 'elped you with so often we threatened to cut off 'is ballocks and make a eunuch of 'im." He made a snipping motion with his fingers, chuckled.

She laughed too. It was good to laugh when everything else was so stifling in its unpleasantness. "Nothing more?"

"Nothing more." Rue shrugged, pushed himself up from the chair and began collecting the charts from the floor, stowing them in their wide drawer beneath the desk.

" 'E never said 'ow much he loved you, did not need to. It was there whenever 'e spoke of you, in 'is eyes, in 'is voice." Rue said the last sharply, critical. Asked direct, "Why did you not come? Why did you leave 'im to sail alone? It broke 'is 'eart - and a pirate's 'eart, *ma chère,* is as 'ard as a two-year old ship's biscuit. It is not easily broken."

She answered with the same blunt directness. "My heart was broken too. We were deceived. I should have realised it instantly, but grief confused me. I ran aground," Tiola admitted settling her hands into her lap, her eyes meeting with Rue's. "As with Jesamiah, I was marooned in a pit of loneliness, unable to scrabble out." She smiled, "Or I thought so, until now. Marrying Stefan was probably stupid but it was the only quick solution I could think of. And now, what I am about to say and do may be stupider still."

Calmly and clearly, she told him what she was.

He did not believe her. First his brows rose, then furrowed. He sat, began to fidget, stroked his chin, drummed his fingers on the desk. His eyes would not meet hers.

"I do not expect you to accept what I am telling you, Rue. Until he saw things with his own eyes Jesamiah did not believe I am of the White Craft either. But he does now, and he does know some of what I can do. That belief, I hope, giving him an anchor to cling to, a reason to stay alive." She paused, spread her hands, pleading. "I am having to trust you with this for we must find

Jesamiah and we must do so now, not in a few days or a week, but *now*. The longer we take the more likely it is there will not be anything of him to save. We will find only the husk of the man he was. Justifiably, he is frightened of Phillipe."

She paused. How to explain? "Mereno is eaten by jealousy; he is so possessed by what, as a child, he saw as betrayal by his mother and father that he has lost his sense of reason. The mind is a complex thing, Rue, I do not expect you to understand, but sometimes human frailty becomes as a beacon to the power of the Dark. It is hard to survive fear and loneliness – despair - easier to succumb to the voices that goad you into hurting others because you have been so hurt yourself. It is a form of vengeance. You cannot take your hatred or spite out on the ones who originally hurt you, so you do so with one who cannot fight back, instead."

Rue sat silent as Finch fetched in the food, and at the quartermaster's solid glare, left again muttering remarks about the untidiness of the cabin and not knowing when he would get chance to tidy it.

Moving to the table Rue sat, ate, tasted little of what he put in his mouth. Finally he said, "As far as Mereno is concerned, I think 'e is a mad man, 'e is like a rat drowning in the bilge – keeps scrabbling at the same bulk 'ead, 'oping to pull 'imself out. If only 'e 'ad the sense to turn round, to swim the other way, 'e would find a footing and survive. Mereno 'as a debt to pay Jesamiah, although to be fair Jes did poke 'is balls with a sharpened stick." He gave a small, half-hearted smile. Had he not been reminded of cobras that night on the Rappahannock?

He smiled at Tiola. "My rational sense is telling me I 'ave been told a sailor's yarn." He pushed the empty plate from him, took a breath. "At sea I 'ave witnessed things with my own eyes that defy belief. What you 'ave told me is beyond my reason." He shrugged, lifted his shoulders, let them fall. "In all 'onesty, I think you, too, are mad, but then, most of Jesamiah's schemes sound like they come from the wrong side of the moon, so, I will believe you."

Tiola laid down her knife and fork, her food barely touched, took a sip of wine. "I believe there may have been a compliment hidden in there somewhere?" She asked shyly.

Pouring a glass for himself, Rue, confirmed there was. "Jesamiah is a man I respect. If I must admit to it I think of 'im as the son I never 'ad. Nor 'ave I ever 'ad cause to doubt 'is judgement. 'E was the one who did not want to go to Nassau, 'e said 'e smelt a rat, 'e was right, I – we – were wrong. Although the rat turned out to be 'is brother, not the Governor." Abruptly he scraped the chair back, stood, offered his hand to Tiola accepting what she had told him and what she intended to do. Use her Craft to find Jesamiah.

Tiola took the gesture as it was intended and placed a kiss on his cheek. A seal of friendship.

"Night is coming," he said, gruff, to conceal the sudden emotion filling him. If Jesamiah was the son he had always wanted, then this lass was most assuredly the daughter. "I 'ave to be on the quarterdeck. Not that we can go any slower than we already are, but to 'elp you stay safe I will reduce sail, let 'er idle as much as I can. You 'ave my word none shall disturb you. I ask you, though, for the sake of God - and for Jesamiah's - to be careful. There is a reason the bowsprit is called the widow-maker."

Ais, she knew. Young Jasper had already told her.

- Twenty Five -

The Atlantic rolled, grey and sullen and bored beneath the languid patches of dismal fog. In the occasional pockets between, the night sky was scattered with countless stars, their brilliance soon swallowed again by the next curtain of mist. *Sea Witch* eased her way forward, her compass heading north until she could safely swing north-west. Until then, they had to suffer the fog.

The first day at sea Tiola had removed her silk stockings, the brocade gown with its tight sleeves and lace cuffs and the impractical layers of stiffened petticoats and tightened stays. She preferred the simple, everyday wear of her plain underskirt and bodice. Before leaving the cabin she slid her arms into Jesamiah's buckram long coat which was saturated with his smell, and folded its warmth – his warmth - around herself. Put her hand into a pocket and discovered another of his ribbons. As she looked at it, tears choked her. Weeping, she tied a lock of hair with it, as Jesamiah did, and made her way out on to the deck and forward to the bow. There was no spray, barely any movement.

She regretted not having better light from the stars, but where she was intending to go no star would be of service anyway. Not Sirius or Orion, nor the blaze of the Sun itself - even were it to defy every law of existence and shine by night.

Darkness covered the ship, the only light glowing from the two stern lamps atop the taffrail and spilling up through the open scuttles and the gratings above the lower deck, making pools of yellow comfort in surrounding blackness. Below, men were amusing themselves with their evening entertainments of singing bawdy songs accompanied by the scrape of fiddles and shrill of tin whistles. Their good humour drifting upward with the swaying rays of the lanterns, to amble away over the rails and be swallowed whole by the yawn of the fog.

The bowsprit stabbed its way forward at the front of the ship, pointing uncompromisingly ahead, the slanted pole sprouting upward from the deck at an angle of 30°. More than eighty feet of slender, wooden spar, a maze of rigging and furled rolls of sails. Nothing below except the vigilant, wooden gaze of the figurehead, and beyond her, the black sea sliding past.

To hesitate would be to become too petrified to move, either forward or back. Tiola's bare feet felt the solidity of the deck, her hand rested on the bowsprit. It was no different than the fore, main or mizzen mast except for it pointing forward not upward. Topmen ran up the masts without a second thought, as if they were climbing stairs, no matter what the weather or wind might throw at them. Men ran out here along the bowsprit, sometimes several times a day to take in or drop sail. Jesamiah would not have thought twice about stepping up, of striding out over the flying sea beneath. He had once told her he often stood out there, especially when the sun was rising or setting. *"It gives a grand view, and a grander feeling. The nearest a man will come to flying. To feeling as free a bird."*

Yet as young Jasper had explained, it was not called a widow-maker for nothing. The spar was narrow and slippery; the rigging salt encrusted and wet and the sea, a long, long, way down. With no coming up again for those who fell.

As Rue had promised *Sea Witch* was making slow headway, her bow easing the sea apart as she progressed forward, the sound of the water glugging as it meandered by. Tiola glanced over her shoulder along the length of the deck. Unlike a normal human, with her ability she could see the outlined form of Rue standing beside Isiah Roberts at the helm quite clearly, despite the fog and the distance. Partially, she regretted telling Rue what she planned to do. Had she remained silent she could return to Jesamiah's cabin and none would be the wiser of her failure. Except herself and Jesamiah, for if she did not do this they may not find him.

Taking a breath of fortifying courage, she hoisted herself upward as she had seen the men do. Felt the light breeze pulling at her hair, teasing the shorter strands into tendrils that patted her cheeks and neck. The salt air stung her face and the cold sent a shiver down her spine. She was glad of Jesamiah's warm coat. Ahead, only fog. Around her, nothing except the sound and smell of Tethys.

Walk quickly, best not run; nor was it wise to feel ahead gingerly with her toes. A matter of balance and to imagine this round pole was a wide, flat surface. As wide as a cobbled street. Look ahead, not down! Her fingers touched the manropes rigged at waist height, although they would do little to save her should she lose her footing.

She reached the cap, the thick block of wood which connected the bowsprit to the narrower spar of the jib-boom and stopped, her heart thudding, teeth chattering; her breath sobbing in her chest and her courage dissolving. To go further she would have to walk out along the footropes rigged beneath, and then grab the fore topmast stay to step up on to the very end of the spar. Willingly, she would have turned back – except she was too frightened to move. In her head, a low, hushing laugh that could have been her imagination or the scorn of the sea itself rolling past, deep, black and endless.

Tentative, Tiola felt with her foot, touched the rope – and slipped! With a gasp of fear her hand curled tighter around the manrope, but she was overbalancing - falling - there was nothing beneath her except the ocean. Desperate, her fingers grappled the lines, her legs kicked... and *Sea Witch* lifted slightly, rising to the next wave, lifted and rolled to leeward - and she shrugged Tiola upward, as if tossing a horserider into the saddle.

With her footing regained Tiola stood in the fog-shrouded darkness, her body quivering, legs shaking, her eyes closed. Tears of despair trickled from beneath her lashes. *I cannot do this! Oh Jesamiah, forgive me – I cannot do it!*

The sea sounded loud in her ears, the roll of the waves, the hush of sound as *Sea Witch* parted the water with her bow, sending it laughing and gurgling its glee along her keel. The ocean, mocking Tiola's fear.

And then the rustle of familiar voices, whispering as wind scurries through the leaves of a tree on a warm summer's day, the guiding voices of Tiola's maternal ancestors, of all those of her past speaking within the spirit that was the peace, and the courage of her soul. Above them all, the stronger, younger, presence of her grandmother.

~ *Tiola. You have already endured desolation. You have already conquered fear. Nothing can harm you. Nothing.* ~

Without conscious thought Tiola stepped down and walked forward as easily as if she were standing on the solidity of the quarterdeck; stepped lightly up on to the very tip of the forward thrusting spar and hooked her arm through the fore topmast stay.

Standing tall and proud she stared ahead – and the fog rolled back, the domed vault of the star-studded sky arched above her. A trail of delicate silver touched everything; sail, rigging and sea, shimmering and beautiful. *Sea Witch* dipped her bow in reverence to the majesty of the glory of night.

The Atlantic trundled beneath the keel and with her mind Tiola entered into the creaking and swaying existence of the ship, becoming one with the rhythmical shift and sway of movement. Aware of every nuance of sound, of every constructed part of her.

Sea Witch was not a dead object, she was made from living things that had once been nurtured by the caress of the sun, soothed by the wind and washed by the soft touch of the rain. Oak from an acorn that had grown a shoot green and strong, and become tall and solid, spreading a canopy of branches and leaves towards the sky, as the ship had masts which billowed a canopy of sail. Masts that also thrust downward, cleaving through the wood and caulking of the decks to where they rested in the blackness of the hold as roots had once plunged into the dark earth. A small, secretive part of the *Sea Witch* had never forgotten her past, that time of living, of breathing, of *being*. She opened that small remaining spark of her soul and invited Tiola to step inside, enfolding her with a wide embrace of joyful welcome, absorbing her as a leaf absorbs the sunlight. Within this secret place, Tiola felt the ache of grief, the feel of loss; a great empty space that wept for Jesamiah, so wanting him. So wanting him to come back to her!

~ *Soon my dear. We shall find him soon,* ~ Tiola soothed. ~ *Together, you and I Sea Witch, together, we shall find him.* ~

Closing her eyes Tiola felt the light wind pushing against the fore topsail, pressing it forward. The braced foremast that took the strain and weight of canvas, held upright and rigid by hawsers, cables, shrouds and rigging; all of it complaining at being bound so tight and so restrained. She felt the upper deck, the planks smooth and blanched by the endless beat of the sun and scoured smooth by the crew scrubbing with the holystone blocks of sandstone, the gaps between water-tight, sealed by oakum, a mixture of old, shredded rope and tar.

Tiola was aware of the great guns, ominous death-bringers, slumbering, fire-breathing dragons, their iron cold and silent beneath her touch. By contrast, the men were delighting in loud jesting and the bravado of outrageous tale-telling. Some were playing dice or cards, mending their clothes, braiding their hair. One man was pricking a tattoo into another's shoulder. Tiola's watching mind lingered a moment. She would like a blue-inked tattoo, perhaps a ship under full sail, rippling on her forearm, or an oak leaf and an acorn, for Jesamiah? Either would be appropriate, but she did not know the men well enough to ask for it to be done. Maybe when Jesamiah was here?

A few of them were already in their hammocks, an arm or a leg dangling over the side; their mouths open, snoring.

In a separate area, away towards the stern, it was dark and deserted. The powder magazine, kept safe behind a draped curtain of wet canvas, while far for'ard, Finch was diligently ensuring the charcoal inside his galley-stove was raked of ash, and the door secured for the night; the iron stove-pipe within the brick chimney properly cooling now the cooking was done. Tiola felt a shudder of fear ripple through the presence that was *Sea Witch*. Fire was the dread aboard a ship. Comforting her, Tiola salved the flickering shadow of horror. ~ *Fire shall not harm you, my dear. Not while I am here to protect you. Nor when Jesamiah returns to care for you.* ~

Below again, going deeper down. Tiola's mind from where she stood, alone and encased by darkness on the jib-boom spar, tiptoed into a place blacker still.

The hold.

Barrels of brackish drinking water, salted meat and weevil infested flour and grain; butter already going rancid, all stored on layers of rock and gravel, the ballast at the very bottom where the rats scurried, gnawing their way into the food. She touched that other place, the bowels of the ship - the cable tier. Smelt its rank, mouldering dampness, the combined foul odour of dead rats and the musk smell of their live companions. Of stagnant water, rot and decay. A place where a man, caught here, would sell his soul to the Devil to see one last glimpse of blessed sunlight before he died.

Unintentionally Tiola's tentative, feeling mind slipped sideways to connect with the same place on a different, red-hulled ship. She heard Jesamiah whimper and abruptly pulled back. For his sake, not hers.

The hull, the keel; the cold sweep of water surging past, the overwhelming sense of slimed, clinging weed, the itch of sucking barnacles and the discomfort of boring worm. The wide, deep, ocean. In daylight the sun would have filtered down, bathing everything green, but the stars had not the strength to light these depths and soon, very soon, as Tiola went deeper and deeper still, everything became black. But not silent. The ocean whispered and echoed with life; the call of the mother whale to her calf, the clicking of the dolphin to his mate, the snap of a shark's cruel teeth and the hurried, flustered, swirl of darting fishes. The lazy flap of the ray's wing or the stroke of the turtle's flipper. The rush and murmur and groan and boom of the sea itself.

The sea bed, the scuttle of crab and starfish. Sand and rock, and coral and shell and weed. The scatter of bones – the gaping corpse of a fish another of a seal. Of drowned men and wrecked ships.

A forest of swaying weed, taller, thicker than a ship's mainmast. A place where it was difficult to decide what was plant and what were the tentacles of a giant squid or octopus. A chasm opened below her, zigzagging across the sand floor, ominous and black. Pitch black, where no light could penetrate. Yet, as she descended, Tiola could see, in the eye that was her mind, as clear as if a flare was illuminating everything with an eerie glow of translucent light.

Deeper! Down deeper! Going down and down to where even the reddish light faded and only flutters of iridescent weird creatures pulsed in the blackness. Where monsters lurked and night was never day. Where such things as stars and moon, sun and sky, wind and rain were distant dreams from an age long, long forgotten.

And through it all, from the foaming surface to the fissure that was the deepest realm of the deepest ocean, Tethys watched. As she watched everything and saw every movement in and around her existence. Every birth, every life; every death. She saw the whelk and the whale, the shark and the shellfish. Had seen the seas when they were silver acid and molten lead. Had witnessed her daughters, the rivers and the lakes and the rain turn to ice and cover her sister the land. Had seen the first creatures live, thrive, and became fossils of stone. Rejoiced at the first birth. Mourned the first death. Witnessed the reptilian beasts drag themselves from the mud and impassively watched them evolve into the terrible lizards they were to became. As, in the passing and passing of time - no more than a rippled sigh to her - she also watched them die.

She had seen the rocks of the ocean bed heave themselves upward to form mountains so high they touched the airless sky. Had seen the great plates of the continents split apart and grind together in earthquakes of destruction, while volcanoes spumed lava to form new, fertile land. She had been there when the world had began. Would be there when it ended.

Tethys.

~ *Who are you who dares enter my realm, mortal?* ~

~ *I am Tiola Oldstagh, Lady, and I am no ordinary mortal.* ~

~ *You are from the creation that is Man.* ~

~ *We are, all of us, created from the stuff of the stars. We are all made from the same breath that created the first simple life, therefore we, both you and I, Tethys, must be kindred of the race called man. Yet, we are not mortal.* ~

~ *I helped create that first life.* ~

~ *As did the knowledge of Craft which I possess and carry. You are therefore my sister, and as your kindred it is my right to enter your ocean realm without the asking. As it is my right to beg your help to find my mate, my lover. Your son. A son who is one of the sea.* ~

In another part of her being, Tiola heard and felt the chasms of the depths of the oceans shift slightly; the bottomless fathoms begin to open like a toothless mouth to swallow something down. Tethys, annoyed, was sinking, preparing to take Tiola with her into the abyss of eternity.

The unseen but oppressive presence of Tethys mocked Tiola's awareness.

~ *You fear me.* ~

~ *I fear nothing except being too late to save my lover.* ~

~ *I can destroy you.* ~

Tiola's turn to mock. ~ *You cannot.* ~

~ You have not the strength to fight me, Witch Child. ~

~ I have no intention of fighting you, Water Woman. Nor do I fear you. I fear nothing and no one, for I have already survived fear. It is those who know they can survive who are to be feared, Tethys. We are the ones who are dangerous, because we have conquered fear. Therefore it is you who fears me, my Lady Tethys. ~

The sea rippled, a wave rolled, driven by no earthly wind. Scurried across the surface of the ocean, gathering speed and power.

~ I can destroy the ship. ~

~ You can. But you will not. ~

~ Will I not? It is my right to take those ships and sailors whom I fancy for my own. It is the price they must pay for molesting my Being. Those I choose must pay the passage for those I reject. ~

Tiola felt the wave of water rise up and crash over her and the bowsprit, a deluge of wild spray that sent *Sea Witch* yawing to larboard, the sea rearing huge, washing over her decks. Tiola heard, from a great distance, Rue shouting urgent orders for men to get their arses on deck.

~ You will not destroy the ship Tethys, because she carries men who admire your wisdom and respect your power. ~

~ What care I for men? ~

~ You care for one of them, Tethys. This ship is his ship. Destroy the Sea Witch and you destroy him. ~

~ I have no care for pirates. Nor for witches. I rule the sea. I am the sea. My word, here, is what shall be and what shall not be. ~

~ You are the currents, you are the surf and the tides, the spindrift in the wind and the foam upon the shore, but you cannot control me or tear this chain of silver anchoring the soul that is mine to the soul of the Sea Witch. Through the power of my Craft

I have become one with her, as she is also one with her master, my lover. And your jealousy, Tethys, cannot divide us. ~

In her consciousness Tiola felt the chafe of the topmast fore stay against her arm, felt beneath her bare feet, *Sea Witch* stoutly rising as she lifted over another onrushing wave, the vessel determined and steady on her course towards the Chesapeake Bay. If Tiola were to glance upward way, away overhead, she would see, tiny and distant the underside of the keel forging through the water. And out on the lonely thrust of the bowsprit, would see herself, her hair and coat and gown billowing around her, glowing with phosphorescence, standing silent and alone in the darkness.

~ Yes. Look! ~

If she looked, her concentration and conviction would be broken. To look was to doubt and Tiola knew she must never doubt her ability. Doubt was weakness. Confidence was strength.

Scathing, Tethys laughed. *~ You are new to your Craft, Witch. Come back when you have learnt how to use what you have. In a thousand, thousand years. ~*

And Tiola answered, proud and confident. *~ The shell that is my body is new, but not the knowledge I carry and use within it. In that I am as old as you. ~*

The ocean shuddered. The fault lines of the continents shifting at the will of Tethys, impotent to do anything against the *Sea Witch* that was the ship, the sea witch who was the ageless woman.

~ It is my right to ask what I will of you, Tethys, for it is the right of the Craft I hold, the Craft given me by the passage of Time, through the generations of Time, from beyond the dawn of Time. ~

~ Time is meaningless to me. ~

~ As it is meaningless to me, but still it is my right to ask. ~ And Tiola altered her voice. Where she had been talking low and coaxing, seductive and harmless, she suddenly snapped a command, the force shattering the near silence, hurling through the

undersea world with its demand to be obeyed. ~ *Where is the ship upon which my lover is held captive?* ~

The sea swelled as another soaring wave rushed across the Atlantic to almost engulf the *Sea Witch* within its white-foamed rage.

~ *I do not concern myself with trivialities. I do not know. I do not care.* ~

~ *You do know, Tethys. You do care. You know all there is to be known of the sea, in the sea and on the sea. You are the sea. I have asked and you* must *answer.* ~

~ *I give no answer unless I get in return. One must be exchanged for the other, as is my right.* ~

Becoming complacent again, Tiola agreed. ~ *As is your right. You shall have something in return.* ~ Her body, standing on the thrust of the bowsprit released its firm hold of the stay and reached for the ribbon, Jesamiah's blue ribbon, from the tangle of her hair. Released it into the night. It was tossed and toyed with a moment by the wind but was soon discarded as insignificant; it fluttered downward into the surf foaming to either side of *Sea Witch's* bow and was gone, taken.

~ *A blue ribbon is pretty but it is not sufficient.* ~

~ *It is a token only, a gesture of my gratitude for your answer.* ~

~ *Payment will be demanded. Payment will be made when I ask it.* ~

~ *What you ask, when you ask, shall be paid. Where is Jesamiah?* ~

~ *Jeshh..a..miah?* ~

Sea Witch rolled dangerously, the Atlantic slamming against her a third time. Her bow lifted and rose higher and higher, seemingly as if she would rise too high and tip over backwards – and then she was breasting the wave and plunging down the other side, her stern now reaching for a sky showing the first hint of dawn, the fog quite gone. In its place, the wind was rising into stronger and stronger gusts. It veered suddenly, took the *Sea Witch's* topsail aback and over and over on to her side she went, the upper dead-eyes of her rigging dipping beneath the water, the mainmast yard arm, beneath the sea. Water sluiced over rails and deck, pouring down into the hatches, flooding into the lower deck and the hold. The once horizontal upper deck now almost vertical, leaning towards the lightening sky. The great guns hanging from their tackles.

Rue shouted something as this third wave engulfed them, his feet slipping on the tipped up planking awash with the sea. He grabbed a halyard, clung on for dear life. From the shout of his first bellow, hands had already been coming up from below, alarmed, running, unsure of what was happening. Attack? Reef? Shoals? Many of them were washed along the deck, some, the lucky ones were sluiced back down the ladders. Three were swept overboard with open-mouthed cries of fear, knowing they were gasping their last breath of sweet air. There was nothing anyone could do for them, except later, say the appropriate words as a form of burial, and pass their meagre belongings to loved-ones ashore.

Tiola saw their deaths and grieved for men who should not have died, and she saw the greed of Tethys reaching out for what was not hers to have. She screamed her rage, the sound renting the sky in a shout of potent fury.

~ Do not dare Tethys! Do you not dare destroy this ship! ~

Sea Witch did not care for such rough treatment, and as the wave rumbled beneath her keel she twisted, righting herself, shaking free of the grappling hold that was pulling her down into a watery grave. She lurched forward, her bowsprit crashing through a cascade of foam and the sail flapped. As if nothing had happened, water pouring from her scuppers, *Sea Witch* calmly ploughed through the next oncoming wave.

"What the Devil was that?" someone called, sodden, bruised, but relieved.

"Did we hit something? A whale? A wreck?"

Rue could not answer, he abandoned the helm to Isiah, was running forward, running to the bow where Tiola should have been. To the bowsprit, where she had stood silent and still through the entire night. Where there was now nothing except a bowsprit, a figurehead, jib-boom and furled sails; all drenched, dripping with spray.

"Mon Dieu!" he cursed as he stepped up for'ard past the heads, the sailors' seat of ease, his eyes peering outward and down expecting to see her body dangling, dead, beneath the rigging. Could he forgive himself if he lost her? He had not said last night when she had spoken to him, for it was a thing he would hold secret to himself, but he had accepted all she had said as a token of hope for Jesamiah. A part of him insisting if he looked after Tiola then he would find his friend; if all was well with her, than so was it with Jesamiah. And stupidly, stupidly, he had allowed her to go out on to the bowsprit!

And then he laughed, his head back, hands on his hips, a lion's roar of relief as a white, slender hand, two, grasped the rail, and a bedraggled, sodden girl began to haul herself upward. He grabbed her arm and dragged her aboard, her hair dripping, her coat and gown soaked and covered by slime and green weed.

"I do declare," he chortled, "we 'ave caught ourselves a mermaid!" He removed the drenched coat, took off his own and set it around her shoulders, picked a crab from her hair and threw it into the sea. She looked as white as death, but she managed a smile for him.

"Mereno went westward. He put in at Charleston," she said breathless and bone-weary tired but bursting with elation. She was grateful for the warm coat and for Rue's arm supporting her waist, desperately needed to sleep. "Phillipe has no love of the sea and he feared the fog. We will find him as he runs north along the coast."

Chewing his lip, Rue wondered whether to ignore her excitement; they could be wasting valuable hours by doing this, and yet... The prevailing wind had returned - the Trade Winds, which blew almost eternally across the Atlantic from east to west – and the fog had lifted to expose miles of a dawn-bright empty ocean. They had no hope of finding Mereno's ship out here in the middle of nowhere.

Jasper trotted up, eyeing Tiola's bedraggled appearance. He said nothing. If the daft woman wanted to stand up here in the bow, more fool her. "Begging pardon, Rue, but Jansy says we need men for the pumps. He says we've got more'n two feet of water in the well."

Rue was not surprised. With the deluge swamping them he had expected much more. They had escaped lightly. "Ask Mr Janson to set the necessary men on to it if you please. As soon as we 'ave canvas set, I willl send more men to 'elp."

Jasper touched his forehead, trotted off away aft.

"Lay 'er on the larboard tack, full and by!" Rue ordered as he stepped into the waist, guiding Tiola before him. "You, get yourself down into that cabin and into Jesamiah's bed. Stripped and dried. Once Finch 'as re-lit 'is stove, I will 'ave 'im bring you 'ot coffee and breakfast."

The crew were scurrying to do as he commanded, swarming up the shrouds and out along the yards, pleased to be free of the fog at last and making way again. No sailor liked to be blind at sea.

"We are going after him as fast as we can?" Tiola asked Rue, peeling away his coat and handing it back to him.

"All 'ands! To braces! 'aul and let go!" he shouted, cupping his hand around his mouth, and sails spilled from the yards. He scowled at Tiola. "If you intend to stay aboard this ship then you 'ad best learn orders are to be instantly obeyed. If you are incapable of getting yourself out of those wet clothes, I am sure I can find one of the 'ands willing to be of assistance."

Imitating Jasper's respectful salute she knuckled her forehead, made no movement to leave. "Jesamiah?" she asked again, her head cocked to one side, her hand lightly touching Rue's arm.

"*Oui*. As long as this wind 'olds. It will take us more than three day's sailing to raise Charleston from 'ere – in the fog we 'ave drifted too far north. If it is the coast 'igher up you will be wanting - take a day off that? We will get our captain back, do not worry."

The men nearby cheered, a sound taken up by those in the tops and those below manning the pumps. A cheer that scurried through the entire ship.

Happy, *Sea Witch* brought her head around and was sheeted home. As eager as her crew she leapt forward. Lying over no more than a degree or two she glided through the water as beautiful as a swan, her rudder balanced perfectly against the full spread of her sail.

Jesamiah, Rue thought as he watched Tiola disappear below into the captain's cabin, was a damned lucky sod to have a fine ship and a beautiful woman. Prayed his friend had not run out of that luck.

'*Old fast mon ami,* he thought. *Just 'old fast.*

- Twenty Six -

"Sail ho!"

"Where away?" Rue responded, peering up the mainmast at Toby Turner who stood precisely balanced on the crosstrees. *Sea Witch* was rolling hard, hove-to with her mizzen topsail backed as they waited, ten miles out from the Carolina coast. Turner was swinging through a wide, curving arc back and forth as the mast ponderously swayed and the ship rocked, everything creaking and groaning with the swell hauling under her keel.

"Hull down, two points off larb'd beam!" Turner shouted, his arm outstretched, finger pointing, totally disregarding the uncomfortable motion as *Sea Witch's* starboard scuppers dipped once again below the foam.

From the rocking deck the crew could see nothing except an empty sea and the grey land-mass of North Carolina spread along the horizon. Taking his telescope Rue scurried aloft his sense telling him to not raise hope, this ship could be anything. This would be the eighth sail spotted coming up from Charleston since sun-up. The eighth disappointment? He hooked his elbow through the shroud and steadied the bring-it-close at what appeared to be a schooner heading north. Too far away to see its hull below the horizon. Rue snapped the glass shut, cursed. It could be any damned ship! Except there were not many of these new slim-line American Schooners on the seas. They were good vessels, fast and expensive. Rich mens' toys – or a pirate's dream. There was not a pirate, yet, who had managed to catch one.

"Keep a sharp eye, Toby. It will be dark in three 'ours, I want a positive sighting before then." Did not add, as the t'gan's'l flapped, nor did he want to lose the wind. If it was the schooner they would be hard pushed to run her down, and if this faltering breeze yet again turned fickle... Rue was not going to think about that. Thoughts brought bad luck.

Toby indicated his understanding as Rue let himself hand-over-hand down to the deck. Tiola had wanted to go to Charleston itself, Rue had firmly refused on two counts. One, it would mean doubling back on themselves and they could easily miss Mereno. Two. *Sea Witch* was not welcome anywhere near Charleston harbour.

"We are pirates," he had scoffed at her persistent arguing *"Pirate ships are not encouraged into respectable anchorages. Not after our last visit there, anyway. We would do better to lay off-shore 'igher up the coast and wait for 'im to come to us."*

He was not as convinced as Tiola about Mereno being somewhere in this vicinity, the feeling of doubt increasing as the hours had slowly passed. They were several days out from Nassau. For almost one of those days they had been tacking up and down this patch of ocean. Getting pirates a bad name, Rue had commented as they had watched yet another laden merchant sail warily by, unharmed and un-threatened.

Now the wind was once again letting them down; the only comfort, there was no return of the fog. Ironically, there were probably storms brewing down in the Caribbean, and Rue could see with his own eyes stronger gusts about five miles away stirring the swell.

He gave order to haul the fore topsail, if for nothing else to at least do something about this stomach-churning rolling.

"All we need is for one of the Carolina guardships to come out and investigate us," he muttered as *Sea Witch* tacked and ceased her sickening motion.

Expecting to see the danger of a patrol ship come immediately into view some of the men glanced uneasily over the rail, crossing themselves or making various signs to ward off bad luck. The Guardship. Pirate hunters. It was not good to be hanging around in these waters.

"On deck! Rue? Rue!" A while later, young Jasper was up the mast having relieved Toby Turner. He called down again, his voice stirring action from the lazing crew. "Sir! It's her, I'm sure of it! It's her, a schooner with a red hull, Mereno's ship!"

Where everyone had been idling with nothing much to do except check *Sea Witch's* westerly drift, life suddenly bounced into a gallop. Men were on their feet, a few running up the rigging to stare south, others leaning over the rails. Peering through squinting eyes, squabbling over a spare bring-it-close.

Rue opened out his telescope, took his time to take a long, careful look. Red hull. A schooner. Figurehead of a red-haired, red-robed lady. He lowered the bring-it-close, snapped it shut. Grinned at Tiola. "I apologise for doubting you. We 'ave found 'im!"

The whoop of chorused cheering lifted upward to the lead-grey sky.

The schooner was at least ten miles distant and she had a wind. They did not. She was also wary of anything suspicious, like a mouse with whiskers quivering, creeping close to the skirting board, certain there was a cat on the prowl somewhere. Or a pirate ship lurking in wait. The mouse saw the cat, flicked her tail - and fled.

Lewd and explicit, Rue swore as she piled on sail, turned her nose and began to race north-east away from the coast and out to the open space of the Atlantic, showing them a wide berth and a clean pair of heels. It meant she would have to tack against the direction of the wind, but to catch her – to follow her - so would *Sea Witch* and first they would have to find the wind that *Ruby*, as the crew were calling her, already had.

With less than two hours of daylight left the sails flapped and collapsed, the patchy wind dropping entirely. Rue swore again. They were going to lose her! "*Merde*," he added as an amen to a particularly explicit oath, thumping his fist angrily on to the binnacle.

"We could always warp her from the boats," Someone suggested, not relishing the idea. Towing a ship the size of *Sea Witch* from the longboats in open sea was backbreaking, bone-aching work, even if it was only to where a wind was riffling the surface a few miles away to larboard. By the time *Sea Witch* got there the breeze could have shifted again and *Ruby* would be long gone.

"Are you sure it's her?" Isiah asked Rue quietly as he tipped his head back and eyed their sails flapping again, lifeless. "No sense in putting our backs into the wrong Chase."

Rue had given the telescope to Tiola who was studying the ship as intensely as Rue had. She lowered the glass, handed it to Isiah who made his own inspection.

"It is Mereno," Tiola said with a confirming nod. "Jesamiah is aboard and he is still alive."

She regarded Rue a moment. Carefully, with small, subtle changes she had altered any recollection he had of her night on the bowsprit. Those of the crew who had seen her for'ard, remembered her with her feet firmly planted on the deck – until that wave had almost washed her overboard. Even young Jasper had no memory of warning her about the widow-maker. Only with Rue had she left something, for she had to allow him to accept her word. The rest of the secret she had shared with him however, was erased from his memory, for his sake as well as hers. What was not known could not be told.

"We need a wind?" she asked, her head cocked on one side as she watched the men heaving the yards around in an attempt to find one.

"Without the wind we can make no progress," Isiah Roberts answered, flatly. "Nature is a cruel mistress. We wait all this while for the schooner we've been trailing. We find her – then we sit here like a hen, arse-tight to her eggs and watch her sail by because she has the breeze and we don't."

"I am learning the requirements of this ship with a speed that surprises me," Tiola announced casually, "but tell me, from which direction do we require this wind to blow in order for us to catch *Ruby* before dark?"

Rue answered gruffly, this was all talk. There was no wind nor, if he knew his signs aright, were likely to get one. "Anything between sou'east through west to north will suit, the Trades blow the total opposite - when they blow. All we can do is 'aul our sails and limp along as efficiently as we can."

"And hope we do not lose her?" Tiola was scornful. "I am not willing to take a risk Rue, not again. Jesamiah has suffered long enough already."

"Well then, *Dieu!*" Rue kicked, furious with the turn of fate, at the helm. "What are you going to do? Are you going to get out and push?"

He was not prepared for Tiola's blithe answer, "If I have to, *ais*." She knew exactly what she had to do – summon a wind. It would be difficult to gradually blur the memory of all of them yet again, but sailors, especially pirates, were a superstitious breed; easier, to let them believe something else had brought it and not her. Those geese winging south for instance?

Casually, she leant her back against the stern taffrail, her eyes watching the fore topsail, that without the pressure of the wind was collapsed into a sagging rag. She concentrated on the yard and braces, the standing and running rigging; the shrouds and the gaskets - the ties used to furl the sails. Thought about *Sea Witch* moving through the ocean, the dip, lift and roll as she surged forward. The curtsey of her bow, the uplifting swing of her stern, her joy and liberty. Merging with the ship, Tiola felt every swaying movement, every shift of settling or bending beam of timber; felt the constant, aching strain on the masts, the push against the sails – the surge of water beneath her keel.

And then Tiola sang. A sound an octave above the pitch of the human ear, and as sweet and pure as liquid honey. A sound that swirled around the three masts and brought with it three enormous snow geese.

Jasper, perched aloft was to swear later a whole flock of birds had flourished overhead, the sky had been filled with them. But then, he could not count beyond a tally of two. Barking and whooping, the birds came in low over the ship, the music of their wings rushing past Jasper's ears, causing every man to look up, point and gasp. Three damned, great bloody geese!

They circled the ship twice, black-tipped, white pinions shimmering in the late afternoon sun, bright against the empty water world of white-splashed grey. Their outspread wings sighing, spread as if they were feathered sails, the birds themselves the graceful, sleek hull.

A higher, clearer singing soared above their mournful cry. More beautiful than a mermaid's love poem, or the voice of an angel; more captivating than a siren's song. An enchantment, the spell of a sea witch fetching up a wind. And in answer, it came, flurrying across the sea from due west, shivering through the rigging, nudging the cordage, the ratlines, the shrouds into their own voice of harp-like song.

The geese circled a third time, caressing *Sea Witch* with their outspread wings as the lifeless sails caught the hurry of the breeze and she began to gather way, her dull lethargy quite gone, quite forgotten. In a wide, graceful spiral the three birds rose, higher against the louring sky. Rue, forgetting them, intent on the rise of the wind shouted for sails to be hauled and set.

"We 'ave a wind!" He bellowed, elated. "Let fall, *mon Dieu* let fall before it fades!" Canvas began to tumble from the yards as eager men leapt to backstays.

"Look alive! Forget those birds - we 'ave a wind! 'Ands to braces. Belay!" Rue was almost dancing in his excitement, his arms encouraging the men, whirling like windmills.

Within minutes all canvas was sheeted home, *Sea Witch* bound forward with an urgency of spirit into the oncoming sea, the hush of her passage as melodious as the wind sighing in above the level of the tide and humming through her rigging.

Tiola, standing at the stern, a smile in her dark, radiant eyes, permitted herself a moment of personal pleasure and released her soul to soar with the geese a while. For a moment only three geese became four. She felt the air currents lift her wings, saw the ocean spread below, mile after mile after mile of unbroken freedom. And below her, two ships. *Sea Witch,* incredibly lovely, her sails wide-spread as she flew, catching up upon the other, red stained and tainted by the spilling of blood.

From up here, high, so high, Tiola could see the entire curve of the world; the infinity of the sea with its islands and continents, the glimmer of ice at the Poles. The slow turn around the sun, the gaze of the moon and the chatter of the stars. All of it, in the sight of her Craft timeless and incredibly beautiful. In her cupped hands, her fingers trembling in exquisite expectation, she held the sky and the sea together with the geese and the wind. And in the centre of it all, rested the *Sea Witch.*

Balancing with the rising motion of the ship as if she had been born to the sea, the one leg bent slightly forward at the knee, the other back, Tiola opened her palms wide and set them all free; the wind to blow, the sea to roll, the geese to become nothing more than three specks drifting away, diminishing and vanishing, as if they had never been.

And *Sea Witch* to fly through the Atlantic rollers, not as a white goose but as the swooping hawk. A peregrine falling from the sky, her wings folded, eyes fixed, talons out-stretched. The fastest creature in the sky, plummeting down on to her selected prey, and at this moment the fastest ship on the oceans. Her prey had no hope of escape, no matter how desperately the Chase tried to haul the wind or twist and turn. Nothing could outrun the spell of a sea witch.

The last notes of Tiola's song faded. None aboard any the wiser of what she had done.

Only Tethys stirring way below, saw and heard the witch. And with a flurry of eager anticipation, understood.

She swayed and crooned; she had been promised a gift of reward and was unable to wait any longer to be given it. She wanted her trophy! She wanted him.

Wanted him *now!*

Twenty Seven

Under fighting sail, reduced canvas to make her easier to handle and keep her stable during the firing of her guns, *Sea Witch* overhauled the *Ruby* – rightly called *Retribution*. Phillipe had named her well for his purpose of vengeance. Two hundred yards to windward, Rue gave command to show her they meant business and fired on the upward roll into her rigging; one-two-three-four-five-six-seven-eight-nine-ten, then riding the strong breeze, a gull now not a hawk, *Sea Witch* came around and fired again. All her shots aimed high, chain shot and langrage to damage men and mast, not to penetrate the hull.

Ruby was firing her six guns indiscriminately, with no discipline or sequence, all haphazard, firing everything she had in desperation. Phillipe had an eye for a ship, a justification for a name but had dolts for crew. From one hundred yards Rue paid *Sea Witch* off to rake the Chase again with another series of well-fired, accurate shots, also on the up roll at the height of the rise, all her shot going home on the same strake through rigging and sail.

The men on the *Retribution,* panic stricken, petrified, surrendered immediately, falling to their knees and crying to God, the Virgin and various other deities to save them, their guns and their master and employer abandoned to the tangle of her broken cordage, ripped sails, shattered spars and broken main mast. Only the officers refused to give ground, firing muskets and pistols at close range as Rue luffed *Sea Witch* alongside, slamming into the schooner's bow with a tearing crash that juddered through both ships. The pirates poured down over the rails to board, swinging on ropes or jumping, their voices shouting the death chant that had shattered the silence of the sea before being drowned by the firing of the canon. A special chant which without rehearsal had come to all their lips.

"Jesamiah! Jesamiah! Jesamiah!"

In the bilge, Jesamiah had heard but ignored it. He was past caring what happened to him, and no longer believed what he thought to be true. Too many hallucinations had haunted him these past days – days? He had no idea if he had been in this black pit for days, weeks or forever. With no glimmer of daylight, no idea of whether the sun shone or the stars gleamed, whether it was morning or afternoon disorientation had rapidly engulfed him.

Twice a day – he assumed a day - they had soused him with a couple of buckets of sea water. He assumed to sluice away his mess of urine, faeces and vomit so that Phillipe did not have to tread in it when he visited, but it added to his discomfort, the salt stinging his wounds and leaving him cold and shivering. They also brought him half a tankard of scum-green drinking water and a meagre portion of food; biscuits that were more weevil than hard tack. In the dark he gulped down the brackish water and sucked at the meagre food, unable to chew for his mouth was too sore, the gold teeth gone. Phillipe had pulled them out, with two other, healthy teeth. Revenge for the ones Jesamiah had punched from his gums all those years ago as an angry boy. At least the salt water had washed some of the dried blood from his face, he could open his eye now. Not that there was anything to see in the darkness.

The first day after Phillipe had tortured him had passed as a fog of red agony and black nothingness, the one misting in and out of the other. Jesamiah's body, where his brother had ill-treated him had been on fire, everything too painful to move, yet too painful to remain still and ignore the cramp tearing at his torn muscles. He had tried, for a short while, to keep himself together, to fight the dark and the wretchedness. Tried, but had soon abandoned the trying.

To keep his mind alert and active he had set himself mental riddles; the most effective way to attack a larger, faster ship; the latitude of familiar places and the points of the Compass Rose. Only, he soon found he could get no further than sou'-sou'-east, and that frightened him. He could not remember! Again, he would start at north, and each time become more muddled until he collapsed into the exhaustion of semi-conscious tears.

And then the days had blurred together into the dread of Phillipe's visits, the hunger and thirst, the smell of the bilge and his own waste. And the rats and the dark. He slept, curled on his side, a half-awake half-asleep place, where he was always aware of the motion of the ship and of his prison; the sound of the sea tearing past on the far side of the keel. Aware of footsteps coming below, scuffing on the wooden ladder and echoing along the length of the hold; of the swinging bob of a lantern's light, growing brighter, coming closer. Phillipe's low, malicious chuckle beside him, and the look of madness behind his eyes. The stomach-sickening dread of being carefully shown what his brother held in his hand to use on him this time. A lit cheroot, a knife, a leather belt. Or worse, when he came with nothing, and his hand went to the buttons of his breeches...

"Why?" Jesamiah had asked once in those first few days, when he lay face down, the tears wet on his cheeks. "Why are you doing this to me, Phillipe?"

He had not expected, nor understood, the reply. "Because when Father left me alone for two years to be cared for by servants, this is what they did to me."

Sometimes, Jesamiah would drift in and out of this insane, semi-aware world and believe he was in his bed aboard *Sea Witch*, could swear he heard Finch bringing him coffee, even smelt it. Or he was on deck, critically watching the trim of the sails - or leaning against a wall in a dark street, blood pouring from his arm, a pistol shot in his shoulder, with a girl who had her arms about him, telling him not to struggle, it would be alright.

Tiola.

He dreamt often of Tiola, and woke each time to the smell of his fear and pain, with fresh tears falling on finding she was only a dream. He was alone with the rats and the dark. And Phillipe's revenge.

Tiola.

~ *Jesamiah. I am coming for you.* ~

And he would again wake with a jerk to find himself naked and chained into this nightmare, knowing he was going mad. Had probably gone mad. Dreading, in his desperation that perhaps he had been wrong. Had he seen a woman who had only looked like her at Nassau? Or wherever it was, he could no longer clearly remember that either. Or what if she no longer cared for him? Was not coming? What if there was nothing except this darkness and Phillipe's obsessive madness?

The only thing of benefit he had discovered, was once he stopped screaming and let Phillipe do what he wanted to him without murmur, the torture had eased. Although that could have been to do with the ship lying at anchor in a busy harbour somewhere. The sounds had been familiar; other ships, the clatter of winched capstans, the shouted calls, the cry of gulls. The bump of a bum-boat coming alongside, shouting the wares they had for sale, and being told in no uncertain terms to clear off by someone on deck. The splash of oars as Mereno's gig was put over the side.

Then they were under way again, moving slowly at first, probably under topsails only; when canvas had been set, they were skimming the sea once again. Phillipe had not come while they were in harbour. A day? Two? Had reappeared once they were at sea and it had all started again. He may be coming in a minute, any minute...

Jesamiah heard his name being shouted and knew for certain he had gone mad. He was hearing voices. Only when the first rolling broadside hit and the ship rocked violently, screeching its own terror, did he come alert, his sluggish mind dragging itself back to a dulled awareness of reality. Guns. When the next roll came he counted rapidly: *one, two, three, four, five, six, seven, eight, nine, ten.* Guns he recognised. Guns he bloody, blessedly so beautifully recognised! *Sea Witch!*

The tearing and splintering, the groans of a ship under fire. The crash of a mast falling, the *pop, pop, pop* of musket and pistol fire. The shouting of men. His men, his wonderful, loyal, precious, men!

"Jesamiah! Jesamiah! Jesamiah!"

The shock of a ship crashing alongside.

"Jesamiah! Jesamiah!"

And a moment later, a long moment later, a different voice; not the vaporing of the pirate's death chant, but sweeter and so much, so very much, dearer.

~ *Jesamiah?* ~

"Oh, Tethys! Jesamiah! My luvver, my dear!" Arms were about him, lips kissing his bruised, bloodied face. Her tears wet, dripping on him. Someone, a man, was swearing a series of blasphemous curses in French, holding a lantern high, its light sending wildly swinging shadows across the low, curved beams. Rue swore again, called orders for clothes or at least a blanket, to be fetched.

A short while later someone else standing there, a black man with a shirt and breeches gleaned from a chest in Mereno's cabin.

Jesamiah's chains went slack, were peeled from the mess of the chaffed skin of wrists and ankles and he was free. Free to move, to get up, to leave. But all he could do was sit there with his arms clamped around the waist of the woman he loved, his face buried into her shoulder.

.

Twenty Eight

Hesitating at the open scuttle Jasper was reluctant to go down into the hold. What was happening down there was none of his or the crew's business. There were some things a man, a captain, wanted to keep private.

He was a good lad, fifteen years of age, fair haired, blue eyed; gangling legs and arms too long for his body. With *Sea Witch* warped to *Ruby* – they refused to call her *Retribution* – the both warped together with sails aback, most of the crew were busy ransacking the hold and cabins for anything of value. So far, there was not much. A few of the men were shepherding the pitiful crew into the launched longboat - rarely did they destroy a ship they attacked, usually stripping it of everything of worth then leaving it for the hands to survive as best they could. Not this ship. Come nightfall there would be nothing of her except pieces of charred wood floating in the sea. One or two bodies among the debris.

Jasper chewed his lip. Dusk would soon be swarming in from the east, the descending sun was striking something white coming in from the north west. Something approaching fast. His mind made, he lifted a lantern from a hook and scurried down the ladders into the lowest hold.

They were grouped at the far end, Rue, Isiah Roberts and Miss Tiola, the men standing, stooping forward holding two lanterns high; Rue's left arm leaning against the bulwark. Miss Tiola was on her knees among the stinking bilge water slopping about, cradling something which Jasper realised with a gasp, must be his captain.

"Sir?" Jasper's tentative voice came as a croak that altered pitch half way through. He coughed, called louder. "Sir? Rue?"

Frowning Rue spun around, snapped, "Go away boy, this is not for you to see."

"No sir, I know, but there's a ship coming up on us." He faltered, wondering again whether he was being foolish. "I can't be sure, I think it's the Guardship."

Rue's expression changed from disgruntlement to alarm. Stooping low he made his way back to the hatch, looked up at the boy. If it was the coastal patrol they were in trouble. Pirate hunters. Sharks. Professional men, usually ex pirates, who were paid a handsome bonus for every man captured and brought in for hanging.

" 'Ow can't be sure are you?"

"I'm fairly certain it's the *Carolina Revenge*. Being the size she is she's pretty distinctive. I had a good look at 'er back in the spring when we 'ad that run-in. I'm certain it is 'er; she's about half hour away."

Rue rubbed at his bearded chin, pinched his nose, thinking a stream of curses. If they were caught here ...

"*Merci* Jasper, you 'ave done well. We will be on deck directly, pass word I want everyone back aboard the *Sea Witch*."

They would grumble at not being able to pick over their Prize at leisure, but they had achieved what they had come for. They had Jesamiah.

"Isiah? Tiola? We 'ave to go. There is unpleasant company on its way." He mouthed the words *"Guardship"* at Isiah, drawing his finger across his throat at the same time.

"I am not sure if we can move him yet," Tiola said looking around, her drawn face streaked with tears, blood smeared on her clothes.

"I'm alright," Jesamiah croaked. "Don't fuss. I can manage. Help me get those breeches on will you? I don't want any o'the crew to see me like this." He tried to rise, got as far as one knee, groaned as stiff, cramped, muscles protested, and half slumped forward, Tiola's arms going out to catch him.

Best to fetch a stretcher? Rue thought. To Isiah he said, "If it is the *Carolina Revenge* we will be done for if they catch us."

Lifting his head at the ship's name, Jesamiah winced. Everywhere, inside and out, was sore. "*Carolina Revenge?*"

"*Oui.*"

What the hell is the Carolina Revenge doing near Nassau? Jesamiah thought, his head aching, his mind confused.

Sensing his muddle Tiola took his hand, explained. "We are off the coast of the Carolinas, Luvver. You have been imprisoned here for seven days."

Seven days? Was that all? Jesamiah frowned, it had seemed a lifetime.

"Help me up," he said to Rue, intending to offer his right arm, changed his mind, offered the left instead. It was rather bloodied, but intact. Sort of.

He allowed Tiola to make him decent, stepping into the breeches that were slightly too large, wincing as she drew them up over his buttocks. Lifting his arms, with a muffled gasp, cooperated as well he could as she eased the shirt over his head. "Leave it loose, Sweetheart, I don't want it tucked in."

He managed a few paces, found his legs were shaking, Rue took one side, Isiah the other their arms entwined around his waist to give support, Tiola moving ahead with the lanterns; Jesamiah biting his lip to stop the cry from getting further than the groan in his throat.

They were being too slow, there were ladders to climb yet - dispensing with nicety Rue muttered an apology, hoisted his captain over his shoulder and scurried above, shouting urgent orders as he took long strides across the open deck. Setting Jesamiah down, he propped him against the gunwale near the bow and marching astern, bellowed further commands.

"We are leaving. Belay what you are doing, you scurvy dogs, and return aboard! Belay it I say!"

The bright light dazzled Jesamiah's eyes. He closed them, rested his head against the bulwark and sucked in lung-fulls of the sweet, cool air, relishing the feel of the cool wind on his grimed face. He was hurting, several of his ribs were broken, as was his ring finger on his right hand. His thighs, buttocks, lower back - internally and externally - were bruised and sore. His limbs were shaking as if they were made of marrow jelly, but none of it mattered, none of it now he was out of that black darkness and out here in the sunlight. Tentative, he opened his eyes, blinked several times, water streaming from them; smiled a lop-sided reassurance at Tiola kneeling beside him, her face lovely.

"I don't think I feel very well," he admitted.

She tenderly stroked her finger down his face, hovering over the bruises, the swellings and the cuts; some would need stitching, one or two would be leaving scars. Her eyes ran professionally over the obvious injuries wondering how deep those she could not see ran. The ones in his mind, especially. She knew how he hated the dark, and had a rough, horrified idea of what Phillipe had done to him. She thrust those thoughts aside, however. "I am a healer I will soon get you better." She had to sound positive, to believe it. "Let's get you aboard the *Sea Witch*, to your cabin." Her arm supporting him, she helped him to his feet.

Shouts. Someone running. Sudden confusion. Someone was slamming into Tiola from behind, pushing her and Jesamiah, shoving them aside by brute force.

Taken by surprise she screamed as they fell, tumbling over the rail, plummeting straight down into the Atlantic that wallowed where *Sea Witch* had swung a few feet outward, *Ruby* being pulled in the opposite direction by the trail of her fallen mainmast dragging in the water.

Phillipe Mereno had seized his chance. Herded with the ship's master and officers on to the quarterdeck, threatened with pistols and muskets, he had fumed, impotent to do anything, failing to realise this was not a run-of-the-mill pirate attack. His anger reached the level of apoplectic rage as it became apparent this was specific, this dross, these dregs, had come to rescue his half brother. He found it incredible someone would actually want to bother.

His disgust was aimed at the filth who were invading his ship and the cowardice of the men who were supposed to be his officers; master, first mate and boatswain. To have surrendered so quickly? To have not put up a fight to the last man? Words failed him.

And when he saw his brother on deck, supported by the woman who was supposed to be van Overstratten's loving wife, his anger boiled over into a livid rage. This son of the whore who had replaced his mother and who had stolen his father's love and attention would *not* see his freedom again!

He was not concerned for his own safety, Phillipe truly believed no one would dare harm him. When something distracted his captors' attention he took full advantage of it.

They had not bound their prisoners, had merely ushered them to the stern and held them there by the threat of weapons. *Guardship!* the word was whispering, running like wildfire. Phillipe Mereno thought these men, this scum, were like frightened rabbits, their scuts white-bobbing as they darted in frantic circles. He seized his chance and hit out with his fist, throwing a punch to a jaw that sent the recipient reeling. He ran, sprinting across the deck, hearing not seeing his officers at last find the grit to fight for their lives. Ran, head down, for the man leaning groggily against the rail towards the bow.

The satisfaction as he watched his brother and that adulterous harlot tumble overboard was as intense as any excitement of sexual pleasure. It was not the end he had planned for Jesamiah but anything was better than seeing him rescued and delivered from misery.

- Twenty Nine -

Tethys crowed her delight, the unpleasant sound clawing through the depths of her undersea world. With the speed of a darting fish she thrust upward towards the surface, her glee trailing behind in a stream of air bubbles.

~ I have come for my payment, for the gift I was promised! ~

~ As is your right. I am of the Craft, I honour a promise made. ~

*

The intense cold shocked Jesamiah into awareness, his fuddled mind snapping to attention as he plunged down through the water. He was bare-foot, wore only a loose shirt and breeches, apart from the shrilling pain had nothing to impede his arms and legs. The coldness of the Atlantic rapidly numbed all feeling, although his mind registered he was going to hurt like hell once he got out of this. Salt water seeping into open wounds would be unbearable. Kicking out, he swam upward thankful that unlike many a seaman he could swim. Saw Tiola floating face down, her gown spread around her as if they were the skirts of a jellyfish. Her arm, somehow, caught on the encrusted barnacles of Phillipe's ship.

And he knew, knew before he reached her that she was dead.

Three minutes? Four? He was in the water no longer. Sailors knew the dangers, were quick to re-act. Seeing Jesamiah come up nearer to the *Sea Witch's* bow than the schooner's, the crew had boat hooks out. Rue and Isiah Roberts leaping from one ship to the other helped to haul Jesamiah aboard as he clung, one handed, to a tossed line, his other arm, aching from the damage Phillipe had inflicted, locked tight around Tiola's limp waist, holding her close. Telling himself it would be better to leave her for she would only have to be put back, knowing he could not. The struggle to free her had taken the last of his strength.

He crumpled on the deck of *Sea Witch*, shivering, his teeth rattling, the unbelievable stinging from the salt hurting his entire body. Everything, internal and external, agony; his hand with the broken bone in the ring finger swollen his joints, knee, shoulder, ankle, all bruised, sore to a point almost beyond endurance. He ignored all of it. The other pain shouted the rest of it into non-existence. She was gone. He had lost her. And this time, this time, there would be no finding her again. This time, it was final.

Rue put a coat around his shoulders, someone shouted for Finch to fetch rum. Jesamiah heard, felt, wanted, none of it.

Tiola had cried out as she fell, the surprise gushing the sound from her lungs. Her mouth open she took in water as she went down and her sleeve snagged against the Ruby's keel, stopping her from sinking. She kicked with her feet but she was caught tight. She tried to tear at it, the material refusing to give, the sharp, serrated barnacle shells obstinately clinging.

It was cold, so cold here in the water, and the two ships loomed, frightening, above her. If they should swing inward, come together while she was trapped here... She tried again to tear herself free and realised it was hopeless, nothing mortal or natural was binding her.

~ *I want my gift. I want him. I want Acorne.* ~

~ *Of what use is he to you, Tethys? He is mortal, his body will decay and rot and then you shall have nothing but his bones as your prize. Do you not have enough of those already?* ~

Malicious. Insistent. Demanding. ~ *Then give me something of his which shall not rot!* ~

For Jesamiah's life, it seemed fair exchange.

Thirty

Jesamiah sat, devoid of all thought staring, blank at Tiola, lifeless on the deck of the *Sea Witch*, her wet hair clinging to a face as white as alabaster. Her lips were tinged blue, there was no breath, no beat of her heart. She had gone. Gone forever from him and suddenly he did not care about anything any more, whether he hurt or not, whether he lived or died. Nothing mattered. Not now. Not ever again

They covered her with the pirate flag and Rue, squatting in front of him, asked what he wanted done with Mereno and the men of the *Ruby*. Jesamiah made no answer.

"Come on lad, let me get you below. Get you dried and warm, *non*?" As if he were a father tending his invalid son Rue lifted his friend to his feet, thread his strong arm around his waist and began to guide Jesamiah towards the sanctuary of the captain's cabin.

For a few steps Jesamiah meekly complied, then he paused to check they were tending Tiola with reverent care and he glanced across at the *Ruby* warped alongside. Saw his brother standing there on the fore-deck, hands on hips, laughing. Openly, derisively laughing.

Phillipe could not resist the opportunity for an extra half mile of vindictive taunting. "Dead is she?" he smirked, safe in the knowledge that the piece of filth he had been forced to call brother was not able to retaliate. Jesamiah was weaponless, beaten and broken. He stank of his own filth and vomit; down in the hold, had been shamed and humiliated, had pleaded to be left alone. Oh, it had been good to see him grovel, to hear him beg!

Swaggering forwards a few paces, arrogantly presumptuous, Phillipe jeered again. "Well, well Jesamiah, my intention was to incarcerate you in the deepest pit of Hell and leave you there to starve or gnaw at your own limbs. I appear to have achieved my aim. I have sent you there!"

Blind rage consumed Jesamiah. All pain, all physical feeling, disappeared with that blood-rush of hot fury. He shook Rue free and ran, yelling something, some wild animal noise of hatred that had no meaning beyond an ululation of bereaved sound. He was up on the rails, a loose line of cordage in his hands, swung across the narrow gap between the *Sea Witch* and the *Ruby*, landed awkwardly, rolled, was up running again, oblivious to everything except Phillipe's malicious crowing. And as Jesamiah ran his hand went to a bedraggled ribbon tied into his hair, tugged it free. It was filthy, but it was a ribbon he needed, no matter its colour or condition.

From the age of almost fifteen, when something, someone – Tiola - had awakened his ability to fight, Jesamiah had been a pirate. Pirates were hard men, piracy a hard life dominated by the stench of blood and the constant threat of the gallows. For a few, for those like Jesamiah who were intelligent, capable men, the life was easier, but they still met their share of staring death in the face and the brutality of killing. Of never knowing if the Grim Reaper was waiting, dark-hooded, on the next chase or at the next anchorage. In the indignity of the noose.

Malachias Taylor had taught Jesamiah all he knew. Had taught him well - how to sail a ship, how to feel her moods, to get that one last, essential knot of speed. To navigate, use a sextant, read charts. How to enjoy a woman, drink rum. And how to fight. How to kill.

"Anyone can kill, boy. Anyone, even drunk, can fire a pistol or stab with a knife - and hope it finds its mark, that the one who's dead don't get up ag'in. I've seen many a good pirate end 'is life by turnin' 'is back an' makin' a last mistake. To kill proper you need to kill quick, clean and thorough. No messin' about, a'tauntin' and pussy-footin' with one o' them fancy swords. I'll show you two ways

of 'ow to kill a man Jes boy, so 'e stays killed. As y'father once showed me."

As he ran Jesamiah's fingers, not feeling the broken bone, automatically tied a particular knot in the centre of the ribbon. A knot Taylor and Charles Mereno before him had used when it was especially needed. Quick and clean and thorough.

And Phillipe realised his mistake. Saw his doom coming straight at him. He screeched his panic and fled; on a ship, there was nowhere to run.

With his back pressed hard against the bulwark he stretched out one hand, a gesture pleading for mercy. As so many, many times Jesamiah had pleaded for mercy from him. He glanced down, below was the grey roll of the sea. Phillipe could swim but not well, and where would he swim to?

Again he looked at Jesamiah approaching at a walk now, menace and intent contorting his bruised face, the wet shirt and breeches clinging to his battered body, the bedraggled ribbon wound around his hands, the length between them stretched taut.

Forcing an ingratiating smile, his gaze darting about the deck desperate for something to use as a defensive weapon, Phillipe spread both hands wide and lied through his back teeth. "Brother! It was an accident, I did not mean for her to drown. Surely you realise that?"

A few feet away there was a pistol on the deck, could he reach it? He inched to the side not daring to glance at what he hoped would be his salvation.

"Jesamiah? You said yourself, we are grown men. Can we not put the mistakes of the past aside? Look to the future?" Another inch; the pistol was beside his foot. "You can have half the plantation. All my ships. Whatever you want is yours. Anything, just name it." Almost added, *"You can have Alicia,"* but thought better of it – he plunged downward, scooped up the pistol and standing upright levelled it at his brother's heart, his quivering fingers desperately trying to drag the hammer back.

Still Jesamiah came on, stepping silently in bare feet over a bloodied corpse its eyes staring, open. Walked on unaware it was there, every fibre of his body, every nerve of his senses focussed on the coward snivelling in front of him.

The sweat on Phillipe's palms was making it difficult to grip the pistol butt, his thumb could not get enough purchase on the hammer to draw it back – he used the palm of his shaking hand to do it, as a woman would – aimed, shut his eyes, squeezed the trigger…

Nothing happened. No flash of a spark striking the flint, no puff of igniting smoke, no sharp bang or jerked recoil. Nothing. Nothing, except an empty, hollow, click.

Urine trickled down Phillipe's legs, puddled in his shoes and stained his breeches. And then the smell of fear, of evacuated, liquid faeces. Terrified, he hurled the useless gun at Jesamiah who neatly sidestepped, not deigning to notice where it fell.

There was no mistaking the focussed hatred in Jesamiah's formidable eyes. Phillipe's voice quivered, rising to a shriek of panic as he began to beg in earnest. "Jesamiah, you cannot do this. I am your brother! We are of the same blood - for pity's sake I beg you! I do not want to die!"

Jesamiah continued walking. Said nothing. Heard none of it.

Terror overwhelming him Phillipe darted to the side, tried to get away but Jesamiah, despite his hurts, perhaps because of them, moved the quicker.

The second method of killing. One he had used enough times to know how to do it well, as Malachias had taught him. Effective and efficient. He lifted the ribbon high, brought it down around Phillipe's neck hooking his hands behind, fast and firm, crossing his arms and locking his wrists together for purchase. The ribbon jerked tight hauling Phillipe, gurgling and sputtering to a halt. In the same fluid movement Jesamiah took one, large, step backwards.

Mereno's hands were at the narrow strip of silk, clawing at the knot pressing into his windpipe, his fingers and nails scrabbling, trying to tear the thing free. Through his choking breath he was still trying to beg, to plead for Jesamiah to see reason. He tried to kick out, tried to stamp down, but Jesamiah knew that trick and was not within reach. His spine bending backwards, Mereno's breath was rattling in his throat, the blood pumping from his heart with nowhere to flow, for the carotid artery was being crushed by the squeezing pressure of a knotted ribbon. A blue ribbon that usually fluttered, innocuous, from Jesamiah's chaos of black hair. A thing worn and valued not for vanity, but for its easy use of killing.

"Save your begging for the Devil, Brother," Jesamiah rasped. "Instead of wasting my time fucking your wife, I should have finished you when we last met, you bastard."

A cannon ball whistled with the familiar *whoomph* of sound across the *Ruby's* bows. Someone shouted a warning. Rue. Jesamiah did not hear.

"Take this as what I owe you, Phillipe," Jesamiah snarled as with the strength of his crossed arms he pulled the ribbon one, last, bit tighter, administering the coup de grace. "And tomorrow I'll meet you in Hell."

Rue was shouting his name, shrieking at Jesamiah to leave it! Leave him!

"Get aboard Jes! It's the *Carolina Revenge!* Get aboard!"

Isiah and several of the men were chopping through the warping ropes securing them to the *Ruby*. Canvas was spilling from *Sea Witch's* masts and she was beginning to move away from the red-hulled schooner, tugging at the last line binding them together. Under immense strain the stretching cordage groaned as she began to gather way.

"Jesamiah! Come on!"

It was only because he had to bury Tiola that Jesamiah released his hold and let the ribbon and Phillipe's twitching corpse fall. He looked up, the breath tight in his chest and throat, the pain of all his hurts returning with a vengeance. He saw the *Carolina Revenge* bearing down on them under full sail and the distinctive white streak of another cannon ball shrieking across the closing gap between them. With a plume of spray it landed short by a few inches. The next one would not.

His brother was dead but Jesamiah wanted to make sure he would receive no Christian burial. No one was to stand beside his grave and mourn. He did not deserve respect, deserved to suffer the fate of the unburied for all eternity. Phillipe was no sailor, he had no gold tooth, no gold earring, had nothing with which to pay the Ferryman to cross, in peace, into the next world. Without remorse or pity Jesamiah dragged the twitching body the few yards to where the bulwark had been shot away. Shoved it over the side. Did not bother to wait to hear the splash.

Willing hands stretched out to catch him as, grasping a length of torn shroud, he swung across the increasing distance between the two ships. *Sea Witch*, knowing he was safe, took her own decision to break free. The last line snapped with a bang, hurtling into the air like a cracked whip-lash and she plunged forward like a greyhound set loose from the slip, the wind taking her. She had her beloved master returned aboard and happy, showed the speed of a fleeing gazelle. By comparison, the cumbersome guardship was a clip-winged duck.

Thirty One

Jackson was a mediocre ship's surgeon when drunk, not much better when sober. He did what he could, but making things hurt more, Jesamiah sent him away. A rum bottle was all he needed. He drank three quarters of it, rolled from his cot and stumbled towards the table where they had lain Tiola. He peeled aside his flag, the skull leering up at him in its parody of death. Revolted, he flung it away.

She lay there ice cold to the touch of his fingers brushing against her cheek. Her beautiful eyes were closed, he would never see her wonderful smile again. Nor hear her voice with its slight lilt of a Cornish accent - how she said *ais* instead of yes; the burr of the 'r' in her words: *surr, luvver.* No more of her easy, teasing laughter. Never more to share the fire in the passion of her love. Gone was the hope of holding in his arms a child made from their union of exquisite pleasure.

He swallowed the bitter, salt taste of tears.

They would come to take her soon, to sew her into a canvas shroud, the last stitch going through her nose to ensure she was dead, a cannon ball placed at her feet to take the corpse to the sea bed. He had already decided when she went she would not be going alone. A ball cradled in his hands would take him down with her. He would not be leaving her.

He lifted her left hand, expecting to see the ring he had given her. He had seen it there, his subconscious recognising it as he had tugged at her caught sleeve, had seen it glinting on her dangling hand. Clearly remembered seeing it - but it was gone, nothing was there except a ragged graze across her knuckles. Vaguely, he recalled dragging her hand over the barnacles as he had torn at the material of her sleeve. The cuts must have happened then, the ring dislodged. She had such slender fingers and the water would have made it loose.

His breath sobbed in this new choke of anguish. Tiola had nothing to pay her passage. He twisted the acorn from his ear - he could not remember being without it, had been surprised that Phillipe had not ripped it from his lobe. A minor hurt compared to the rest of what he had suffered, but Phillipe had never been sentimental, had probably not understood its significance, seeing it purely as an adorning trinket. As most people assumed the ribbons to be.

The tears were beginning to fall, the sorrow dragging him into a place of misery far deeper than any he had so far visited.

"You can use this instead, m'darlin'." He tucked the earring into the curl of her hand, would make sure before they came to take her that someone bound it there, safe. He had nothing of his own now as payment, did not care. He could always find a coin somewhere, it should suffice.

"If I'm delayed arguing my passage, wait for me on the other side, darlin', please?"

He rested his head on her breast, his arm sliding around her waist. His tears falling like the tumble of rain. "If I cannot follow, at least I'll know you will not be condemned to wandering the depths for eternity."

"I will not be condemned to anything. I have the Craft. I am a witch."

Jesamiah yelped, scrabbled backwards. His body, finally having enough of the abuse it had endured and being swamped with a generous excess of rum, crumpled on to the deck.

Swinging her legs from the table Tiola smiled at his absurdity, the light of her ageless soul shining as it always did through her eyes. She knelt beside him, cupped his poor battered face in her hand and wiped the trail of tears with the gentle healing tips of her fingers.

"Fine pirate you are," she chided. "Look at you, all muddled in a heap."

He stared. Said nothing, just stared.

She leant forward, touched her lips to his. She felt warm, smelt as she always had of summer meadows and fresh-cut hay, but now the scent was mingled with an additional, faint, aroma of tar and the sea.

"You do take some convincing that I am a witch, do you not my luvver? I am not immortal, but there are only certain ways I may die. And drowning is not among them."

He slid his arms around her waist, buried his head in her living, breathing, comfort. And wept.

She held him, let him cry, let him freely release the terror, pain and the grief. The relief. Nature's way of healing, tears or laughter, both a catalyst to cleanse the tight-tied knots life so frequently tangled itself into.

There was much work to do to put him together again for he was damaged and broken – but not irreparable. She knelt, holding him, rocking him as if he were a child, stroking his blood-matted, wet hair. Removed the one remaining ribbon. He would want new ones.

Tiredness was swamping him, the ache of exhaustion gradually replacing the outpouring of tears. Suddenly, all he wanted to do was sleep, to curl up in his cot with Tiola, his arms secure around her, and sleep.

"Promise you will never leave me again," he said looking into her eyes, scared he might see something there he would rather not. That she no longer loved him, was not prepared to live aboard a pirate ship. Or, he swallowed hard, frightened of saying it, had to know.

"Or perhaps you are wanting to return to your husband? To van Overstratten?"

"Now why would I be wanting to do that?" Tiola kissed him, careful of his hurts. "You are such a fool Jesamiah Acorne. I swear, I do not know why I love you."

"Ah," he said, attempting a lop-sided, awkward grin, the pirate trick of making a pretence of bravado and confidence. "Think how tedious it would be to always know everything."

Broken, but not irreparable. He was a pirate, was already mending. And she was a witch, already protecting and healing him.

*

Beneath the oceans where light was unknown and unwanted, Tethys clutched a ring. It had belonged to the witch, and before her, to the man, the pirate. The one who had taken his name from the pattern etched into it, Acorne.

She was a cunning one, that witch, with her look of innocent youth but ability of ageless competence! Tethys would need be careful of her, of the black haired witch who smelt of the warm earth of the land and the tang of the sea.

~ You tricked me. ~

~ I offered you his ring. You accepted it. ~

~ I do not want a ring. I want him ~

~ He is mine Tethys, the sea shall not have him. ~

~ He is of the sea, Witch-Woman. I am the sea and therefore everything of the sea is mine. ~

~ Not everything. I too am of the sea, for I have become part of his ship, as his ship is a part of him. We are inseparable, joined as one of three as the body, the shadow and the reflection are one of the same. Those who respect and love and need each other Tethys, can never be separated. ~

~ I will have him, Sea-Witch. I will. ~

Annoyed, Tethys sank deeper and deeper into the mud at the very bottom of the oceans. She did not understand this human emotion called love, for she had no such feelings of her own.

She released the gold ring, let it drift, unwanted, with the current. She could wait for her prize, could wait for Jesamiah, for he was mortal and she was not. There would be other opportunities for the collecting of trophies, for gathering the drowned bones of men. The bones of pirates.

The sea rolled with the swell of the tide and the surf hushed on to the shore, echoing the faint and distant whisper that was the murmuring, lonely voice of Tethys, crooning for what she wanted.

~ *Jeshh..a..miah......* *Jeshh..a..miah* ...... *Jeshh..a..miah......* ~

Author's Note:

Jesamiah Acorne did not exist, nor were pirates the charming rogues made familiar in movies and stories. They were ill-mannered thieves and murderers who never washed and were, more often than not, drunk on plundered rum. Heroes in novels cannot be like that. Jesamiah certainly is not – although he may not always be quite the "nice guy" you expect him to be. He is, after all, a pirate.

The background details to *Sea Witch!* however are mostly accurate, although I have taken liberties with dates. I have enjoyed researching the men who were the cut-throats who sailed under a skull and crossbones flag, the *jolie rouge,* the ships they sailed in and the era of the Golden Age of Pirates in the Caribbean (roughly 1680 – 1725) when Port Royal in Jamaica was known, for a while, as "the Wickedest city in the World". But thorough research, an accurate historical time-line and interesting stories do not always sail well together.

A quote I adore was from the superb UK comedy duo *Morecambe and Wise*, in a sketch parodying an orchestral concert Eric Morecambe was playing the piano - very badly. When the conductor, André Previn, berated him for playing the wrong notes he quipped, "I *am* playing the right notes but not necessarily in the right order." Well, I am using the right events, but not necessarily at the right date.

For instance, Captain Woodes Rogers and his companions *were* in Cape Town but in 1711, not 1716 (William Dampier in fact died in late 1715). Rogers became Governor of Nassau in July 1718. I considered 1711 to 1718 too long a time-span for a novel such as this, and so I have compacted the dates and eased my conscience by adding this confessional apology. There is one other slightly inaccurate date: the Spanish Treasure ships sank off the Florida coast in a storm on the 31st July 1715 – not 1716 as I have portrayed. Henry Jennings made his fortune by raiding the warehouse where the salvaged gold was stored – if he had a pirate called Jesamiah Acorne with him it was not recorded. The only other fabrication regarding Jennings; he was not Vice Governor of Nassau. He did, however, accept a pardon and settle down to a respectable life on New Providence Island, so perhaps his role as mediator was not recorded either...

Many pirates elected their captain and de-elected him if he was no good, usually by marooning him. The second in command, however, was the quartermaster not the first mate as in the Royal Navy and pirates did not have lieutenants or midshipmen. One disappointing note, there does not appear to be any evidence of pirates making their victims walk the plank. Pity.

I have based *Sea Witch* on a combination of two famous – and real – pirate vessels, the *Whydah*, which ran aground off the Florida coast, and Blackbeard's ship the *Queen Anne's Revenge*. I have tried to be accurate with my sailing details and beg forgiveness from anyone who knows their subject better than I. Errors are all my own work and not the responsibility of more knowledgeable, sea-farers who have most generously given me advice.

As for the plundered haul of hats, the event really happened. I thought it would be fun to give the honour of it to my own loveable rogue, to Jesamiah Acorne.

Long may he sail, with a following wind and a calm sea – and Tiola to keep a sensible rein on his more outrageous exploits.

Helen Hollick
2006

Glossary

Aback - a sail when its forward surface is pressed upon by the wind. Used to "stop" a ship.

Account - see On the Account

Aloft - up in the tops, at the mast-head or any where about the yards or the rigging.

Articles - Each man when coming aboard "agreed the Articles". Some pirate ships were run on very democratic lines, the crew elected their captain, agreed where to sail, divided the "spoils" fairly etc. Most rules were sensible things like no naked flame below deck; each man to keep his weapon clean and ready for use and no fighting aboard ship.

Bar - a shoal running across the mouth of a harbour or a river.

Bare poles - having no sail up - the bare mast.

Belay - stop that. "Belay that talk!" would mean "Shut up!"

Belaying pin - a short wooden rod to which a ship's rigging is secured. A common improvised weapon aboard a sailing ship because they are everywhere, are easily picked up, and are the right size and weight to be used as a club.

Bell (Ship's bell) - used as a clock, essential for navigation as the measurement of the angle of the sun had to be made at noon. The bell was struck each time the half-hour glass was turned.

Bilge - the lowest part of the ship inside the hull along the keel. They fill with stinking bilge water or "bilge. Can also mean nonsense or foolish talk.

Binnacle - the frame or box that houses the compass.

Bow - the front or "pointed" end of the ship.

Bowsprit - the heavy slanted spar pointing forward from the ship's bow.

Brace - rope used to control the horizontal movement of a square-rigged yard.

Broadside - the simultaneous firing of all guns on one side of a ship.

Bulkheads - vertical partitions in a ship.

Bulwark - interior wall of ship.

Cable - a long, thick and heavy rope by which a ship is secured to the anchor.

Cable's length - a measure of 120 fathoms or 240 yards.

Capstan - drum-like winch turned by the crew to raise or lower the anchors.

Careen – the process of beaching a ship, heeling her over to her side and cleaning the underside of weed, barnacles and worm; making essential repairs to the part of a ship which is usually below the water line. A careened ship will go faster and last longer than one that is not.

Cathead – vertical beam of timber protruding near the bow, used for hoisting the anchor.

Cat o'nine tails, or "cat" – a whip with many lashes, used for flogging.

Caulk – to seal the gaps between planks of wood with caulking – see oakum.

Chain shot – two balls of iron joined together by a length of chain, chiefly used to destroy, masts, rigging and sails.

Chandler – a merchant selling the various things a ship needs for supplies and repairs.

Chanty – or shanty, a sailor's work song. Often lewd and derogatory about the officers.

Chase – or Prize. The ship being pursued.

Cleat – wooden or metal fastening to which ropes can be secured. Can also be used as a ladder.

Clew – the lower corners of a sail., therefore *Clew up* – to haul a square sail up to a yard.

Close-hauled – sailing as close to the direction of the wind as possible with the sails turned almost 90°

Cordage – rope is called cordage on board a ship.

Colours – the vessel's identification flag, also called an ensign. For a pirate, the Jolly Roger!

Courses – lowest sails on the mast.

Crosstrees – wooden platform partway up a mast to keep the shrouds spread apart.

Doubloon – a Spanish gold coin.

Fathom - a measure of six feet of water.

Fore, or forrard - toward the front end of the ship, the bow.

Forecastle – pronounced *fo'c'sle* ; raised deck at the front of ship.

Fore-and-aft rig - sails set length wise not at right angles (square-rigged) to the hull

Flukes – the broad parts or palms of the anchor.

For-and-aft - the length of a ship.

Forestay -the rope leading from the mast to the bow.

Galleon -a large three-masted square-rigged ship used chiefly by the Spanish.

Galley – ship's kitchen.

Gasket – a piece of plait to fasten the sails to the yards.

Grape-shot – or grape, small cast iron balls bound together in a canvas bag that scatter like shotgun pellets when fired.

Gunwale - pronounced *gun'l* ; upper planking along the sides of a vessel. "Up to the gunwales" - full up or overloaded.

Halyard - pronounced *haly'd*. The rope used to hoist a sail.

Hard tack – ship's biscuit. Opposite is soft tack – bread.

Hatch – an opening in the deck for entering below.

Hawser – cable.

Heave to - to check the forward motion of a vessel and bring her to a stand still by heading her into the wind and backing some of her sails.

Heel – to lean over due to action of the wind, waves, or greater weight on one side. The angle at which the vessel tips when sailing.

Helm – the tiller (a long steering arm) or a wheel which controls the rudder and enables the vessel to be steered.

Hold – space below deck for cargo.

Hull – the sides of a ship which sit in and above the water.

Hull down – a vessel when it is so far away from the observer the hull is invisible owing to the shape of the earth's surface. Opposite to hull up.

Jack Ketch - the hangman. To dance with Jack Ketch is to hang.

Jollyboat - a small boat, a dinghy.

Jolly Roger - the pirates' flag, called the jolie rouge – although its original meaning is unknown. The hoisted flag was an invitation to surrender, with the implication that those who did so would be treated well – and no quarter given to those who did not.

Keel – the lowest part of the hull below the water.

Knot – one nautical mile per hour.

Landlubber or lubber - a non-sailor.

Langrage – jagged pieces of sharp metal used as shot. Especially useful for damaging rigging and killing men.

Larboard - pronounced *larb'd*. The left side of a ship when facing the bow (front) Changed in the 19th c to "port."

Lee – the side or direction away from the wind i.e, downwind.

Lee shore - the shore on to which the wind is blowing, a hazardous shore for a sailing vessel particularly in strong winds –can easily be blown on to rocks etc.

Leeches - the vertical edges of a square sail

Letters of Marque - Papers issued by a government during wartime entitling a privately owned ship to raid enemy commerce or attack enemy warships.

Luff - the order to the helmsman to put the tiller towards the lee side of the ship in order to make it sail nearer to the direction of the wind.

Maroon - a punishment for breaking a pirate ship's articles or rules. The victim was left on a deserted coast (or an island) with little in the way of supplies. Therefore, no one could say the unlucky pirate had actually been killed by his former brethren.

Mast - vertical spar supporting the sails.

Oakum - a material used to waterproof seams between planks on deck etc. Made of strong, pliable, tarred fibres obtained from scrap rope which swell when wet.

On the Account - or the Sweet Trade; a man who went "on the account" was turning pirate.

Piece of eight - a Spanish silver coin worth one peso or eight reales. It was sometimes literally cut into eight pieces, each worth one real. In the 1700's a piece of eight was worth a little under five shillings sterling, or 25p - this would be about £15 today. One side usually had the Spanish coat of arms, the other two lines symbolising the limits of the old world at the Straits of Gibraltar, the exit into the Atlantic Ocean from the Mediterranean. In later designs two hemispheres were added between the lines representing the Old and New World. Pieces of eight were so widely used that eventually this sign was turned into the dollar sign - $.

Privateer - an armed vessel bearing letters of marque, or one of her crew, or her captain. A privateer is theoretically a law-abiding combatant.

Quarterdeck - the highest deck at the rear of a ship where the officers stood and where the helm is usually situated.

Rail - timber plank along the top of the gunwale above the sides of the vessel.

Rake - when a ship sweeps another with a broadside of cannon.

Ratlines - pronounced *ratlins*; ropes beneath the yards on which sailors would stand while adjusting the sails.

Reef - (1) an underwater obstruction of rock or coral. (2) To reduce the size of the sails by tying them partially up, either to slow the ship or to keep a strong wind from putting too much strain on the masts.

Rigging - the ropes which support the spars (standing rigging) and allow the sails to be controlled (running rigging).

Round shot – iron cannon balls

Rudder - blade at the stern which is angled to steer the vessel.

Run - sail directly away from the wind.

Sails - in general each mast had three sails. See diagram at the front.

Sail ho! - "I see a ship!". The sail is the first part visible over the horizon.

Scuppers - openings along the edges of a ship's deck to allow water to drain back to the sea rather than collecting in the bilges.

Sheet - a rope made fast to the lower corners of a sail to control its position. Sheet home – to haul on a sheet until the foot of the sail is as straight and taut as possible.

Ship's Biscuit – hard bread. Very dry, can be eaten a year after baked. Also called hard tack.

Ship of the Line - a war ship carrying at least 50 guns.

Shrouds - ropes forming part of the standing rigging and supporting the mast or topmast.

Spanker – a square sail wide at bottom and narrow at top attached to a boom that projects straight back from the mizzenmast along the axis of the ship.

Spar - a stout wooden pole used as a mast or yard of a sailing vessel.

Spritsail – pronounced *sprit'sl;* a sail attached to a yard which hangs under the bowsprit.

Square-rigged - the principal sails set at right angles to the length of a ship and extended by horizontal yards slung to the mast.

Starboard –pronounced *starb'd.* The right side of a vessel when you are facing toward the bow.

Stay – strong rope supporting the masts.

Stem – timber at very front of bow.

Stern – the back end of a ship.

Swab - a disrespectful term for a seaman, or to clean the decks.

Sweet Trade – see On the Account

Sweeps – long oars used by large vessels.

Tack / tacking - to change the direction of a vessel's course by turning her bows into the wind until the wind blows on her other side. When a ship is sailing into an oncoming wind she will have to tack, make a zigzag line, in order to make progress forward against the oncoming wind.

Taffrail – upper rail along the ship's stern.

Transom – planking forming the stern.

Trim - a term used for adjusting the sails as the wind changes.

Waist - the middle part of the ship.

Wake – the line of passage directly behind as marked by a track of white foam.

Warp - to move a ship by hauling or pulling her along on warps (ropes); also the name of the ropes which secure a ship when moored (tied up) to a jetty or dock.

Weigh anchor - to haul the anchor up; more generally, to leave port.

Widow maker – term for the bowsprit.

Windward - the side towards the wind as opposed to leeward.

Yard - a long spar suspended from the mast of a vessel to extend the sails.

Yardarm – either end of the yard.

To be launched ~ Spring 2007

Pirate Code

Being the 2nd voyage of
Cpt. Jesamiah Acorne and his ship, *Sea Witch*.

Jesamiah has received his pardon from Governor Woodes Rogers -
but Stefan van Overstratten will not release Tiola from her
marriage - either she returns as his dutiful wife or she must
suffer the consequences.
How can Jesamiah get her back - and how does he become a spy
for the British during a brief upsurge of war with Spain?

The answer is simple.
He must return to sea as a pirate!